and the

Fall to Pieces

"Tishy shows us tough and tender Nashville with a pedal-to-the-metal plot. Warm as a New England fireside, her Kate Banning scans the South with 20/20 laser vision. Great reading."
—Lisa Scottoline, author of *Legal Tender*

Cryin' Time

"This second Kate Banning novel is a real treat, as Tishy combines believable characters with a lively view of country music and Nashville life."
—*Booklist*

"Carefully crafted and thoroughly detailed . . . the Nashville setting and country music subject will appeal to many."
—*Library Journal*

"An entertaining series with a twang."
—*New York Daily News*

Jealous Heart

"An enticing tour of Nashville, with goosebumps enough for the ride."
—Linda Barnes, bestselling author of *Snapshot*

"Entertaining and provocative . . . Cecelia Tishy is brilliant."
—*Nashville Banner*

Praise for Cecelia Tishy
and the Kate Banning mystery series

Other Books By Cecelia Tishy

Jealous Heart
Cryin' Time

FALL TO PIECES

Cecelia Tishy

A SIGNET BOOK

SIGNET
Published by New American Library, a division of
Penguin Putnam Inc., 375 Hudson Street,
New York, New York 10014, U.S.A.
Penguin Books Ltd, 27 Wrights Lane,
London W8 5TZ, England
Penguin Books Australia Ltd, Ringwood,
Victoria, Australia
Penguin Books Canada Ltd, 10 Alcorn Avenue,
Toronto, Ontario, Canada M4V 3B2
Penguin Books (N.Z.) Ltd, 182–190 Wairau Road,
Auckland 10, New Zealand

Penguin Books Ltd, Registered Offices:
Harmondsworth, Middlesex, England

Published by Signet, an imprint of New American Library,
a division of Penguin Putnam Inc.
This is an authorized reprint of a hardcover edition published by Dowling
Press, Inc. For information address Dowling Press, Inc., 1110 Seventeenth
Avenue South, Suite Four, Nashville, TN 37214.

First Signet Printing, August 2000
10 9 8 7 6 5 4 3 2 1

To Bill, Claire, and Julia

ACKNOWLEDGMENTS

First thanks to Bill Tichi, superintendent of the Kate Banning plot hatchery. Thanks too for Claire's and Julia's input on Kelly, for Mary Ellen Logan's advice on Tennessee brush and brambles, for Thad Davis's advice to add tincture of murder, for the support of mystery buddies, Cae Carter and Billie Laney.

Once again, my gratitude to Barbara Bennett for legal counsel, to Marilyn Murphy for awesome art and Bruce Gore for dashing two-tone graphics.

Every mystery novelist owes a great debt to the mystery retailers and to the organizers of gatherings of mystery writers and fans across the U.S. Thanks also to the Middle Tennessee Sisters-in-Crime chapter and to the organization nationwide.

Finally, my warmest gratitude to Maryglenn McCombs for anchorage at Dowling Press, to Joe Pittman at NAL Signet, and to Susan Thomas for her editorial eagle eye.

Johnson City, Tn.—Country music star LilyAnn Page reportedly escaped serious injury when an electrical fire damaged her tour bus and destroyed the singer's stage wardrobe. According to her manager, Ms. Page and her band were released yesterday from a Johnson City hospital where they were treated for smoke inhalation. One of the singer's road crew was fatally injured last month when sound equipment tumbled from a truck during unloading. A spring concert tour is expected to proceed on schedule.

CHAPTER ONE

Inept was the core feeling. How could she stall out at a light for the second time in twenty minutes? The Navigator lurched, bucked, engine died, and Kate felt sweaty as she turned the ignition key again. And again. The nice Nashville drivers behind her waited quietly because this was the South, not the Bos-Wash corridor. Nobody honked. Nobody yelled in road rage here at the intersection of Harding Road and Tyne Boulevard. Right now, Kate Banning was glad to be in Nashville, not in Boston.

But why did the vehicular silence sound louder than horns?

Don't think about that now. Focus. Signal a right and this time do not mistake the windshield washer for a turning signal. Sitting stiff as a board, Kate nudged the gas and turned the wheel—trying to resist her own *déjà vu* rerun of age sixteen with a learner's permit and a Massachusetts State trooper in the passenger seat.

So admit it, *inept* was the core feeling. Why did she agree to this "loaner" vehicle? More important, why did she, an editor, let the new sales director talk her into making a sales call this Saturday afternoon? Not just any sales call but a pitch to a real celebrity. She never sold anything in her life, had no training, no experience—worse, no faith in the project in the portfolio in the backseat.

Did she harbor some deep-down hope of actually

meeting a *bona fide* queen of country music? Nine
months in town, Kate could count two country music
star sightings—Reba McEntire in Dalt's having a
burger, and Alan Jackson in the audience at the
Ryman Auditorium. Both were pointed out by com-
panions who knew the music scene. Maybe she agreed
to today's sales pitch on the off-chance of actually
talking to a big star—Kate Banning in her late thirties
in celebrity-obsessed America, angling for a stardust
moment.

And sales—talk about a fish out of water. But there
was no turning back now. What was that saying, No
Way To It But Through It?

Minutes later, just at 1:00, Kate slowed for the right
turn onto Claridge, where the lots ran to a couple of
acres, then to Mosely—numbers eighty-one, eighty-
two, then eighty-three. She braked and eased the Navigator onto a graveled drive and stopped.

Stopped and stared.

Eighty-three Mosely could turn a sunny day somber.
It was a Nashville gated fortress with fifteen-foot high
spikes at the top, an austere prison-bar look with one
clear message: Keep Out. Kate reminded herself again
that this was the boundary line a celebrity had to
draw, even in Nashville. The fence was a reminder
that fan was short for fanatic.

She picked up her car phone, dialed the number
given at her office and heard a businesslike female
voice ask her to wait, somebody would be right out.
The voice sounded nothing whatsoever like LilyAnn
Page, its rhythms nothing like the signature song,
"Break of Dawn."

Yet Kate had a moment's foolish fantasy of the star
herself coming to the gate. Her pulse quickened, and
despite herself she began to hum "Break of Dawn,"
the song up there with "Stand By Your Man," with
Dolly Parton's "Coat of Many Colors," and Linda
Ronstadt's "Blue Bayou." If you were alive in the

U.S.A. and not raised by wolves, you probably could sing a few bars.

But here at this gate, deep down in the inner corridors of the self, Kate had to admit to herself that her agitation, her very pulse rate went beyond the mothlike lure of celebrity, the sales call, the balky SUV. Face it, this was personal. Admit it, Kate knew Lily-Ann Page's "Break of Dawn" by heart—literally, as a matter of the heart—for reasons beyond the casual claims of pop culture.

Here at this security gate, Kate gave into the surge of memory. The fifteen-year-old breakout hit still touched her deeply and transcended country & western music. It was one of those songs more entwined with the soul than the *Billboard* chart. The nostalgia rolled in a wave of yearning and regret. The tune and lyrics spiraled down to the time of Kate's own first love and marriage and into early pregnancy, then the newly-marrieds' impatience, the nastiness, the baby, Kelly, the irreconcilable differences and the divorce.

At this minute she stewed in an autobiographic musical mix of hope and dread here at the gate of the Lily of the Shenandoah Valley with her auburn hair "skunk" streaked at the temple, a fragile face, soulful eyes. She never seemed to age, at least not on TV.

Thank heaven for the sound of an approaching motorcycle—a Harley? No, it was a John Deere lawn mower, green as grass with bright yellow trim. The young man in the seat had blond slicked-back hair, camouflage pants and hunting boots, and a quiver of arrows in a holster on his hip. He peered at her through the fence, opened the gate with a remote, made a U-turn and waved her to follow his trailing plume of blue smoke. She moved at 5 m.p.h. along a winding drive through stands of trees that screened the property from the road. The John Deere exhaust was choking. She slowed from five to three. He slowed too. The arrows bristled at his hip. Kate took shallow breaths.

Finally, in a clearing, the manicured green lawn and the main house appeared. Kate had expected something from *Gone with the Wind* or maybe Graceland. Wrong. The house was a large gray two-story timber with bright white caulking and a wide porch with four big rockers that looked purely decorative. The squared-off timbers and river rock chimneys at either end suggested something between an estate and a lodge with a hint of Davy Crockett. There were blossoming dogwoods and ornamental specimen cherry trees undreamed of in days when Crockett "cilled a bar," or was that Daniel Boone? Despite herself, Kate felt impressed and curious. How did a country music legend live? Surely not with log furniture.

But the John Deere forked left and away from the main house toward a matching cabin about two hundred yards away in a stand of pines with jonquils blooming in the sunny spots. Somewhere dogs were barking. It occurred to Kate that Tennesseeans were notching logs when her ancestors, New Englanders, carved decorative moldings for formal Federal style houses.

Never mind. She pulled left and parked between two new gleaming green Land Cruisers and jumped out. Maybe the sales manager was right about the upmarket auto image. She dropped the Navigator keys in her bag because it seemed silly to lock up. She tucked the portfolio under her arm and smoothed her sienna linen skirt and jacket, and made sure the silver neck chains were not caught on a button. She checked her supply of business cards.

The John Deere was throttled back. Dogs continued barking. "Head in there. Dottie'll be with you. We're still off track. With the fire and poor Carnie, things are crazy." He growled off as if the entire compound were his.

Kate tried not to gag on fumes as she approached the cabin door, which was opened by a woman who motioned her inside while talking on the phone. There was no sign of LilyAnn Page, which was disappointing but somehow a relief. This woman—Dottie?—was forty-ish, about five-five, slender with dark bobbed hair. She drummed fingers on the tabletop as if it were a keyboard, and her phone voice sounded more like Chicago than the sunny South. She wore all black—jeans, a black silk shell and jacket, black sneakers and socks, and the lightest makeup of dusky lipstick, eye accents, darkened brows. She reminded Kate of the fashion designers on TV, their new seasonal lines flashy-unto-gaudy while they themselves receded to the background in *matte noir*. So much for the notion of polyester as country music's favorite fabric.

The woman pointed Kate toward a stack chair but continued to talk on a flip phone as streamlined as herself. The cabin felt, actually, like the inside of a supply cabinet with a long trestle table, a fluorescent lamp, computer and printer, an old Selectric, a fax machine, TV, two telephones, three sets of "in" and "out" baskets. The one personal item was a large framed photo of two teen girls, one dark, apple-cheeked and curly-haired with soft, rounded features and a sweet smile. The other was more angular around the nose and mouth, the hair long and straight, the eyes hinting the soulfulness of LilyAnn Page. It occurred to Kate that she knew nothing about the country music star's personal life.

She looked to the left where six steel file cabinets stood in a row. There was also a raised platform with one red upholstered easy chair, a table lamp and little rug, all of which looked unused, like a homey little stage set. Turning, Kate saw a big stone fireplace, which was notably messy, its charred logs mixed with cigarette butts, peelings, apple cores, foil wrappers and bright globs of something pink—bubble gum?

Right now Dottie's midwestern voice rose impatiently. "You touch those car keys, Deb, even a thumbprint, you're grounded for a week, seven whole days. And if the kitchen's not cleaned up, don't even ask for my Visa card. And no dates, no Saturday night, I don't want to hear about Farley or any of them. Especially not Farley. This mess you and Angie made in the fireplace here at the office—no, I'm looking at it right now, gum and wrappers and garbage and God-knows-what. All we want is a little consideration, the fire, the accident—No, not tomorrow, you've got today to clean it up, period." She folded the phone and put it in her jacket pocket. "Kids."

Kate smiled, "Sounds familiar." She reached out to shake the woman's hand and noticed her eyes, puffy and bloodshot. "I'm Kate Banning, Fleetwood Publications." The woman's palm was dry as paper.

"Dottie Skipwith. You have kids?"

"One fourteen-year-old daughter," Kate said.

"She gone boy crazy yet?"

"Uh, not yet."

"Just wait. It's boys, boys, boys on top of everything else."

Kate said, "Right now my daughter's selling house plants door to door in a strange neighborhood. I thought about buying the whole lot to keep her at home. But you can't say no to everything when they're teens, can you?"

Dottie shook her head and moved from foot to foot as if ready to break into a jog. Her energy could be taken for girlishness, or vice versa. "I'm running behind, Kate. Kids, they're a constant pain in the neck, but I'm nonstop here with all kinds of problems, insurance people about wardrobe replacement, the whole morning on depreciation, which is one of those big gray areas." She shook her head. "Timing's terrible. Lily's got a new album coming out, and they're scheduling the video shoot for next week, and all I do these days is yell at the girls and talk to insurance people, assessors, claims adjusters, lawyers. Last month, same thing, and poor Carnie, God rest his soul, that was just a terrible thing."

"I'm afraid I don't know—"

She tossed her head to flip the bob into place. "Twenty-three-years old and the first time out on the road crew, and it was just a crazy thing. Big heavy guitar case, it was stacked way high in the truck and probably shifted out on the road. We think it just let loose, came down like a rock slide on a highway, boom, like that. Young kid, not even a regular, hit him on the temple and now he's gone. One of those bizarre things. Billy D, the blond guy who let you inside the gate, he was off taking some course in archery. He goes deer hunting with a bow and arrow every year. It's his passion. Would it have happened if Billy D was out with them? We'll never know. The truck was leased, and so were the monitors. Two different companies. We're insured, of course.

"The lawyers will say, 'Where's the training program?' " She leaned toward Kate. "Shoving guitar cases and monitors in and out of a truck or a trailer, there's not a road manager in Nashville who runs a training program for that. You treat a country artist like they're General Motors, it'll have an effect with promoters, venues, management all up and down the line. It's already sent a chill through all the artists' management here in Nashville, I can tell you that."

Kate nodded. The core and the gist, a road crew substitute died when heavy equipment fell on him. Deadly liability everywhere. Yet the manager seemed far too talkative, especially to a stranger not even in the music business. Was she normally like this, or did recent events send her spinning?

Dottie Skipwith sighed. "Okay, we appreciate your time today, Kate. Let's talk about your deal."

Spotlight on Kate. Pretend that sales is second na-

ture. She handed Dottie Skipwith the glossy portfolio
which was put together by Don Donaghue, Fleetwood's sales director. She cleared her throat and
worked to sound energetic. "As Mr. Donaghue—
Don—told you by phone, Fleetwood wants to max-
imize audience outreach and take the burden off the
star and the star's management. We aim to profession-
alize all communication from stars to fans, including
mailings and web pages."

She stopped. Boring. Like those deadly dull meetings with an overhead projector. No Way To It—

"You of course have the promotional materials sent
over from our sales director. And if you've had a
chance to look over them—" In fact, Kate could see
the whole folder lying in a pristine state on the trestle table.

Should she now offer her business card? Not yet.
"Fleetwood has over ten years experience publishing
trade magazines under contract," she said. "Our current clients are insurance companies, one regional airline, and several other businesses. You'll find sample
copies of our *SouthWing* and *Roadways/Sealanes* magazines. We're a Nashville company, privately owned.
It makes sense to offer our experience to country
music. . . ."

She hesitated on stars or legends. "To country music
artists." Relief. In Nashville every solo singer was
an artist. Talk the talk. She smiled, looked Dottie
Skipwith in the eye and said, "As you know, we're
on Second Avenue only minutes from Music Row.
As chief coordinating editor, I assure you we'll welcome the chance to offer creative suggestions for
LilyAnn's Page and to propose additional media for
fan outreach."

She did not, could not say right here and now that
she thought the whole notion of subcontracting country music fan magazines a dumb detour for Fleetwood.
Or that she half-expected the project to be shot down

by the company president, an umpteen-generation Old Nashville aristocrat who thought country music's rise meant the decline of Western Civilization. If Don Donaghue only listened when Kate offered him that particular info byte in the office last month, she wouldn't waste a warm Saturday in May adlibbing in this cabin-turned-boiler-room.

Across from her in the big black office chair, Dottie Skipwith's eyes oddly both glazed over and yet focused as she said, "So you're not in sales."

That obvious. Kate felt a flush rise up her neck. She said, "It's not my job, that's true. But Fleetwood puts out first-rate products, and I'm proud to be a part of the effort. Our sales director particularly asked me to come here today."

Dottie's gaze had not changed. Something was wrong. Then Kate remembered, here in the South people often wanted the personal side. She said, "Let me just add that I've personally considered LilyAnn Page's 'Break of Dawn' to be a cherished classic."

She stopped and felt her cheeks flush. The declaration felt cheap and verged on an outright lie. One powerful song deep in her personal past did not make Kate Banning a fan of LilyAnn Page. Business was business, but this was too much.

But Dottie Skipwith's gaze narrowed further. Somehow in these moments, Kate realized she had felt more scrutinized than listened to. She pictured specimens pinned to a board.

Finally the woman drew a deep breath, extended her foot and pushed off a few inches as if launching a boat. "With many artists," she said, "their families run the fan club. John Michael Montgomery's mother, Kenny Chesney's sister-in-law. They keep it all in the family. They run it out of a Florida room or a weatherized garage.

"*LilyAnn's Page,* now, I rough it out and a freelancer comes in and adds spice. We feature the up-

coming tour schedule, the appearances and the Tick-
etmaster phone numbers. We scan in some photos of
LilyAnn with her fans." She paused, pushed up a
sleeve to reveal a huge watch. There was some micro-
calculation in Dottie's eyes. "Just tell me this, Kate,
if we hired your company, would you be included in
the deal?"

Kate said, "All Fleetwood's resources will be committed and available."

"I mean, do we get you?"

"Of course I'd oversee the project, be involved,
work to assure the highest standards—" She stopped.
Cut back this dreary jargon. She looked at Dottie's
no-nonsense face. "Frankly, at this preliminary stage
we don't assign staffing. It wouldn't be worth our
time."

Dottie tapped her black shoes on the plank floor
and looked up. "To be equally frank, Kate, we might
be especially interested—if you're the key person. I
didn't want a sales rep here today. I wanted to talk
with you. Maybe that's surprising."

"We have a first-rate staff. Several very compe-
tent—"

She cut Kate off with a wave. "I'm sure your company will work hard, Kate, but there's a definite reason you're here this afternoon." Dottie Skipwith
paused, looked around as if to make sure no one was
hiding in the cabin's corners. She stood and went to
the fireplace as if looking for a listening device among
the gum wrappers. She then went to the screen door,
opened it and gave a one-eighty gaze before coming
back inside to sit back down again.

She wet her thin lips. "I've worked for LilyAnn
Page for the past nine years. I do a little of everything,
and we get all kinds of come-ons, some legit, some
crooked. We have a policy—if a venture seems prom-
ising, we look into it. We do a little research on the

side. In your case, on your company, we got the rundown."

Kate nodded.

"The company checks out. We made a few calls. We already have some sample issues of *SouthWing*."

"Very good." The best Kate could do, actually, to produce a seat pocket magazine for the airline whose major hub was Fort Smith, Arkansas.

"And we got the rundown on you too."

"Me?" Kate's voice echoed back like a shrill bird.

"That you moved here to Nashville last September. Before that, you were an investigative reporter in Boston. Isn't that right? The magazine was *New Era,* and three years ago you won a prize for exposing industrial fraud in pharmaceuticals. Then your magazine went bankrupt."

This Is Your Life? Kate worked to keep cool.

"Prior to that, you were a police reporter."

"Wait a minute, that was years ago. It's so deep in my resume, it's nearly buried." But Kate now sat up, curious. "I can't believe you research every sales rep's background this thoroughly—?"

But Dottie Skipwith shook her head and smiled wearily as if she knew this scene by heart. She said, "Kate, we've hired a fair number of people over the years, and we have to check them out. As for employment history, it's like privacy." She shrugged. "There's not much out there hidden, is there? As an investigator, you know how easy it is to get a few facts."

"I'm no longer an investigator."

"When you need them. And we need them." Her voice changed, dropped lower.

Quietly Kate said, "Did you hear me? I'm not an investigator. I mean, not now. As for my work in Boston, just for the record, it was mostly consumer fraud, public health issues, corporate misconduct. I also wrote feature articles, one piece on umbrellas for *Good Housekeeping.* You can't get more—"

"But you were a police reporter."

"So long ago it feels like another life. My daughter was a baby." She stopped. "Maybe we could get back to Fleetwood's proposal."

Dottie swiveled a few degrees in her big chair. She said, "I heard some rumors about cases you got into in Nashville too. The town's not that big. Word gets around."

Murder and mayhem always got around. The Brandi Burns death, a certain disappearance. The smell of brick and mortar chipped by bullets aimed for her head in a Nashville warehouse that was also minutes from Music Row. New England to Nashville, open borders for crime. Where was Dottie Skipwith going with this? What was on her mind?

The bobbed hair shimmered. Dottie sat forward. A new expression was moving in, less aggressive. Around her mouth, Kate thought she saw a tremor.

Her voice was even lower. "You need to understand, LilyAnn Page is my friend, my boss, and one of country music's greats. Eighteen albums, four Grammies, she's an artist that's taken the music to a new level. We've known each other since high school, and there's nothing I wouldn't do for her. And I'm not alone. You don't know how many job requests we get, people wanting to work for her, road crew, lights, gofer, anything. People worship the ground she walks on—and I don't mean the fans alone. I mean veterans in this industry. The entire industry."

Dottie paused, gripped the sides of her chair. The industry, Kate knew, was a shorthand term. In Rochester, it meant Kodak. In Minneapolis, the Pillsbury Dough Boy. In Nashville, a multi-billion dollar ride on vocal twang and the slide guitar. Plus some big bucks crossovers into rock and pop. And of course, certain country standouts like LilyAnn Page.

Kate sat still. Through this testimonial, Dottie Skipwith's knuckles whitened from the grip on her chair.

"Young kids just cutting their first album, the women'll tell you they learned country from singing along to Lily's albums when they were in grade school. And she's a special personality, Kate, very tough in her standards but also delicate. I say this because there's something . . . you know about the fire."

"The man on the mower mentioned—"

"A heater in the bus stateroom, they said a wire shorted out. Except Lily swears she didn't turn on the heat back there."

"Oh?"

"And then the accident."

"The crew member who was killed."

"Killed by LilyAnn's own guitar case, Kate. You have to understand, Lily likes to take her own guitar out of the truck personally. It's a good-luck thing with her. It's her signature guitar, you've seen it."

"No."

"Yes, you have, the custom Martin Dreadnought, with the big white mother-of-pearl lily inlay on the body. It's her symbol, like Emmylou Harris's rose. When LilyAnn's onstage, you can see it from the back row of the last balcony. You can see it from the bleachers. It shines white. We put it on the T-shirt for the *Love Me Not* tour. Now you remember?"

"No, I . . ." Trapped. How many times did you tell your own child to be honest, not to lie, not to fake it. At least you'd save yourself embarrassment. "Frankly, Dottie, being from New England, I never exactly really got into country music. I mean, 'Break of Dawn' is fantastic, one of the great classics. But I don't actually collect country albums."

It was technically true, though since her move to Nashville, a shelf of country CDs was growing steadily, thanks to Sam Powers who brought them to her with each visit, like lessons.

"So you're not a fan."

Kate shook her head no.

Another look at the quarter-pounder watch. Then, abruptly, Dottie Skipwith sat back in the big black swivel chair as if braced for some g-force. "That's okay," she said, "maybe even better, for the sake of objectivity."

"Objectivity?"

"Because somebody's trying to kill her."

Kill her. They sat. Dottie now looked as though her chair were nearing the sound barrier. She repeated, "Trying to kill her."

The moment was silent. A songbird outside began an aria to the spring. Through a window Kate could see a dogwood, its pink blossoms seeming to float in the warm air. Over the week, the tree had lost a good many flowers. The days grew longer, but beautiful springtime was on the wane.

Kill?

She looked sidelong at the woman across from her, dressed all in black in a big black chair. She was stark but not self-dramatizing, a committed employee of a country star. Kate detected no sign of hysteria.

Nor any sign that a good murder scare would be a publicity gimmick for a longtime star. No sign of anything, in fact, but a statement of bottom-line belief.

Nevertheless, Kate used a tactic of counselors and shrinks, who repeated terms back to force a person to hear their own thoughts. Slowly she said, "You think someone is trying to kill LilyAnn Page."

"That's exactly what I said. That guitar case meant to fall on her head like a rock the minute she touched it. That bus fire, I'm sure it was set. Ten minutes earlier, she'd have been in her stateroom. We'd have lost her."

Kate said, "If she thinks her life is in danger, she ought to go to the police."

"That's just it, she—" Dottie pushed at her silver bracelet, crossed and uncrossed her ankles. "She doesn't know . . . she doesn't think. . . ."

"You mean, she doesn't agree with you."

"It's not about agreement. She . . . I haven't brought it up, not directly."

Kate stared. Was there an *in*direct way? Subtle hints about a killer on the loose? Outside, another half-dozen pink dogwood blossoms tumbled on the breeze. Two thoughts occurred, that the country legend's business office looked strange from the inside, and that the Fleetwood sales director owed her for this.

Dottie now sat forward. "I'm not ready to upset Lily, Kate. She needs all her strength. She has to focus. People think a country star's life is glamorous, but they don't see the wear and tear. You wouldn't believe her schedule. Two hundred-plus concert dates a year, most on the road. And here in town she's in the studio every free hour working on an album. This new one, *Against the World*, it's a miracle she got it done. Every time we got the studio scheduled, she got the flu. We joked about calling it *Flu Season*, and it's scheduled for late summer release, but we're all going nuts with the schedule. You have no idea—"

Kate nodded. Maybe this woman was so over-worked she was delusional. Her puffy, bloodshot eyes suggested a lack of sleep. Stressed out, she could easily imagine that a couple of serious mishaps amounted to attempted murder.

Dottie went on. "And Lily works on other artists' albums too, Kate. The longtime stars and the New Country youngsters, they all want her to sing a duet or a harmony backup. Take today; she's in the house for fittings, Manuel and DeSoto both working double time to get her wardrobe ready for spring tour dates. Then she goes into the studio to check some overdubs; then later this afternoon she interviews with *Seventeen*."

"*Seventeen* Magazine?"

"A feature on show-business mothers and daugh-ters." She pointed to the framed photograph on her

desk and to the blonde with the angular features.
"You know LilyAnn has a daughter?"

"No."

"This was Angie two years ago. She's seventeen
now." Dottie then pointed to the apple-cheeked,
curly-haired girl. "My Deb was fourteen." She shook
her head and paused in reverie. "Miracle of the day.
Those girls actually sat still and posed." She chuckled.
"Lily and I both laughed because the girls refused,
put up a big front, said it wasn't worth their time."

She looked across at Kate. "Picture it, the two of
them on summer vacation, all the time in the world,
and it wasn't 'worth their time' to sit for a portrait."
She chuckled again, looked back at the photo. "I guess
it takes a pro. Anyway, it was Myers, the photographer that worked with Lily on her picture autobiogra-
phy, and he got them to pose like angels. Clicked off
roll after roll, and we were thrilled with the result.
But they're a handful, the girls, though I don't expect
Lily to go into those details for the *Seventeen*
interview."

Now Dottie turned back to Kate and was all business. "Anyway," she said, "that's just one hour in her
schedule, then there's a reception at the Vanderbilt
Plaza. Next week we shoot the video for the album.
It's nonstop. There's no downtime." She kept looking
at Kate. "As far as your company is concerned, my
thought is, if you work on the fan club media, you
can investigate on the side. LilyAnn wouldn't have to
be troubled."

Quietly Kate said, "If you think somebody is trying
to kill LilyAnn Page, you ought to tell her."

"She's one of the most beloved stars in country
music."

"Forgive me, Dottie, but after ten months in this
town, you learn every female country vocalist is dearly
beloved. Reba McEntire builds Habitat for Humanity
houses, Emmylou Harris supports a food program,

Dolly Parton provides jobs and scholarships for half the state of Tennessee. The PR is terrific."

Dottie Skipwith's impassive face flushed. It had to be anger. Kate paused. As the Fleetwood business proposal lay on the trestle table, Kate's official role solely to talk it up and answer a few questions. "I'm sorry," she said. "That's out of line. I came here to represent my company. This is simply a business proposal for Ms. Page's consideration."

"But you were a police reporter."

Kate sighed. "Mostly, Dottie, a police reporter is on the scene after—as in aftermath. You see a lot of yellow police tape and . . . spatter."

"Blood, you mean."

"I mean, the job is to report, not investigate," though she hedged. Kate routinely made the extra calls outside the line of duty. More than once, even back then, her editor recited the job description of a police reporter to reel her in. More than once she had gone ahead anyway, beyond the harbors, beyond the buoys into the open sea. And been threatened, finally shot at, including the spray of gunfire a few months ago right here in inland Nashville.

She said, "If you believe somebody wants LilyAnn Page dead, Dottie, you better start asking who and why. So far, your description fits somebody who sets booby traps and sits back to enjoy the action. And it sounds very much like an insider." She leaned forward so that her knees nearly pushed against Dottie Skipwith's. "That front gate tells me somebody around here is security minded."

"Good intentions, anyway." Suddenly Dottie seemed flustered. "The gate's turned out to be a good front, period. It was installed when the stalker tried to get at Lily three years ago. He went to prison. What a relief that was." Dottie looked at Kate. "He was released from Riverbend last month. Paroled early because they're so crowded."

"And—?"

"So far, no sight of him. I gave everybody his photo, the band, the road crew, people on the property here. Problem is, he's so nondescript looking, you'd never pick him out of a crowd. I called Metro Police, but they can't do anything unless he shows up. He's under court order not to come within a thousand feet of her in public places. If we see him on the property, he'll go right back to prison." She bit her lip. "He's probably long gone."

But Dottie looked through a window as if to spot the stalker in the grass and trees. She said, "Actually, I doubt he'll be back. I think we've seen the last of him. But you never know, Kate. So many crazies, somebody might take his place. We're always on the lookout. We try to keep up security, but there are so many in and out." She touched her silver bracelet and counted on her fingers. "Different work crews, the lawn guys, the roofers here last month to put in skylights. The cleaning service, dog groomer. Maybe you heard the barking, Bismarck and Freezee, a boxer and a mutt. They bark so much they're useless as watchdogs. Useless."

She shook her head. "Then there's kitchen and bathroom contractors. And subcontractors. Lily gets restless, she wants new wallpaper and furniture. And antiques, she's a collector. So decorators are here too, dealers, gallery people, their assistants. Delivery trucks."

"Family? Friends?"

"Sure. Lily's brother. He's a contractor. In fact, one of his crews is finishing up a fence along the east side of the property line. That ought to help us out. Then there's distant cousins. Billy D is Lily's third cousin, and he works around the place, keeps an eye on the grounds and cleans the pool. He's around a lot practicing his archery. And a housekeeper looks after Angie, but try to find reliable help, you can't, so there's been a string of them over the years. We sometimes joke it's Grand Central Station.''

"What about fans?"

"She gets everything, pleas for money, love letters, hard luck stories, messages from Jesus. I keep them in special files."

"Any threats?"

Dottie bit her lower lip and looked away. "Some of the sex letters are pretty hard core. She doesn't see them, of course. We screen out the porn and the crazies to spare her."

"How about feuds? Grudges?"

Dottie looked back at Kate. "It's a high-profile life. Like anybody, LilyAnn's had her share of misunderstandings. Her divorce from Angie's dad was bitter. It got into the media. And there's a few people that feel wronged for this or that. Some hard feelings along the way. It's inevitable." She shrugged and looked back at Kate. "You see, Kate, you could work with me on this. You and your company, it's optimal, the perfect setup."

A setup all right. Kate fingered her silver chains, felt this woman's eagerness like a rapid pulse. Dottie made the would-be killer sound as likely to be one of the roofers or dog groomer as the embittered ex-husband. Was she casting a wide net or diluting the mix? Did she have her suspicions, or were the possibilities really this wide open?

And what about Kate? Wasn't adrenaline juicing her heart rate? Wasn't she a top candidate for the LilyAnn Page Patrol the minute Dottie Skipwith showed her ace card, which was Kate Banning's job history? And deep down didn't Kate really want it that way? Didn't the day-to-day routine office job duties bring a yearning for a kick?

She looked very closely at Dottie Skipwith. There was no sign that this woman was actually savvy enough to lure Kate into the fan magazine project

with a death threat as bait. There was no sign that
she had the dimmest knowledge that "Break of
Dawn" was a song that touched Kate's soul, that it
was a hotline to her first real romance, marriage,
maybe even to the personal failure sealed in the divorce from Kelly's father.

Dottie Skipwith could not possibly know, what's
more, that Kate Banning saw boredom over the horizon of her nice new job at Fleetwood and that she
repeatedly found her way to trouble the way ants find
their way to a picnic.

But she must be self-protective too. LilyAnn Page
probably sang "Break of Dawn" at each and every
concert to this very day. A song so entwined with
Kate's own life, with love and marriage and bitterness
and divorce—who needed that baggage?

Go slow, she told herself. Steady as she goes.

Now Dottie folded her hands and sat back as if to
give Kate a little elbow room. "A couple of years
back," she said, "LilyAnn made a TV pilot. The show
was called *American Dreams*. It didn't get far. We all
agreed it was just an experiment. No hard feelings, we
just closed it out and moved on." She looked directly
at Kate. "Think of this as a pilot project between Lily-
Ann Page's management and Fleetwood—and yourself. Just a pilot, Kate. An experiment."

CHAPTER TWO

"Mom, you won't believe it, the whole Richland neighborhood, every front door, we must've listened to a hundred speeches about African violets. Like we really care how much plant food to put in the water, or how much morning sun or Gro lights. It's like the plants are pets."

"That's door-to-door sales for you, Kel. It's person-to-person, one-on-one." Kate pulled the kettle off the stove before the steam whistle shrieked, and mother and daughter bumped hips by the kitchen countertop near the fruit bowl. Nineteen African violets sat in little crocks in rows to the left, plus two bruised ones in small mustard jars.

Kate reached for mugs and Lemon Zinger teabags, poured in the water and decided not to point out the parallel of the mother-daughter afternoons on the sales floor. She said, "Years ago, lots of consumer goods were sold door-to-door, like vacuum cleaners and brushes. Like our bathroom nail brush with the black bristles?"

"My great-grandmother's?"

"Nana's, yes. It came from a door-to-door Fuller Brush man. Nana bought it that way." Kate paused. This could lead quickly into the sad family facts—of Kate's parents whom Kelly never knew because they died in the plane crash in Kate's early childhood. And of Nana who stepped in to raise Kate but who did not live long enough to know her great-granddaughter.

Their new Nashville condo, like their longtime Boston apartment, had a few memorial objects, a chest of drawers with Chinese pagodas on the front, a nondescript side chair, and the one sturdy relic of the Fuller Brush Company. But Kate did not want to linger now on the family history that never was. Go with consumer history, the nonstick kind. She said, "Companies like Fuller Brush sort of disappeared when so many mothers started working outside the home. Nobody was left to answer the doorbell. Now it's mostly kids like you selling candy and plants for fundraisers."

"Well, we hardly sold any. We went to every single house on Central and Richland Avenues. We smiled and were really nice. 'Our concert is a week from this Wednesday,' we said, 'free and open to the public'." Kelly sighed. She spread peanut butter on banana halves, sat down at the kitchen table and licked a glob.

"This bald guy, Mom, he talked to us for fifteen minutes. We explained the violets are for the band trip to Disney World. We were really polite. He did this good-old-days number about his trumpet and marching in some big parade in Chattanooga to win a trophy. His eyes got that misty look, Mom, and I thought, great, he's definitely buying two, maybe three violets for sure."

Her face was now the picture of indignation. "Then he made this long speech about how music is good discipline and builds character. And then he didn't buy even one violet. Not one. He said his wife takes care of the greenery—he called it the greenery. He 'donated' a dollar. Big deal, one measly dollar."

"Maybe it's all he could afford."

"Are you kidding? His driveway had two Mercedes."

Kate dipped her teabag a few times and pulled it from the mug. "Well, Kel, you know those sayings."

"About rich people, yeah, well I am not impressed.

I can't believe nineteen African violets are left. The whole afternoon for six crummy sales." She sighed. "We're supposed to turn in the money by Thursday. And I have to do a nature journal with *Walden*."

"Henry David Thoreau, that's wonderful." Kate smiled. "You've actually been to Walden Pond."

"I don't remember."

"You were just a toddler. Anyway, *Walden* is a New England classic, actually universal, full of wisdom." Kate tried to recall some lines, mostly from calendar captions. "Wait, I remember—'Simplify.' That was a motto."

"Oh yeah, that. I saw it on a Gap ad."

Give it up.

Now Kelly jabbed the knife into the peanut butter jar. The season's first spring sun had lightly tanned her face. Her dark gold hair was pulled back into a ponytail, her cheekbones beginning to give her oval face a womanly shape and a beauty she had not yet discovered. At this rate she'd be taller than Kate by the year's end.

Kelly's mouth drew to a pout. "Mom, the four violets you promised to buy, would you . . . would you buy the ones that dropped?"

"Sure, Kel, sign me up for those two in the mustard jars." She looked at the thick furry leaves with pink flowers. If only she liked them better. Kate patted Kelly's shoulder. "It'll be okay. Selling is a tough business all around. You did the best you could, Kel. I'm thankful you're back safe and sound."

A scowling Kelly looked over at the little crocks as if each signified a personal failing. " 'Safe and sound, safe and sound.' " She said it in a voice of sing-song mockery. "Safety again, Mom. Safety, safety. You always nag about that."

"I am always concerned."

"No, you nag. Nag." She paused. "I just think it would be lots easier if we had a cart to pull them—

no, a wagon like when I sold Girl Scout cookies in
Boston." She looked at Kate. "Hey, where is my
wagon?"

"I gave it to Goodwill." Kelly stared. "I gave it
away when we moved."

"You gave my wagon away?"

"Kelly, we couldn't bring everything."

"You just gave it away? You didn't ask me?" Incre-
dulity. Her brow was now like a dark cloud over a
mountain. "I loved my wagon."

Kate said, "Kel, it was wonderful when you were
six and seven. It mostly stayed in the basement after
that."

Kelly's eyes narrowed. "First you make us move,
then you leave my stuff in Boston." Her eyes narrowed further. "I bet you brought all your stuff, Mom.
I bet you didn't give your stuff to Goodwill."

"That's not true. My old ice skates, winter boots—"
Kate stopped. She did not owe her fourteen-year-old
an inventory of jettisoned personal possessions. In
fact, she could start to feel bad herself, especially at
certain times of the year, such as right about now,
approaching the third Sunday in May, which was Lilac
Sunday at Boston's Arnold Arboretum. She and Kelly
always took a picnic lunch with Italian cold cuts and
bought the current year's lilac poster from the gift
shop. Three framed lilac posters hung in the living
room of their Nashville condo. These May days, Kate
could barely look at them.

The mood across the table was dark as a weather
front. "I can't believe you gave away my wagon."

"Kelly, please, that's enough. It went to Goodwill.
Some needy child in Boston is delighted. Let's drop
it."

"I'm needy too. And you aren't even sorry. Easy
for you, Mom. You had a cool afternoon with LilyAnn
Page." Her face struggled for control. "Well big deal,
she's on the oldies station."

"Oldies?" Kate heard the surprise in her own voice.

"Sure, oldies. Your generation. Like Linda Ronstadt and the Supremes. And Elvis."

"They're quite a bit before my—"

"Sometimes we listen in case somebody wants to do a really cheesy imitation in the talent show. Like 'Teddy Bear' or 'Blue Bayou.' I mean, really cheesy."

Cheesy and old? Not classic and timeless? Somehow it was jarring to think of LilyAnn Page as an "oldie." When did a star become an "oldie?" Did that make Kate's own life an "oldie?" To a fourteen-year-old, of course. Keep it in perspective.

"So did she sing for you, or what?" Kelly raised her face in a mock expression of heartbreak. " 'Pale sky at morning—' " Now she actually sang. It was the opening of "Break of Dawn," but a taunting version, as if Kelly sensed her mother's weakness. " 'All sailors and cowboys take warning—' "

Kate tried to manage a neutral look at Kelly, who was surely unaware that the song was a link to her own mother and father, to their broken marriage when the young doctor-father and the young police reporter-mother realized they were staring across chasms of mistaken identity, mounting resentments—and one wonderful infant.

" 'Pale sky at morning—' "

The wonderful infant now in adolescence. Enough of this. Stop it with conversation. "I didn't actually meet LilyAnn Page, Kelly. She had some other appointments."

Kelly bit the last of a banana half. "So where was ol' LilyAnn today?" Again that warpath tone.

Kate said, "She's busy replacing her wardrobe because her tour bus caught fire a few days ago."

"Oh yeah, now I remember, it was on TV. Her clothes are toast." She licked a peanut butter drop from the table. "So did somebody torch the bus?"

Kate snapped to attention. But this was not about

information, she saw, only defiance. She put down her mug and looked closely at her daughter's face. "Fires," she said, "are always terrifying. They move very fast, and burns are one of the hardest injuries to treat. You've seen burn-scarred skin—you remember that little boy in second grade, the hot grease?"

"Dennis."

"So why would you say a thing like that?"

Her lip quavered, ready to exit this hard-shell pose. "Because . . . because in Nashville you can't even sell five-dollar violets to somebody with two Mercedes. Stupid ugly African violets. The best purple flowers are lilacs." She stopped. "Hey, what about Lilac Sunday? We're going to miss Lilac Sunday! Can we go? We could fly up to Boston for the weekend. I have some money from my allowance. I'll contribute."

Now Kate took her daughter's hand and spoke in a low-key voice. "It's . . . it's not the right time, Kel. We need to learn to live in Nashville. I thought we might take a drive down the Natchez Trace with a picnic over next weekend. I understand there are great waterfalls and walking trails. The Trace is a historic trade route that went all the way to New Orleans." Kelly did not respond. Kate said, "We need to be patient, Kel. You'll be in New England with Liza at summer camp in a couple of months, and we need time to make friends and settle in here. They say the first year's the hardest." She hoped it was true. She paused to remind herself that a year was a teen's eternity.

Now Kelly pointed to the window of their four-unit condo. "Are you making friends with those magnolia trees, Mom?"

"I don't understand."

"You don't have a new friend here yet. Nobody like Maggie."

"I talk to Maggie on the phone the same way you talk to Liza on the phone. I'm busy at my job. I be-

lieve that in time I'll make friends." Yet Kelly had a
point. Their small condo cluster had just four units
tucked amid magnolia trees, and Kate knew the neighbors only on a casual first-name basis.

But some sixth sense told Kate this wasn't entirely
about red wagons or friends or even the Boston-to-
Nashville move, but the teen years. She thought of
Dottie Skipwith on the phone this afternoon to her
own daughter over the mess in the office fireplace.
Bubble gum, a red wagon, whatever could be used as
a blasting cap.

"You think Sam will buy some violets?"

"For a bud vase in the cockpit of the Learjet?"
They both laughed. For now, the storm had broken.

"Probably he will," Kate said. "Wasn't he your biggest customer for Girl Scout cookies?"

"Yeah. When's he coming?"

"Tomorrow evening."

But now Kelly clapped her hand to her mouth. "Oh
Mom, I forgot."

"What?"

"Sam called. While you were at Kroger's. Something about air traffic control, and he's trying to get
here but there's a delay, like a radar failure but it's
fine, we shouldn't worry. He'll let us know." She
rushed on, undisturbed. "And some woman called too,
Dottie somebody."

"Dottie Skipwith? She called already?"

"She wants you to come back to her office tomorrow. I wrote her number, it's here someplace." Kelly
bounced up to her room.

Dottie Skipwith's number turned up minutes later
on a Post-it nearly black with doodlings of The Simp-
sons. But Kate was in no rush to get back to Dottie
of the flip phone. Didn't the woman believe in week-
ends? The sacred Sabbath here in the Bible Belt?

More worrisome was Sam's message. Filtered
through Kelly, it was garbled. His weekend destination

was Nashville, but his current whereabouts unknown.
He could be on the ground in the Northeast or Texas,
or at thirty thousand feet in the cockpit of the Lear.
She turned on TV and let a CNN cycle play through—
a bus bombing in the Middle East, a drug bust at
the Mexican border, a vice-presidential tour of flood
damage in Ohio. Nothing about radar failures or avia-
tion mishaps.

Most probably, he was simply delayed. Most probably too, he'd arrive with CDs meant for Kate's quick
course in country music. It wasn't exactly true that she
was totally ignorant. Thanks to Sam, Kate now had
Hank Williams, Dolly Parton, Emmylou Harris, Willie
Nelson, Tammy Wynette, George Jones, Charley
Pride. And a few others, such as those two men with
great voices and the names Kelly liked to joke about,
Ernest Tubb and Lefty Frizzell. Classic, top-quality
country, Sam said. Maybe on this visit, it would be
LilyAnn Page's latest.

Though *visit* was an awful word for time with your
lover. It sounded so . . . institutional. She tried to
suspend the angst and stay by the phone. And start
dinner, a quickie special, frozen ravioli, salad and tomato sauce with pesto. She reached past the pots of
violets to tune in the kitchen radio to WSM FM, one
of Nashville's major country music stations.

These current hits were mostly fast, jingly tunes,
heavy on the snare drums and cymbals, the slide guitars like cats in heat. These songs sounded nothing
like "Break of Dawn," the singers nothing like Lily-
Ann Page.

It struck Kate that in half an hour, not one song by
LilyAnn Page had been played, the star's name not
mentioned at all. She turned to the other big station,
WSIX, 97.9, which sounded exactly like its competi-
tion. Again, no LilyAnn Page.

It was nearly six o'clock when she mixed the salad
greens and wrestled with the jar lid of the Classico

sauce, held it under hot running water and then twisted with a pliers-like, medieval device until the vacuum popped. Mentally she wrote a note to Classico ("Dear Mr. and Ms. Classico, Your lids are too tight"). It was one more consumer letter in the internet of her own brain. On WSIX, a song by a vocalist famous for her navel piercing was now announced as number two on the *Billboard* country chart. Her voice was thin and drowned by a tambourine. Next a male vocalist rhymed "battle" and "cattle" in a song about Nevada which sounded more like rock 'n' roll than country. She turned off the radio before calling Kelly. Still no LilyAnn Page.

Mother and daughter ate quickly, Kate resisting the urge to ask Kelly what she knew about recent country music here in Nashville. Skip the chance to be patronized by a fourteen-year-old. An amiable Kelly agreed it was her turn to clean up the kitchen.

Kate listened to a few more current songs. Tweedle Dee, Tweedle Dum.

Still no song by LilyAnn Page.

Still no call from Sam.

Into the living room, she sat for a few moments, just sat with her thoughts. Ignore the lilac pictures. Ignore the telephone and the clash of pots and plates as Kelly made loading the dishwasher a contact sport. Ignore the laughter bursting through the closed door of Kelly's room upstairs moments later. Settle into the nice sofa the color of golden wheat, thankful for the Nashville job that got her and her daughter a condo and a health plan and education money set aside each month.

Time out. Give a few moments' thought to the phone call to Dottie Skipwith. Whether LilyAnn Page was an "oldie" or a star, she was a celebrity on national TV. She turned up on Leno and *Regis and Kathie Lee* and was sprinkled through those media

"People" columns too. Her face was recognizable at airports, restaurants, any public place.

So what would it mean, shadowing a celebrity? Once at a party in Boston, guests told of their moments in the presence of stars. One described Elizabeth Taylor's eyes, another Garbo's cape, a third the chiseled face of Robert Redford, who commanded sidelong gazes of a roomful of people trying not to stare. All the while Redford himself tried not to look like somebody constantly stared at.

Then too, Boston was a town that also made stars out of professors, such as the revered, world-famous Nobel Peace Prize winner who stole a taxi in the pouring rain from an eight-months-pregnant friend of Kate's, throwing a body block as he announced in his thick inflection, "I need zees cab!"

Tally them up. The Nobel offensive lineman, the exhausted-looking Senator in the airport, the elevator ride with *My Fair Lady*'s Rex Harrison, and the two female giraffes identified on a Manhattan street as *Vogue* supermodels. In Philadelphia six years ago, she had attended a lunch honoring a billionaire and was distracted through every course by the phenomenon of the small wiry figure picking at a stuffed tomato two tables away in a cheap suit and richer than certain states of the Union.

But the singer of "Break of Dawn?" This was the vocalist whose song cut to Kate's own life—plaintive, elusive, yearning and searing. The lyrics and vocal delivery held promise and desire, and a kind of fatalism from someplace deep and dark. For Kate, it cut to the soft tissue of the soul. Working to protect LilyAnn Page from harm, what would Kate feel? Awe? Dazzle? Stardust on her shoulders like flecks of gold? Or like heavy metal dragging her under?

"Break of Dawn"—

She shifted on the sofa and moved a cattail-pattern throw pillow behind her back. What about LilyAnn

Page's jeopardy? A tour bus fire, a cascade of heavy instrument cases—did two freak incidents amount to attempted murder? Or was her personal manager paranoid, maybe overwhelmed by the insurance work, various duties and the onslaught of her own daughter's teen years?

Assume malice for just a moment—the bus fire, also the truck in which the singer's guitar case was loaded. Touring itself would connect the two. If LilyAnn was performing on the road some two hundred days per year, then two-thirds of her life was spent away from Nashville. If somebody had a grudge, a kind of rage boiling against her, would they try to kill her "accidentally" in her accustomed home away from home?

But if Kate took this assignment, what about her own danger? There was the physical side, of course. The four elements—earth, air, fire, water—she had nearly succumbed to them all.

But there was a different peril here and now. Kate turned on a table lamp in the gathering dusk, and the lamp itself made the point. It was one of a pair with Chinese basket bases on brass, solid and durable, a middle class lamp, the kind she'd never had in all those years when Goodwill was not just a donation site but a furniture store.

But as Dottie Skipwith's undercover agent, she'd put her own job at risk, her new Nashville life in peril. The opening at Fleetwood came up so abruptly at the eleventh hour when Kate faced no prospects and mounting bills, when Kelly's very sneakers were a test of economic failure. Then suddenly, a light at the end of a dark tunnel of unemployment checks. Steady income in Nashville, no more scrounging. Only a fool would put all that at risk. This was not about materialism but safety and common sense.

She paused. From inside the middle class, maybe life was all about fear. Fear of losing your status and your stuff.

And your kid's future too. Besides, who would take care of Kelly? These accidents happened on tour, and she'd have to spend days on the interstates in Lily-Ann's tour bus. Leave Kelly alone or with a hired stranger? Out of the question.

So turn Dottie down flat. She would phone at once. She stood.

Then stopped. Foolish Kate. She wasn't a free agent at all but a Fleetwood employee, tethered to the company. As dumb and shaky as she considered the fan magazine project, it was a formal Fleetwood proposal. The new sales director, Don Donaghue, pushed it hard, asked for Kate's support. She'd agreed to play corporate doubles.

So the proper procedure was to bow out of the Lily-Ann "case" but talk up the advantages of the Fleet-wood deal. Kate went to the kitchen Post-it. Dottie's flat Chicago voice sounded so pleased to hear Kate say she'd come back to the cabin office tomorrow morning at eleven.

Once again it was the borrowed Navigator, the SUV or Suburban Assault Vehicle lumbering along Harding and Tyne feeling like a Sherman tank. No sign today of the bow-and-arrow man on his John Deere as she was clicked through the 83 Mosely gate and followed the crushed gravel lane to the office cabin at 11:15, surprised to see a Fiesta and a Camry. The weather was pleasant. She heard barking dogs as Dottie came to the cabin door and stepped outside.

"Apologies, Kate. We're backed up, but you're about to see what a major star is up against." Dottie Skipwith lowered her voice. "It's a quality thing. One look at LilyAnn Page, you know she's a class act. No ratshack low-rent promotionals for her. If it's top of the line, let's put it on LilyAnn's table. She shoots most of them down so nicely they don't know what hit 'em. She will not suffer fools. You'll see it all. Come in."

The fluorescents were off, the log cabin interior so much darker than the bright sunshine outdoors. Then Kate saw the semicircle of stack chairs facing the far platform area with the red easy chair and rug and also the lighted lamp. Kate sat down as if selecting a church pew.

Before her in the red chair on the platform sat a small-boned figure who seemed to bask in her pool of lamplight from head to toe. The high collar of a snow-white tailored shirt set off the alabaster skin, the fragile face and soulful eyes and auburn hair with the trademark skunk streak. LilyAnn Page wore a long chocolate skirt and matching vest. Her legs were crossed, and the tip of a cowboy boot pointed out from the hem of her skirt. She looked both smaller and larger than life. The lamp light marked a territory that looked both inviting and yet off-limits.

Kate tried not to stare, tried not to feel like a worshipper at this very hour when ninety-five percent of Nashville was settled into church pews. In the semicircle of stack chairs, three people faced forward as if to an altar. A gaunt young man in a green golf sweater at Kate's left cradled a small cardboard box in his lap. To his left sat a twosome who looked enough alike to be brother and sister. They balanced a large sketch pad and satchel. Dottie Skipwith was seated in her big black leather swivel desk chair. Were these fans? Supplicants? It felt like a Sunday service for Lily-Ann Page.

Dottie apparently was Ms. Command Central. She wore black on Sundays too. No, correction, her shell top was dark gray. She nodded to the gaunt man and said, "Okay, let's hear it, Eddie." LilyAnn's face, Kate noticed, looked noncommittal, as if withholding judgment and enthusiasm too. It was the expression of someone who knew how to conserve energy.

The sweater man reached into the cardboard box and took out a little rustic house with snow white patches on the ceramic roof. He looked prematurely wizened, as if from boyhood he'd worked up from secondhand things, used textbooks or skimpy towels or flea market tables of chipped plates. He turned a crank under the little house. The music box sound was fast and tinny.

Dottie turned to Kate. "You recognize that tune?"

" 'Break of Dawn'."

"And would you buy a music box with that sound?"

"I'm . . . I'm not sure."

"A diplomatic answer, meaning no." Dottie Skipwith turned back to the man. "This lady knows a signature song, but she's too polite to say how terrible it sounds." He squirmed. Dottie said, "What about our agreement?"

He said he'd tried his best. LilyAnn Page still looked neutral.

"Eddie, this is important to us. Signature collector products are something new for Ms. Page. And we want to help you out, believe me, we do." She swung around in the black chair, and her voice rose. "In fact, we're bending over backwards so far our spines are cracking. How can LilyAnn Page license a Christmas music box that sounds like a tin can?"

Dottie Skipwith pointed her finger like a schoolmarm. "Don't say I didn't warn you three weeks ago. Now it's deadline, and we've got a situation. Would George Strait license a song that sounded like a three-year-old going tinkle? Would Garth? Reba? Shania?"

Eddie protested that all music boxes sounded miniature. He did not look ahead at the Queen of Country Music enthroned before him.

The room fell silent. Finally LilyAnn Page shifted in the easy chair, leaned forward and spoke. Her voice, like Dottie's, was surprisingly Midwestern but rubbed soft by the South. "You forget . . . Eddie, is it?" He nodded as if forced out from hiding. "Well, Eddie, we tour Europe, we tour Germany and Austria and Switzerland. Their music boxes, well let's just say you'd be proud. This one you've got there, it's from—?"

"Taipei."

"We've toured East Asia too, Japan, Korea." She wet her red lips. "But pride is the issue here. Pride is what we're talking about." The voice, Kate noticed, was as firm as it was soft. "Of course, I'm not an expert on products like these souvenirs."

"Collectibles." Eddie sat up as if stung. "With all due respect, Ms. Page, these are not souvenirs. This is fine porcelain ceramic. These are Harwell Collectibles."

He waited for a response. Silence. He said, "You heard of the Franklin Mint? They make offerings to the public, collectibles every one. Harwell is top quality."

The country star's face was still in neutral, though she cleared her throat and tipped her head back as if to peer down at the pitchman before her in the dim light.

"Eddie, let me put this in my terms, music terms. There are certain songs I won't go into the studio and cut, and they're songs we've been working on for months, sometimes years." She paused. "I have one song about a father and daughter, and it needs just one line. But that line hasn't come along yet. I can work with a rhyming dictionary and come up with all sorts of filler, but I won't settle for so-so."

She recrossed her leg, adjusting the skirt so that the tip of the boot pointed like a bodily punctuation mark. "That song won't go to copyright with my name on it until it's right. Now you hear what I'm saying?"

Kate heard the word, somewhere between *saying* and *sayin'*. It was unhurried but fluid as a moving stream with a certain velocity. Kate noticed she did not meet his eyes, that her gaze fixed at a point high and off-center, perhaps the top of his forehead. An-

other personal energy conservation tactic? Surely it'd
be maddening to be stared at like that.

Deadly maddening?

Dottie took a cue. "You know we want a deal,
Eddie. The Christmas Village concept is a good
promo. We're ready to announce the product in *Lily-
Ann's Page,* see it in *Parade* with the Sunday papers,
see it on TV. It'll hit just right with the NBC Christmas special. LilyAnn will sing 'White Christmas' and
a song of her choosing. It could be 'Break of Dawn'
to help promote the music box Christmas House.

You folks are halfway there, and Ms. Page will be
the first to say so. The very first."

All eyes turned to LilyAnn Page, who seemed to
wait for expectation to rise. Indeed, the small group
seemed to hold its collective breath until at last, when
it peaked, she nodded her confirmation that the Harwell folks were indeed at the halfway point. The
group, Kate too, let out a collective sigh.

"There you are," said Dottie. "Upgrade that music.
It's your move. That's it in a nutshell."

The dismissed Eddie flushed and murmured about
his deadline, about Taipei and holiday delivery guar-
antee. His face grew more pinched as he spoke. "We'll
rethink," he said, almost cringing. "We want you to
be happy, Ms. Page. Harwell Collectibles wants its
Stars of Country Music licensees to be happy."

LilyAnn Page smiled ever so slightly in his direction,
her full lips in a curve Kate had seen close up on TV.
It was a smile just a little crooked and somehow more
appealing for that. But the smile, Kate now saw, was
also ambiguous. It might signal encouragement or
scorn, pleasure or contempt. Kate hoped no one ever
smiled at her like that.

Dottie swiveled again as the rueful Eddie nodded
briefly, boxed up the little house and scuttled out.
They heard an engine coaxed to life, the Fiesta.

Dottie turned immediately to the twosome, not

pausing to introduce Kate. "Okay, Clark and Babs, let's see what you've got." She glanced at Kate. "It's nonstop around here, Kate. Sundays too, never a letup. You're next, don't worry, your time's coming." She turned. "Okay, Fan Fair time, let's hear it. Kate, you do know about Fan Fair, right?"

"Fan Fair? Sort of a country music festival, right?"

Suddenly the room went dead quiet, as if the electricity had failed.

As if Kate, too, had brought a product that bombed.

The country star did not blink.

Dottie's sigh was all exasperation. " 'Festival,' that's an understatement." She turned to Kate. "Biggest convention of country music fans anyplace in the world, Kate, that's Fan Fair. One week every June out at the state fairgrounds, all the stars are there. The Judds, Wynonna naturally, but Naomi too. They hold a big charity auction. There's celebrity softball, that's a fund raiser. Tim McGraw, Clint Black, Faith Hill, all of them. There's even fan clubs for stars who've passed away, Roy Orbison, Hank Williams. A few years back, Garth showed up and signed autographs for nearly twenty-four hours straight. It was hot as Hades that year. Most years it hits ninety and pouring down rain."

She shook her head dismissively and went on. "Fans don't care a bit about weather. There's concerts, fan club galas, autographs, chance to get your picture taken with the biggest stars, a private moment with just you and the star at the booth. National TV coverage too. People come from every state in the union and a bunch of foreign countries. Acres of campers and RVs, every hotel in town full, traffic backed up all over Nashville. Fan Fair tickets are usually gone by January, and they're a hundred dollars a pop. That tells you something."

Kate nodded, felt a flush up her face and the scope of her mistake. Ignorance was never bliss.

Dottie Skipwith went on like a carnival barker. "So Clark and Babs, what have you got?"

The couple sat up straight. In a navy blazer and khakis, Clark was sandy-haired with pale eyes and a certain passive slope to his shoulders, while Babs was all angles from her close-cropped hair to her brows, her suit lapels and sharp-toed shoes like a geometry exercise with a protractor.

He spoke in a high tenor voice. "We're thinking the booth's theme should be . . ." He flipped the sketch-pad and held up a drawing. "The Fifties! We think Formica and chrome kitchen table and stools, a Waring blender, a Mixmaster, a fridge. We'll have fridge magnets holding recipe cards with titles of Ms. Page's hits. 'Break of Dawn,' of course, and 'Destiny' and 'Chisholm Ridge' and 'Royal Flush,' 'Stones and Stars'—"

"I don't think so." The voice from the lamplight was low and clear and icy hot. The face kept its composure, but LilyAnn swung her leg. The skirt rippled. The cowboy boot kicked forward like an exclamation point. "I don't think so."

"That means no. N-o." Dottie smacked her palm against the table and brushed the carcass of a bug to the floor. "No Fifties, no kitchen, no Lucy and Desi. You want to push kitchens, kids, try Loretta Lynn, that's her gig." Kate recalled the highway signs for Loretta Lynn's Kitchen, home cooking. "You forgot who your star is. LilyAnn Page is a younger generation. Mature but very much younger. Much younger than Loretta. Much."

Kate looked from one to the other. Age, clearly a sensitive point. An awkward moment ticked by. She looked at her watch. It was eleven-thirty. She'd spent half an hour basically waiting in line.

Babs said, "The Fifties is hip. Maybe a lava lamp."

"It's not LilyAnn." Dottie Skipwith's dark brows arched up. "It's not who she is. Look kids, you've got a reigning queen of country music right in front of you. Authentic classic country music. Quality."

Babs started to open the sketch pad as if to continue the presentation. Dottie's finger jabbed. "Put that away. What part of no don't you understand? That was Lorrie Morgan's hit, Kate, just so you know where the reference is from. I'm applying it here."

Dottie drummed fingers on the tabletop. She said, "Your theme ought to follow the new album. I sent you that tape, Clark. How about the title cut—"

" 'Against the World.' " He sounded like a pupil reciting.—"*Against the World,* absolutely." Dottie's voice now turned sarcastic. "*Against the World,*" she repeated. "Now, what's that got to do with the Fifties and lava lamps?—pure nothing. Here come LilyAnn's most devoted fans, with their vacation money saved all year for Fan Fair. They're on the road to Nashville, they're flying in, they're ready for a preview of the new album and the Fan Club party too. And you want to give them Loretta's kitchen."

"Dottie, I'm sorry, it's a misunder—"

"It's a disaster, that's what it is. *Against the World* is eleven songs about courage and moving ahead. If you listened to the tape, you would have figured that out. Your job's to design a booth that makes fans feel like they can hardly wait for the album release and the video."

Clark said, "It would really help if we could see the video."

"We're not shooting it till next week." Dottie's cheeks were a bright pink, her voice now paved with sarcasm. "Kids, believe me, if we had a video, you would have a copy in hand. We would not deprive you. But as it happens, the video shoot is scheduled for next Saturday, which is too late for you. In an ideal world, the schedule would be different. If you ever find that world, let me know."

They sat silent.

"Okay, here's the thing, we need a booth concept to tie the new album to LilyAnn's career hits. Think big, kids. Think about facing life against the odds. But no water, not after that year with the lily pond." She let out a sigh. "And what about the Fan Club party at the museum? I suppose you had a kitchen theme in mind for that too?"

Babs's hangdog look confirmed it.

"Some old fridge in the Country Music Museum lobby? A classy reception with catered wood-fired chicken and petite artichokes, and you want to. . . ." Exasperated, she clapped her hands together. "Tell you what. Go tour the museum exhibits and adapt a theme. Endurance and classic South. Brave and coping. Beauty, good taste. Do it today. But nothing tacky, no polyester. Think leather and silk, dignity, courage, you can't lose. Remember, Kip's crew's ready to build whatever you want. If LilyAnn Page's own brother didn't have a construction company, I shudder to think." She shuddered. "Let's finalize tomorrow. Tuesday at the latest. Make it good."

Clark and Babs started their retreat, looking uneasy, almost frightened. No wonder. This was some good cop/bad cop duet act Dottie and LilyAnn Page worked out between them. The star sat like the reigning dignitary on a parade float while the manager ranted and raved. LilyAnn Page might or might not be targeted for murder, but if anybody felt homicidal, Dottie seemed like the likelier mark.

In her halo of lamp light, LilyAnn Page tapped her wrist and murmured that she was needed at the house. She stirred from the red easy chair, stood, then stepped off the platform. Somehow it was shocking to see her move, come down to earth. At ground level she stood five-three at most. But in the half darkness, she seemed to take the lamp light with her, as if she glowed.

Dottie said, "Lily . . . Ms. Page, this is Kate Banning, with the plan for the *Page*. Kate, you stay put, we'll talk."

But the country star was already near the door, her Sunday morning audiences over. Vaguely she said, "Dottie'll take care of you," then smiled and glided past. The door hissed and clicked shut. Was that scent her perfume or the jonquils?

A moment passed. Letdown. Dottie was obviously waiting until LilyAnn was well out of earshot. The manager went to the door, stared out for a moment, lingered as if for a moment of rest herself, then turned on the fluorescents, returned to her desk and shuffled some papers.

Kate turned to look into the fireplace—at yesterday's trash, butts and pink gum globs. So Dottie's daughter was not scared into action by the phone ultimatum. Maybe the woman's bark was worse than her bite. Suppose the various staffers and beggars and freelancers thought so too. In which case the real center of fear defaulted to LilyAnn Page, whose slightest gestures were really Doppler radar storms.

So much speculation. The LilyAnn Page life drama, however, was just that, a showcase exhibit. For Kate, it was NA, not applicable. She had her viewpoint and her bailout statement all ready.

Moments passed. The wait seemed endless. At last Dottie looked up. "It's a tough business, Kate. It's rough."

"I can see that."

"Those designers, Clark and Babs, we've worked with them for five years. They're supposed to be so hot, they win awards. Me, I think they have lava lamps for brains."

"It must be frustrating."

"Asking for a video that doesn't even exist."

Kate nodded but said nothing. She waited for a calmer moment. Dottie shuffled some more papers, went to the red chair, turned off the lamp. At last she stepped back and looked up at Kate, who cleared her throat and tried to speak slowly.

"Dottie, I'd help you out if I could. The Fleetwood deal is well worth your consideration, but as for the . . . the investigation, I've given this a lot of thought pro and con, but I have to bow out. I don't feel my responsibilities can extend that far. Let me recommend—"

But just then a thump and wheeze distracted her. It was the screen door again. The next sad soul in the Sunday lineup of appointments? "I want to say in confidence, Dottie, that I appreciate—"

But Dottie's face suddenly looked like clay, no, more like stone. She was staring into some distance behind Kate.

"The door—" Kate heard a small, familiar voice say behind her. "Dining room door—" The voice sounded Midwestern, rubbed by the South.

Dottie Skipwith's face was now white as marble and staring off past Kate's ear.

Now Kate turned to see the chocolate skirt and vest, the white shirt and skunk streak and the soulful eyes. The hair was messy, the vest askew, the skirt dusty and torn as if trampled and stepped on.

As if crawled in?

The hands were dirty, the face streaked. The glow was all gone. She and Dottie stared as the figure stepped forward, lurched left, clawed the wall for balance with the left hand while the right arm hung, angled out.

"Door—"

And it took Kate a moment to realize that between the wrist and elbow, LilyAnn Page had an extra joint in her arm.

"Damn door came down on me . . . dining room. Fell down." Slurred speech. That skunk streak white as snow.

Snow. Kate's thoughts flashed to a New England

winter scene from a chair lift, a woman below, skis
crossed, one leg with an extra joint below the knee.
Broken, Kate had realized. A broken leg.

"Damn door."

A broken arm.

"Came down on me, fell real hard like . . . can't
walk any . . . more."

She did not finish. The next moment blurred as the
figure took a step, sighed, and then pitched forward
as Kate and Dottie rushed to stop LilyAnn Page from
falling face down and unconscious on the hard plank
floor.

CHAPTER THREE

Monday morning, 8:06, and Kate sat at her desk and tried to settle an issue; literally a magazine issue for readers ranging from Ski-Doo sales reps to dude ranch managers. Would they enjoy a tongue-in-cheek account of a crazy romp through today's health spas? On the desk before her were two thousand words on massage wet packs, waxing and pummeling, all in bombast and bravado. *"I felt like a home renovation project when Jacques scoured my cellulite with a brick . . . but it felt like the embrace of an octopus when the multi-suction nozzle was clapped to my thigh. . . ."*

The piece went on about body wax like boiling oil, a steam room like a Yellowstone geyser; a personal trainer like Paul Bunyon. And on. Kate had tweaked these paragraphs for a week now, with no noticeable improvement. The Fleetwood design department needed the copy text by ten. Would this piece seem cute or just stupid?

She flipped once again through the approved, edited articles in a stack all ready to go. Suppose she slotted "Wrapped in Plastic and Left to Sweat" after the earnest piece on shiatsu message. Actually, this issue needed a little more bulk. She looked back at the text.

"I felt like a loaf of whole wheat when the trainer kneaded my ribs with his toes. . . ."

Enough, this was deadline. Go with it. There was lots to do on *SouthWing,* and she needed the time. She clipped the hardcopy, slipped the disk into a plastic sleeve, bundled the whole issue into a big envelope, and stood to take it downstairs.

Then Kate paused to look through her fourth-floor office window overlooking the Cumberland River. On the east bank, an NFL football stadium was rising. The mayor, nicknamed Pharaoh Phil, was the big daddy of the deal. From her office window, Kate had the daily view of his pyramid scheme. Nashvillians' grandchildren would still be paying for it. It looked like an aircraft carrier in dry-dock.

She turned back to her desk. If only the morning's work and the view blocked the mental reruns of the scene in the cabin yesterday. In memory's aftershock, she relived the deadweight feeling of LilyAnn Page's body as she collapsed and fainted. Dottie and Kate pulled her in a weird dance, a *trois;* the cowboy boot heels dragging across the floor. They'd got the rug under her and smoothed it for a pallet, then laid Lily-Ann down as Dottie called 911, and then opened the electric gate.

Kate stayed long enough for the ambulance, for the EMTs who rolled out the stretcher. When Kate's own helpfulness slid into voyeurism, she went home. A call to Dottie later in the evening went unanswered. Kate left a message, still unanswered this morning. Nothing on local TV news or radio so far, ditto the morning's *Tennessean.*

Time to drop off the edited issue, find Don Donaghue, and give him back the Navigator keys. If only Sam made it into Nashville tonight so she could tell him about the LilyAnn mess, get his read on this situation so far. If only her corporate pilot was not ordered to fly off two or three time zones into the distance for most of the week.

She slipped on her lightweight camel-suit jacket and went down to the Fleetwood Design Department one floor below on three. It was enemy territory because visuals were everything, words and print columns despised. She put the envelope on the design chief's desk, smiled at the cute green-eyed male intern with the brush cut and walked down the third floor hall to Don Donaghue's office in Sales.

His door was partway open, his back to her. Kate caught sight of the pink scalp shining through the reddish brown hair. A year from now, comb-over.

He swiveled and grinned. "Kate, just the woman I want to see. Perfect timing. Perfect." The grin stayed in place. In his mid-thirties, Don was boyish with a fair complexion with freckles. A short upper lip left him just shy of TV-ad handsome. His office decor, one month into the job, was a wall-mount basketball hoop over the trash can. His sportcoat jacket was on a hook, ready to grab for a meeting, a huddle, a twenty-five-yard dash. Some day Kate would ask why he wore his white shirts big enough to look like blouses.

"Morning, Don."

"Great morning, Kate. Hated to bust into your weekend, but this is a big one. Big one. We could score a knockout if we play it right." Even his voice was pumped.

Keep this pleasant but focused. She said, "I just want to go over the . . . the meeting with LilyAnn Page's manager. Two meetings, actually, Saturday and Sunday both. Your staff will take it from here. I think LilyAnn Page's management will consider Fleetwood seriously." Kate reached into her jacket pocket and held out the key to the Navigator.

But Don made a palm-up stop sign. "Not so fast, Kate. You're only at the second inning."

Tiresome sports talk. Why wasn't he reaching for the key?

"Sit down a minute, Kate. Please."

She smoothed her light camel-skirt and perched on a gray tweed and chrome side chair exactly like her own. His office, she realized, was directly below hers.

She could tap dance on his head. "Kate, I need a favor."

Again? Here in Nashville, the courteous response was, "Like to help you out if I can, Don." The new sales director, however, was from Oil City, Pennsylvania. His recent stint with a company in Atlanta was too brief for southern etiquette training. She said, "What favor?"

"It's the follow-up for the LilyAnn Page proposal. Damnedest thing, Page's representative—Dottie Skipwith? She just called me back. They want to see you again. You personally."

Shabby manipulator. Kate felt a hot pulse. "Sorry, Don, I gave at the office."

He loosened his tie another notch. "Kate, I know you pinch hit on this, and I'm damn grateful." He cleared his throat. "You made one hell of an impression, pardon my Swedish. This Dottie wants to talk in detail—but only to you. She hopes you might even stop out there sometime today. 'Fact, I thought she sounded a little pushy."

"Like a bulldozer in size two."

He put hands on knees and leaned forward. "But we could get a KO on this, Kate. Fleetwood could lock in the country music fan magazine market. Get the advertisers, that's the key." He looked at her. "Get on board with me on this, how about it? Help out Sales and Planning, and you can call in a favor for Editorial anytime. Any favor."

She paused, wishing she'd put the brake on this a week ago. "Don, I have real doubts. This project's not a good fit for Fleetwood. I think the fifth floor will veto it, and there could be fallout."

"What, from Amberson? He's a Teddy bear."

She said, "Hughes Amberson is the company president and very active in the firm, a family firm, let me remind you. And what's more. . . ."

"Kate, if you only had a business outlook. Maybe

if you had an MBA. . . . Look, it's simple. You cut
the fan fees and the production expense. Circulation
skyrockets. More fans than ever. I'm thinking, soft
drinks, snack food, automotive, maybe tobacco products. I tell you, it's a gold mine."

"Not for Fleetwood, Don. It's a bad match." She
worked to keep her voice steady. Like talking to a
brick wall. "Look, it's an image problem. Country
music fanzines—they're totally alien to Mr. Amberson
and his circle. They'd seem degrading, like *Penthouse*
or *Hustler*."

Don laughed. "When Amberson sees the bottom
line, he won't feel so degraded. Wait'll you get your
year-end bonus."

"Or pink slip."

He blinked. "Oh, hey, so you're worried about job
security? Hey, Kate, forget it, this is modern times."

"I like this job. I moved from Boston for this job.
I intend to keep it."

He shrugged. "I lived in five cities over the last
six years. Maybe another six ahead. There are other
Fleetwoods in the league. You gotta make your opportunities. It's a fast-track scene. You gotta be your
own free agent."

"Don, I have a daughter to support."

He shrugged. "Sounds like yesteryear's thinking to
me, horse and buggy. Hey, we got a great opportunity
here. LilyAnn Page's people are the gateway. And
they want you."

Like a Marine poster. She put the Navigator key on
the edge of his desk. "Don, I've got a heaping plateful
to do on *SouthWing*. I did my share on this, pitched
the plan to LilyAnn Page's people. It's in your court
now." Kate tried to keep her own sports talk to games
she might actually play. She thought of Kelly, her
condo. "Your court, Don."

"Kate, don't blow me off, please. It's touchy, but
we've got a strong offense. Dottie's serious about our

plan. Loves the idea of bigger circulation. Wants to
talk to you again ASAP. C'mon, be the Fleetwood
rep one more time. I'll take the heat from Amberson.
Full responsibility, it's on my shoulders. Help me out
just once more. Look, I need this for Sales and
Planning."

She hesitated.

He frowned, cocked one brow. "Hey, nothing happened out there over the weekend, did it? Nothing
odd?"

" 'Course not."

"I just thought for a minute . . ."

"Nothing at all. No way." She shrugged it off, then
realized if she truly wanted out, on-the-spot honesty
to Don Donaghue would fling the exit doors wide
open. If the Sales Director thought the *LilyAnn's Page*
contract would come red-taped to a mission that might
hang him out to dry, he'd back-off like lightning. She
was sure of it. If Kate Banning wanted out, this was
the moment.

"Actually, Don, I. . . ." But somehow she still hesitated. Nanoseconds ticked. Then a riverfront horn
sounded. The *General Jackson* was docking from its
run from the Opryland Hotel a few miles upstream.
From the window, the *General* looked so good. That
was the trick, distance. That was key to Disneyland
America, corporate America—don't look too close,
the rule of thumb also for much of her job here at
Fleetwood. So much puffery all around, reality syn-
thetic and virtual. And not enough to keep the mind
alive, the spirit.

As for the *General,* Kate knew its red paddle wheel
was fake, the "steamboat" engines really diesels, the
upholstery in the saloon one hundred percent vinyl.
In her bones, she needed to know things like that. She
looked and poked and pushed for core facts that kept
her grounded. "X-Ray Kate," a college roommate
called her.

LilyAnn Page of "Break of Dawn" collapsed against her with a broken arm. How real was that?

As real as a publicity stunt that got out of control just when a new album was about to be released?

Or was the star merely accident prone this spring?

Or was there a murderer at large? If so, by next month the oldies station DJ's might play tributes to the late LilyAnn Page. Album sales of *Against the World* would be posthumous.

Would "Break of Dawn" then trouble Kate's conscience as it now scoured her soul?

She kept her perch on the tweed chair. Upstairs on her desk lay three articles ready to edit. Routine and dull—but safe.

LilyAnn not safe.

Could she find out why? Clear her conscience and kick the boredom too? And yet put herself at risk—

Maybe this was a moment when a decision surfaced, when she both won and lost a debate circling deep within. "—about to say, glad I made a good first impression, Don. If LilyAnn Page's manager wants to go another with me, I guess I could be persuaded. Just remember, you do owe me. Oh, and thanks much for the Navigator test drive, but from now on, I'll take my own car. The old Buick wagon may be a junker, but it's user-friendly." She stood, left Don with his one-man high-five that morphed into a failed three-pointer from midcourt.

At 3:05 Kate was clicked through the 83 Mosely gate. Dottie slid into the passenger seat and said, "Drive over to the house, Kate. You have to see that dining room door." Reading glasses dangled from a black and white cord around her neck, and a janitorial key ring banded her wrist like a bracelet. The unseen dogs barked as Kate followed the crushed gravel to the back of the main house and parked. They went into the back door.

The kitchen was long but narrow, with a high-ceiling, recessed spotlights and three wide windows. The walls were finished in a terra cotta orange, and there was a lot of stainless steel, the double sinks, the pots and pans hanging from S-hooks, the Vulcan six-burner and Sub-Zero. The cabinets were birdseye maple. In the middle of the glazed tiled floor stood an old butcher's block with slots for six knives. Two of them, she noticed, were missing, probably in the dishwasher. At the kitchen door entrance, a long, wide hall went straight through to the front of the house. At the kitchen's far end, in the pantry area, stood a small drop leaf table with two rush-bottom chairs. No, it was not Loretta's cozy country kitchen. In all, it looked like a designer's show place and production center.

Dottie led Kate past the butcher's block and out into a spacious dining room with two small windows that looked like Tiffany glass. The dining room was dominated by an oak trestle table big enough for a testimonial dinner.

Dottie tapped the oversized door, which was thick solid wood beautifully finished in a soft milky cypress sheen. Right now it was off from its hinges and propped against the wall.

Kate whispered, "This is the door that fell—?"

"Don't whisper, she's not here. Nobody's here. Yes, that's the door." They stared briefly. "How it happened, Lily came in through the kitchen. Nothing was out of the ordinary. The dining room door was shut, and Lily opened it and walked through."

Dottie reenacted the moment. "See, she turned right here and started around the table toward the hall. The door let go and crashed down. Lily said she felt it coming behind her, intuitively sensed it. Then she turned—like this." Dottie turned toward the right.

"When Lily saw it coming, she tried to back off and also to catch it at the same time. It just missed her shoulder." Dottie touched her own shoulder. "She lost her balance and fell, and it landed on her arm and broke the bone. Her radius. She made it back to the cabin through sheer will power. She fell and almost fainted the whole way on that driveway. The doctors say she's lucky, it's a clean break. She'll be in a cast for the next six weeks."

Kate stepped up to the door, then to the doorway. She touched the hinges, which looked like old brass, newly refinished. "These are loose-pin hinges," she said. "They're good for removing a door without having to remove the hinges too. Just pull the pins, and the door's free. Where are the pins?"

"Exactly. Exactly my question."

"You mean somebody pulled the pins out?" Dottie nodded. "And they left the door closed so it looked okay." Another nod. Kate said, "So the first person to open the door was going to get hurt."

"Or worse."

The two stood silent for a moment. Dottie said, "The bus fire and Carnie's 'accident' happened out on the road, but this brings it home. Whoever it is, they're right here. You have to find who it is."

Kate looked at Dottie. "I'm not a bodyguard."

"I know that. We're hiring one, a fella who used to work security at Opryland. His name's Turk Karcic. Lily knew him from her Geo Theater concerts out there. He's worked private security since the amusement park closed. We're putting Turk on staff as of tomorrow morning. You'll meet him. Where LilyAnn Page goes, he'll go."

"What does Ms. Page think about this?"

"That she's humoring me. She thinks it's all a streak of bad luck, bad Karma. She sees how upset I am, and she OK'd Turk for my peace of mind." Dottie shifted the ring of keys. "As I see it, the plan is simple, Kate. Turk watches out for Lily, and you find out who's trying to kill her."

Simple as that, like chess pieces moved around to

protect "Queen" LilyAnn. Suddenly Kate felt hot anger rise. She said, "Dottie, your call to Fleetwood this morning, it's a pressure tactic that almost backfired. I nearly bailed out. One more maneuver like that call to Don Donaghue, and I'm gone."

The ring of keys jangled, and one foot tapped the wide plank floor. Dottie's cheek twitched. She said, "Okay, fair enough, I hear you. I understand. Apologies. Consider it history."

Or desperation. Kate said, "What about the files of letters from the crazies? I need to see them. Who holds a grudge against Ms. Page? You said her divorce was bitter. What about the ex-husband?"

"Keith. Keith Grevins. He's a businessman now. He lives in Hawaii."

"Ms. Page has custody of their daughter?"

Dottie nodded. "Angie spends summers and every other Christmas with her father. They finally worked it out."

"It was difficult?"

"It was hell on earth. Keith's his own worst enemy. He made life miserable for everybody. I never want to go through anything like that again."

"He's remarried?"

"Not that I know."

Kate paused. "Would you say he's living in the past?"

"He's living in Hawaii." She looked at Kate. "Five thousand miles away. Let's say he's like a storm blown out to the Pacific Ocean."

Nice to think so. "Okay. What about the stalker that just got out of prison last month?"

"April third. His name's Walter Sian. They found a shrine to Lily in his room when they arrested him. Flowers and rocks and little branches, and lots of cutup photos and women's underwear on a home-made altar. Elaborate lights too. He's got some crazy ideas."

Kate said, "Does he have a connection with Ms.

Page? Did he work for her? Most stalkers have some link with their victims."

Dottie shook her head, then suddenly nodded. "Yes and no. He never worked for her, and Lily doesn't remember meeting him, not even once. But I feel guilty about this, Kate. He started sending weird notes, and I treated them like ordinary fan mail. At first I mailed him autographed photos."

"So he felt encouraged."

"I guess. He's got this twisted idea about Lily and the environment. Her song, 'Stones and Stars,' he thinks it's some kind of earth song. He used to send her mailing tubes." Dottie stopped, as if reluctant to go further. "I'm just relieved that's all over."

"What was inside the tubes?"

"Nature stuff. Pussy willow branches and snake skins, and skulls of little animals. Stuff little boys find in the woods. And he put in crazy notes in some kind of code. He scared the hell out of us at the time. He's got a serious criminal record. I'm thankful that episode's behind us."

"If it is."

"Oh, I doubt he'll be back. I think Walter's history too. It's just creepy to remember, brings it all back. Look, I'll get you the files, but I can't do everything. I can't be in two places at once, and I wear a lot of hats around this place. That Fan Fair booth, the Fan Club party, Clark and Babs, our schedule's never been this tight. And now there's all kinds of hassle over the video shoot out at The Waterfront next Saturday— you know The Waterfront?"

"The river?"

Dottie shook her head no. "More like a little lake. It's off Metro Center Boulevard by the Fountain Square movies. They used to have ducks and paddleboats and a shopping mall. We took Deb and Angie and shopped at Esprit, they had such cute kids' clothes."

She smiled at the memory. "We'd feed the ducks, have lunch. There was a country music stars' promenade, and the stars put their palm prints in wet cement plaques. Lily drew her flower in the cement, a lily outline. There was a special ceremony. . . ."

She lingered with the memory, then frowned. "But then the shops all failed. They moved the star plaques out to Opryland, and they're probably in storage. It feels deserted. But that's why Blue Sky Productions wants to shoot the video there—you know, the desolate background with Lily singing 'Against the World.'"

Dottie sighed. "She thinks it's too dreary, and she's worried about the cast on her arm, whether they can get the right camera angles. And the production people need official clearance from Waterfront Management, and there are issues over the script too. Lily sent it back three times for rewrite. It's one more hassle on top of everything else." She stopped, and Kate noticed that tremor again at her right cheek.

Now Dottie took a deep breath, sniffled, blew her nose and murmured "allergies." She said, "Just for the record, a day like this, I also have to be mom to both girls. Angie and my Deb need prom gowns, and we've been all over Green Hills and Cool Springs, the three of us. They cut school today so we could go look, and we've been to every Dillard's store in middle Tennessee. I never saw so many ugly dresses."

She ran a hand through her smooth short hair. "So much of it falls to me. I have to go shopping because LilyAnn gets recognized, and everybody wants autographs, and the girls just freak out. It's their prom, their dates, mind you. They're entitled. But it's a real time problem."

She patted her hair back flat against the scalp. "I'm not a whiner, Kate, but it's damn hard to do the regular things in the middle of this crisis. But I'll get those records together by tomorrow. And you and I will sit down to talk too. I'm making a list in my head of any individuals who might possibly go over the edge. Maybe a drummer who worked with us, Bucky Sibbett. He got hurt, and we had to replace him. You got me really thinking. I want to help."

"Good." Kate wanted to ask more about Bucky Sibbett and his injury, but the timing was off. Maybe Dottie threw out his name like a bone to a dog. Kate turned. She said, "Let's talk about this door. It looks newly refinished."

"It is. That door was stained dark walnut when Lily bought this place five years ago. She had it stripped and hated it from the get-go. The idea of milky cypress caught her fancy. The refinish job took a couple weeks. The door was just delivered and re-hung late Saturday afternoon, maybe an hour or so after you and I first talked."

"That's seventeen, eighteen hours between the installation and the . . . the injury. And nobody went into the kitchen in all that time?"

"Oh sure, but the quickest way from the front or the upstairs is straight down the hall. The dining room door is mostly closed unless a caterer's here to do a party."

"Nobody here cooks?"

Dottie paused. "The way we're handling it this year, a woman comes in Wednesday afternoons and cooks for the week. Her name's Maria Basco. We tell her how many are staying in the house, and she shops and prepares the meals for that whole week. Some go into the freezer, some the fridge. Anyway, Maria wasn't here."

"Who was?"

"Well, I've got a list." Dottie reached into the breast pocket of her black T-shirt, unfolded a small sheet and put on the reading glasses. "Mind you, this isn't my list. I had to ask Billy D and the kids too, because after you left on Saturday, I was alone working in the office. I didn't leave till about nine o'clock that night."

"You heard nothing through the screen door?"

She shook her head. "I closed and locked the office main door right after you left because I wanted privacy. I'm like a hermit when I work on the monthly payroll. I wouldn't even let the girls in to clean up the fireplace. I shut off the phone for total concentration because payroll makes me so nervous."

She smoothed out the paper. "Anyway, Billy D let some people in through the early evening. You remember Billy, Lily's cousin, the guy on the John Deere?"

"—hunts deer with a bow."

"Hunts anything that moves, squirrels, raccoons. That boy was probably Robin Hood in another life, and you hear more about archery equipment than you ever want to know. But he cleans the pool and a hundred other things. He's the caretaker, more or less. He's worked here for the last two years, lives in the loft in the old barn. Billy comes from Indiana. Sometimes he works road crew when Lily's short. Very conscientious. Mister Dependable. I count on Billy. Anyway, he and Lily's brother are her only family here in Nashville. So this is his list. He let in a florist and a woman from DeSoto delivering Lily's new stage clothes. A photographer came, too, but it turned out he had the wrong date, so he'll be back next week. He left."

"That's it?"

"No, couple more." She straightened the glasses across her nose and looked back at the sheet. "Farley Eckles came to pick up a trailer hitch. He's on Lily's road crew, and my Deb thinks he's the hunk of hunks, but Billy says he got the hitch and left. Then Lily's brother stopped by, Kip. Valley Construction, that's Kip's company. He wanted to check the fence his crew's finishing up across the east side of the property.

Then two or three landscapers came with some new dogwood trees to be planted, trucked them all the way from McMinnville, sort of the landscape capitol. But they need special equipment to dig the holes because of the limestone rock."

Dottie gestured toward the windows. "The trees are out there with burlap wrapped around the root balls. Lily can't get enough specimen trees. This batch is supposed to have cream-colored flowers. Billy D turned the hose on 'em so they won't wilt. Anyway, Angie and my Deb and their friends were here too. Strictly girlfriends. No boys allowed because the fireplace mess isn't cleaned up. They rented a couple movies and went out to Pizza Perfect about ten o'clock. They were back here by eleven thirty, because I called. Deb stayed the night. Those girls can talk for days on end about their proms."

Dottie looked down at her list. "That's it—no, wait. One more, Brent and Joel. That's Brent Landreth and Joel Cain, they're band members. They came to pick up some tapes."

"Current band members?"

Dottie nodded. "Brent's on rhythm guitar. He's been with Lily forever. I mean, forever. He's from the Shenandoah Valley too. Joel's the new drummer and still learning the music, so he needed tapes that go way back because some of Lily's albums are out of release."

"Joel replaced the injured drummer, Bucky Sibbett?"

Dottie shook her head no. "Bucky was two drummers ago." Her eyelids fluttered. "For some reason they don't last long. Actually, I don't think Bucky's drumming these days, not after his hand. . . ."

"What happened to his hand?"

"A car door slammed on it. It was nobody's fault, just one of those things, but Bucky's convinced it was personal. I hear he's mouthing off about getting back."

"At Ms. Page."

Dottie shrugged and gestured around the room, the house itself. "I'll tell you, last night I couldn't sleep. Payroll does that to me. I lay awake at two o'clock and ran through every possible weird-o and creep I could think of beside Walter Sian. Bucky kept coming into my mind, the way he's talking in public about LilyAnn and the Iron Works boys these days. I think Bucky's political. It's like he believes he ought to have an estate too, like the star and the band should be some kind of commune."

"You think he'd try to kill Ms. Page?"

Dottie paused. "These days, I can't shrug it off."

Kate said, "But he wasn't here last Saturday evening?"

"No." She looked deflated.

Kate looked Dottie Skipwith straight in the eye. She said, "Dottie, on Saturday when you told me about the bus fire and the deadly guitar case, it seemed like somebody out on the road with Ms. Page and the band." She wet her lips. "Now that it's inside the house, it seems more like collaboration. I'm sure it's entered your mind."

"Conspiracy."

"Yes." Kate kept her gaze steady on Dottie, ready to gauge response. None was obvious. Dottie dropped her reading glasses as if to show Kate her naked eyes—though doubtless this woman in black realized that a conspiracy could include herself, that Kate Banning would have Dottie on her own list of suspects. Wasn't it clever, for instance, that Dottie Skipwith read Billy D's list instead of urging Kate to talk to him in person? Was the list a device to control the information flow? She said, "Dottie, I'd like to talk to Billy D."

"Sure. Just get ready to hear about compound bows and nocks and fletches and arrow spines and—"

"And talk to Ms. Page too."

She did not blink. "Every country music fan would, Kate. You'll have to get in line. Hey, that was just a little joke. Thing is, she's so busy."

"I'm sure she is, but I'll count on you to arrange it." Kate turned. "Who installed the door?"

"I was getting to that. The refinishing was handled by a gallery where Lily's bought some art and antiques. She collects Tiffany glass. You see those windows? Authentic. The gallery is called the Evelyn Galleries at . . . let's see, it's at Cummins Station." She handed Kate the paper. "I can't vouch that everything's covered from Billy D, but it's a start."

It was 4:45 when Kate crossed the Demonbreun Street viaduct and slipped into a metered spot along Cummins Station, the former industrial warehouse now occupied by professional offices, retail and business start-ups. She went to the directory and scanned the names, the usual attorneys, architects, CPAs, plus a bank, ad agency, the Nashville Symphony and a psychiatric group.

The Evelyn Gallery was listed at 106-07A, and its window lettering crossed retro with contemporary. Kate stepped in to see Art Deco glass vases and lamps from the Arts & Crafts era of the 1910s to the Fifties. Not a price tag was in sight, which was the definition of *gallery,* simply too tasteful for crass dollars. A Cranbrook table with two chairs at the side was casually strewn with current issues of *Architectural Digest, Art-Forum, Art in America.*

The woman who came forward was about five-ten with a narrow face, hazel eyes, high forehead, wavy dark blond hair with the kind of high-end streak job that looked as if the sun personally kissed each hair on her head. She moved confidently, almost like a runway model in slow motion in her mocha pullover with a sailor collar and pants a tone darker. Her spring sandals were sling-backs. She looked somewhere past forty.

"Hello. I'm Kate Banning."

The response was a workplace smile, more functional than warm. "Taylor Evelyn."

Long-e Evelyn. Taylor, of course one of those first names that sounded like last names. No twang in this voice of the cultured South. The voice sounded like butterscotch. "Pardon the confusion," she said. "I'm expanding my space to show contemporary art, and we're mounting a show by an artist from Houston. I was just at work on my mailing list. How may I help you?"

"If you have just a few minutes, I have a few questions about a recent transaction."

Taylor Evelyn almost concealed her slight perplexity and annoyance. "Oh why not?"

They went back to her desk, a teak oval probably dating from the Fifties. Kate sat in a plywood chair, a familiar shape. She said, "Charles and Ray Eames?"

It was as if the sun broke through. "Wonderful, somebody who knows, especially down here in the land of Queen Anne and Regency—where I fight a losing battle to bring in the twentieth century. You'd think it would be safe, now that it's history. Anyway, your voice, it's not from here—"

"Boston."

"I thought so. My favorite place on earth. I spent the best years of my life in Boston." Her face was now animated. "Oh, let me gush a little, it's been so long. At Boston University, I just camped out at the museums, the Museum of Fine Arts and the Gardiner."

"How did you happen to—"

"Go to school in Boston? Just to be ornery, to give mother and daddy fits. I spent every cent on the Amtrak to New York. The MOMA, the Whitney, the Dia Center." She smiled at Kate but clearly dwelt in memory. "Let me tell you something, I came upon an old punched Amtrak ticket in a thousand-year-old purse of mine a month ago, and I just sat and cried. Actually wept."

The look in her eye was an ironic twinkle. "I'm a girl of the South, you see. The family plan for me was Hollins College in Virginia, or maybe Agnes Scott, then marry a nice boy out of Washington and Lee or The Citadel." Her grin was sly. "Instead, I went to Boston and swore I'd never come home. Never." She fixed that wry look on Kate as if to gauge response. "We southern expatriates all take that vow. We're never coming back. Then we do. Faulkner mapped us all, we are doomed." Her eyes narrowed. "How about you? You been here long?"

"Ten months."

"Oh, culture shock. Poor thing. Is your family with you?"

"My daughter. She's just fourteen." Kate decided not to name Sam Powers, her frequent flyer. She said, "I'm divorced."

"Everybody's divorced. It's a rite of passage. What brought you to Nashville?"

"I work for Fleetwood Publications."

"Hughes Amberson's company." She obviously saw Kate's mild surprise. "The Ambersons go way back. For that matter, so do the Evelyns. You helping Hughes get richer?"

Ignore that bait. "I'm an editor. But here at the moment I'm not in that role, not exactly." She said, "I'm trying to find out who installed a refinished door at the home of LilyAnn Page. I understand your gallery arranged it. To come to the point, the door fell from its hinges soon after it was re-hung last Saturday evening. The hinge pins were not in place."

Taylor Evelyn blinked, as if confused. Then her expression turned to dismay. "That's awful. Was anything damaged?"

"Ms. Page broke her arm."

"Oh, God." Taylor Evelyn looked genuinely shocked. She bit her lip. At last she said, "You know, that doesn't make one bit of sense. Sonny Burkendahl did that door work. I've known him all my life. He's worked for me and my family and my clients for years. He's an old hand, literally refinished wood for thirty or forty years. His daddy was a cabinet maker and his granddaddy before him. Cabinets, doors, mantles, everything." She reached for her Rolodex. "I'll give you his number and address, but it's a waste of time for sure." She jotted and handed Kate a mauve paper slip. Then she pressed her palms together. "Dreadful, just dreadful. You think it was some kind of practical joke?"

"We don't know."

"It's just so helter-skelter out there with those different work crews, a real circus. The dogs bark non-stop, and the grounds are always dug up with trenches, and as for the inside—let's be kind and call it a work-in-progress. I hear they had an awful time shooting that photobiography of LilyAnn—what was it, *The Page of My Life? My Life's Page?* Something like that. Anyway, the place looked like a war zone, and the photographer was going out of his mind. I said, 'Put her in Scarlet O'Hara's hoop skirts and you can recreate the Battle of Nashville'."

Then Taylor Evelyn looked a bit sheepish, as if she'd gone too far. "Actually, if I could take that back . . . Look, I'm not one to go on about the Old South. As for the balls, the social life here in town . . . let's say I'd have more gallery business if I kept up certain club memberships. But we still tell family war stories about women burying the silver to hide it from the Yankees hours before they overran us. It's a cliche but it's true."

"The Civil War—"

"The War of Northern Aggression. It's all relative, Kate. It happened in our backyards and our fields.

Around here, old houses have grapeshot and minnie
balls buried in the wooden walls. Every so often the
Nashville metal detector clubs ask permission to work
your front lawn." She looked at Kate. "The stuff they
turn up, you could open a lead mine out around Battery Lane." Her smile was rueful. "I don't want to
sound pious or sacrilegious either. It's just that every
time I'm out to Mosely, I need a couple Gentleman
Jacks to calm down. Do you know LilyAnn's band
even rehearses out there sometimes?"

"The Shenandoah Iron Works?"

"Rehearses at the artist's home. In Music City,
that's unheard of." She looked back at Kate with that
frank stare. "You're not working for her?"

"Not personally."

"You a fan of hers?"

"Of 'Break of Dawn'." Taylor nodded. Kate said,
"You know Dottie?"

She paused, straightened the Rolodex, replaced her
pen in a carved rosewood cylinder and finally spoke.
"Anybody dealing with LilyAnn Page knows Dottie
one way or another. One way or another." She wet
her lips. "LilyAnn Page is a good client of mine, I
guess Dottie told you that. Tiffany glass and Mission
furniture, that's her passion, and I have some private
sources and handle certain sales. Did you see her
house?"

"Only the kitchen and dining room."

"You've got a real treat coming. She has some marvelous pieces. Get Dottie to take you through. I mean,
if you're still on speaking terms by the end of the
week."

Kate blinked. Whatever that meant. She put the
mauve paper into her purse and handed over her own
business card.

Taylor studied it. "Fleetwood Publications. Chief
Co-ordinating Editor." She seemed to ponder the information. "And you were an editor in Boston?"

Kate flushed. "No. In Boston I worked as an investigative reporter for a magazine called *New Era.*"

"Oh, I remember it. Sort of like *Mother Jones.* Consumer activism, environmental rights, business fraud. Very New England. Didn't it fold?"

Kate nodded.

"So that's why you've come to the Athens of the South." Across from her, Taylor Evelyn cocked one eyebrow. "I get it now. You're investigating this door accident, aren't you? You're trying to find out if somebody pulled those pins?"

Kate managed a weak smile. She began to feel as though a pickpocket got her wallet and now, card by card, put her identity on display. She said, "Maybe I ought to take up bourbon."

Taylor Evelyn laughed. "Kate, I don't mean to be rude. But when I came back South, I didn't agree to give up my ornery side. There's a saying, 'Be sweet.' Southern mamas send children into the day telling them to be sweet. Me, I'm running for Vinegar Queen."

Kate looked her in the eye. "There are too many queens in this town, Ms. Evelyn. I can't keep up with them."

"Taylor. Call me Taylor." The woman looked at her. Her butterscotch voice was low and sounded sincere. "I feel for you, Kate, coming all this way. Nashville's no suburb of Boston, that's for sure. You need somebody to talk to down here. You've got to have a bad case of homesickness. This time of year in Boston, let's see, there's that flower festival—not camellias."

"Lilac Sunday at the Arboretum."

She nodded, sat back and locked her hands behind her head. "Marvelous place for a spring or summer stroll, look at the trees, feed the goldfish in the pond."

"My daughter and I fed those fish."

Taylor smiled. "Sweet painful memories." She sighed. "Maybe it's my own nostalgia for Boston.

Maybe we're like two little children in parallel play.
Maybe it's my hope that we'll see each other again,
have lunch. It's so good to meet new people from out
in the world."

She crossed her legs and pushed back her rose gold
bracelet. She leaned toward Kate. "Now I'm going out
on a limb, caution to the winds. Let me say, I learned
Boston can fool you. When you talk to people up
there, it seems so direct, all open and aboveboard. I
thought it was refreshing.

"But I was naive. It took me a while, you see, to
realize the talk isn't so frank as it seems up there.
New England currents run deep underneath that spare
style. Here in the South, now, it's different. We love
to talk, and story telling is our birthright. But the
meaning's in a maze. You have to walk that maze.
LilyAnn Page might be a maze, Kate Banning. She
and Dottie are some pair. It will be the hinges today,
something else tomorrow. Her music's fantastic, but
people get hurt and used up. Let me say, it hasn't
been easy completing glass and furniture deals."

"You mean, getting paid."

"I mean the whole business from start to finish.
LilyAnn Page has a certain reputation. And I've heard
some things around town. People have long memories.
People have stories to swap. From what I hear, there
are people who'd line up for the chance to pull door
hinge pins out and break both that woman's arms."

CHAPTER FOUR

It was just past six when Kate got back home and pulled into her slot among the magnolias. Fred, one of her new neighbors, looked up and waved, a fifty-ish man in horn-rimmed glasses just picking up his mail. This past March he'd moved in with his wife, Alice, who also waved whenever she walked their Yorkie, named Mitzy. They seemed like a breezy and pleasant couple. Total strangers. Thus life in the live-and-let-live four-unit condo cluster.

Kate dumped her canvas tote by the coat closet, called out "Kel, Kelly, I'm home" and heard her daughter upstairs on the phone to a friend. She paused, waiting for an interval.

"—yeah, some of them wouldn't even come to the door. Three o'clock in the afternoon, and this woman in her bathrobe hid behind the curtains. We rang her bell about fifty times. We wanted to drive her psycho. That's when that whole armful fell on the sidewalk and two of the pots broke. Yeah, my mom bought them." Kelly's laugh was loud and harsh.

Kate hesitated. More African violet talk, but not quite the version she'd heard. Kelly said nothing about driving anyone "psycho." Did she exaggerate for the friend or sanitize for mother? Would Kelly knowingly, deliberately harass somebody? Her Kelly? Was it possible?

This new doubt moved in along with the question of the hour—was LilyAnn the beloved Lily of the

Shenandoah Valley, or a woman so disliked that some
wished her harm?

Wished her dead?

Kate checked the time. Sam ought to be here within
the hour. For once, let his schedule and her needs
match. Let him also know something about LilyAnn
Page. It wasn't a farfetched wish, since Sam Powers
was such a longtime country music fan. Maybe rumors
circulated among the fans. Didn't Hank Williams
drink, Dolly have implants? Did the Lily of the Shenandoah Valley ever make the *Enquirer?*

She opened the phone book. No listing for Buck or
Bucky Sibbett, but several likely music shops that
might know a drummer's whereabouts. There was
Sam's Music, Corner Music, Cotton Music—and a
half-page ad for Fork's Drum Closet. All were closed
for the day. Shelve the book, wait for Sam.

She hoped they could have a talk about Kelly, a
reality check. Sam was no Dr. Spock but knew Kel
well enough to venture a thought on the new teen life.
Above all, she needed him here with her. That country
song about "Lonely Street," sometimes it applied to
a certain condo in Nashville, Tennessee.

In the kitchen Kate stood a minute and thought
about the evening. Your lover as sounding board, was
that fair? Sam would need to unwind from bucking
the crosswinds. She wanted to spare him dull domes-
ticity. Why not make the two of them a real dinner
for the later evening. Maybe that Moroccan chicken
with pickled lemons where you simmered minced veg-
etables so long and slow.

She opened the pantry cabinet door, rooted for the
gift jar of pickled lemons, stopped and pulled back.
No, not now. The timing wasn't right. Even the food
processor felt like too much effort. She was too caught
up in this LilyAnn thing, as if others were writing
scripts for her to follow. Conflicting scripts. She called

out again "Kelly, I'm home." No response this time either.

She went upstairs and changed from her workday suit into jeans and a green plaid shirt Sam especially liked and moved to the alcove where the computer now cohabited with the ski machine. One machine for the brain, one for the body. She called into the bedroom hallway, "Kel, I'm here on the web."

"Oh, hi, Mom. On the phone." Kelly's bedroom door snapped shut.

More talk about driving the Richland neighborhood residents psycho? Don't think about that now. Wait for Sam. Kate rolled the mouse, clicked, went through Netscape, typed h-t-t-p slash slash to pay a visit to the LilyAnn Page website, which came up in vivid colors to feature stunning portraits of the country star smiling against a dell of lilies of the valley and scenes of the Shenandoah Valley. The web visitor could click on links to her albums, to her record label, her Grammies, her concert schedule.

And her bio. Click. LilyAnn Page—Vocalist, Guitarist, Songwriter. First prize in a talent contest at age eleven in Leesburg, Virginia, launched Lillian Corinne Padgett's musical career, though fans are surprised to learn that the birthplace of the Lily of the Shenandoah Valley is not Virginia but Evanston, Illinois. From childhood, the Grammy-winning artist acclaimed for such Billboard *chart-making singles as "Break of Dawn" and "Dark Eden" was slated for ballet and classical music as the daughter of a manufacturing executive and a mother devoted to the symphony. The one-time Lillian (Lily) Padgett practiced on a tiny violin under her mama's watchful eye.*

Kate paused. So LilyAnn Page had not grown up learning guitar chords on a folksy family rural Virginia porch, had not actually been LilyAnn Page but Lillian Padgett, child of a businessman and his symphony-subscriber wife. The Midwestern sound in her voice,

as in Dottie's, was the Chicago flatland, not the rolling
hills of the southern Appalachians. She was a country
music transplant and makeover. Did her fans know?
Care?

*Dad's corporate transfer to Virginia's Shenandoah
Valley sprung the future country star from classical to
country, but it was stepbrother Kip who became key to
his sister's career start-up.*

She stopped, reread. Stepbrother. This was the contractor Kip who stopped by 83 Mosely the day before
LilyAnn's "accident." He came about a fence, nothing
related to music. Why the stepbrother in the web page?
Genealogical accuracy or a family faultline?

Founder of the country garage band, The Recliners,
*guitarist (and sometime claw hammer banjo-man), Kip
persuaded "Sis" to fill in for an ailing vocalist. According to LilyAnn, there was no looking back. At first
Kip and LilyAnn were the featured duet, which led to
LilyAnn going solo backed by the Shenandoah Iron
Works. . . .*

Kate stopped, reread the last lines, which sounded
like standard pop culture press-release style. Yet one
phrase caught her attention, the little term, "led to."
The brother-sister duet apprenticeship with the Recliners "led to" LilyAnn's solo career. Maybe the Recliners simply ran their course, then Kip bowed out
of the duet and band and wished stepsister Lily all
the best.

But "led to" had darker uses. True, it always
sounded innocent, so simple, a useful link from this
to that. As writer and editor, Kate used the term herself from time to time. The two little words were everywhere. The historical plaques you saw on school
field trips were full of "led to" phrases. One event
"led to" another.

It was the nature of those events that often got
Kate's attention. Usually they were feuds, takeovers,
killings, wars, every kind of disaster. It was as if no

actual human decisions were particularly involved, no person or group to be held responsible. One thing simply led to another, as if natural and inevitable. Nothing could have been done to stop that wreck, fire, flood, massacre. "Led to," Kate had decided, was often a crucial phrase because of what it could conceal. "*Kip and LilyAnn were the featured duet, which led to LilyAnn going solo backed by the Shenandoah Iron Works. . . .*"

Was there an untold tale? Suppose stepbrother Kip was forced out when Sis moved on and up. Years of smoldering resentments only now to reach flash point—? Kate took a big breath and exhaled slowly. Find out where Kip was in the scheme of things. At least she had her own question to ask, not Dottie's and not Taylor Evelyn's but Kate Banning's very own.

Ready to scroll through the rest of the bio, she was stopped by the phone—rather, by Kelly's open-door announcement that Sam broke through on call-waiting to say he'd be here in half an hour.

Great. Wonderful. Turn off the computer screen and hit the *Twenty-Minute Menus* book once again. She stood, went down to the kitchen, pulled on her red apron, opened the cookbook, decided on spicy peanut chicken with rice and asparagus. The great thing about *Twenty-Minute Menus,* it told you exactly which steps to follow, a do-this, do-that for those who were brain dead at the end of the work day but up for a decent meal. She'd used it so much the binding was collapsing. One day she'd write a fan letter to author Marian Burros. So to the peanut chicken recipe. The boneless breasts were at hand, and the cumin and cinnamon and even a can of jalapeño chiles.

She reached into the pantry for the peanut butter jar, unscrewed the lid. Empty. The next edition of *Twenty-Minute Menus* should warn the cook to beware the household teen. Kate stared again into the hollow glassware. The most neurotic scraping would

not produce anywhere near the called-for two table-
spoons. She remembered that her Boston friend, Maggie, compared teen kids to carpenter ants and
termites, literally eating adults out of house and home.
Back then, it sounded only humorous. Now, like a
time-release message, its moment had come. The
stealth snacker had hit.

Well, onward. She flipped forward to the mustard-
coated chicken, a good fall-back recipe because Kelly
did not make runs on Grey Poupon. Kate trimmed
the chicken, shook out the bread crumbs and cut a
lemon. Skip the side dish of brussels sprouts, a hella-
cious veg. Spring asparagus, everybody's fave.

And then the doorbell, and in seconds Sam Powers
stood before her, filling the doorway with all six feet,
his flight cap and bag in hand, his dark blue uniform
jacket hooked by one finger and slung over his back.
The early evening light from behind made a silhou-
ette of his solid frame, his square shoulders, sculp-
tured head, the jutting jawline in quarter profile. He
closed the door, dropped his bag on the foyer tile,
tossed jacket and cap onto a side chair, looked into
Kate's eyes and softly said, "Hi there."

"Hi there." The gold flecks in his brown eyes.

It was if shyness got them both, as if they needed
a moment to pause, reconnect, find their own territory
just before an embrace. Then they moved toward one
another, kissed, and stayed a full moment in the hallway as if the space existed solely for renewal. Kate
ran fingers through his thick dark hair, fingered the
cowlick at the back by the crown. He caressed her
neck, cradled her head. It was as if they must read
one another like Braille.

At length Kate murmured, "Oh, I forgot to take off
this apron."

"Sexy apron."

Sexy apron that should have been in last week's

wash. She chuckled. A gallant lie. She said softly, "You smell like airplane."

"Good thing." He pulled back a bit to see her face. "Good thing I smell like a plane. That means I've still got a job."

"Oh Sam, don't tell me—"

But he put a finger across her lips. "Shh. Nothing to tell. We made a nice landing, no tailwinds. I tied down the Lear, finished the paperwork, no problems."

"Your passengers—?"

"The whole tent load of company top brass walked off the tarmac into a limo and drove off for meetings and golf."

"And Hacksaw too?"

"Hacksaw first and foremost." They caught the ironic glint in each others' eyes at the mention of the company CEO whose nickname was the stockholders' term of endearment. And a term of terror for down-the-line employees and ex-employees by the thousands. Lately Sam felt a kinship with the latter. He said, "Hey, how about a beer? And where's Kelly?"

"Upstairs. With the phone grafted to her ear. Talk to me a minute first. Let's have a drink." She flipped off the apron, opened his usual Michelob dark, then poured herself a cranberry juice with a splash of soda and lime slice. She opened a can of smoked almonds and dumped them into a plain glass bowl. They went into the living room, sat side by side on the sofa, clinked glasses, kissed again and held hands. Sam ate a handful of almonds.

"If you're really hungry, we can have dinner right away. I'm using *Twenty-Minute Menus*." Sam replied that a thirty-or forty-minute menu would work fine. It was a ritual joke between them. Kate leaned toward him. "Tell me about that radar failure."

"Radar—? Oh, you mean last Saturday when I left the message with Kelly." He shrugged. "Not much to tell. The air traffic control center in Westbury nearly

shut down for ten hours. Dust from a new ceiling installation made the Long Island controllers choke and
tear up. They couldn't see, they couldn't talk. Result—
gridlock in the skies."

"Skies, plural?"

"You bet. Like a major storm hitting a hub airport,
it disrupts the whole system. Planes were grounded
from LA to Maine. They kept us in Dallas for eight,
ten hours. My passengers were, to put it mildly,
pissed." He sipped his beer and shook his head. "But
you know something, Hacksaw and his fleet of VPs
turned that delay into one more reason to sell the
Lear and buy a Gulfstream."

Kate knew this did not refer to ocean currents and
shrimp. "The Rolls Royce of private corporate jets."

He chuckled. "Rolls and BMW, they both supply
the engines. And Grumman makes the tail, the wing
belongs to Textron, and Honeywell supplies the avion-
ics. It's a hybrid." He shrugged and managed a short
laugh. "All those hours stuck in Dallas, the guys were
lapping up the Gulfstream brochures and specs. They
have their eye on the G V. It can fly nonstop from New
York to Tokyo. Hacksaw and eighteen of his henchmen
can fly halfway around the world in fourteen hours without refueling. The Lear can't do that."

"You've never flown those guys to Tokyo."

"Maybe they want to see the Ginza at night. Maybe
they want blowfish sushi for breakfast. Most likely
they want the status. Kate, we're talking about a plane
that costs well over thirty million bucks green, unfur-
nished. Not a lick of paint."

"Custom interiors, of course."

"Custom fitting like you can't imagine—at twelve
thou per square foot." He shook his head. "Pig suede
and embossed iguana seat covers if you want 'em. One
customer did. Hacksaw heard that male whale sex or-
gans make the softest seat covers. He wants to look

into it. We're heading to Savannah next week to see the planes."

"So they're actually going ahead?"

" 'Considering options,' that's their pitch."

"And the boards and stockholders go for it?"

He drank again. "Here's the deal. The CEO and top people pull down their yearly tens of millions, right? So figure their cost per hour, and the numbers are staggering. That's where the efficiency argument comes in."

"I don't understand." Kate paused, drank. "Oh, now I get it. The top executives' time is supposedly so valuable that a gazillion-dollar plane actually saves the company money."

"You got it."

"So it starts with these golden calves you fly around."

"Prime beef on the hoof, babe, and let's not forget it." He ate more almonds and shook his head. "But hell, Kate, to be honest with myself, if it all collapsed tomorrow, I'd still hang around little airports and try to get myself an air-taxi job. Flying, it sounds mushy, but it's my church, my temple." He put down his beer and held his hands in front of him. Kate got the feeling Sam was mentally beginning to fly at this very minute.

He said, "Today, for instance, it was fantastic, clear skies from Denver on out. A clear day, there's nothing like it. You're up there with wraparound glass with all that continental big geology and the human fingerprints all over it. You can see the rivers really are Earth's arteries. And the farms—there's something downright spiritual about the fields. They're laid out so neat in green and brown, and you feel for the people that cleared that land and still farm it today. And the irrigation circles over the Southwest too, like clock faces on the earth. And the country roads in the middle of human nowhere." His fingers curled. Kate knew at this moment he was in his cockpit at the controls. He looked back at her face. "Those guys in the back of the plane, all they see down below is property and deals and too many hours between their destinations."

Sam picked up the beer bottle, drank and swallowed. "It can make you philosophical. I'm up at thirty-one thousand feet, and I figure, I might be the only one in the plane that really knows how to live. The guys back in the cabin, some of our nation's leading executives, they don't have a clue what they're missing."

He dug at the Michelob label with his thumbnail. "But face it, they're the ones that keep me in the sky in a great flying machine. Without them, I'm grounded." He looked again at her face. "Kate, if I have to nurse them along while they get themselves a G V, if I have to get recertified to fly it, then I'll do it. It's the price, and I'll pay it. And gladly. Anyway, it's a good airplane. I wouldn't mind logging some hours to Asia. Maybe I'll learn to eat rice for breakfast. But hey, for a while let's forget corporate America, let's talk about us."

She didn't speak right away. This wasn't about corporate America but the personal side, the push-pull. Moments like this were rare with Sam. Each such moment needed to be set apart, not run on with trivia or a day's cares. Sam had just spoken both his declaration of independence, and dependence too. Had he saved it for her ears? Or did it somehow take him by surprise, an impromptu outpouring criss-crossed with conflict but straight from the heart? She squeezed his hand. They were quiet a moment longer. This was not for discussion but for taking in.

Then it was back to the kitchen. They held hands, and then she put on the rice and worked with the chicken while Sam offered to prepare the asparagus. He ran the whole bunch under cold rinse water and bent each stalk until it snapped. "New trash bag?"

"Hey, you're throwing out those perfectly good stalks," she said. "I peel them. Asparagus soup. . . ."

"Too skinny, too much work, there'd be nothing left," he said. "Forget the New England thrift for once. Anyway, this is my job, and I'm a heartland boy, plus we're in the Southland now. You know, 'where the livin' is easy.'"

She snorted and felt a guilt twinge as the green ends dropped into the waste can. "Speaking of heartland," she said, "did you know LilyAnn Page comes from a suburb of Chicago?"

"New factoid of the hour?" He was arranging the spears in the steamer. "Nope, didn't know that. But Willie Nelson was born in Fort Worth. Johnny Cash was born in Arkansas. Vince Gill's from Oklahoma, and Reba too. How's that for country star data? And I've got more." He looked at her face and stopped. "Hey, what's up?"

The canola oil crackled in the sauté pan. The chicken was rolled in a mustard-yogurt coating. This was not the moment for hints or bombshells. "I'm trying to find out personal stuff about LilyAnn Page. Fleetwood is pitching that deal to her management."

"The fan magazine idea? From that sales director from Atlanta?"

"He's from Oil City, Pennsylvania. And yes, it's his idea." She added, "I've been listening for LilyAnn on the radio. No luck."

Now Sam snorted. "Country radio? Top forty *Billboard* country? Kate, you could listen till the end of time. Forget it, nobody over thirty gets radio airplay on country music stations. Don't you know that?"

She flushed. "I guess not." As though she'd been on Mars.

"Hell, Kate, it's been a big sore point for years now. The record labels mostly sign sound-alike kids." He shrugged. "They spin through the revolving door too. Their albums go gold once or twice, but they get dropped because the companies want platinum, double platinum. The system these days makes for a few blockbusters and a lot of very short careers."

"But why can't the radio stations play a lot of different acts? Is it the advertisers? Are there just too many records competing?"

He dried his hands on a kitchen towel. "That's all part of it. The rest is, the radio stations use focus groups to pick winners. Eight, ten kids off the street, and they play them fifteen seconds of a new song and ask, thumbs up or thumbs down? That's it, they're the jury. It's sort of like those instant lottery scratch cards. There's no chance at all for an audience to catch onto a song slowly, fall in love with it over some weeks of play. Some really good newer people like Mandy Barnett can't get airplay. And the established artists can't get their songs played either. George Jones, Tammy before she died, Emmylou Harris, Dolly, Willie—"

"The legends."

"The legends. And anybody else the radio market people happen to think is off-center. The Mavericks, Steve Earle, Nanci Griffith, Lucinda Williams, and Mandy Barnett."

Kate sighed. So many names to learn, songs to hear. She covered the rice, turned the chicken, poured in the yogurt sauce, covered it and turned down the gas. She said, "I just hope LilyAnn Page's people don't think Fleetwood can get her on the radio."

Yet Sam's comment gave her a new inkling of why Dottie Skipwith was at first tantalized by Don Donaghue's pitch. If the star's radio play was blocked, she was doubtless looking for other promotion avenues. The music box suddenly seemed less frivolous.

And the singer's personal demands less understandable. If LilyAnn needed the Harwell Collectibles to help her career, shouldn't she be nicer to Eddie, the music box man? Was she too accustomed to playing the diva?

"Tell you what," Sam said, "after dinner let's hit the web and look up LilyAnn together. No colorful stories about her come to mind. Maybe a web page'll jog my memory."

"Good. You see, I've already—"

But at that moment they heard the bounce on the stairs, two at a time to trigger Kate's worry about a fall. Kelly arrived in the kitchen full of energy as a puppy. "Sam!"

"Kelly Banning!" Their hug, Kate saw, was very real but a little less tactile than last year. Kelly now turned a bit sideways, and Sam held her more like a dancing partner to show affection but not intrude on a maturing body. He tousled her hair, and she protested. "So Kel," he said, "how's the band's Disney World campaign? How many poinsettias to sell before you kids can charter a bus to Orlando?"

Her voice rose in mock exasperation. "You know it's not poinsettias, Sam. That was *last* semester, Christmas. It's African violets now."

"Edible flowers?"

"You know they aren't."

Straight-faced. "Sorry. Pilots only buy plants we can eat. Sky snacks."

Kate watched this routine. How Kelly would fume if she tried this. Sam's banter would be mother's stupidity. She stood on the sidelines to tend the dinner, set the flame under the steamer and the chicken. It was Kelly's job to set the table. "Five minutes to dinner, Kel. How about the table? Maybe Sam'll get the drinks."

"Aren't we having the peanut chicken? Oh, yuck, Mom, mustard."

Kate said, "Mustard by default. Who put the empty peanut butter jar back in the pantry? Not moi."

"That was on purpose to remind you to get more, Mom. It was a signal. And don't forget to recycle the jar. You put the pickle jar in the regular trash yesterday. I grabbed it out for recycle."

Kate sighed. Surrender. The dinner went on, with Sam and Kelly in a lively chat as the now fourteen-year-old made a great show of denuding her chicken of every trace of sauce. The notion of cleaning Kelly's fish tank did not arise as a topic, even though the neons were barely visible through the green murk. *Walden* was described as a deadly dull act of personal persecution. Kate held her tongue. At intervals Sam winked at Kate as if to reserve their own time together.

And at last they had some. Kelly was sealed in her room with history and math homework.

He said, "How 'bout that web page?"

"Sam, I also need a word about Kelly. I overheard her on the phone earlier and was . . . almost shocked. Her voice sounded like somebody I don't know, callous, nasty."

He laughed. The bass-baritone was hearty. "Kate, you've got a *bona fide* teenager."

She waited until the laugh subsided to chuckles. She said, "That's it? That's all you can say?"

"Nothing else to say. Think back to age fourteen. Didn't you step out of line?"

"Well. . . ."

"Well let's hear it. Come on."

They stood at the bottom of the stairs. She said, "Let's look at that web page."

"In a minute. This first."

She said, "Okay." Things she hadn't thought about in years. "One Halloween we maybe ran some summer porch furniture up a flagpole."

"Good for you. And—?"

"And what?"

"Gotta be more."

"Why? That's plenty."

He raised a warning index finger. "One more. This is for your benefit, you'll feel better. Let's hear it."

"Okay, okay." She was smiling at the awful memory. "We had an English teacher nobody was crazy about, and it was water gun season."

"And you—?"

"Squirted her. About six of us in different seats. We all let her have it on cue. Some squirts hit her, some hit the blackboard and trickled down. First she cried. Then she got mad. We all wrote 'I will not bring water guns to school' about a thousand times."

"Did you regret it?"

She paused. "I felt bad when she cried. She was young, and we knew it. But . . . secretly, it was a great moment."

"And pretty innocent." He put his hand on her shoulder. "Hell, water guns, this is the age of AK47s and semiautomatics."

"Don't you see, that's what I worry about, that Kelly could get so far out of bounds."

"And so you wouldn't care if Kelly's principal called to complain that she'd squirted her English teacher with a water pistol?"

"Of course I'd care. I'd be mad."

"So she's supposed to be Goody Two Shoes?"

"No. She . . . hey, what is this?"

"Food for thought. Kelly's right on schedule. She's a great kid. Let's see that web page."

So they climbed to the alcove, Kate feeling both buoyed and corked. She sat down with Sam at her shoulder and brought up LilyAnn Page's bio. Any more "led-to's?"

Sam leaned close. *An early marriage faltered in months, but LilyAnn was already turning heads of Nashville music execs for her rendition of "Valley Winter," released by tiny Fleur de Lis Records. Performing in clubs, county fairs, even supermarket openings, Lily-Ann tried her hand at songwriting and soon remarried, this time to Shenandoah Iron Works manager, Keith Grevins. Daughter Angela was born three years before her mother rocketed to stardom with the chart-buster "Break of Dawn."*

It went on, a scroll-down, upbeat story all the way, a triumphant march of albums and Grammies and world tours and awards by the Country Music Association, the Academy of Country Music, a humanitarian award for honorary chairing of fundraisers for two dread diseases, the possibility of Hollywood film roles.

One point surfaced, the end of the second marriage, which was slipped in as minor data, not as a storm worth media footage. Fair enough, a star's web page was not a scandal sheet. But even this site of cyber puffery showed many personnel changes in the band. Shenandoah Iron Works seemed in constant flux. Over the years, only one player, the rhythm guitarist Brent Landreth, had stayed the whole course. Kate remembered the name. He was on Billy D's list which Dottie read through. He and the new drummer, Joel Somebody, were at LilyAnn's house hours before the door accident.

Here he was onscreen on the web page holding his guitar, his broad smile showing a remarkable set of even white teeth against a dark complexion. Brent Landreth had bright, dark eyes, bushy brows and a mass of curly black hair. Kate lingered at his image. Fifteen years in LilyAnn Page's band, fifteen years of water under the bridge, and Brent Landreth could be a reservoir of information. As for the "political" injured ex-drummer, Bucky Sibbett, no sign of him on the web page of smiling young guys. The current drummer, Joel, had blond shoulder-length hair and a radiant smile.

"Sam, when band members leave, are they usually fired?"

"Downsized?" The ugly word hung in the air for a moment as if threatening to spread. But Sam shook his head no. "There's a good deal of changeover. Always has been, and the musicians understand that. It's not personal. This isn't the era of the Jordanaires."

It was a relief at least to recognize Elvis's sidemen.

Sam went on. "Artists often want a new sound, so they replace a band member—sometimes the whole band. Emmylou broke up the Hot Band and the Nash Ramblers, and Rodney Crowell moved from the Cherry Bombs to the Cicadas. Lord, some years ago a charter plane crash killed Reba McEntire's entire band. The pilot failed to clear a mountain." Sam's voice turned unnaturally calm, steely calm. It was the voice of a man who understood his last words might be heard on a tape in a black box recorder.

Kate saw him force attention back to her, to the topic. "And some band members," he said, "just get sick of the road, the constant touring. They want regular lives." He crossed his arms across his chest. "And some of them sort of evolve. Like Barry Tashian started out as a rocker, then joined Emmylou's Hot Band as lead vocalist on electric guitar. Now he's a duet act with his wife, Holly, and they're into acoustic music. They have their own albums, tour with their own band, write songs." Sam pointed at the computer screen. "See Chuck Springer's name there? He got a record deal and left Shenandoah Iron Works for a solo career. I bought his album. It's pretty good."

"What happened to him?"

"Who knows?"

"You mean the album failed?"

"It's a hard business, Kate."

She sighed, said she'd seen enough for now. Sam too. They stepped away, and the screen saver came on, an aquarium scene. She refrained from mentioning Kelly's foul fish tank in her room. That was between Kel and Sam.

Back downstairs in the living room, Kate turned on

the basket lamps, ready to tell Sam the real reason
she was pelting him with all these questions.

Instead, she found him looking at her. "So, Kate,"
he said, "are you ready to tell me what's really going
on? You're about as subtle as a fire truck with flashers
on." He laughed. "Something's up, don't deny it.
You've got that blood-in-the-eye look. This isn't just
about a fan magazine, it's about the Lily of the Shenandoah Valley. What's this all about?"

So she told him.

His response was a sigh and a moment of reverie.
"To think, I was dumb enough to believe that in Nashville you'd settle down."

"As if you'd quit flying."

"And lead a nice humdrum life."

"Like yours."

"Except on the splendid occasions when yours truly,
Captain Sam, comes into town."

"Make it arrival by interstate highway. If Nashville
only had passenger train service. . . ."

"And no more crime cases."

"No radar blackouts, especially the ones at thirty-
thousand feet."

"And happily ever after." He stopped. "I like that
one, the happily forever after."

"I like it too."

"So forget the crime investigations."

"Forget wind sheer."

"Okay, okay. Truce." He held his hands up for surrender. "You think my flying life is crazy, and it's
vice versa on your damn cases. And nobody's giving
an inch."

Quietly she said, "We do a lot of giving. Quite a
lot." He turned and kissed her, once, twice. Were they
both thinking of how long before Kelly finished her
homework and sank into a deep sleep and left them
really alone? Sam drew back and said, "Kate, let me
put in a word. For one thing, there's a country music

research library practically under your nose in Nashville. It's the Country Music Foundation Library, and
it'll save you time. You probably pass it on the way to
work, looks like a cross between a church and a barn."

She nodded. "At the end of Music Row. With tour
buses out front."

"Right. You can see Elvis's gold Cadillac and everybody's guitars. But downstairs is the library. Use it,
and you won't have to depend on LilyAnn Page's han-
dlers. That's just a practical tip." He looked closely at
her. "But there's something else. This 'case' is different because it's got a personal streak. You told me
once that 'Break of Dawn' was tough to listen to. We
were at my place, and I hit the reject button pronto
and played us some Mingus. Now you're in 'Break of
Dawn' country. You'll have to work a little harder to
keep your head about this. Maybe it's like flying. You
have to turn off the emotions to do your job. That's
the secret of it. You hear me?"

Easier said than done, but she nodded.

They kissed, and the night passed in late and furtive
love, too little sleep, then early morning with Kelly's
breakfast and school lunch, shower, a trying moment
at the clothes closet, the day's choice of beige and
burnt orange and a set of museum Chinese beads to
pull the colors together—and all done in semi-quiet
so Sam could sleep in before heading to the airport
and off to Wilmington, Delaware.

Kate left him a note, dropped Kelly at school and
headed toward downtown on West End-Broadway.
Tuesday morning traffic was moving nicely, and she
was early. The air was mild, overcast. People had
warned her about tornado season, but all that seemed
remote, like TV footage from Oklahoma or Arkansas.
With no meetings scheduled today, it would be steady
office work on *SouthWing*.

But at a long red light near the I-40 interchange,
she reached into her purse for a mauve slip of paper

with the address of Sonny T. Burkendahl, cabinet maker and refinisher of woods. Maybe this was the moment to pay a call on Sonny T. The address Taylor Evelyn gave her was ten minutes from here. She could zip easily back into town. Give this forty-five minutes max.

So she hit I-40 West, exited at Jefferson and made her way from Albion to Clare, where she slowed and looked for number 374.

S. T. Burkendahl & Son was two long sheds with a small white cottage in the back. A van and a panel truck were parked in the front, and Kate pulled in under a tree that dropped pale spring green seed pods onto her hood. The door of the nearest shed was ajar, and she stepped in at the call to "Come in," expecting bandsaws and table saws but hearing instead the rhythms of hand tools. Planes, chisels. She breathed the aroma of wood and sawdust in a neat and orderly interior, with tools hung on wall hooks and stowed in open cabinets along one side. Before her stood a card table—Sheridan?—minus its fourth leg. A man stepped forward. "Yes, ma'am, may I help you?" He put down a Stanley plane.

"I'm Kate Banning. Are you Mr. Sonny Burkendahl?"

"Junior. Some call me Sonny. What can I do for you?"

"Junior" was at least in his mid-sixties and rail thin in a blue-and-white striped short-sleeve shirt with a carpenter's pencil in the pocket. His crewcut hair was the color of wood shavings, and his nose looked planed to a narrow wedge. His handshake grip was surprisingly soft for a man handling boards and planks and tools. She said, "Mr. Burkendahl, I represent Ms. LilyAnn Page's management. I'd like to ask a few questions about the installation of the dining room door at her home last Saturday. I understand you refinished the door."

"Refinished and rehung it too," he said.

"And you did all that yourself?"

His steady pale blue eyes gave no sign he found the question unusual. He said, "Yes, ma'am. When we brought that door into the shop, we took off the hinge sets for cleaning. Tindall—that's my assistant—he rubbed them with Brasso. Sat on that bench back there and rubbed like no tomorrow." He pointed, and Kate saw the bench where a coffee mug now sat steaming. No sign of Tindall or the Brasso. Sonny Burkendahl's voice was midrange and twangy. He said, "Tindall rubbed both hinge sets like sailors do brass. When we got the door ready, you'd think they were eighteen-karat gold."

"And you personally hung the door."

"Like I said. I screwed the hinges back on and carried the door back out there to Mosely in my van. Beautiful place she's got out there, reminds me of a park. Anyway, I hung that door, dropped the pins in, tapped 'em with a hard rubber mallet to prevent any dents or dings. That door's got real good balance."

He made a sleek wavy gesture with his hands. " 'Course, I swang it closed a few times to test it out. B'lieve I left it closed, but I couldn't say for sure. Might've been open when I left." He sucked his teeth and looked aside. "I'm real sorry to hear Ms. Page had an accident with it. Accident or whatever it was. I don't know a thing about that. Miz Taylor called me."

Kate felt annoyed. So much for the surprise element. Yet so far this was, as Taylor Evelyn predicted, a routine verification. Kate said, "Have you done other work at Ms. Page's home?"

"Been out there a few times. Ms. Taylor calls me and we work it out. I put in some picture-glass windows a few months back. Beautiful colors when the sun shines through, reminds you of a church. And I made some cabinets for the kitchen last year. Made 'em from blueprint plans. Solid birdseye maple. You don't get to work with wood like that very often, not with new construction. These days, folks'll pay up for crown molding made of plastic. Eighteen-foot ceilings, million-dollar homes with plastic molding. Cryin' shame."

Kate nodded. "When you hung the dining room door, Mr. Burkendahl, did you notice anything unusual?"

"Unusual? Well, it was raining that morning, I remember, and you always think about wood swelling on you."

"I mean, apart from the weather. Were people around? Anybody you noticed?"

He paused. His eyes flickered and his mouth tightened. "There was two fellas lookin' all over for music tapes, I remember that. They looked in a lot of the drawers. One of 'em I seen there before, I don't know his name, got good solid arms and dark hair that's real tight curly." He paused, shifted his weight. "And then somebody came in with big bouquets of flowers, and rock 'n' roll music was playin' real loud upstairs on a stereo or somesuch. I remember 'cause it's all noise to me. I went to the van for the rubber mallet, and I seen a big car go around the back drive. A sedan, I think it was a Jaguar. I don't know who that was."

"Color—?"

He squinted. "Tan, metallic. Like silver ash, and that's a hardwood you don't see these days."

"And that's all?"

He paused. "More or less." He now seemed uneasy. Kate too paused, as if not to disturb a mental door possibly swinging on its own hinges. At last Kate said, "Since you already spoke to Ms. Evelyn, Mr. Burkendahl, I don't have to tell you there's a serious injury as a result of the hinge pins gone from that door. Ms. Page will be in a cast for many weeks. Anything you remember might help."

He stood, shifted from foot to foot, looked skyward

as if hoping rain might put a stop to this. At last he said, "I don't mix in family matters. I'm a cabinet maker and wood refinisher. Some restoration." He pointed to the table. "Like a new leg for that table over there. That's the kind of work I do. No drink, no drugs either. You need your eye and your hand. I'm not a general contractor. I don't do construction." He looked at Kate. "And I don't expect a general contractor to say he can do my kind of work. Most times, he can't."

"But somebody did? A contractor there on Ms. Page's property?"

"More like an estate, I'd say, the size of it. But again, I don't mix in family business. If Ms. Page's brother thinks he can make cabinets or refinish a door, I got nothing to say on that."

"You must mean Ms. Page's older stepbrother, Kip. I know he's a contractor."

He wet his lips. "It's none of my business. I work through Ms. Evelyn. She can tell you I'm cold stone sober every day of my life. I'll just say, that one oak armchair, it was near ruined time it got to me. Even smelled like rye whiskey. I don't want bad blood, but I laid down the law after that one. Nothin' harder to undo than a bad repair job."

Kate blinked. Such a southern kind of statement, bits and pieces buried and half dug up. LilyAnn Page's stepbrother, the contractor, evidently drank and crossed into Sonny Burkendahl's turf. Did that make it a guerilla turf fight? Would the "kid" brother pull those pins?

Sonny stood with feet together as if ready for a pledge of allegiance. "The one time I seen Ms. Page at her home," he said, "I got an autographed photo. But I came real close to sayin' something right in front of him, he got her so upset, I didn't have the heart. I was installing the picture glass windows. I just worked along. They got all riled up. He had a claw hammer

in his belt. I tell you what, I worried he'd try it on
her. Some kid brother. That's all I got to say on it. I
don't mix in."

Kate paused. "Mr. Burkendahl," she said, "you've
been very helpful. Thanks for your time." She shook
his hand and went out toward her car. Her thoughts
were on the web page bio, on the stepbrother who
left the Recliners, who swapped guitar for a toolbox.
Who swapped his claw hammer banjo for a cold
forged claw hammer. Suppose she was right, one thing
led to another, and the brotherly link was Kip.

CHAPTER FIVE

Forty minutes later, in the office, a map of the state of Arkansas was spread across Kate's desk. Her coffee cooled in the "World's Best Mom" mug, and voicemail was set to take her messages for the next hour. She put one finger on Fort Smith and peered at rivers, state forests, a myriad of roads. She needed magazine features on enticing Arkansas vacation spots—and fast. She traced her finger from Fort Smith to Fayetteville, Pine Bluff, Little Rock. *SouthWing* was supposed to lure passengers to Arkansas for fly-and-drive packages. Kate scanned the map like a prospector hoping for a gold rush. Any rush.

"Stay Over a Weekend for an Arkansas Adventure!"

Some of the place names—Texarkana, Arkadelphia, El Dorado—sounded like failed utopias a century ago. With a pencil eraser, she tracked the major interstates. I-30 ran into Texas and I-40 cut all the way West.

"Arkansas—From Interstates to Back Roads!" Ugh.

Roaming the map, she noticed the several springs, Hot Springs, Eureka Springs, Siloam Springs, Sulphur Springs.

"Arkansas!—Land of Springs!"

Awful. Flat. She sighed, sat back, sipped coffee, acknowledged the distraction, the time ticking by. Doubtless many fine recreational spots shimmered throughout the state of Arkansas, and she'd better find a way to do them justice, and fast. Meaning she

better forget the Lily of the Shenandoah Valley and
get past her Yankee snobbery and, as they say, embrace Arkansas. *SouthWing* ought to run a seasonal
events calendar. Did the Ozark Mountains feature Fall
foliage? Eco-tours?

She put in a call to one Shawnlee Davis of the Arkansas Democrat Gazette. Time to network, pronto.
Sam said the state's best writer was Lucinda Williams,
and she'd searched directory assistance before remem-
bering the woman wrote songs. Kate tried to sound
nice on her voicemail speech to Shawnlee. Remarkable how these days you never expected to reach anybody on the first try.

Not even Dottie Skipwith.

Kate had a call in to her too, to schedule a little
talk ASAP on the subject of stepbrother Kip of the
claw hammer. Why did Dottie fail to mention his tem-
per? His drinking? Surely she knew the inside story
of the Padgett-Page family situation—unless she was
in charge of their family secrets.

Or maybe kept out of them, the main house off-
limits much of the time, the key entrusted only on an
emergency basis. Could that be? Could her Deb spend
the night with LilyAnn's Angie, with Dottie herself
virtually barred from the house? Not likely.

And the new bodyguard, this Turk Karcic, sounded
right out of central casting. For sure, he took a load
off Kate by his very presence. Starting today, LilyAnn
Page was his full-time job. And Kate Banning's hobby.
Good term. Less pressure. But could he shield her
from the deep pangs of "Break of Dawn?" That remained to be seen.

For now, set aside the Arkansas map and work the
phone to try finding out where Bucky Sibbett kept
himself these days. Cotton Music said sorry, they dealt
mostly in guitars, and Corner Music thought they
knew the name but couldn't be sure. Fork's Drum
Closet said Bucky wasn't drumming anymore, as far

as they knew. Someone in the back of the Closet, however, mentioned he might be working at Tennessee Stage and Studio Supply, Fourth Avenue, downtown.

Great, an easy walk from Fleetwood, practically under her nose. She stood to take a break when her phone rang. It was Mary Fortune, the assistant on the fifth floor executive suite to say that Kate's boss, Hughes Amberson, wished to see her.

"Now? At this minute?"

Mary's voice was always so smooth. Yes, preferably now, though later on this morning would be possible. Either way, Mr. Amberson would call upon Kate in her own office.

Why did a talk with the company president feel more like a threat than an opportunity?

She spent the next ten minutes on office housekeeping, as if he might cite her for clutter. Kate straightened stacks of papers, gathered all loose pens and pencils into the crock, moved spiral binders off her red loveseat, put her jacket back on. The company president had never before come to her office. What if he brought an ultimatum on the *LilyAnn Page* project? How would she handle it?

Hughes Amberson's knock was soft yet percussive, the sound of *noblesse oblige* faking democracy. She opened up. "Mr. Amberson, good morning—" She stopped before "sir."

He smiled. "Kate, good to see you. Much appreciate your time." He shook her hand and sat on the loveseat, a tall mid-fifties, blond-fading-to-gray man in a custom tailored window plaid suit with a dark red tie and Italian loafers the color of oak.

"Kate," he said, "I hope you and your little daughter are appreciating one of the loveliest spring seasons we've had here in Middle Tennessee."

"Beautiful." She spoke from her desk chair. Was

this an inspection? Was the fan magazine project on his mind?

"The dogwoods have never been nicer." His eyes that watery blue. "Kate, I'll come to the point. I need your advice."

"Whatever I can do."

He looked toward the river, back at her. "You've been with us a year now?"

"Closer to nine months, actually."

"It seems longer, Kate. I hope you take that as a compliment. Fleetwood's clients are pleased. I take it *SouthWing* is coming along for us?"

Her palms were damp. "It is. We're developing a roster of Arkansas writers. The new expanded format will debut with the Fall issue."

"Good. Very good."

She felt her shoulders tense. The last time Hughes Amberson summoned her for a talk, he dumped the dopey *Distant Lands* on her desk, a fake travel magazine. Back then, he exuded seductive charm. Now his jawline looked stern.

"Kate, I've been talking to Donald."

Don Donaghue. She almost flinched.

"And he tells me we're moving ahead with a pilot project involving magazines of the country-and-western music singers." He paused, looked her in the eye. "I don't suppose you're taking the lead on this?"

"Uh, no."

"I wouldn't think."

She felt her face flush. She could dump this all on Don. It was tempting. She looked her boss in the eye. "But the Editorial Department is involved, Mr. Amberson. We're cooperating at the departmental level." She swallowed hard. Some department, Kate herself and the two free-lance copy editors. She said, "The Sales and Planning Department conferred with me, and together we're proceeding." She kept her voice firm.

Two furrows appeared across his ever-tan forehead. "Kate, you know I don't interfere in day-to-day operations, but we are not a presence in the Nashville entertainment industry."

A.K.A. low life, riff-raff country music. Wasn't Mrs. Hughes Amberson on the symphony board? The ballet? She braced for the obvious, the plug pulled from *LilyAnn's Page* and a reprimand.

He shifted on the loveseat. "And yet," he said, "Fleetwood must think of the future, of the new generations." She nodded, waited for other shoes to drop, a cascade of shoes on her head. "I understand, for instance, that young people nowadays wear ear plugs when they go to these big concerts in the Nashville Arena, the ones with the huge television screens—"

She nodded. What was this about?

"The young people insert earplugs. That's how loud the music is. I never heard of such a thing."

"My daughter might have mentioned it." Actually, Kelly had not.

"So we must be open to the future."

Kate nodded. Was he saying that Fleetwood must remain a corporate pot of gold for the Amberson family progeny, even if that meant redneck fanzines?

"Though we must also be prudent. 'Conservative' is not a term we need defend."

"I understand."

"And so, Kate—" She felt called to attention. "So I seek your advice." He looked her in the eye. "Donald is too new here to put his stamp on the company with innovative ideas. Your work, however, has already proven to be in our best interests. If you assure us that this pilot project is right for the Fleetwood Corporation, we will accept your judgment. Otherwise, Fleetwood will withdraw before any contract is signed. We don't need to be in country-western music."

Don't need to be. It was a phrase she'd heard several times in Nashville. Mild as it sounded, it was hot-

ter than Tabasco, a southern term of censure that
broadcast the Fleetwood chief's deep hostility to the
fan magazine venture. She looked at Amberson's
hands lying loosely in his lap, hands that held golf
clubs, sterling letter openers, julep cups.

Hands that held the reins.

And her job on the line. No matter how well you
did, your job was always on the line.

But for LilyAnn Page, life itself on the line. A
woman evidently disliked, maybe even hated, but the
voice of "Break of Dawn." And Kate felt caught. Her
job against her . . . mission.

Goodbye, *LilyAnn's Page?*

Hello, murder?

Hello, unemployment?

Murder . . . murder.

"Mr. Amberson, the pilot project may not be Fleetwood's typical venture, but at this time, I believe we
should support it." She forced herself to look him in
the eye. "Country music sales are tabulated in many
millions. Garth Brooks, and, um, Alan Jackson and . . .
Reba McEntire, Shania Twain. Male and female vo-
calists both. Their sales range in the tens of millions,
and their own marketing tools include fan magazines
and websites."

She held her gaze. "For Fleetwood, these may become more than a niche market. The Sales Department sees a good future for advertising revenue. I'm
sure Don Donaghue has forwarded the projections to
your office." She wet her lips. "My advice is to move
forward, at least with the pilot project." She added,
"Sir."

They shook hands on it, his palm warm and firm,
hers clammy. Then he left. Duty and stupidity, weren't
they just opposite sides of the same coin? She looked
around the office, the furniture, Tizio lamp, great view
of the Cumberland. She must earn them every day.

Yet just seconds ago she put them all at risk by

lying to a generous boss whose trust she'd earned over nine long months in Nashville.

But wasn't LilyAnn's life worth more than a few quarterly profit points?

Wasn't Kate Banning out on a thin limb? A cracking branch?

Now she breathed deeply and stared out at the river, which caught an ochre yellow light, the sky ever more drab as the morning wore on—so much for partly sunny. On her desk lay the cycle issue and a *SouthWing* prototype. And Hughes Amberson's cologne in the air, probably private stock from London.

Take a break. Take five. Or fifteen. Get out of the office. She didn't want to eat, just get some air. Maybe check on Bucky Sibbett's whereabouts. She walked down to lower Broadway, turned the corner onto Fourth and walked halfway down the block. Tennessee Stage and Studio Supply was a one-story brick with plate glass windows. Inside was crammed with sound equipment, and a lanky guy in jeans and sneakers was looping electrical cord around his left elbow and palm. He looked up as Kate entered. "Help you?" Kate asked for Bucky Sibbett.

"Bucky? I don't know a Bucky." He paused. "We got a Frank Sibbett works part time. Hey, Lisa—?" A nasal "yo" came from somewhere in the rear. "That new guy, Frank, does he go by Bucky? He does? You sure?" He looked back at Kate. "There's your answer. Pays to ask." He put the coil of cord on a glass showcase so scratched it looked like seaglass. "B'lieve Frank—or Bucky—is out on a job right now. I could look it up."

"The job, it's with a band?"

"Band?" The look was quizzical.

Kate said, "Frank—Bucky—he's a drummer, right?—but the folks at Fork's Drum Closet said he's not drumming these days."

Still quizzical. "Well, nothing to say on that score.

Django Reinhardt played guitar with three fingers, so it can be done. Anyhow, Bucky's on a crew putting up a stage out in Hermitage. You want to leave a message?"

"Uh, I'll catch up with him later. Thanks."

Down the block, she regretted not asking more. What about the fingers? Try for a light touch, and you can miss a cue. Did Bucky Sibbett need an extra day job, like so many Nashville musicians, or did the injury that Dottie mentioned force him off the drummer's stool?

Force him into deadly rage—? Was it politics and maiming both fueling his wrath?

Questions without answers. She stood on the sidewalk, checked her watch, felt the breeze, closed her eyes and listened to the traffic, the good city sound of cars and trucks. Then a tug at her elbow. She jumped, squealed.

"Kate Banning?"

He had tight curly hair, narrow-set dark eyes, bushy brows, thin lips and a very serious expression. He sprang to life from LilyAnn's web page. "Are you K-Kate Banning?"

"Are you Brent Landreth?"

It sounded more like a challenge than a greeting. Neither one smiled. So he'd followed her, tracked her. Why? He held her elbow. He said, "I want to talk to you."

She pulled her arm free. "Some people make appointments."

He shrugged—no, twitched. He wore jeans and a dark crewneck cotton sweater. Surrounded by a hundred public places, they stood on this corner. He looked back and forth as if in search of a plan. "Jack's," he said. "Let's go over there. Please." He steered her across Broadway and into Jack's Barbecue.

She sat opposite him in a slatted wood booth, and

the barbecue smelled delicious. Jack's was gearing up for the lunch crowd. Kate had no appetite. Brent Landreth waved to a counterman and put both palms down on the table. She imagined him with a guitar.

"So, Mr. Landreth—"

"Brent."

"Kate, then." The pause was awkward. Neither seemed eager to break it. They peered across at one another, and he thrust out his jaw. She said "I believe you're the rhythm guitarist of the Shenandoah Iron Works."

"And Dottie says you're working on *LilyAnn's Page.*"

"My company is developing a pilot project, yes." Kate said, "Actually, I've been wanting to talk with you. But I don't like being followed."

He said, "It's better this way." He sounded more anguished than boastful. He looked around. A group came in for lunch.

Kate decided to play it his way. She said, "I know you've been with Ms. Page for quite some time."

"From the beginning. Since the Ironworks started." He looked at her closely. "Dottie told us about the *Page* shakeup."

Kate nodded. "A fan magazine needs a new look from time to time. It's like anything else." She added, "How about a band? Does a band need a shakeup too?"

He looked wary and looked around again. He said, "People come, people g-go. Everybody's different. Everybody's got their reasons."

"But you've stayed on."

"I have my reasons."

Kate nodded. At this rate, the two of them could circle one another until sundown. She said, "What's on your mind?"

He paused as if sizing her up. "I want to know what you're really up to."

"I don't understand."

He leaned forward. "This fan magazine stuff, I have no problem with it. I just don't b-buy it. I want to know what else is going on."

She took out a business card and slid it across the table. He didn't even glance down. Kate said, "Have you talked to Dottie?"

"Everybody talks to Dottie. She's great, great for Lily, great for the g-girls, and they're a big handful these days. But she's got the manager's lookout. For me, it's different. I'm on the road, in the bus. I'm in the studio too. Over the years, I make it my business to know what's going on. My boss, she's got trouble. She's a beautiful woman, but her arm's in a cast and it's not pretty."

Kate nodded. She wanted to ask him about stepbrother Kip, about Bucky Sibbett. She wanted to ask about the bus fire, the dead crewman, his own visit to the Mosely house the day the pins were pulled from the hinges. But first, his roadblock of suspicions.

He said, "*LilyAnn's Page,* it works good. Nobody should mess with that."

"We'll work closely with Miss Page. No changes will take place without her approval."

His close-set eyes like lasers now. "You know, Tammy Wynette sued the tabloids and won. They smeared her, and she went after them."

She nodded, puzzled—then suddenly got it. "You think I'm secretly working for the tabloids? Like the *Enquirer?*"

"Maybe."

Her laugh stopped at the look on his face. He thought her a double agent and summoned her here to find out. It wasn't unreasonable, more a mark of his own private vigilance.

"Brent, believe me, I am not a spy for the tabloids. I'm on the Fleetwood Company payroll. We publish magazines for the insurance industry, travel and recreation, retail, building trades, one airline."

He waved her to silence. "Some people in this town want to dish dirt. They don't last long."

"I'm not in the gossip business. I was an investigative journalist back in Boston, and it's a big transition here in Nashville. Maybe old habits die hard, but I'm not here to libel Ms. Page."

Brent Landreth did not look satisfied. He said, "Even if that's true, you're in this short term. You'll redo the *Page* and split. You're here today, gone t-tomorrow."

"Fleetwood is a Nashville company."

"No, that's not it. Not it at all. Listen to what I'm saying. P-please." He spread his arms as if to signal his command of the scene. His eyes never left her face. "The difference between you and me," he said, "is I'm a lifer. The Iron Works is where I am. It's the long road, and I travel every mile. I'm there in the good times and the bad too. I mean, I'm *there*."

Kate nodded, folded her hands, listened.

His voice was low. "LilyAnn goes on tour, I'm in the b-bus in my bunk, and I'm on stage for sound check on the dot. Fifteen years, I missed one tour. Tell you why—appendicitis. Four concerts missed, that was it. I even changed my own wedding day to fit a road tour."

She nodded. Why was he telling her this? Two couples sat at the next table with barbecue plates. They smacked and laughed and bit morsels from bones. Brent leaned closer toward Kate. She smelled mint on his breath.

"You read the liner notes on her albums," he said, "and every one of them says 'Rhythm guitar: Brent Landreth.' Year to year, the producers change, and the session players change, and the Iron Works road band too. B-but not Brent Landreth. And I'm proud of that. Proud LilyAnn Page wants me on her records.

I was in the studio when my little boy was born. That's
how it is with me."

"I understand."

He leaned even closer. "Nobody really understands
that hasn't been there. You play the state fairs in late
August, September heat, the d-dust nearly chokes you,
gags you. We had yellow-jackets swarming, had rain
come pouring down through a roof. You wouldn't believe what backstage looks like at fancy clubs."

She nodded. It was like a prepared statement. "I'll
just tell you, a year ago at this one particular stadium
c-concert at Boone, North Carolina, we had gale-force
winds, and the road manager wanted to pull the plug
because of the lightning. It was flash-boom, flash-
boom. That close."

His shoulders seemed to squeeze at the memory.
"Lily's contract called for a certain number of songs,
and she decided to go for it. She told the band we
could bag it, she'd sing solo and take all the risk. The
other guys r-ran to the shelter."

"But you stayed onstage with her."

"Absolutely. That's my message. I'm with her."

Kate said, "Are you telling me Brent Landreth is a
body guard."

"No, I am not. I'm saying Lily is my b-boss, and
she can count on me. When something's not right, I
try to fix it. Somebody with a scam, somebody out to
cheat her, I try to watch that no harm's done. I'm the
guy that spotted that stalker when they arrested him.
I'm like a scout. My goal's a hundred percent."

Kate nodded. "Brent, I'm not here to do harm. I'm
not part of some scam."

"I hope not." He spread his fingers and then curled
them into fists. "I h-hope not. You know about the
bus fire?" She nodded. "About Carnie? The road
crew accident?"

She nodded again. "I'd like to know more about
that."

"So would I. The fire too. I mean, things can happen, accidents. Trisha Yearwood had a bus fire on tour, burned up all her clothes. So it's not unheard-of." His eyes darted back and forth. "But this is too much. Carnie's dead, decent kid. Now the door and Lily's arm. It could have been her head, her spine. It could of crushed her. We're all jumpy, the band, the road crew. It s-stresses you out."

"Yes."

"Lily's cool about it, and the guys say it helps. They say, if she's not worried, why should we?" He leaned close. "But that's just why—because she's n-not. Do you get it? You have to worry for her. She's got her own stuff, but she needs a lookout. Me, I spent one summer in a fire tower in Yosemite when I was eighteen. You spend the whole day watching the trees on the lookout for smoke. That's what I do for LilyAnn— I look out."

Kate looked at him. Was he in love with LilyAnn Page? Did it even matter? Today he was here to put his loyalist card on the table and to issue a warning to Kate. Could she get him to talk more if he thought Kate, too, stood watch in a fire tower?

He licked his lips. "Thing is, I'm not a guy that t-takes chances. I don't gamble. When Lily and The Ironworks play Reno or Tahoe, the hotel gives us free chips, but I give away my share. I walk through the casino with my wallet in my pocket. You understand?" He stopped.

Kate said, "You mean, it feels risky talking to me, is that it?"

He said, "It's not the way I like to handle things."

Kate paused. A fly settled on a dot of catsup on the tabletop. First fly of the season. Kate said, "Brent, it feels risky talking to you too. At this point, everybody comes under suspicion. That means close friends and strangers. Musicians, crew, grounds workers. Everybody."

He bit his thumb. "I heard from Dottie you're not just a magazine editor."

"I mentioned my background when you and I sat down here—"

"I know, I know." He leaned his arms on the table and rubbed his wrists. The fly now rubbed its legs together. "Dottie says you're working on this . . . this thing. Unofficially."

She gave the smallest nod.

"Billy D thinks it's all Walter Sian's doing. Like a plot."

"Is that what you think too?"

"I think Billy watches too much TV, when he's not out in a field somewhere shooting his arrows." He scratched his head, fingers dug deep into the mass of curls. "Not that Walter doesn't matter. Believe me, I'm watching out for that s.o.b. Love to see him locked up again. All the t-trouble he caused Lily, I'd throw away the key. But he's a loner, that's my read on him. Anybody with a plot, they have to be a leader. He's no leader."

"But you think there's a plot?"

"Yeah, a plot. That's on my mind." He kept his fingers in the tangle of his hair.

"How about Bucky Sibbett?"

He shook his head. "He couldn't keep quiet long enough."

"So he's disqualified?" He said nothing. "I hear he hurt his hand—"

Brent sighed. "Yeah, he got his hand hurt, but the accident didn't drive him out of the band, his drumming did. That and his t-temper. He lost his ear for the beat. A drummer off the beat, he drove us crazy. Bass and rhythm guitar had to take over." He looked disgusted. "Lily fired him, and then he stuck his own hand in the car door. That's the truth."

As if a bad drummer could not possibly plot a homicide. Or was it a Nashville thing—that musicians could not possibly be killers? She said, "You must be more like a family member after all this time, Brent. You must know all LilyAnn Page's people, like her stepbrother. . . ."

His eyelids fluttered, like a visual stutter. "Kip's a decent enough guy." It sounded dutiful, as if for Lily-Ann's sake. "He needs his space. Gets strung out sometimes."

"Strung out? That's interesting." She looked at his face. "Brent, where I come from, that term connects to drug problems."

He chewed his lip, eyelids flickering faster. "Hey, I'm talking work, life, whatever. Look, it's not Kip on my mind. What I'm thinking . . . you know Keith Grevins?"

She nodded. "Ms. Page's ex-husband. I understand he lives in Hawaii."

"Mostly. But he's in t-town now. In Nashville." Kate tensed but did not blink. So much for Dottie's five thousand miles. Brent said, "I saw him at the Exit/In last Friday night. He was in the back. I doubt he saw me."

She worked to look neutral, open. "Is this the first time since the divorce?"

He shook his head no. "He comes to Nashville once in a while. He has a business here."

"What business?"

"Laundromats. Nashville Wash-O-Mat, that's Keith." Brent fixed her with a stare. He rubbed at his wrists, tugged the cuffs of his sweater. "Anybody in this t-town could run into Keith. He has his old friends, they go out, the city's not that big."

"So he's in and out—but this time it worries you?"

Brent fingered the handle of his coffee mug. "I mean, if we're on tour, maybe Keith comes into town for a few days, it's no big deal. Even if we're all here, Lily, the band, no problem. Nashville's big enough.

But with Lily's arm, with the fire and Carnie's accident . . ."

"You think Keith Grevins is behind all this?"

Distress in those eyes. "I don't know. I think maybe—see, Keith's from the old days. He managed the Iron Works when we all s-started out. He was married to Lily then. We had some good years." He looked at Kate's face. "You know the whole story?"

"I understand the breakup was rocky."

"Terrible. Onstage, that was fine. The t-tour kept our heads on straight. I mean, onstage you go into a tune, you're in that world. You're in the music. Same with the studio. Every place else, though, it was . . . like poison."

"Poison?"

"The atmosphere."

A man at the next table rose, went to the cafeteria area, returned with three pieces of pie, handed them out around his table. Kate said, "The divorce was, what, six, seven years ago?"

"Feels like yesterday. Feels like last Tuesday. Keith's got one big problem, he nurses a grudge and he's jealous."

"Jealous of LilyAnn?"

"Of everything. People. Stuff he owns. He always carried a gun."

"Concealed?"

"He has a permit. The idea was to protect Lily. He waved it around now and then, nothing serious as far as I knew. But he's . . . like this one time he flattened a guy for touching his truck fender. The guy put a hand on the fender in a parking lot, and Keith decked him. Knocked him unconscious. He treated Lily like that truck. Anybody near her, he got furious. I mean, he protected her too, so you have to say that part was good."

"And the other parts? How about your years in

close quarters with LilyAnn? Did you have trouble with Keith?"

Brent sat back, inhaled, exhaled. He said, "Ups and downs. He got along good with Kip. They were tight. Me, I tried to be mellow. I'd see him around. Even day-to-day after he and Lily split. That kind of contact, it felt okay, like I knew where I stood with him." He crossed his arms. "I'm more worried now. Angie's older, and maybe she doesn't want to go to Honolulu on spring vacation, and he takes it hard, like Nashville's all against him. Last time I talked to Keith, last winter it was, he hinted maybe Lily and I are getting together. He ragged me about it"

"And was he jealous?"

"It feeds his fires." He shrugged. "Hawaii, you think surfing, you think beaches. Keith, though, he's like a volcano. Forget Kilamanjaro or whatever it is. He boils inside and erupts. Blowout."

"But blowouts are sudden. We're looking at somebody who sets traps, somebody cunning. The dining room door, the bus fire and Carnie's death—they were rigged, plotted." He said nothing. "Or would he hire someone?"

Brent neither nodded nor shook his head. He leaned forward and spoke in low tones. "I heard this new rumor. I got it from a source I trust. Keith had a few drinks a couple nights ago and started saying he'd get Angie back. More like bragging about it."

"A new custody fight?"

"No, no court stuff. No lawyers, no judges. More like he's t-taking it into his own hands."

She hesitated, putting this together. "So you think Keith Grevins is the mastermind of a plot to get his daughter back by harming LilyAnn." He nodded, though reluctantly. "By eliminating her?"

His eyes looked wild. He tried to speak, but the sounds were a jam of consonants.

Kate said, "You think the plot is already in motion with these . . . these accidents?"

His fingers were taut. "L-look—I . . . I . . . t-t-t-tell—" He stopped, pushed back his chair, looked down and away from Kate. He closed his eyes. A moment passed. He opened his eyes and spoke slowly, as if from a distance inside himself. He said, "I know K-Keith. I know how he is. He was a genius with Lily's career. He ate, slept, breathed her career. He launched her. When he wants something, he g-goes for it. He lives it."

Kate paused. "Brent, have you talked to Dottie?"

He looked her in the eye. "I t-tried. I sat down with her, but what happened, she started telling me her troubles. When it came right down to it, I couldn't bring it up. I helped her clean out the fireplace in her office. Ashes and garbage. Gum stuck all over. Her eyes were all red, I thought she was gonna cry. Believe me, Dottie's very tough. She doesn't cry."

Kate nodded. "What about the police?"

He shook his head. "No police."

"They could help."

"I have my reasons."

She stared across at him. The fly went to the edge of the table. Brent reached, slammed it with his palm, stepped on the remains, wiped his fingers with a napkin. His nails were even, neat. He looked at Kate as if for a plan of action.

She said, "Brent, I know it's tough to talk to an outsider. Believe me, I do. I appreciate your time." She wrote her home number on the back and gave him a card. "Let's stay in touch. Work or home," she said. "Call me anytime at all." She stood to leave, and the last thing she remembered was his eyes. They looked scared.

CHAPTER SIX

It was hard to concentrate. Her stomach growled. A go-box from Jack's Barbecue would have been smart. She was grateful for the call from Shawnlee Davis at the Arkansas *Democrat Gazette,* who promised to e-mail back a list of Arkansas feature writers likely to moonlight for Fleetwood with articles for *SouthWing*.

Great, an actual, normal business arrangement. Nothing cloaked or camouflaged. No guns. Keep this going. Get into normality. Kate sorted a folder of proposals for the varied magazines she supervised, then reached for the "in" basket's bulging folder of magazine maybes. She dutifully dug into a piece on mountain bikes for a cycle issue. She turned to ready a thick pack of proofs for the printing plant, sat back, rolled her shoulders and rubbed her neck and thought about Brent Landreth, who idolized LilyAnn after all these years and mapped a trail directly to a homicidal ex plotting to kill his country star former wife. How could Dottie refuse to face this?—unless she was so scorched by their break-up that the Pacific was her pacifier.

Or unless Brent had an agenda of his own. His Keith was a monster, but Kip merely "strung out." He pushed the stalker into the background, and the drummer too. But wasn't Keith Grevins actually Brent's biggest rival over the years? The loyal rhythm guitarist could have special motives for fingering his beloved LilyAnn's ex. The loyalty was disarming, the stutter and humility too. Factor in these variables.

Kate reached left, grabbed the Metro phone book and thumbed through. Nashville Wash-O-Mat had eleven locations, no headquarters. Probably a parent company she'd have to research. For now, maybe take Sam's advice and check out the Country Music Foundation Library, a ten-minute drive. Call it Fleetwood research. Maybe combine it with a check on Kip. Call to the building trades unions? No, they protected their own and stonewalled. Instead she found the Nashville number of the Contractor Licensing Board and the Permit Office, the Old Howard School Building, Second Avenue, hours eight to four.

It was 1:51 when Kate came out of the building with her list of permits issued to Valley Construction. Two were business permits, a hair salon, Chez Robert at the Bellevue Mall, and a Wyoming Steakhouse on Nolensville Road. Just what Nashville needed, another chain steakhouse. Three others, including 83 Mosely, were residential, scattered in West Meade, Green Hills, Granny White. Granny herself supposedly had kept an inn for travelers in the old days. Her name was now commemorated in a two-lane blacktop along a very pleasant stretch of country dells. So grab a sandwich and head out Twelfth to Granny White Pike, then loop back to the country music library.

Number 3323 Granny White was a brick Tudor with bright blue plastic sheeting dangling on the left side. No yard sign for Valley Construction was in view anywhere. Kate pulled in and parked, wadded the tuna sandwich wrapper, grabbed her purse and approached the house. At first she did not see the slight, white-haired figure who rose from a flower bed by the front door, a woman in a green rubberized gardener's apron, hat and gloves.

"I didn't mean to startle you," Kate said. "I'm Kate Banning."

"How do you do? I am Miss Marjorie Styles." She began to tug at one garden glove. "I need to get these begonias into the ground."

"I don't mean to interrupt," Kate said. "I'm considering Valley Construction for a renovation project at my home. I understand Mr. Kip Padgett is working for you this spring, though I don't see a sign."

The woman stared. "Working? I don't know that 'working' is the right word." Now the pale blue eyes flashed. "Do you know Mr. Padgett?"

"We haven't met."

"Very charming, very winning young man. But if you'd like to come around to the side and back of my home, it's a picture worth many words. Watch your step."

They walked in silence to the blue plastic area at the side and back of the house, where a wall was torn out and covered with additional plastic. Kate stared. In the yard were a pallet of bricks, a small bulldozer, a cement mixer, two trailers, piles of lumber, frames and trusses. It looked more like a contractor's storage yard than an active building site. Weeds were sprouting between the wood members, and the lumber was settling in the earth. Miss Styles said, "My brother, who is currently in North Carolina in a convalescent home, plans to come live with me. He cannot climb the stairs, so I need a first-floor bedroom and bath. Mr. Padgett started the work in early March. He demolished the wall and hung the plastic, but I haven't seen him or his workmen since the fifteenth of that month. That lumber is sinking down in the mud, and it's warping." She added, "Believe me, he has been paid handsomely. I'm heartsick."

Kate said, "Contractors take too many jobs and spread themselves thin."

The voice was quiet but firm. "This isn't thin, Miss Banning. This is neglect. This is dereliction of duty. Mr. Padgett doesn't answer his phone. He doesn't return my calls. His voicemail fills up so a person can't even leave a message. And the letters I've written, not one reply."

She said, "He was so nice, I was fooled. I suppose we'll meet in court, although the building inspector's office tells me the bad ones just start up another company. They move their money and equipment to the new name, so you can't recover."

Her voice stayed calm with evident effort. "Sharon at Metro Codes, she's on my side, and they know all about him. He used to be good, but not anymore." She pushed back her hair against her forearm. "I try not to take it personally. Homeowners all over Nashville are in a fix with that man. I pulled the Valley Construction sign out of my yard like a weed. My advice is, don't let Mr. Padgett fool you. He'll gladly take your money and disappear."

Kate thanked her, wished her well and went back to her car, which now smelled of tuna. She started the engine. What did Kip's vanishing act mean?—that he was overextended, for sure, that the residential contracts were lowest on the construction totem pole, a convalescent brother no match for a national franchise steakhouse like Wyoming. As Kip himself might be the first to admit. Besides, talk to any homeowner about their renovation, and it was always a tale of major surgery from the incision on.

Yet one image stuck, the tall weeds around the piles of lumber. And Kip's dead silence despite the calls and letters. Ms. Styles struck Kate as just the kind of client you could stall with a little personal attention, a little framing here, a skylight there, a few licks of paint. Contractor sweet talk would be cheap. Bottom line question: did ten weeks of no-show by Valley Construction connect to the attempts on LilyAnn Page's life?

Maybe the country music library files would help. She nudged the accelerator, cut over to Demonbreun and finally the Country Music Museum and Hall of Fame came up on the right, a building she'd passed countless times, its style c.1960 Barn Moderne. She pulled in and curled two dollar bills for the honor-system parking slot—really, a slit. Who could roll up paper money this tight besides cokeheads? All over the city, Nashville parking lots ideal for cokeheads.

Inside, a tourist group jammed the museum lobby, oohing at the dark polished walk-of-stars floor and a black guitar the size of a ticket booth. Cheerful young staffers directed her downstairs.

The library reading room was glassed, and a ruddy-faced man pored over documents at the far end by a Xerox machine. A staffer, Sandy, smiled and agreed to bring material on LilyAnn Page.

The folders were brought to the reading table, five, six of them stuffed with newspaper clippings, press releases, black-and-white glossy photos, magazines covering the last fifteen years. Also the book, *Lily-Ann—A Life in Pictures*. Kate opened it to find early family snapshots of Lillian in her cradle, in her stroller, on Santa's lap. The scene shifted to the Pad-gett backyard summer family barbecue, the business-man dad in his chef apron, the mom with a bowl of potato salad, little Lily with her hot dog. And Kip in his Little League uniform on the pitcher's mound squinting at the camera as if ready to release his bean-ball. So the stepbrother and sister were together as children.

Kate peered closely, as if to see a violent glint in the boy's eye. Impossible. She turned the pages to find the Padgetts at church, in their driveway with a new family station wagon, vacationing in the mountains. Model nuclear family.

Then "Part Two—Country Stardom." It was Lily arm-in-arm with lanky, all-American Kip of the banjo, then the major record deal, whereupon Kip and the Recliners gave way to the Shenandoah Iron Works as

the photos became arty, stylized, sumptuous and lush
right up to the present. Kate recognized the timbered
wall of the Mosely main house, the photographs clev-
erly arranged to suggest country living, with no sign
of the chaotic house and grounds which Taylor Evelyn
described. No photo in *A Life in Pictures* showed a
drummer. The Iron Works were a soft-focus
background.

On to the newspaper and magazine clip files, in
which the Lily of the Shenandoah Valley was the dar-
ling of reviewers from Helena to Prague. "Lily Wows
Crowd at Newport Beach," "Flower of Country Music
Blooms in Detroit," "Shenandoah Valley Enchants
Lake Champlain." LilyAnn's performances were
"breathtaking," "fabulous," "delicate as her floral
namesake." The newspapers were exuberant, even
worshipful. Most carried photos of the star.

Most were yellowed with age.

None carried photos of former husband Keith
Grevins.

Kate tried to find Bucky Sibbett among the numer-
ous drummers. Was he the full-featured one with
shoulder-length hair? The black guy with an afro? The
scowling one who looked like a latter-day Ringo? She
could not spot the drummer with the political grudge.

Brent Landreth, however, looked like a swarthy
sentinel, unsmiling, wary, ageless, a constant presence
onstage just behind LilyAnn.

Nothing of Kip in the clip file.

But plenty on the divorce. "Courtroom Erupts,"
"Heated Custody Battle," "Lily of Valley Held in
Contempt," "LilyAnn, Estranged Hubby in Restaurant Fracas." Photos showed Keith Grevins with a
high forehead, narrow nose and a salt-and-pepper
beard and moustache that hid much of his face. He
seemed to be shouting at the photographer. LilyAnn,
on the other hand, looked somewhere between stony
and stoic.

Kate carefully read the newspaper columns, which reported midnight shouting matches in parking lots, on the front lawn, in the courtroom itself. LilyAnn called her husband a rottweiler. Grevins's name for her was said to be unprintable. The battle raged over fourteen months over division of property and custody of daughter Angela Lyn. Grevins fought for sole or joint custody but got only visitation rights. At one point, he was arrested for endangerment with a firearm, and LilyAnn Page was granted an injunction against him. Many quotations from both professed parental love for their only daughter. Both vowed to give her the home she deserved.

Kate paused, fingered one clipping, stared at a blurry image of bearded Keith until it dissolved into dots. Upon LilyAnn's death, would he gain custody of daughter Angela? Was he in league with the stepbrother to make it happen? Or with someone in the band or household?

She had to get going. She straightened the folders, began to close *LilyAnn—A Life in Pictures* when the title page caught her eye. Photography credit to Myers Fatenza. Myers, a familiar name, the photographer whom Dottie praised for capturing the girls, Deb and Angie, in charming poses. This was Myers's work.

But something was odd. The book was "with" Myers Fatenza, but his name appeared in tiny print and photo copyright was held by LilyAnn Page.

Why would LilyAnn hold copyright on Myers Fatenza's pictures? To control their use, certainly, but what about the royalty income? What about the money? Why did his name practically need a microscope? Make a note to check out Myers.

Back at the office, she found two e-mails from Arkansas writers delighted to sign on for *SouthWing* features. She had just turned to the day's mail when Delia phoned up to announce a messenger in the lobby with a package marked "personal and confi-

dential" for Kate from Dorothy Skipwith of Page-
One Management.

Kate skipped down four flights of the back stairwell.
In the Fleetwood lobby, receptionist Delia of the ever-
larger hair was busy charming the messenger, who
held a big puffy mailer bag. Kate signed and watched
Delia slip the deliveryman two crisp singles as if the
receptionist had a graduate degree in sleight-of-hand.
Kate felt awkward.

Then she tromped back up to four, bumped the
office door shut with her hip, moved the mail over
and opened the bag, which spewed gray insulation like
prison-issue confetti. She dusted it aside and pulled
out a bundle of folders with a note.

> Kate—Enclosed find your Fan Fair badge and the last
> two years' *LilyAnn's Page* for Fleetwood plan. Also
> recent years' weird-o/sick-o mail. FYI. Read them on
> your schedule, bring them back whenever. Brace
> yourself.
>   Dottie.

Kate put the badge in her purse and looked at the
stack of folders. More folders, days of folders. The
LilyAnn's Page file lay underneath, but as for the top
files—pure, pulsing temptation. Those come-ons celebrities get, requests for money, pleas, threats—here was
the real raw data inches away. Who could resist the
urge to take a look at the weird-o/sick-o stack? Just
for a few minutes? She sat and reached for the file.
This was the Day of the Files. And this was the under-
belly of the glowing press reviews at the Country
Music Foundation Library.

First impression—such labored, childlike script.
These specimens professed undying devotion, love and
lust. Both men and a few women sought pleasure and
pain in specific requests for S-M, for bondage. Would
LilyAnn like to whip? Manacle? Phone sex? Would

she lie face down naked on a glass tabletop? One
doggerel poem from "Kathy" fetishized her western
boots. That was folder one.

Folder two got more serious. In this batch, the reli-
gious fanatics condemned LilyAnn as a practitioner of
witchcraft, a Jezebel who must die, a reincarnated Eve
acting on Satan's orders. Kate jotted names of the self-
appointed avenging angels' names as she went, Albert,
Seth, Pinger, Nordon, RF. Not one last name. No return addresses.

Then came the letters thick with vengeful fantasies
of unrequited love. Some of them were one-time-only,
others clamped together in chronological series that
tracked the route from idolatry to rage—to the
psychotic.

Scanning the first few, Kate saw the cycle. They
began with rapturous praise for LilyAnn's music or
body. They knew she sang for them alone in the studio
or the audience of thousands, how her eyes locked
on theirs in the twenty-fifth row, balcony, loge. They
demanded meetings, dates, rendezvous, and vowed pil-
grimages to Nashville. Graphic descriptions thick with
anticipated intimacy and ecstasy.

Unanswered, the letters turned to bewilderment.
Why no call, since their love was destined? Must meet.
Dates suggested. Then phase three, the rage of be-
trayal, accusations and threats of the jilted. The
predictable if-I-can't-have-you-nobody-can and if-you-
won't-love-me-you-must-die. Scanning the pages, Kate
found drawings mixed with terms of maiming and tor-
ture. They involved fingernails, electric devices,
knives, nails, pins, and fisherman's leader wire. The
race to rage took about three letters per writer. Dottie
clipped the envelopes to each. A few were typed. Kate
wrote down more names, Carleton, Ramor, T. Ernest.
The letters were posted in Evansville, Indiana, Way-
cross, Georgia, Columbus, Ohio, plus four from towns

in the Carolinas, three from Alabama, two in Pennsylvania . . .

She was making notes and just turned to the third folder when the phone rang. Kate cradled the receiver against her shoulder and checked the time, 4:01. She said hello.

Dottie's voice was high and fast. "So Kate, you got my package? What do you think, could any of those perverts be involved?"

As if the woman had a surveillance camera right here in the office. As if Dottie was the elementary school teacher with eyes in the back of her head—and Kate mentally right back in third grade, denying everything. "In fact, Dottie, I've been at work on several projects, I just don't know—"

"Don't bluff me, Kate. Those slime files are irresistible. How about the garroting with fishing wire, didn't that chill you to the bone?"

"All threats must be—"

"Taken seriously, right? That's why we need you. Nine years of these things, a manager can get jaded, like it's ordinary junk mail. I had to stir things up." The line crackled. "Let's not make excuses, Kate. We both understand the curiosity factor, so don't pretend you didn't open that bag and dive into the muck. It's human nature. I'll take full blame for playing the psychologist. That's how desperate I am to get to the bottom of this thing. I'm out of my mind worrying, and I want you involved, involved, involved."

Another breath over the line. "Listen, Turk's here with me. We're going over the protection plan. So can you come out right now?"

"No." No beck and call. "Sorry, Dottie, I'm tied up."

"I have the file on our stalker here on my desk."

Our stalker? Our Walter Sian?

She wanted to bring up Kip and Keith Grevins. Save

them for the face-to-face. Keep the irritation down.
Kate suggested five-thirty. They settled on five.

Kate sighed as she hung up, pushed these LilyAnn
Page files aside, scraped up more bits of that gray
package insulation. She dumped it in the trash can,
brushed it off her lap.

Not enough day in a day.

It was 5:18 when she pulled into 83 Mosely. The
sky was still cloudy, and it looked like rain. Beside
the familiar Land Cruiser sat an army-brown Jeep
Wrangler with its canvas top rolled back. Kate parked
beside it, got out, stuck an umbrella in her purse,
heard the usual din of dogs barking as she approached
the cabin. She expected to hear voices.

"Kate? Is that you? Come in."

The screen door opened, with Dottie in a black
sweatshirt and jeans. The desk fluorescents were on,
the cabin interior otherwise shadowed in gray light.
She expected Turk to be standing on the very spot at
which LilyAnn Page collapsed some forty-eight hours
ago. She looked around. No Turk.

"Where's the bodyguard?"

"At the house. Billy D's showing him the dining
room door. I'll bring him in in a few minutes." Dottie
patted her forehead with a white handkerchief.
"We're lucky Turk's available. I spent all day with
him, briefed him. He understands the situation. He'll
stay close to LilyAnn, whatever it takes. He feels hon-
ored, and that's a break for us. Far as he's concerned,
LilyAnn's the First Lady of Country Music now that
Tammy's gone."

Dottie's voice grew confidential. "You know, Turk's
a former Marine M.P." She almost whispered it. "He
was at Starwood last season, Kate." She made Starwood sound like a badge, like a sheriff's star.

In fact, Starwood was the Nashville-area open-air
amphitheater down I-24, like D.C.'s Wolf Trap or
Massachusetts's Great Woods. A bank officially had

renamed it, but everybody still called the place Starwood. Security there would be fairly serious.

Yet Starwood was seasonal. What did Turk do with
himself from November to June? Kate said, "Security
work must take him indoors in the winter months?"

"Turk spent last winter in Kansas City, Kate. A
woman judge very well known in Missouri politics got
death threats. Turk caught the creep and wrestled him
to the ground. He held him for the police. He'll be a
key witness at the trial." She smiled.

Such a big glow for this man. Such a big buildup.
Yet as she described him, Dottie seemed almost co-
quettish. Odd for a woman otherwise so strict. Did
she have something going with the new bodyguard?
Or maybe Turk's pay package was low, the flattery
meant to bulk his ego instead of his wallet.

Dottie said, "Turk surveilled the property all afternoon, and I'm about to give him a quick house tour.
We'll be right back here. Give me twenty minutes."
She stepped to her desk, tapped the thick stalker
folder with a pencil. "This is the file on Walter Sian.
Help yourself. In fact, take one of the photos on top,
there are copies galore. The crew, Billy D, the band—
I make everybody carry one just in case. So take your
time, get comfy. Just steer clear of the red easy chair,
okay? It's reserved for Lily."

"Actually, Dottie, I have a few questions for you."

Dottie stood in place but tapped her foot impatiently. "You and everybody else, Kate. I've had calls
all day—like about Lily's ex. He was spotted at Planet
Hollywood and Hard Rock."

"That means—"

"Means it's mistaken identity. Got to be a looka-
like." In the fluorescents, Dottie's cheek was pale,
voice strained. "But you know rumors, they spread
like measles. It's all hearsay. If I thought Keith was
really back in town—" She shuddered and looked
through the screen door. "Never mind. Give us twenty

minutes. You can take the file with you if you don't
finish up." But her voice was distracted.

Kate felt placated with paper and crayons. She
wanted to ask about the ex-husband and about Kip.
She wanted a real talk instead of these brief encoun-
ters. "Actually, Dottie, there's an issue with LilyAnn's
ex and her stepbrother—"

"*Brother,* Kate. We don't nit-pick on titles. I have
to meet with him too, you know, because his guys are
building the Fan Fair booth."

Kate paused, chilled. Claw hammer Kip let loose
again. Plus Keith. But Dottie was paying no real attention, was virtually out the door. Bad timing, too many
odd moments on this manager's schedule. It occurred
to her, Dottie Skipwith played ringmaster to perfec-
tion. She snapped her whip, stamped her foot, blew
her whistle, and everybody jumped and fell into line.
What did Taylor Evelyn call the Mosely scene—a circus? Dottie's circus? Barking seals, dancing bears—

And Kate, the Wonder Dog?

Enough of this. Anger rose, hot but focused. Exit
this animal act and third-grade moments with Dottie
Skipwith at the teacher's desk. Enough. Kate stepped
toward the cabin door but turned, blocked the doorframe and faced Dottie. She kept her voice low and
slow. "I want to ask you about Brent Landreth. He
cornered me today. He followed me. We talked. How
much did you tell him about my involvement?"

She shrugged. "Not all that much, really . . ." She
blinked. "Okay, okay, I told him who you are. Why
not? Brent's worked for Lily since forever. He's like
Lily's German shepherd. We're all tense, all except
Lily. She's got her arm to worry about. I've got everything else. Now the damn kitchen knives are
disappearing."

"What?"

"Maria came to cook this afternoon and she can't

find the boning knife and a carving knife. They belong to a set in the kitchen.''

"I saw that set. Two of the knife slots were empty when you took me into the house last Monday. I noticed.''

"Well, gold star for you.'' She flushed. "Hey, sorry, Kate, that was out of line.'' She shrugged. "Thing is, they're not in the utensil drawers either. Maria says she's turned the kitchen upside down. Nobody knows a thing, not Billy D, not the girls. Maybe they got tossed out in the garbage. If it was potato peelers, nobody'd worry. But two knives, it's on your mind.''

"Of course. And you'll let me know if and when they're found, right?'' Kate held her ground in the doorframe. "Right now I want to ask you about step-brother Kip too.''

Dottie blinked. "Just plain brother, Kate. Family's family. Turk's waiting.''

"I'm also waiting, for some information. You insisted I come over. Now I want some attention. Look at me, Dottie. I want you to answer some questions. First, you said Kip's here quite often.''

"As brother and contractor. Valley Construction, that's Kip.'' Her voice shifted to an emcee's warmth, as if to close out this talk.

Kate ignored it. "And the two are on good terms?''

Reluctant now. "I told you, he's over here at the house all the time, in and out.'' She pointed as if to indicate the far horizon through the cabin fireplace wall. " 'Fact, his crew's worked on the fence for the last two, three weeks. Kip's a real jack-of-all-trades,'' Dottie's eyelids flickered. "Kip and LilyAnn love each other like a brother and a sister through thick and thin.''

Then she looked sharply at Kate. "Surely you don't think—'' Dottie gave a short, harsh laugh. "Hey, Kate, Kip started his construction business in Nashville years before Lily moved here. Valley Construction, they do great work. Kip's reputation is rock-solid. He's doing great. He has all the jobs he wants. People wait months for Kip. He put in my own new bathroom the year before last. His clients line up to give A-1 references, and believe me, you know what bathrooms cost, so I checked him out. Now I really should catch up with Turk."

"Just another minute, Dottie. If he's on the property regularly, does Kip Padgett have a key to the main house?"

Dottie looked over Kate's shoulder toward the outside, then nodded. "Sure. Sure he does."

"And does he have access to his sister's tour bus?"

"The bus is leased, Kate. When they go out on the road, the bus pulls up to pick up Lily, and off they go."

"Kip is never inside her tour bus?"

"You're thinking about the fire." Kate nodded. Dottie shrugged. "Well, I asked for this, didn't I? It's your job to be suspicious, to take nothing for granted. But 'never' is a big word."

She looked at her watch and sighed. "Okay, here's the drill. Now and then the bus parks here overnight if Lily and the band come through Nashville in the middle of a tour. Like from Louisville to Atlanta, they might stop off for a night at home with their families."

Dottie brushed at her shoulders, another gesture of impatience. "You're going to ask whether they stopped off here on the way out to Johnson City where the bus caught fire." Kate nodded. "I can't remember. I'd have to look it up. I'll make a note and let you know. Like the knives."

She made no note. Her foot beat time on the planks. "You might hear rumors they're fighting. Lily and Kip are no Donnie and Marie Osmond, that's for sure, and they will get frank with each other no matter who's around. But neither one means anything by it. Neither one of them holds a grudge."

"Fine, Dottie. I need—"

"I need too, Kate. Need to see about Turk and a thousand other things. The girls are due in here too. They're out shoe shopping for the proms. It's boys, boys, boys, and platforms and spikes. I say they'll break their necks. But hey, don't even think about Kip that way. He's a peach, good-natured as they come. He understands about the music life because he used to play guitar."

"And banjo?"

"Anything with strings. Listen, I'll be in the house. Give us twenty minutes. The stalker file's right there. Remember, you're welcome to take the whole thing. Welcome to it. I trust you."

The last sentence felt like a slap. Dottie Skipwith's great skill, putting others on the defensive. For now, hold further questions about Kip and about the "Rottweiler" ex with the illegal firearm. In fact, from now on avoid the Dottie pipeline as much as possible. Branch out. Find Kip by yourself. And be alert for sightings of Keith Grevins. How would Kate know him—Aloha shirts? A flowered lei? Coolly she said, "I do want a word with LilyAnn and Turk. And Billy D too. I need to talk to all of them."

"Of course you do." She brushed past Kate with a whoosh.

Somehow the cabin air felt stagnant instead of peaceful. The fireplace, Kate noticed, was once again a target for silver wrappers and gum wads. The smiling teens in the picture frame on Dottie's desk—apple-cheeked Deb and the lithe Angie—seemed to mock the whole scene. Kate took a notebook and pen from her bag and went to the trestle table folders. Where to sit down? The forbidden red chair looked like an empty throne.

She sat in Dottie's black leather chair, noticed a file to the right marked Personnel. A sheet stuck out, a form filled out in ballpoint in backslanted script. It was a W2 for Arvin Deal Karcic—Turk. He was on the Page-One Management payroll for a three-month period, an official taxpayer. She even saw his social security number, starting with 423. The prefix might be useful since it located the state of issue. Kate tugged the form out a bit further, clicked her own ballpoint, and copied the full nine numbers. Back in Boston, she scavenged her share of data. Never hurt to have a social. Now she prepared to open the file marked "Sian, Walter: Stalker."

Yet she paused. So far, whoever was trying to kill LilyAnn Page made it look accidental, at least like an act of possible negligence. It was easy for a man in Kip's position to hide behind construction tools, easy for him to work a scene of truck loading, bus wiring, carpentry. There'd be no need to keep a log of Kip's presence, he was a fixture on the property.

Suppose he had a deal with Keith. Suppose Mister Valley Construction needed money while the ex-husband and father wanted his daughter full time. Kip might be a beneficiary in LilyAnn's will. Or maybe Grevins offered him a deal.

In Dottie's chair at the Page-One Management trestle table, however, Kate realized how much she was thinking in the past, the very run up to last Sunday when the country star collapsed with a broken arm.

Time, however, did not stop while a bone knit, did not pause even one tick while Kate—or this Turk— tried to find out who rigged the guitar case, set the bus fire, pulled the hinge pins. Clock and calendar moved.

So focus in the here and now. How to guess what the killer, or killers, planned to do next? Where the traps were to be set? Kip Padgett's crew was slated to build the Fan Fair booth. It was less than a week away—six days. Would Valley Construction build a death trap to kill LilyAnn Page in front of her most ardent country music fans?

Kate bit her pen tip, shifted in the black leather

chair, squirmed. There was business at hand. Focus on the Walter Sian file. Do the assigned homework. The stalker was his own plot.

She opened the folder, looked at the press photos and was struck by Dottie's accuracy about the convicted stalker's appearance. The round head, the bland features, he looked like a cartoon white everyman, like *Peanuts'* Charlie Brown or a young Jesse Helms. Pick him out of a crowd? Never.

Kate did take one of the photos, stuck it in her bag and moved quickly through the clippings that said Walter Ben Sian, a handyman, was arrested in McMinnville, Tennessee. Prior to that, he had served time for auto theft and armed robbery. He was convicted on nine counts of stalking, harassment, trespassing, disorderly conduct, intimidation. According to the clippings, he should now be thirty-two years old.

His message started with short notes probably saved from the mailing tubes. They were cryptic but filled with images of nature. "Spying the dead fox she suddenly ceased her hounding, as if struck dumb . . . I greet you from the lips of the lake . . . In this chopping sea, with clouds and storms and quicksands, only a great calculator succeeds." They all continued in this vein. Kate imagined these notes tucked into the tubes among dried frogs, feathers, animal bones. No wonder Dottie said he wrote in code.

But then Kate picked up Walter Sian's Love diary, a spiral notebook with thick heavy pencillings, like heavy breathing. Filled front to back, it was evidently sent to LilyAnn as some kind of gift before its author went to prison.

The lines sounded sexual and environmental. "When I think of you, I think sacred laws of love, obedience to the surface of the earth and your body. You are moonlight amid mountains. I lay the foundation of true expression and praise the volatile truth of our words."

Kate paused, tapped her pen top on the table. The rhythms and word choice sounded vaguely familiar. It was not a romance novel or poetry, but what? She turned the page. Walter wrote on one side only, his pencil pressure embossing the paper. He repeatedly compared LilyAnn to earth in springtime, her body a mass of thawing clay, her hands spreading leaves, her nose a congealed drop. Much was made of thawing and growing vegetable cheek bones, breasts and labia. "Myriads can be sacrificed and suffered to prey on one another . . . squashed out of existence like pulp. . . . My head is an organ for burrowing into you . . . I sculpt your flesh and blood and bones as my own."

On and on, all the same. Confused, obsessed. The entries were written over months spanning summer, fall, winter. Though Kate noticed something odd. Whether an entry was dated November, January or July, it was always springtime in the Love diary. A hundred handwritten pages insisted on a perpetual spring.

She paused. McMinnville, Tennessee, didn't Dottie mention it? Yes, those specimen trees for the Mosely property, they were trucked in from the "landscape capitol," McMinnville. Any connection?

"Stand fronting the sun, and you will feel it like a scimitar dividing you through the heart and marrow. Life or death, we crave reality. So you will happily conclude your mortal career."

Kate felt a prickle at the back of her neck. Dottie was wrong to think Walter Sian was history, wrong to make him into a bad memory from the past, like the lightning at last season's outdoor concert. Dottie spoke of the stalker almost as an exotic pet, the alligator mascot in a backyard pond. But a million women and nearly a half-million men were stalked every year. They sent victims into counseling, drove them out of their homes, cost them job time—and their lives.

The fact of the spring season in the diary was itself important. Released early from prison this past April, Walter Sian could believe himself destined to sculpt LilyAnn Page's flesh this very season.

Sculpt it with a scimitar?

Kate paused, tapped the pen in useless nervous energy, suddenly realized how much the horizon line had changed. She was not looking through a notch in the Tennessee hills only for a single killer or even one homicidal conspiracy. Add Walter Sian to the mix, and the danger to LilyAnn Page was that much greater. Walter might not trouble to pull hinge pins or rig a bus fire or any other complicated trick or trap. But Walter's notes and diary were full of hawks and snakes. He could come out of the wild blue nowhere and strike at any time.

A beep and buzz sounded beside her. A pager? No, a fax. She stared as it rolled through, finished, beeped again, as if Walter Sian might be sending. Kate's glance caught the letterhead, Go-forth Productions. Something urgent for Dottie? Something that required a response by the close of the business day, perhaps Eastern time? She looked across through the window, the screen door. Turk and Dottie were still at the main house, nobody in sight. The ethics of faxes, what to do? Go get Dottie?

Kate looked back at the fax, skimmed it. She read sideways. *To:* Dottie Skipwith, *From:* Ronnie Healy, *Subject:* Venues. Then the message: "Ticket sale projections suggest nec. rethink venues. 3-5 thousand optimal/max. Working on openings . . ." Then dates months into the future, followed by names of states and a string of venues.

Kate paused to decipher. This was about smaller venues, about opening for the headliner instead of being the main act. Was LilyAnn Page downsized too? Those country radio stations, LilyAnn was missing from the playlists. And then Kelly's crack about oldies.

So could all this horror be a publicity stunt after all? A broken bone, a dead crewman . . . and Kate somehow playing into a scenario capped with the release of the new album and video. In fact, LilyAnn could take a page from George Jones, who got national publicity for his new album and concert tour when he totaled his Lexus against a bridge railing outside of Nashville and spent time in the hospital ICU. The smashed Lexus was hoist up a flag pole as a warning to drive safely, with Jones himself on radio and TV urging safe driving for all. The timing was as exquisite as it was purely accidental.

Against the World, it was a perfect title for the country diva besieged by hostile forces. Maybe crewmen were expendable, a broken bone and incinerated wardrobe the cost of doing business. LilyAnn could hit the talk shows in August as a brave survivor.

Kate looked away, felt sick. Was the voice of "Break of Dawn" a conniver's, callous enough to sacrifice an employee, to break a bone and practically walk through fire? A song was a script, the vocalist an actor who lived or died through record sales and concert tickets. In a slump, maybe a star took radical measures. In this age of dysfunction, calamity was capital.

So count LilyAnn Page as a possible mastermind of the cruelest comeback plot. And Dottie as potential accomplice. Farfetched, maybe, but all channels were wide open.

CHAPTER SEVEN

"Kate, meet Turk Karcic."

Kate twitched in Dottie's chair as the door opened and the two figures entered.

"Kate, this is Turk."

He came forward. "How you doing?" He mumbled, his voice both southern and flat. She got up and extended her hand.

His closed over hers like hot wet felt. Turk Karcic even looked like a bodyguard, from the buzz cut to the lugsole lace-up boots. He was stocky, with sloping shoulders and a short neck. A half-moon scar curved up from his right ear, and aviator dark glasses hid his eyes. He wore olive twills stuffed into the boots, and a dark brown sweater with stars stitched across the shoulders in a vague suggestion of military rank. No holster was in evidence, no bulge to indicate a concealed weapon. He looked too young to be a retiree of the Marine Corp or a police force.

Kate said, "Good to meet you."

"Same here."

Why didn't it feel one bit good? Why awkward, as if she'd broken into a private conversation? Kate looked at this bodyguard, her designated partner of sorts, Turk's two hundred-plus pounds of muscle to guard LilyAnn Page's person while Kate played the brain. If this was Dottie Skipwith's notion of the body-mind connection, it was downright grotesque, a division of labor, his and hers, circa 1958.

Kate said, "Dottie, I think a fax came in a few minutes ago. You might want to check—"

The manager fairly sprang to the machine, began to read, turned her back to Kate and the bodyguard. Kate kept her voice pleasant and businesslike. "I understand you work privately, Turk? You're not with an agency?"

"Like Wackenhut or Brewer? Not at this time."

"And your background, is it law enforcement?"

"Mostly."

From her side vision, Kate saw Dottie's shoulders stiffen, her hands grip the fax as if it were a proclamation. Kate said, "Dottie tells me you spent some time in Kansas City, Turk."

He barely nodded, as if reluctant to divulge such privileged information. Then he hitched one shoulder, maybe trying for six-foot-one. He said, "I put myself out of a job up there in KC. That's how it goes when it's workin' right." His voice sounded like corroded metal. "Believe it, we'll nail this one too." He cracked his knuckles and flashed the aviator lenses Kate's way as if to hint what it might feel like to be nailed. "We will." Kate heard Turk Karcic's "we" as a territorial marker that emphatically excluded her.

Yet she would be forced to spend some time with this man, to cooperate with him at some level. She wanted to see the eyes behind the mirror lenses. "Turk," she said, "I'd appreciate a tour of the property."

"I already did that. Walked the line, every inch. Surveilled."

Kate nodded. "But I need to walk it too. There's still daylight, so this is the perfect time."

He frowned. Dottie rejoined them. "Turk's going to walk the property with me, Dottie."

"Billy D could take you sometime, Kate."

"Sure, I'd like that," Kate said. "I'll talk with Billy D very soon. But right now I'd like to see it through

Turk's eyes—the security professional's." The mirror lenses did not move. "Of course, I could just walk it by myself, no big deal."

"I'll go with her. I'll take care of it. First I gotta put my Jeep top up, looks like rain. I'll be out there." He stumped outside, though his movements were surprisingly quick, almost lithe. Kate could imagine him running down an s.o.b. Or an innocent.

Then another car engine was heard, a horn tapped lightly. It sounded like a vehicle just outside on the driveway but running at open-road speed. Dottie snapped to. She said, "The girls. The girls are back. Too damn fast. If they keep this up, they'll total another—" But she did not finish. "Look, they're heading to the main house. I'll catch up with them there. You go ahead with Turk. Those girls. . . ."

She looked suddenly smaller, almost lost. Kate turned away. Sympathy?—no, save it for herself, for this little forced march. She went to her own car and put the file folder in her tote, slipped on a pair of driving moccasins she kept in back, joined the bodyguard. She said, "I'll follow you."

"South." He pointed. "This way." They set off up and over hillocks in a straight line toward the sound of the barking dogs. The clouds were passing now, the evening sunlight beginning to shine.

She tried to match his stride, but her hem hemmed her in. The kick pleat would surely rip. In body language, he gave her the cold shoulder, his pace just a half-step ahead of hers. Behind his left ear, she saw the nicotine patch. Just her luck, a man extra surly as he tried to break his habit. But he showed no shortage of breath as they strode across the season's just-mowed grass, doubtless gratis Billy D and the John Deere.

They passed the specimen dogwood trees with the wet, burlap-wrapped root balls. They passed ornamental cherry trees whose blossoms lay on the grass like

pale white stars. No sign now of the big-dig projects
Taylor Evelyn described. No sign of the dogs either,
though they heard them. Kate said, "It looks too
peaceful and beautiful for such trouble." It was meant
as a lead-in for a talk about the stalker. Turk merely
grunted and quickened the pace. She felt the threads
of her skirt pleat give. She did not slow.

About two hundred yards from the southern boundary, the land sloped sharply down, and Kate saw on
the right a tennis court and about four hundred yards
to the left of that two archery targets and a kennel
with a fenced dog run. Inside, a brindle boxer—Bismarck?—and a fluffy white dog with a curled-up tail
and a pointed snout raced back and forth with full-
throated barks. She remembered the name of Bismarck's pal was something that sounded cold—
Freezer? Freezee. The dogs had spotted Kate and
Turk and jumped against their fence.

Mixed with the barking, though, Kate heard other
sounds, female voices back over the hillocks. They
were loud, louder, and they rose from up over the
grounds. Alto and soprano voices rose and fell, cried
out, even screamed in near-hysteric tones. The one
lower voice sounded like Dottie. Probably the two
girls shrieking. An adult-teen confrontation. It continued. She and Turk both looked away, studied the kennel and the targets, studied their own fingernails. Then
something slammed, an engine roared, and the only
remaining sounds were the dogs. Turk's face was without expression. A moment passed.

Kate said, "Uh, these dogs, you hear them bark all
the time. Dottie says they aren't great watchdogs,
though."

"Hunters either. Not even sniffer dogs. They went
crazy this morning over a ball of gnats, those two.
Just useless."

"So you were out here this morning?"

He turned his mirror lenses on her. "Lady, when I

said I walked every inch of this property, I meant
every inch." He fell silent. As the evening shadows
lengthened in the deep sunlight, they moved in march
steps to the right toward the tennis court. Surrounded
by chain-link fencing, it was green-painted asphalt,
newly lined. But the net was torn, the court surface
cracked. Spring weeds were sprouting. Kate said, "I
didn't know there was a tennis court on the property.
It can't be seen from the office or the back side of
the main house. It's hidden, like the kennel, isn't it?"
She added, "Looks like nobody plays much tennis."

He stopped, wiped the back of his hand across his
forehead. "She's gotta get some lights out here." He
pointed to the fence. "Run 'em up the steel posts,
beam 'em all around. You can get pretty fair coverage.
Problem with this place, too dark. Three sides of the
property, there's no lights."

She nodded. Beyond the tennis court were thickets
of evergreens and wild cherry, brambles and grasses
and vines. Kate recognized the Osage orange and the
full-grown yews that seemed to mark the entire
boundary in double rows about five feet high. Landscapers had trimmed them neatly across the top for
the hundreds of yards that Kate walked with Turk as
their own shadows lengthened before them.

In silence they moved to the east side, though he
took her by surprise with a sudden military pivot that
redirected them northeast toward the main house.
Grass stain covered the tips of her moccasins, his
boots too. Then, in a little dell, she saw the tiles, the
patio, the kidney-shape and aqua tint.

"Just so you see the pool," Turk said. "Nothing out
of the ordinary, standard in-ground pool, and all set
up for summer." He wiped his sleeve across his forehead again. "I advise against anybody swimming until
I check out the electrical wiring at the pump."

He said no more, but Kate was heartened. Maybe
he was thinking about the electrical fire in the tour

bus—that a killer might send a deadly current through the pool. Maybe Turk Karcic was not such a cement head. Do not mistake oafishness for stupidity. The two of them, this odd couple on a walk, might actually cooperate if they could find common ground—literally, the ground of LilyAnn Page's estate.

He pivoted again. Now they headed toward a cluster of oaks that framed a small barn where the south and east property lines joined. Picturesque, the wood siding was darkened a deep tobacco brown. This had to be the barn where Billy D lived. At loft level, she saw windows cut into the walls. An air-conditioner protruded from one window on the east side, where Kate now saw the new fence in progress, a heavy stockade fence about eight feet high. Some trees were cut to make way for it. So this was brother Kip's Valley Construction project.

She saw at once why LilyAnn might want the eastern property line secured. And why Dottie would urge her to. On this fence side, there was no thick barricade of yews, only scraggly growth of trumpet vines and blackberry canes, of locust trees and more Osage orange with thorns that she and Turk moved sideways to avoid.

He said, "This land was probably a farm at one time. They'd plant Osage when they couldn't afford barbed wire." He made it sound bobbed. "Hey, watch out for that poison ivy."

Against the tree trunks and over the ground, the three-leaf pattern grew bright and prettiest green. Kate stepped around it, saw where the workmen had cut it back. The new fence was nearly finished, only another ten or twelve feet to go. Thick posts were already sunk in cement to prevent rotting. Another day or two of curing, and the stockade pickets could be attached. Kate scanned the property line as they walked it. There was no break in the yews or the new fence. "Turk, you walked these grounds today . . ."

"Twice, some spots three times."

"Any sign of an intruder?"

He looked past her shoulder. "That's for me to know and you to find out."

Infantile and cold. Kate said, "If somebody trespassed, how would you know?"

He shrugged. "It's an art. Takes time. You get a feel for it."

"But you're sure you could tell?"

"Like from tracking? Sure. I make it my business." He paused, took a box of wood matches from his shirt pocket, snapped off a match head and stuck the stick in his mouth. He chewed for a moment. Cellulose instead of a cig. The silver sunglass lenses flashed her way.

He said, "You gotta think surveillance, counter-surveillance too." He pointed toward the main house. "Let's say somebody cuts through the bushes to dump poison in the pool. Let's say acrylamide. That's an industrial product, water soluble. It comes in crystals and the reaction's delayed. Very toxic, you inhale or swallow it, you got brain damage no doc can fix. That's on-site sabotage."

Kate nodded. So toxic crystals were the sugar plums dancing in Turk's head.

He gestured at the property line boundary. "You got a residence on one side, and a buffer strip on the other." He pointed into the distance. "Let's say a perp stands at the line with a camcorder, maybe a still camera, he or she's lookin' for footage, wide angle, telephoto, whatever. That individual does not set foot on the property, but they get what they're lookin' for. Got it?"

"Got it." She said, "Too many hiding places in those bushes."

"You get night vision or you get outflanked." He swept the property with his left arm. "Okay, lady— Kate—here's the thing. My line of work, I don't mouth off. You're workin' your side, I got mine. My business is security." He rolled the matchstick to the downturned side of his mouth. "You do paperwork, that's fine. But Ms. Page, she deserves the best. She's a great lady of country music, she's gotta have protection, guys looking out for her. Like me, I walked this place, every inch. I'm on patrol. My job's learning this place like the back of my hand."

They both looked at Turk Karcic's outstretched hand, dark hair at the knuckles, a chunky silver ring with a stone the color of the swimming pool. He folded his arms and scanned the property and said, "I'm not much for talk, but this place is open like a sieve. They gotta cut all that shrubbery way back at the line. She needs motion-sensitive exterior lights that are high enough so that anybody at ground level can't disable them. She needs a loud exterior alarm. Inside, it's another story."

Kate nodded, wishing he'd tell that story. He did not. They stood as dusk drew on. With a hand across his forehead like a visor, he scanned the western side. Kate stepped downward toward the fence construction spot. The land dipped into a gully there, and she gazed down at last season's leaves, dead vines, mold, wet. The shadows deepened into twilight, dark gold to pale gray. The familiar leaf shapes caught her eye—maples, oaks, the local hackberry she now recognized on sight. Somehow she thought of beach combing in New England at this time of evening, the scallop and razor clam shells on the sand. Here in the Tennessee woodland, she identified the pointed maple leaves, the rounded oaks. And one dark arc too—a black semicircle partly covered by dead vegetation. It was too rounded to be a leaf, much too big for a bottle cap. She began to pick it up.

She stopped. Whatever it was, Turk would take it over, claim it as if by right. She wanted the first crack at it.

So she leaned one hip against a tree for balance, murmured "twig in my shoe," bent down as the skirt kick pleat seam ripped further up while Turk scowled in his macho lugsoles. Kate's left hand deliberately loosened, removed, wriggled the left moccasin like a puppet while she bent at the knee and stretched out her right hand to grope the leaves, to palm the rounded object and see it up close.

It was a camera lens cap. She stuck it into her skirt pocket. Not as slick as Delia but not bad. Kate put her shoe back on. She felt smug. Fooled him. He now stepped down the gully toward her. They marched left, right, left in the mulch and compost.

Woodland animals were not on Kate's mind. She did not think about moles or even foxes as her right foot slipped, ankle turned in a burrow hole. She fell suddenly sideways in the gully in the near-darkness and felt at her skirt pocket to secure the lens cap. She tucked it deep, felt the wet through her skirt, then struggled to rise.

And felt the hot damp grip at her underarm. "You need help. Let me." His fingers tightened against her ribcage.

She said, "No, I'm all—"

But his laughter broke in like a third dog's bark. He grabbed her. "Relax. Just relax." He pulled. He yanked. She felt something in her shoulder pop. "You ladies need a helping hand."

"Please, no. My shoulder, ribs. You'll bruise my . . ."

"No sissy stuff now. A lady falls down, she's gonna have Turk. That's what I'm here for. Get it through your head and ease your mind. I'll be looking out 'cause I'm the man."

The phone number for Valley Construction was answered with a taped message. Ditto the number for Kip Padgett, General Contractor. It was 7:45 a.m.,

Wednesday, with no sign of rain. Construction crews would be hard at work outdoors all over Nashville. Where was Kip?

At the bathroom sink, showered and slathered with the Gap's Grass body lotion, Kate rotated her ankle for the umpteenth time to make certain it was not sprained, then smoothed foundation base over her face, quickly worked the eye pencil and examined her ribs in the mirror. She turned to view her back. There were two light greenish bruises, Turk's calling card last evening. She'd held cold compresses against them until bedtime while distracting herself with the Walter Sian file.

Were the bruises deliberate? She'd actually purpled her own palm while clapping at a moth in the kitchen a couple of weeks ago, so a mistake was possible. Still . . .

Still, she needed to know whether a couple of bruises were a cheap or costly price for a Nikon lens cap. She'd washed it off, dried it, stuck it in a drawer, moved it to her purse. It had surface scratches. Was it Kip's? Did the contractor bring a camera to take photos of his work at different sites?

Or as a pretext to spy on his sister and her compound in order to plan the next attack?

Or did somebody else stand at the property line as Turk Karcic said they might? Walter Sian had cut-up photographs in a homemade shrine to LilyAnn at the time of his arrest. Did he come back for a new 35mm supply here in the actual springtime? Was a photo shoot merely practice? Would he use bullets or buckshot to "sculpt" LilyAnn's body and so end her "mortal career"?

Maybe it wasn't Walter but the photographer who collaborated on LilyAnn's book back for another round of photos. Telephoto exclusives for sale to the tabloids, photos LilyAnn could not copyright? Could a shutter be the warm-up for a trigger?

And what about the disgruntled former drummer, Bucky Sibbett, who might go for a film roll instead of a drum roll with political fires smoldering? At flashpoint?

Or was the ex-husband involved, the five thousand miles between Nashville and Hawaii not nearly enough? Dottie took too much comfort in the Pacific Ocean. Everybody had their blindspot, and that was hers.

Finally, consider the lens cap simply as the kind of junk that was fast becoming the earth's newest ground-cover.

Kate shivered. Time pressed. Get going. She quickly finished the light makeup job and went to her bed-room closet to select a wheat jeans skirt made of tough denim with a copper rivet at the kick pleat. Plan ahead for construction site visits. She reached for a wine-colored silk blouse she'd bought at half off from a final markdown rack, a bit wintry but vivid.

She lingered a bit before clipping the tag that still dangled from the cuff. It said how this garment had undergone a special wash process to give it a unique appearance. "Variations of shading, texture and un-evenness give this garment its natural beauty and are not to be considered imperfections."

Weren't such tags multiplying lately? The shirts, pants, jackets at the turn of the century all manifested their natural beauty from weaving, dying, and sewing proclaimed to be irregular. You used to find paper slips saying the garment had been inspected and passed by number 17 or by Rosita, whose name con-jured the image of an actual person on your side, the quality side. Now you got propaganda cardboard to persuade you that bumps and fades were planned and actually made the clothes look better, that flaws weren't flaws but signs of "natural beauty."

Could she try this as editor—"Variations in spelling and punctuation give this page its natural beauty and

are not to be considered imperfections. . . ." Whole
new approach, Fleetwood could cut out the copy editors, shrink the payroll. The Accounting Department
bean counters would love it.

She cut the tag, swept the annoying plastic T into
the wastebasket, put on the blouse and buttoned it.
An OK belt and tan pumps got her ready for the
day, for Kelly to school with a club meeting and band
practice, and Kate to start off with a few calls from
right here at the condo.

Start with Fleetwood. She phoned Delia's voicemail
to say she'd be out of the office until later this morning. Any urgent calls, she could be reached by cell
phone.

First, phone the publisher of *LilyAnn—A Life in
Pictures* and get the name of the star's literary agent.
Make this a Thursday morning fishing trip into the
Eastern time zone, but do not give Dottie Skipwith a
rod or reel or worm. She got the number.

"Maxine Kramer Agency." The tenor voice almost
whispered, doubtless a fledgling assistant.

"This is Kate Banning of Fleetwood Publications."
Kate's best Northeast fast talk kicked in. She said,
"This is in reference to a photo book you agented two
years ago for LilyAnn Page, the country music star.
The book is *LilyAnn—A Life in Pictures.* Our company may offer a contract to the photographer of that
book, Myers Fatenza, for a certain corporate project.
We're phoning to verify that the Kramer agency also
represents Mr. Fatenza—?"

"One moment please." The entry-level whisper
soon gave way to a female whiskey voice. "Max
Kramer here."

Kate started over.

She was interrupted. "No, Ms . . . Banning, is it?
No, we did not represent Mr. Fatenza, then or now.
His work was simply fee-for-service." There was a
phlegm cough. Then Maxine Kramer said, "Fatenza

had no agent. We all wished he did. The transaction would have been much easier. Much."

"I see." But Kate needed to "see" more. She said, "We can't get bogged down in contract problems. If Myers Fatenza might be difficult—?"

"Let's say he's complex." Another short cough. "Mr. Fateneza was under the impression that he would be named co-author of Ms. Page's book. It was a terrible misunderstanding on his part. It caused many problems." Maxine Kramer's voice rasped. She sounded like a snow-scraper blade over concrete in a March blizzard. "You do know, of course, about the Hollywood episode?"

"Frankly, I don't."

"Oh, I forgot, you're calling from Memphis."

"Nashville."

"Well dear, here on the East or the West Coast, you'd probably know the story. I don't have the time to rehash, but if your project has a tight time frame, you'd be smart to reconsider. I do some work with the Coffening Agency. Alix Coffening represents top photographers all over the world, the best of the best. I'll fax you."

Hustle, hustle. Kate said thanks, hung up. Didn't New York always get its kicks this way? Zap, you're provincialized. Zap, you don't know the Hollywood story because you're in the outer darkness of Memphis, Nashville, Knoxville, Chattanooga, Dubuque, Tulsa, Burbank wherever. In election years, you're in the dear heartland. Otherwise, it's the sticks. Zap Zap.

She sighed, checked her watch and immediately dialed Fatenza Photographic Services to hear a nice female answering service voice explain that Mr. Fatenza was out on assignment for most of the day.

"Oh gee," Kate said, "I'm calling about a telephoto lens Mr. Fatenza wants. I have it for him. He's expecting it by this afternoon. You wouldn't know where I might catch him?"

In fact, the sweet voice thought he would probably be at Soper Avenue. She gave a street number as a baby began to wail in the background. Answering service, a.k.a frazzled mother trying to boost the household income. Been there.

Then Kate tried Valley Construction, which still answered with a tape. She left another message,

Head down there? Not just yet. Kate got out the paper slip she'd saved from the office cabin and at 8:03 phoned for a listing of the Department of Employment Security in Kansas City, Missouri. The voice was male, young, eager. "Hey," Kate said, "this is Kate at the St. Joe office. Hate to start the day with complaints, but our screen's down. How 'bout yours? Is it the whole system?"

"We're up."

"Great, glad it's not the whole system. Look, I need wage credit information on one account. B'lieve this is out of your office. Can you help me for a few minutes?"

"Sure thing. You got the social?" She read off Turk Karcic's social security number. A keyboard clicked, a minute passed. "This individual has wages for the first quarter of this year."

"What do you show?"

"We show $5,236.87 at the Excalibur Security Corporation."

"How about last year?"

Slight pause. "For the last two quarters we show $10,012.91. Also at Excalibur."

"Okay. Any claims?"

"He filed an unemployment claim a year ago last February 4, and he was entitled to $123.47 per week for seventeen weeks."

"Uh-huh. And where was the last check mailed to?"

"That'd be 453A Carstairs Ave. here in Kansas City."

"Good. Just one more thing, do you have the address of the Excalibur Corporation?"

"Let me go to my other screen . . . yes, it's 3305 14th Street, KC."

"Great. Hey, if your screen's ever down, give us a call here in St. Joe."

"Will do." The line went dead, and Kate paused, rose, stuck a cup of coffee into the microwave. King Arthur's sword, Excalibur, jammed in a rock until Arthur himself drew it forth. It took no imagination to picture the logo of the Excalibur Corporation. Kate retrieved her mug, sipped, then phoned Kansas City information for the number of Excalibur on fourteenth. "This is Pat. How can I help you?"

"Pat, Kate Banning here at Page-One Management in Nashville, Tennessee. Need a little help this morning. We're checking references on a former employee of yours, Arvin Karcic. He goes by the name of Turk. He's applied for a security position here at Page-One, and he lists Excalibur as a former employer of . . . let's see, about nine months, ending in the first quarter of this year." Pat seemed to be cracking gum. "We understand he worked for you last year and the winter of this year."

"So you want to verify the dates of his employment?" She sounded cautious.

Kate lowered her voice. "Well yes, verify, but of course we'd welcome any additional information. This is a sensitive position."

A keyboard clicked. "I can tell you the individual in question was an Excalibur employee during the referenced time period."

"And he remained an employee in good standing?"

"Our position would be affirmative on that." More silence. More gum.

Kate said, "Pat, the position in question here at Page One Management involves personal security and very confidential information. We need to have total confidence in Mr. Karcic. Can you refer him at the highest level?"

She could hear a metallic click of a lighter, then Pat inhaling, exhaling, all the while a keyboard clicked and a file drawer hummed, rolled out on bearings. Then, "Kate, the evaluations of Excalibur employees are confidential. One area, though, any company would research this, so it's a courtesy to you."

"Okay, appreciate it."

"Excalibur requires all employees who have served in the military to show honorable discharges. Our records show that since Mr. Karcic could not produce his Marine Corps discharge, we initiated our own background check under Freedom of Information, which showed . . . it's right here, it's a general discharge. He was a private at the time. Company policy required termination of employment. He left us as of March of this year. That is all I'm at liberty to reveal."

"Well that's a big help. Could I also verify his Kansas City address as 453A Carstairs Ave?"

"That is correct."

"Thank you." Click.

Kate sipped her coffee. So Turk made enough trouble for the Marines to dump him. The toughest of the tough ejected the self-styled Marine Corps M.P., stripped him down to private. Why? What else lurked in his background?

She paused, checked her watch, got out her old black notebook that went way back to Boston days, to the countless times when Redi-Real Estate came in handy with its instant microfiche lookups on property owners, no pretext required. In moments, for a modest fee, she got the name of Bendix R. Washington as the owner of 453A Carstairs. Back to directory assistance.

The voice was gravelly. "Washington here."

"Mr. Washington, sorry to bother you. I understand you're the owner of a property on Carstairs, number 453."

"That damn water bill again? I told them six times, I'm not—"

"No sir, excuse me, nothing to do with water. It's a tenant of yours I'm trying to track down, Arvin Karcic. I've got three big boxes of his personal belongings stored in my garage, and I have to clear them out. I can't seem to get hold of him. His nickname's Turk."

"Yeah, the mountie."

"Excuse me?"

"Like in Canada. Can't help you, he moved out couple months back. No forwarding."

"Turk Karcic? You think he went to Canada?"

"Doubt it, he's an Alabama boy. Wouldn't know where he went."

"Sorry, sir, thought you said 'mountie'—"

Bendix Washington's belly laugh sounded like it came out of a smoky blues club. He then said, "Never gave me no trouble, Turk, but he had a red jacket, looked real official. Acted like the watchman on the block. Got physical a couple times with different folks. The lady next door called him Sergeant Yukon."

"Yeah, well, he's kind of cop-minded."

"Got plenty of cops in Kansas City, we don't need the mounties too. Sorry, can't help you. Maybe the Post Office."

"Thanks." They hung up. Kate eased from the chair. Her side and shoulder were sore. And so, presumably, were the others' with whom Turk got "physical." Should she contact the Gaylord Corporation to look into his record here in Nashville at Opryland?

No, not now. Lock up and get going. At her car, she found a sort of poster under her wiper. Condo meeting tomorrow night, called by Fred and Alice who promised strudel and coffee. Subject: Security Improvements for All Units. Kate sighed. Mitzy, their Yorkie, was not good enough as pitbull? They wanted, maybe, a gatehouse and guard? Call it a timeout to meet the neighbors. Sure. She put the sheet on the seat beside her. The shell game of the day—where was Kip?

Probably not putting a kitchen into somebody's house, not with a permit to build a new franchise restaurant of a national chain just coming into the midsouth.

And Wyoming Steakhouse was big. A good job building one could lead to bigger contracts. Valley Construction might well ignore homeowner clients and put the hair salon under the dryer to free up all workers to please the corporate powerhouse. Kate plotted the route to Nolensville Road—by way of Soper Avenue. The lens cap wasn't burning a hole in her pocket, but maybe a talk with Myers Fatenza would be useful. It was cooler today, in the mid-fifties and breezy, the sky mottled blue and gray-white.

It was almost nine fifteen when she found Fifty-seven Soper, a brick cape with short columns. A classic MG roadster with a MYERS vanity plate was parked in the drive, which led into a cluster of large trees where the house stood—its roofline bashed by a fallen tree as thick as an artillery cannon. The huge root system, exposed in the air, was sidestepped by a thin, tall, orange-haired man in pleated black pants and a green silk shirt who circled the scene with a camera. Kate parked behind the MG and heard the click of the shutter and whir of the motor advancing the film as she approached.

"Mr. Fatenza?"

He turned, his gaze a cool appraisal. His handshake felt like cold moss. She said, "I'm Kate Banning."

His mouth tightened. "So you're the Kate that called my answering service?" She nodded. "What's this gobbledygook about a telephoto?"

She met his gaze. "I wanted to find you."

He paused. "Mission accomplished, but I have work to do."

"I won't interrupt. Perhaps we could schedule a talk."

"If you need photographic work—?" He took a card from his shirt pocket.

Kate took the card but shook her head. "I need to talk with you about LilyAnn Page."

"No thank you."

"You made the photographs for her book."

"Been there, nothing to say." He moved around the tree roots, snapped three shots in quick succession. It was a 35mm. A Nikon? she couldn't see. "Big booby-traps, these Nashville trees," he said.

"You're documenting for the homeowners?"

"It's too rocky around here for deep roots, and the trees just keel over in a stiff wind. Even the oaks. If it's live wood, watch out." He glanced her way. "State Farm owns every exposure on this roll. Homeowners' insurance claim."

Quietly Kate said, "Is that the camera you used for LilyAnn Page's book?"

He didn't look at her. He brushed a streak of yellow pollen from his trouser leg. His bare arms looked chilly. That hair, was it a henna rinse? "I used a couple of cameras," he said. "It was a big project."

"I saw the book. I notice that LilyAnn Page holds the rights to your photographs."

He stopped, turned, faced her. "What do you want?"

"Just a few minutes of your time." She gave him her card.

"Chief Coordinating Editor, Fleetwood Publications," he read aloud. "So you want pictures, or what?"

"My company is involved in a magazine project for LilyAnn Page."

His mouth tightened. "Good luck. You'll need it."

"Mr. Fatenza, I don't want to play games. I'm trying

to get information for planning purposes. We might
want to use a few photos from *A Life in Pictures*."

"So use them. I can't stop you. She owns the
rights."

"Forever?"

"Only until hell freezes over."

Kate did not smile. "Isn't that unusual?"

"Unusual?" He let his camera hang from his neck
and stuck his hands in his pockets. "It's 'unusual,' Ms.
Kate, when you devote yourself twenty-four hours a
day for months and months, and shoot a hundred rolls
and travel in a funky tour bus where the highest form
of humor is bodily functions."

His features narrowed. "Let's say it's 'unusual' right
up to the moment when the contract arrives, and the
promised fifty-fifty split turns into minimum wage for
yours truly. Then you find out what the word 'unusual'
really means."

He took his hands from his pockets and cracked his
knuckles. "Do I sound bitter?" he said. "Just let me
tell you, LilyAnn Page doesn't own all my photos. I
have others. I have a separate file, if you're interested.
We could discuss it."

She nodded. "Does LilyAnn know about them?"

He laughed like a terrier barking. "Look, whether
she does or doesn't, life goes on, it's live-and-let-live.
I'm from the West Coast, never in my wildest nightmares thought I'd end up in this burg." He paused,
looked up at the treetops. "But here I am. For now
anyway."

He looked down at Kate. "And you know what I
like best about the South?—violent weather and highway carnage." He met her gaze. "Truly. Every tornado, every flood, every tractor-trailer pile up is a
photo op. I document the damage—houses, boats, au-
tomobiles. School buses too. Even a train wreck. The
insurance companies love me. Give me devastation,
I'm through with celebrities. But I tell you this—a

deal with LilyAnn Page is a deal with the devil." He scratched his chin, cradled his camera. "So if you want, we can talk. For *A Life in Pictures,* F.Y.I., since you asked, I used two cameras, a Hasselblad and a Nikon."

"Thank you, Mr. Fatenza. I'll be in touch. You've been helpful."

She held out her hand, and he extended his. At the shirt cuff, she saw his wrist, which flared pink in splotches with Calamine lotion. This was not eczema but poison ivy. She recognized it on sight.

Kate left Myers Fatenza changing his film, got back in her station wagon and headed for Nolensville Road. No point asking the photographer whether he dropped a lens cap in a secret visit to the Mosely property line. Or whether his "other" file photos included salacious shots he hoped to peddle to the tabloids for a sweet twosome of money and revenge.

Or whether his vengeance was a series of accidents to befall LilyAnn Page? Myers Fatenza knew the routines of LilyAnn's touring, knew the layout of the tour bus, knew the Mosely property where he had intimate access for months. When *LilyAnn—A Life in Pictures* went under the contract that pared his income to small change, did he become a self-appointed paparazzo killer? Did he have an accomplice among the various work crews, the landscapers, the road crew?

The Shenandoah Iron Works?

Ex-husband Keith Grevins?

It took about twenty-five minutes off I-440, the truck route that pretended to be a parkway. She exited at Nolensville Road and turned left. Soon every place in America would have every single franchise, the fast fooderies and pizzerias and the sit-down places, the Pargo's, Houston's, Denny's, Friday's, Red, White and Blue Lobsters.

The Wyoming Steakhouse was on the right, the construction well along. Cinderblock walls were up on three sides, and interior aluminum studs. Inside, the workers were everywhere, carrying beams, yellow insulation panels, framing. Some climbed ladders. All wore hardhats. Most were notably dark-complexioned. At the front and side were three Valley Construction trucks, a flatbed and two new Dodge Rams, plus the junker vehicles of the crew members parked off to the far left.

Kate pulled in beside an ancient cream Granada with its backseat ripped out. She pocketed her key, shouldered her purse and then stood scanning the scene.

The standard Wyoming Steakhouse profile was unmistakable, a two-story operation with the signature Old West storefront that pushed the facade another twenty-five feet and profiled two Rocky Mountain peaks. Another few weeks, a huge sign with a red lariat would rope in customers for campfire beef and all-you-can-eat desserts for the whole family.

For now, it was banging hammers and the scream of table saws. To the right, Kate noticed, a backhoe was digging a trench, and a cement mixer was churning. She stepped closer on the clay earth, scanning the workers, trying to pick out Kip. Then some workers began to spot her, to point her out to the others, who promptly turned their backs. With each step she took, more backs turned as if on cue. They seemed to slow their work and almost huddled, like exotic programmed beetles.

"Help you?"

She whirled. A lanky man in jeans and a blue plaid shirt flashed a wide boyish smile just inches from her face. He had soft gray eyes, a freckled nose and reddish gold hair that fell in bangs across his forehead. With a sunny smile, a bump in his cheek, and a hardhat, he looked like a young outfielder with a batting helmet. Kate said, "I'm looking for Kip Padgett."

"Tell you what, ma'am, you found him."

"Oh." He stood very close, as if up close and personal was nature's way. She said, "I'm Kate Banning. I'd like to schedule a talk with you."

His smile did not waver, but his gaze narrowed. He said, "Are you with the INS?"

"Immigration and Naturalization?" He nodded. She laughed. "No Feds, I'm with a private company, Fleetwood. We're located on Second Avenue."

Kip Padgett's eyes did not leave her face, but his shoulders relaxed as he waved toward his crew, who immediately broke rank and went about their business. Hammers and saws resumed. One tool of the trade was evidently missing on site, green cards. Kate said, "I realize you're busy."

"Sure am, fighting a deadline. But let's talk a few minutes. How 'bout let's step into my office."

He steered her to one of the Ram pickups and opened the passenger door. Kate stepped up, and he closed the door, came round to his side and got in. He put his hardhat on the seat between them, started the engine and turned on the fan. "Quieter here," he said. "We can hear ourselves think."

Kate gave him a business card, which he read and pocketed without comment. She said, "I tried your number under Valley Construction."

"And got the tape?" He shook his head. "Dang it, you try to put every dollar into equipment and the crew, and the office gets neglected. I admit it, can't seem to catch up. I'm sorry. What can I do for a magazine editor today?"

Kate said, "My company is working on a project for LilyAnn Page through Dottie Skipwith and Page-One Management. It involves Ms. Page's fan magazine and the web site."

"Great."

"But we want to be careful about pictures that could show too much of her private property. I understand you're Ms. Page's brother, and Valley Construction is completing the fence at Mosely."

"Not the fence I'd like to put in, I'll tell you. Tried my darndest to talk her into a brick wall. Nothing doing."

"For property values?"

"Heck no, for protection. For safety." He rested a wrist over the wheel and peered through the windshield. "These days, everybody's gotta be careful. We built the gatehouse and stone walls at Kensington Trace North—you know that area?" Kate shook her head. "Homes out there start at a half-million. Stone masons, they're real scarce these days. Anyway, I sent two of my best carpenters over to Mosely today. Hated to do it 'cause they're needed right here. One of my guys is out with poison ivy from that fence job. Got it all over his arms, down in his throat. Been over a week, he's still out."

Kate said, "My daughter got it once. Souvenir of Brownie Scout camp. Awful."

He nodded, then rubbed his eyes. "Nasty stuff. Hate to begrudge a man, but Wyoming, they want the work done yesterday, and we're busting our you-know-what. And good labor's so hard to find." Just then his eyes darted left. He said " 'Scuze me," opened his door, climbed half out and stood calling up over the cab, "Mike, face it out. No, wrong way, face it out. Tell Xavier, out. Yeah, OK. You got it."

He lowered himself back onto the seat and looked right at Kate. "Mexican labor's half of Nashville construction these days, that's a fact. The downtown arena, the football stadium, they'd still be holes in the ground without the Mexicans."

He scanned the site through the truck windows. "If the INS would just give us a break. Their last sweep, I lost two stone masons. Sent 'em back across the border. You can't get Americans to do that work, banging away on stone with a fifteen-pound hammer."

He draped his wrist back over the wheel and said,
"I couldn't get Lily to go for a stone wall either. Says
she'd feel walled-in like a prisoner in her own home.
We had big fights over it."

"Fights?"

He laughed. "Oh, not *fight* fights. We yell some,
make noise. But I'm real thankful you came to see
me about the pictures. You don't want to show the
fence in any publicity shots, no details, not even if
she wants you to. There's crazy fans, and my sister's
accident-prone."

"Accident prone?"

"Since we were kids. And like things come in
threes, she's sure had her three lately. That's my
thinking." He shifted on the seat, leaned an elbow on
the door frame. "Dottie, now, she sees the dark side.
You talked to Dottie?"

Kate nodded, looked him in the eye. "She seems
to believe somebody is causing these problems. She's
persuasive. She makes a good case."

"Yeah, she's like a lawyer. But accidents do happen.
Guys on any crew can get hurt, and tour buses do
break down. And that door at my sister's house, I
swear the old guy forgot to put the pins back in. He's
old, he's losing it." He gestured toward the workers.
"You don't see old guys out there."

Kate said, "No, you don't. But back in New England, I knew a mason who worked with his father.
They climbed ladders and hopped around three-story
rooftops to fix the brick chimneys of antique houses.
They were in great demand." She held her gaze at
Kip's gray eyes. She said, "The son was sixty, his father was eighty-something."

Kip shrugged, then grinned. "Okay, you got me on
that one. And heck, I could use those guys. Maybe
they'd like to come South." He shook his head. "It's
just that folks make mistakes and accidents happen.
Dottie's spooked, but my line of work, with the

OSHA regulations, I watch out. I see stuff go wrong from plain old screw-ups. Dottie sees the dark side, but then she's got a lot on her mind with the girls. You seen Lily's arm?"

"In the cast?"

He nodded, then shook his head. "It's like she won't protect herself, and we all got to do it for her. Lily's my kid sister, and I'm used to looking out for her. I stayed in the Recliners—that's our old band—lots longer than I wanted to just to keep an eye on her. For Dottie and the roadies, I know how rough it is."

He shook his head. "You heard about the stalker?" Kate nodded. "I can't believe he's out of jail. A government worth anything, they'd lock him up instead of deporting good workers." Then he paused, rolled down his side window and spat a stream of tobacco juice as brown as whiskey.

Kate caught a whiff. Pungent, sour. Could tobacco be mistaken for whiskey on Kip's breath? Rye whiskey? Could Sonny Burkendahl be mistaken? A lifetime of woodworking with solvents, maybe his sense of smell was warped. Maybe he mistook the brother-sister frankness for hostility. Maybe Kip was right about him "losing it" and Dottie correct about Kip, the "peach."

Looking at his face now, it was clear that Kip's boyishness was not youth. The tan face was weathered, and a sense of weariness seemed to lie just beneath his anger and his cheer. He said, "We're installing the best wood fence money can buy at Lily's place. It's top-quality stockade, every picket a full round four-inch pole, custom fitted. Best I can do."

"Sounds like you're building your sister a real stockade."

He grinned and nodded. "You got it. Not only that, we're putting up a Fan Fair booth this weekend out at the State Fairgrounds. A young woman, Babs Somebody, she brought me sketches, but I gotta turn

her pictures into specs and build the thing. Takes time
I haven't got. Well, I gotta get back. I gotta climb the
Rocky Mountains and set the example."

He pointed to the top of the facade, then opened
his door, got out, reached for his hardhat and came
around to assist Kate, who was already stepping down,
her ribcage bruises in protest. "Anything I can do, just
holler. Take care now." He shook her hand, and then,
hardhat on, jogged fast into the building and started
up a ladder.

Kate began to pick her way around piles of beams,
a stack of plywood sheets. She crossed behind the cement mixer and looked up to see Kip already up high
at the top of the Wyoming peak. He seemed to wave,
but the motion was the upstroke of a hammer. She
watched his arm come down once, twice. She looked
down and walked toward her car, crossed at the front
of the building, just past the center, the backhoe
growling, circular saws shrieking.

She was just at the foot of the Rocky Mountains
when it happened. Her bag was over her arm, and she
just reached for sunglasses when the first wave hit.
Like a jaw with teeth, she thought, a bite at her shoulder. Her shoulder, but then her head felt the crush.
Crush and crash. Like rain, metal rain. It was sharp
and loose, a torrent to pound her head, rattle her
skull. It was a waterfall of steel, and it kept up, so
heavy. She could not seem to move, could not work
her legs, her feet. The black iron rain on her head. . . .
She thought how her ears now closed and rang, how
her knees gave way, how the bright daytime turned
patchy black as the clay earth rose up to meet her
face.

CHAPTER EIGHT

Blue and white swirls on a screen, and a bird flew across. It was the sky. And faces swam in and out. At her sides, Kate felt something soft and rough. And odors, of leather and sweat, tobacco, wood, oil. She saw a moustache, brows, more faces in and out, blurred and dark against the blue sky and clouds. Men in hats, helmets. The dark faces formed a circle.

Then came a set of gray eyes, red-gold hair and a freckled nose. "Ma'am," this face said. "Ma'am, can you hear me."

A sunny voice, but Kate's tongue felt thick.

"Ma'am?"

Talk to the freckles. She heard herself grunt. A huge ache, like a tide across her skull.

"Ma'am."

She managed to say "Kip?" He nodded. The rough at her fingertips felt like cloth—a blanket? Kip in the middle of the sky circle. She was on her back on a blanket on something hard. "Where am I?"

"Layin' on my truck tailgate, ma'am. You had an accident."

"My shoulders," she said. The circle of dark faces peered and nodded, and not one was smiling. "My head."

"A paper tub of nails spilled down on you."

"Your hammer."

"Tub of nails from way up high, it just tipped over."

"Up at the top."

"The top peak." The faces stared like swarthy druids. "Nails just got away from me. I grabbed for 'em but too late. You were right underneath. How're you feelin'?"

Kate paused, felt the headache like a land mass on a map. "Headache."

"I'll bet, the way that whole tubful fell over on top of you. I should've made you wear a hardhat." His red-gold head turned and talked to the dark faces. Kate heard "ice," "back to work," "okay," and something that sounded Spanish. Kip's eyes were back on her. "Get you some ice. Get it right quick."

A moment passed, and then plastic rustled against her head, felt like cold rocks. "Ouch."

"Easy with that ice. Maybe we better get you to a hospital, get you checked out. How 'bout it?"

"I don't . . . I don't think—" She paused, tried to think, dragged memory into this fog of pain. The time in Boston when Kelly fell off the swing set, hit her head. Signs of concussion, you looked for dilated pupils. Kate said, "My eyes . . ."

"Wide open, ma'am."

"Can you see the pupils?"

"Sure can. They look just fine. They look regular."

She said, "Let me sit up." He eased her slowly into a sitting position. She touched her scalp. Tender, beyond tender.

Before her, Kip Padgett's face looked solemn. He said, "How 'bout we head out to an emergency room, just to be on the safe side?"

She tried to think, sort out the ER reality, not TV. Hours of paperwork, gurneys, X-ray. Test the limits of her Nashville health plan? Spend the day?

Kate looked at her watch and read the dials. And registered the fact that she was doing so. And moved her hands, brushed off her skirt, watching herself do these things. She touched the tip of her nose with one index finger, then moved her finger sideways and followed the movement with her eyes. Coordination intact.

To the hospital emergency room? No, not today. She saw her bag beside her, reached in and said, "Couple of Tylenol. How about water?"

"You got it."

Kip returned immediately with a thermos cup. She put the ice pack down and swallowed the pills. "I think I'll be okay."

"You don't want to go to a hospital?" Kate noticed a worker standing by, thickset with glasses. Once again Kip said, "You sure you don't want to go to a hospital? You don't want us to call you an ambulance?"

He said it slowly, each word distinct. It sounded something like her Miranda rights, probably to limit his legal liability in case this ever ended up in court. The worker was doubtless the designated witness. Kate said, "I think I'm fine. I'll take it easy today."

"We can drive you home. Drive your car."

She considered, eased down from the tailgate, stood. "Let me just walk around for a minute."

And they did. At Kip's signal, the worker backed off, and Kate and Kip Padgett strolled the grounds of the soon-to-be Wyoming Steakhouse on Nolensville Road as traffic whizzed by and the construction saws and drills shrieked. Her head felt like a pain superdome, but her vision was clear, her arms and legs strong enough. She said, "Kip, I think I can drive okay."

"No problem to drive you." He looked concerned.

They walked toward her station wagon. Kate got out her key and said, "I'll be okay. Thanks." She opened the door and got in and sat a minute.

He leaned against the opened window toward her face, his gray eyes all sympathy. "You take good care of yourself now," he said. "Go slow and stay safe." Then he lowered his voice and almost whispered very slowly into her ear, "Lucky it wasn't bricks. Lucky it

wasn't a hammer. Hammer would have killed you."
He backed away, stood steadily watching as she
started the engine, eased out.

Kate watched him recede in her rearview. In the
mid-seventies and sunny, she felt a chill move from
the headache down her spine. Bricks and hammer,
why did he say that? Why bring up death? A cascade
of nails, wasn't that enough?

Her head pounded. She wanted quiet. People with
migraines, didn't they drink strong black coffee at the
onset? Gas station coffee—try it. She passed a BP, a
Texaco, then spotted a Burger King on the right. She
pulled in, parked and went inside, got a large coffee,
sat in a back booth and began blowing and sipping
and trying to think.

It was nearly 10:30. Give herself fifteen, twenty minutes. She leaned her head against the wall, closed her
eyes, tried to consider the case of Kip Padgett, who
was all good-natured sympathy, the self-appointed
guardian of his sister and builder of the fence stockade, Fort LilyAnn.

And a rock-solid believer in bad, bad luck. He could
say his sister crossed paths with black cats and walked
under ladders and broke mirrors. He could say Dottie
Skipwith brooded and saw plots.

He could swear that accidents will happen—case in
point, a three-story rain of nails less than an hour ago.

With Kip himself the rainmaker.

"Tub of nails from way up high . . . nails just got
away from me." Got away because he dumped them?
Were the nails a deliberate threat? Sunny, smiling Kip
Padgett, would he specialize in his own Olympic hammer throw? This time nails, next time bricks. Hammer? This time life, next time . . .

Was he his own sister's very worst luck?

She shuddered, she sipped. It was 11:03, and her
headache pulsed. She brushed at her skirt—as if the
denim and rivets were body armor. How naive. Reck-

less of her to enter the Valley Constructon site. Dottie doubtless told Kip who she was, the newest face in LilyAnn's crowd, the off-the-books investigator.

So give her a souvenir headache to drive her off, was that his message? Leave a clear path for a stepbrother's well-planned "accident." Each near-miss upped the odds, but maybe the guitar case and bus fire and door pins turned into the fun of it. Maybe Kip liked the cat-and-mouse game he planned to win in his own good time. Maybe he was planning more gothic events before the big one. Another broken bone? Voltage? Black-cat Kip?

Kate reached into her bag, took out one more Tylenol, downed it, the liquid temperature drinkable because of that crazy McDonald's case of the lapful of hot coffee. Question: if Kate Banning won nearly a million bucks in a hot coffee lawsuit-lottery, would she still subject herself to the Kip Padgetts of this world? The Turk Karcics? A whole roster from the past, the future? Avoid the sane answer, the very answer which her own Sam Powers hoped she'd give someday.

This wasn't someday.

It was time to head out. With one last swig, Kate dumped the coffee and went to her car, walked carefully, measured her steps. Settled into the driver's seat, she looked at her eyes in the rearview mirror. Pupils normal size. No sign of concussion or hemorrhage. Just plain rotten headache, just the general sense of being beaten down.

Perfect frame of mind for a meeting at work. By 11:45, she was in the third-floor conference room. Time for a session on graphics and layout. A consultant for the insurance magazine urged a new format, and Fleetwood must respond. Kate represented the interests of editorial, meaning watch-dogging the print columns. Turf patrol. From the conference room window overlooking the Cumberland, she watched a tug push two barges of scrap metal between bridge pilings

against the gray backdrop of the football stadium. She
hoped some enterprising kids would load up on spray
paint and give it an artistic upgrade in the dead of
night, some neo-Keith Haring and his crew. Nashville
could use more spirited graffiti art.

For now, make it office politics with the rumpled
Fleetwood art director, the business manager in his
usual chalk stripes, the insurance company consultant
in a tweed suit with a thigh-high skirt and skin the
color of a latte, a supervisor from the printing plant,
Don Donaghue with a sport jacket taming his bil-
lowing mainsail of oxford cloth.

They said their hellos, all opened folders, clicked
pens and set out calculators, discussed, debated. The
consultant urged cost cutting with more "core" con-
tent. Kate argued the case for print-column "hard"
information. The art director countered with the vir-
tues of at-a-glance pie-charts and bar graphs. From
the business manager came cost analysis. "Leverage"
seemed to be the business verb of the moment. Everybody wanted to leverage their opportunities upward.
Always upward. Fleetwood committed to every upward opportunity, leverage-wise.

Then it was lunchtime, and the group broke up and
walked over to Broadway to the Merchant's Restaurant, a renovated old brick counting house. They took
a downstairs booth, and the sound system was loud.
Pearl Jam with this headache? Kate ordered a grilled
halibut sandwich, ate most of it, left her share of the
check and excused herself to walk back early. Too
soon for more Tylenol.

Back in the office, Kate checked her pupils in a
compact mirror—normal size. She found e-mails from
Arkansas and promptly assigned articles on historic
bed-and-breakfasts, bicycle tours, state parks, things
to do in Little Rock. Official letters and contracts
specifying fee-for-service terms would follow. She got
out the letters.

Then she faced this month's sign-off on *Distant Lands*, a dumber-than-dumb travel magazine which Fleetwood published as a favor to its president's old Nashville prep school buddy named Buford Kincaid. Doubtless Buford and Hughes Amberson shook hands on *Distant Lands* on a gently sloping green of the venerable Belle Meade Country Club. Tapping their balls in for eagles, birdies, or whatever the ornithology, they'd probably sealed the deal, finished up the back nine and headed into the men's locker room for some fine old Tennessee sippin' whiskey.

Leaving Kate, so to speak, to caddy, or carry the water. Articles ranged from "Alhambra by Moonlight" to "The Dear, Dear Danube."

She worked on, forced herself to get this done.

But she was still not through at three as the sun shifted to backlight the Cumberland. Enough. Wrap it up tomorrow. Two more stops on this workday. She took more Tylenol, began to pack up her tote, checked the mail center on the way out of the building to pick up the latest slushpile batch for an evening half-hour at home.

"Heading out, Kate?"

"Got to check out the Fair Grounds, Don. On Dottie Skipwith's advice. Don't want to miss angles for *LilyAnn's Page,* not with Fan Fair next week. See you tomorrow."

She walked first, however, up Broadway to Fourth and stopped at Tennessee Stage and Studio Supply. A woman in denim overalls looked up and spoke in a nasal voice. Kate said, "You must be Lisa. I'm looking for Bucky Sibbett. I thought he might be back here."

"He's still out. He should check back in by six at the latest."

"Thanks." Kate looked at her watch, frowned and said, "I'll probably stop by tomorrow." She hurried to her car. Traffic was thick but moving, a straight shot out Wedgewood to the Tennessee State Fair Grounds.

It was 3:32. There was plenty of parking, but the
campers and RVs were already settling in for Fan Fair
week, their pop tops and little awnings out over the
vast acreage. And cheery welcome signs, the Flickers
(Jim and Sally) from North Dakota, Bert and Millie
Sarendis from Omaha, the Maurices from Tallahassee
with palm trees and tomahawks on their trailer.
Nomad neighbors on the grass and blacktop. Colored
pennants were strung everywhere. It felt pastoral, not
a danger sign anywhere. No headaches for these fans.

Kate flashed her ID badge against a background of
hammers and saws from the cinderblock buildings and
open sheds inside the guarded gate marked "Authorized Entry Only." Little green and yellow John Deere
trucks scooted everywhere with supplies from soft
drinks to fire extinguishers.

"I'm looking for LilyAnn Page's booth."

The uniformed guard pointed to a long, narrow
building. Inside, on both sides of a long center aisle
were country stars' booths in various stages of decoration by helpers who clustered like bees at hives.

Each booth had a theme, she saw, starting with a
rustic "lodge" with rustic rafters and wall-mounted
stuffed bass and snow shoes. Further on down, a
staffer for the Lorrie Morgan booth was fastening
a big wavy border of musical notes and mounting a
sparkly "25" to celebrate the singer's years in music.
Pam Tillis's "Hits" were baseballs bulging like so
many eyes against a cyclone fence batting cage, and
Wynonna Judd's booth was a carnival with skeet ball
and a ring toss. A girl about Kelly's age was sorting
balloons while another strung colored lights.

Several booths had room fans churning the moist
air to boost the AC. Each had electrical power for
light, for air—for a fatal "accident" awaiting Lily-
Ann Page?

All booths, Kate also saw, had waist-high counters,
like store counters with merchandise piled behind

them. The George Strait volunteers were stocking back shelves with souvenir T-shirts, mugs, backpacks, totes, water bottles, bumper stickers and Christmas ornaments. So were the others, the Clint Black booth, the Trisha Yearwood, Kevin Sharp. Every country star had an array of personalized paraphernalia.

But each counter was also a physical barrier between the star and fans. Presumably Walter Sian could not simply lunge. Nor a killer.

Not unless that person was already a booth insider.

Like Clark and Babs? She spotted them at a booth lagging well behind the others in decoration. In jeans and LilyAnn Page T-shirts, they were unwrapping forms shrouded in sheets. Mannequins? They turned briefly to give her distracted half-smiles.

"I'm Kate," she said. They stared. "We met last Sunday at Miss Page's office. You were presenting Fan Fair ideas. The kitchen?"

"Oh Lord, that." Clark frowned. "I remember you now." Babs winced. Her T-shirt sleeves were ironed like crisp wings, her jeans creased. She said, "That was truly bad, mixed signals." He said, "But we're on track now, pressing ahead. You, uh, need something?"

"My company's on a project for Miss Page. Dottie said to check out the scene here before Fan Fair starts. Seems like good advice."

"Whatever Dottie says. She's the boss." Babs sounded resigned and resentful.

Clark grinned. "Just wait till Dottie sees *these* beauties." He tilted the unwrapped forms upright, three huge molded figures each holding aloft a torch. Against the back wall of the booth were red, white and blue banners that read "*Against the World.*" A pile of wood slats and panels on the floor.

Kate said, "The Statue of Liberty? Is that the theme?"

"Lady Liberty enlightens the world. That's it, both

patriotic and classic. LilyAnn loves it, and Dottie thinks it's super." Clark struck a Miss Liberty pose.

To the left, however, Kate saw a gold-painted door propped against the counter. She said, "Tell me about that door. Is it a decoration too?"

Babs was pulling on workmen's gloves. "The door's about the poem on the base of the statue. 'I lift my lamp beside the Golden Door,' that's the quote on the Statue in New York at Ellis Island. See, the Golden Door is, like, America."

"Interesting." Kate looked from Clark to Babs to the door. Heavy as the Mosely mahogany? She said, "It looks like it weighs a ton."

Babs shrugged. "The Valley crew can handle it." She pointed to the lumber on the floor. "They have to put that wood thing together anyway. It's sort of a ramp with a chair, like knock-down furniture so we can use it again from year to year. There's an inner box and an outer box too. He planned it. He calls it a module."

"Kip Padgett?"

"The one and only." Babs's cheeks turned a bright rose at the sound of Kip's name. She smiled broadly. Kate's head pounded. Then Babs brushed her hair away and stepped back. Clark began moving big pots of lilies.

Kate said, "It reminds me of the Fourth-of-July. Surely no actual fireworks."

Babs shook her head. "Let me tell you, this was a very tough assignment. The Love-Me-Not year was a whole lot easier. We did flowers—he loves me, loves me not. But 'Against the World'—?" She shrugged. "We tried different heroines, it didn't work out. Last Sunday night we brainstormed. Even with the Statue of Liberty, there's a real down side about being tired and poor, and wretched refuse and huddled masses. I mean, nobody comes to Fan Fair for that stuff."

"I believe it."

"But patriotism's always good. Red, white and blue.
It's like the Statue of Liberty stands for freedom
against the dark forces, and LilyAnn Page is like that,
against the world. She's Lady Liberty. Notice the
lilies."

"Bright white."

"Patriotic."

Just then a Deere truck approached on the concrete
floor to unload four-foot metal poles with heavy bases.

Clark said, "This should give you some idea of how
many folks line up for autographs."

"You mean the fans snake around those poles? Like
an amusement park? Like the movies?"

"And out the door and down alongside the building
too. By the time you get inside to the poles, you're
almost home. Folks'll wait outside three, four hours
in the broiling heat to get their own private moment
with the star. They're devoted."

Now Clark gave her a sidelong look. "You been out
to the Fair Grounds before, Kate?"

"I've been meaning to."

He wrinkled his nose. "Livestock get shown right
here in this building at Tennessee State Fair time. The
4-H kids sleep in the straw right here with their animals, heifers, lambs. And then the flea market's here
the third weekend every month."

"I haven't yet—"

"Don't s'pose you're a NASCAR fan either?"

"Auto racing. No."

"Well then, you come on with me. Come on right
now. We need to catch you up real quick. If Dottie
says you should see the scene, then you should see it.
Boss's order." Clark took her lightly by the wrist, and
they walked out of the building, turned a corner and
moved toward a cement and girderwork area that
looked like a stadium.

It was. They emerged into a grandstand section, before them a huge oval of a motor raceway. Kate saw

the track straightaway, the banked sides, the ads for
Little Caesars, Custom Exhaust, First Union. Inside
the grassy inner oval was an enormous stage facing
these bleachers. Crews were beginning to install huge
speakers, giant TV screens, microphones. Banks of
lights were up on a truss arch.

"So, Kate, you can sit on these bleachers next Monday at eleven and hear LilyAnn sing a short set right
out there. Half dozen songs, old and new, live and in
person." He pointed to the track. "If you want, you
can even walk past on the race track while she sings.
You can take all the photos you want. If you're in the
Fan Club, that is."

"You mean people can walk on the track right up
in front of that stage?"

He nodded. "Lily might reach down and shake a
few hands."

"Surely not with her arm in a cast."

"Oh, never underestimate LilyAnn Page. Of course,
security keeps folks moving."

Kate squinted. So close up, the singer would be exposed. No buffer zone despite security. She thought
of Walter Sian. She said, "LilyAnn's schedule is set?
No possible changes?"

"Set in stone and printed in the program. It's on
the web too. See, it goes by the labels. Monday all
the Mercator artists perform, Jackie Norman, Jay Cal-
loway, Richie Havering, the Diamondbacks. 'Course,
Lily's featured. Her fans get a taste of the new album,
sort of an appetizer."

Kate nodded and scanned the scene and even wondered what Turk Karcic would say if he were here.
Actually, she didn't have to wonder. "And how does
she actually get to the stage?"

"Easy. In her bus."

"Her tour bus?"

"Drives right up. See, over there." He pointed to
an asphalt area inside the oval. There were two parked

buses, an assortment of tractor trailers, cars, panel trucks, pickups.

Kate said, "Whose vehicles are those? Different crews?"

"Crews, musicians, caterers, officials from the labels, you name it. Great space. By the weekend, it'll fill up."

Space for murder? It was far too open. A sniper in the grandstand, a sneak attack from the buses . . . How hard could it be to get an ID tag and slip in? Or buy a ticket in advance?

She said, "Big place."

"Oh, this is nothing. Just wait till next Monday. Thousands of people all right here."

"But how do the stars get from the stage to their booth?"

He smiled like a veteran to a recruit. "There's full escort to and from the booth and stage. The crowd makes way. Metro Police are out in force, and people are very nice. The stars get star treatment at Fan Fair, and the fans are the guests of honor. There's never been a problem." He cocked one eyebrow. "But Kate, tell me, please, do they pay you to look that worried?"

"What?"

"No disrespect, but it's as though the worries of the world are on your shoulders."

She tried to smile. Her headache kept the beat with her pulse. "It's all a little overwhelming, I guess."

"You'll love it. But let's get back to the booth. I don't want Babs to think I ducked out on her. We've got some work to do for the Fan Club reception too."

"At the Country Music Museum?"

He nodded. "Tuesday night. Kind of a tie-in with the booth, bunting and stars-and-stripes. So colorful. We found this incredible red, almost iridescent." They now walked back toward the booth building. Kate kept pace, head throbbing. Clark seemed lost in the color pallet of reds and blues. Babs stood waiting at the booth, her hands anchored on her hips. "Thought you'd never get back. Guess who was just here—Bucky."

"Bucky Sibbett?"

"Got his spit all over my shirt. Like always."

Clark rolled his eyes. "The man's obsessed. He ought to be put away."

Kate said, "Then he's right here at the Fair Grounds . . . installing equipment?"

They nodded. "Stage and lights. He works crew for a stage rental company." Babs said, "I thought he just might turn up. Good thing it's only us here."

But Kate said a swift thanks and goodbye, left the building fast, headed back to the grandstand and down the concrete steps to the raceway. She half-vaulted, half-clambered over the cinderblock wall and went straight to the inner oval stage. Workers were everywhere. No way to spot Bucky. She looked for a Tennessee Stage and Studio Supply truck. Most had no lettering, the anonymity probably to foil highjackers. Bucky Sibbett?—she asked a guy with a wrench, another with black cord over his shoulder. They shook their heads no. Then a lanky redhead with wirecutters pointed her to a truck. "Tennessee Stage and Studio Supply, it's that one. You could wait."

She simply stood by the door, waited fifteen, twenty minutes. It was 4:45 when a stocky man with long sandy hair, a tool box and a walkman came to reach for the door handle—reach awkwardly with a right hand whose middle two fingers were crooked and withered.

"Bucky Sibbett?"

He took off his headphones. "Yeah?"

"I'm Kate Banning. Could I talk to you a minute?"

He ignored her and called to an older man in a tank tee, "Hey, that coupling was loose. It's not going anywhere now." He opened the door, started to put the headphones back on.

"Mr. Sibbett, could I talk to you for just a couple of minutes before you go."

"Lady, I'm clocking out."

"Just a few questions, please. I've been looking for you. It's about the Shenandoah Iron Works."

He seemed both to cower and brace for a fight. He slid the phones around his neck and looked her up and down. "What for? You LilyAnn's lawyer?"

She shook her head. "I'm with a company that's working on media for her management. It's a bit complicated."

His head was cocked. "So did Dottie send you out? You another one come to shut me up?"

"No."

"Don't lie to me. She's LilyAnn's mouthpiece." He made a mock-soulful face. "Miss LilyAnn Page, all sweetness and light, and Dottie the battle axe." He shifted. "Well, they won't scare me. You go tell them Bucky's not scared. And I'm not gonna go away either. I got a lawyer that's real interested in my case."

"And what case is that?"

"Don't play dumb."

"What case?"

"This." The injured hand was thrust at her face. His close-set eyes gave him a hunted look. He said, "This right here, this is my case. The bitch slammed the car door on my hand."

"Dottie."

"Oh, not Dottie . . ." He spat the word in disdain. "Not Dottie, she wasn't even there. LilyAnn Page, that's who. The goddamn queen of the Shenandoah Valley. And don't tell me you didn't know."

His flying saliva hit Kate's cheek. Kate said, "I didn't."

"Shit you didn't. You work for her." He paused, wiped his mouth on his arm. "You think I slammed the door on my own hand? I'm a drummer, for god-

sake. 'Least I was." He tried to make a fist. The two
withered fingers stayed stiff as sticks.

"Got my eyes opened," he said. "You think somebody's looking out for you, well, nobody's looking out.
You get hurt, you're garbage. Bust your hump to
make somebody rich, they throw you out like trash.
Shitty system." He gestured toward the stage. "Rich
bitch stars and labels. Blow it all up and start over."

Kate said, "Maybe your lawyer—"

"Another parasite. That's what it comes down to.
You know what they want? Half. It's my hand that's
wrecked, but every dollar out of my own flesh and
bone in some courtroom, a lawyer wants half. Preda-
tors. Cannibals." Kate saw his face, the mad-dog look,
the insight turned to blind rage.

Murderous rage, but would he actually do it? She
said, "I'm sorry about your injury."

"Tell it to LilyAnn. Tell it to the hospital. You
wanna see the bill? Tests, X-ray. Roll of gauze, forty
bucks. You wanna know what they didn't cover. The
doctors, another bunch of vampires. They'll sue me.
So sue me, I'll sue them back. I'll do worse than that.
I can tie knots with my teeth. At least I'm alive. At
least I'm not shot dead."

She blinked. "Shot?" Rabid man. Kate backed off
slowly. "What do you mean, dead?"

"Landreth."

"Brent Landreth?"

He thrust out his jaw. "Don't play with me. Cops'll
probably be out here any minute."

"What about Brent Landreth?"

"Hell, I worked on the stage all day with a million
guys. I got an alibi a mile wide. It wasn't me."

"Bucky . . . Mr. Sibbett, what are you saying?"

"It was just on the radio. Somebody shot Landreth
right outside his house. Hit him in the neck. He's
dead." He stepped up into the truck and slammed
the door.

Kate went to her car as if taking shelter, turned the key, tried to reach Dottie, heard Bucky Sibbett's last words about the curse of LilyAnn Page. She turned on the radio and punched every button. Traffic reports, ads, late-breaking news about the stock market, the NASDAQ, more ads. Nothing from Dottie.

She hit 650 AM. Dick Lehman in the newsroom, today's news-on-the-hour. First, the mayor's budget, the school board fight, a business bankruptcy, then ". . . found shot to death outside his home in the Sylvan Park section of Nashville . . . Landreth a long-time member of country star LilyAnn Page's band, the Shenandoah Iron Works . . . leaves a wife and son . . . Police suspect robbery." On to a three-car collision on Briley Parkway.

Kate punched in Dottie's number again. Busy. She got to a phone book and found "Landreth, B.," was listed at 471 Colorado, a Sylvan Park address.

A white bungalow, as it turned out, with neat squares of green trimmed lawn, rose bushes along the side, a maple tree and bike in the front yard—and yellow tape and three police cruisers around the perimeter. She parked down the block.

Things were winding down. Cops in twos and threes stood talking, their radios cracking inside the cruisers. Neighbors huddled in small groups and kept their distance as if fearing contagion and wary of the police. The front window blinds of the house were pulled down. In the driveway sat a white van and a late-model Celica with driver's side door open.

Kate approached, stood near enough to see the front walk, the flagstones splashed a darkening red that trailed toward the house, stopping about eight feet short of the front door. It looked as though Brent was shot near the street, tried to make his way into the house but never got there. By now the body was gone, his wife probably inside continuing police interviews.

Kate stepped up to a pony-tailed mother who clutched the shoulder of a downcast little boy with a G.I. Joe and two Ninjas. In Boston, fourteen years ago, she would talk to neighbors like this only after flashing her press pass and going inside the crime scene, the cops grudgingly cooperative. Now, lockout. She'd wanted it this way, she reminded herself. No more gore, no survivors in shock.

Now she stood before Brent Landreth's house. The curly-haired sentinel who kept watch for forest fires and guarded LilyAnn with his guitar and his very life—now a fallen ranger. Was he the victim of a robbery, a drive-by—or did somebody hunt him down?

Kate took a deep breath and stepped closer to the pony-tail mother. "I heard it on the radio," she said to the woman. "You must be a neighbor?" She nodded. "The radio said robbery, is that it?"

"We never had trouble over here. It's real quiet."

"The radio said he was shot."

She shrugged. "The police sirens, that's the first I knew about it. Neighbors all came out. The paramedics were here with the ambulance." She smoothed the little boy's hair. "Seems like he just got home, got out of his car and somebody pulled up and shot him and drove off. We think he was gone when the ambulance got here. He just bled to death. It was real fast."

"So it wasn't robbery."

"I think they can't find his wallet. That's what they're saying."

Kate paused. A uniformed cop walked across the grass and went to the front door and then inside. A breeze twisted the yellow tape like party streamers. Two girls put a bouquet of flowers on the ground just outside the police tape, folded their hands and prayed. They backed away. Kate asked the woman, "Did you know Brent Landreth?"

Her nod was firm. "Real nice man. One cold spell, he gave us a hand with the furnace. Always said hello,

very polite. My Davy here played with his little boy
once in a while, didn't you, Dave?" She rubbed her
son's shoulders. He hugged the G.I. Joe to his chest.
The mother said, "I guess now the wife can go back
to Virginia."

"Brent's wife?"

"All her people are in the Shenandoah Valley, and
that's all she talked about, how she never could get
used to Nashville in all these years. Sometimes the
Lord's ways are a mystery."

"Indeed."

The woman guided her son back toward their own
house, and Kate stepped closer to the tape and looked
at the Celica. The open door meant the cops hadn't
yet dusted it. It looked as though Brent just got out
and was shot. So why wasn't the lawn bloody? Blood
marked the walkway, which was perpendicular to the
street. It seemed Brent left the car, its door still partway open, went toward the street, and then was shot
and tried to make it down the walk to his own front
door.

"Miz, if you'll step back. This is a police line."

"Sorry, officer."

Kate moved off to the side. "I know you need to
keep the scene clear for your investigation."

"Ma'am, we do." She was a young cop.

"I guess you wouldn't even want to shut that car
door in the driveway."

"Part of the investigation, ma'am. Don't want to
disturb a crime scene."

Kate nodded. So the Celica door was open when
the cops got here, doubtless open when Brent was
shot. Still, this was an elementary geometry puzzle
with straight lines and triangles. Unless he had a fetish
about keeping off his own grass, Brent Landreth
would have shut the door and cut across the lawn to
his front steps. But the blood indicated otherwise. It

seemed he was either ordered at gunpoint to the
street—or drawn there, perhaps by someone he knew?
   Grevins?
   Now the front door opened, two uniforms and a
plainclothes officer coming out. One glimpse of a pale
delicate hand with a wedding ring, and the door shut
tight. Would the police tell Kate anything if she identified herself as a friend? Probably not. And she'd
rather not get her name on a police list here on the
scene. As Brent might say, she had her reasons.
   So Kate shouldered her purse and stepped back and
looked at the cut flowers lying in cello wrap. Her head
pounded. Wouldn't it be nice to lay flowers at the
scene and pray and walk away? Wouldn't it be a relief
to leave it all in the hands of the Lord and the Metro
Nashville police? Wouldn't it be easier not to be what
the late Brent Landreth called a "lifer?" Wouldn't it
sometimes be a whole lot easier not to be the person
you actually are?

CHAPTER NINE

One of these days she'd take a yoga course. Or maybe hypnosis. She'd learn relaxation, find the calm center.

It was early Thursday morning, two days to the scheduled video shoot, four to Fan Fair. Too many loose ends, loose beginnings. What Kate achieved so far was a scalp so tender she couldn't bear to shampoo.

Dressed for work in blue wool gabardines, she sat on the edge of her unmade bed. Wake up, and guess what? Brent Landreth is still dead. A police investigation was underway, an autopsy scheduled, though early reports indicated a hemorrhage from a gunshot wound to the neck as probable cause of death.

"Not an enemy in the world" was the mantra. From Dottie, from TV news and today's *Tennessean*, the same message was unvarying. Brent was the thoughtful neighbor, the Iron Works good buddy, the doting father, a Nashville musician's musician. LilyAnn Page was said to be in seclusion following a condolence visit to the Landreth home. Funeral arrangements were incomplete.

"It's an I-40 problem," Dottie said when Kate finally reached her on the phone close to midnight. "You live near an interstate exit, you are asking for trouble. There was nobody like Brent, he was the rock. Of course Lily's devastated. None of us will get an hour of sleep. The girls need help. Listen, there's robberies in all those neighborhoods off I-40. Brent and Suzanne stayed in Sylvan Park way too long."

Kate had bit her tongue to keep quiet. Talking to the manager at the stroke of midnight was like being in a Salvador Dali painting.

Dottie, we need to talk about Keith Grevins. That was the message Kate wanted to send. Not last night, she couldn't. She sent her sympathies and said she'd be in touch.

She stood and went to the window. It looked like rain, the sky a weird greenish color. She called out to Kelly, who was quiet as they got into the car. The radio said storm cells were moving east from Little Rock and would cross into Tennessee. Tornadoes were possible later in the day.

Tornadoes . . . people's lives reduced to bits of wood and cloth. If they still had lives at all. Do not talk about tornadoes. Telling Kelly about the band member's death was enough. She promised to pick her up at the regular time. "You okay, sweetie?"

"I guess. 'Bye, Mom." Kate watched her get out, resisting an urge to call her back, somehow tell her everything would be all right.

Wouldn't it be nice to think so.

In twenty minutes she was in her office, door closed, coffee steaming. No sign of a black funnel cloud across the river where the gray hulk of the stadium loomed.

Was the gun that killed Brent buried deep in the river muck?

If only Brent . . . had lived in another neighborhood? Or told the police about Keith Grevins's rumored threat?

As for Grevins, was he still in town or perhaps at thirty-thousand feet headed back to Hawaii? Whoever was closing in on LilyAnn could remain right here in Nashville. With so much anger against her, Grevins would have plenty of help in Music City.

From whom—Kip? Myers Fatenza? Bucky? Or

some anonymous workman or crew member? Mix and match. For certain, the next move was in the planning stage.

And Kate now in limbo. Though Brent's death might gain her some time. Perhaps there'd be a period of mourning. The video shoot would surely be postponed, and LilyAnn would bow out of Fan Fair. A disrupted schedule could actually help.

Some background on Grevins could help too.

But the deadline on *Distant Lands* was today. How to work on magazines with Brent Landreth in the morgue? How to reconcile trivia with mayhem?

Edit, edit . . . She opened the envelope, slid out the *Distant Lands* packet. Edit, edit this bimonthly narcotic for subscribers so cocooned that they couldn't bear to encounter a word, phrase, or visual image that might stir the least vibration. Who were they?—the Sun City crowd in their no-children-allowed compounds? The tender ladies who found Hummel figures too racy?

Don't get mad, she told herself. Catch the renegade commas, the howlers like the Leaning Tower of Pizza. The freelance copy editor had already fixed spelling and run-on sentences. Kate scanned the lines, "Moonbeams dip their lovely fingers into charming pools. . . ."

Moonbeams with fingers? Finger-lickin' lunar light? The circulation, she saw to her dismay, was up some eighteen percent this calendar year, ad revenue too. Leverage *Distant Lands* into the very upper atmosphere.

The light outdoors had changed when she finally finished at two, sent the whole mess to production, tended her mail and e-mail, the FedExes. She ordered in a cheese steak with onions for greasy comfort and started to research Nashville Wash-O-Mat when Delia phoned to say that Davidson County was under a tornado watch until further notice.

Davidson County was Nashville.

Kate needed no further notice. She threw on her
jacket, exited and just pulled her car out to go get
Kelly when a fluttering sound came from her bag—
her phone. Last thing she wanted. One hand on the
wheel, she felt around her wallet, her hairbrush. She
said, "Kate Banning."

"Miz Banning?" Static sound. She said yes. "This
is Billy D. I'm at Fountain Square with the girls, with
Angie and Deb. We came out to a movie. I can't get
hold of Dottie. She's tied up with the Brent thing.
We're all wrecked."

She was looking at the greenish sky. "What can I
do for you, Billy?"

"Pretty sure she'd want me to call you. Like I say,
I'm with the girls. We just got here to go to a movie.
But I just saw him. Ten-to-one, it's him."

Keith Grevins?

"He went into *Desire Mountain,* that one about the
bear hunter. It was not five minutes ago. If I could
just get hold of Dottie."

"Billy, who exactly are we talking about?" She
nudged the gas. "Who did you see?"

"Walter, Miz Banning. It's that stalker." She hit the
brake, barely stopped at the bumper in front. "Miz
Banning, you there? Hello?"

"I'm here."

"You know where Fountain Square is? The blue
roofs right next to the big pond and the mall that went
bust. It's called The Waterfront."

She blinked. The Waterfront, Dottie's words for the
site of LilyAnn's new video. Did Walter Sian know
about the video shoot? Was he scouting? She said,
"Listen, Billy, you stay right there. Try to reach Dottie. I'm on my way to get my daughter, then I'll be
there. Promise you'll stay."

"Yes, ma'am, I'll watch out for him. You know

where Fountain Square is? It's Metro Center Boulevard."

"Do you know about the tornado watch, Billy?"

"Yes, ma'am. Springtime, we get quite a few."

"You don't see a black cloud right now?"

Was that sound his laughter? "No, ma'am. I think you're safe on that score. We're more or less used to 'em."

" 'Em" meaning warnings or actual storms? She did not seek clarification but drove on in thick, slow traffic. Finally, the sight of Kelly with a handful of other kids with backpacks and instrument cases. She recognized *Walden* under Kelly's arm and read her daughter's posture—sullen—when the back door opened, the pack tossed inside, the passenger door shut.

Kate said, "Kel, I need your help. Get the atlas from the backseat pocket. Find the best route to Metro Center Boulevard."

"There might be a tornado."

"I think we're okay for now. Is there a route through downtown."

"The interstates look better. Let's turn on the radio for the weather."

Could they be partners in this? Kate sketched the situation for Kelly. "—so this matters a lot because they're going to shoot a video for LilyAnn Page's new album out there."

Her daughter said, "Wow."

"I know, the stalker thing's so scary."

"Yeah, that too." The radio said to stay tuned. Kate glanced at her daughter, who said, "See, Mom, I'm thinking about those girls who can go to movies on a school day. Maybe if you're in high school and your mom's a country star, you go to the movies whenever you want."

So off the point. Though not to an eighth grader. Still, do not talk about priorities now. Drive.

Twenty minutes later, the first bright blue roofs

came up, and just past it the marquee full of Hollywood titles with vehicles clustered in the front lot.
Kate pulled in. "Kel, you wait here. I'll try to be fast."

But the passenger door flung open. "Not a chance,
Mom. I'm not some baby you can . . ."

But a trio was headed for them, the blond Billy D
and two teen girls in jeans who looked as though
they'd stepped out of the portraits on Dottie's office
desk. Kate knew them on sight, Dottie's apple-
cheeked and spunky Deb, and LilyAnn's long-haired
Angie who looked like a budding teen folksinger. She
held a huge Pepsi, and Deb had the bag of popcorn.
They all blurted without introductions.

"He went into theatre four. We were all in the
lobby."

"At the snack bar. I just got the popcorn and
Pepsi."

"He got popcorn."

"—and went into *Desire Mountain.*"

"And if I just had my Mach-Flite Four and a couple
carbon arrows, I coulda—"

"Billy D would stop him."

"—rigged with a nockset and stabilizer, I'd be all
set."

Deb said, "Two hours of a dumb grizzly bear.
Movie for retards."

Kelly smiled at Deb's crack as if hoping to be considered a high schooler's equal. Kate said, "You're
certain it's Walter Sian."

Billy D nodded and gestured toward The Waterfront. "We came from that way. I think he was walking behind us."

Deb said, "I saw him *first* first."

"She did," Billy said. "It's true."

Deb now twinkled at Billy D, who looked like he
played the good-natured older brother with these two.

Kate said, "So he's definitely in the theater."

"We've watched the exits. We'd know if he left."

"And you just happened to be out here—"

"My mom thought it would help us, like, feel better. We stayed home from school because of Brent—" Angie's tone faltered. "Anyway, after lunch Billy brought us to a movie. It's extra-credit for history class too." Her tone was both flat and slightly world-weary. "It's about the French Revolution."

"And Billy D had to drive us, like we can't even drive ourselves, my mother gets so freaked out. Today worse than ever." Deb added, "But I saw the creep first. I win that prize."

Billy D said, "Deb's got eagle eyes. She'd be a great archer. Start her with a compound bow equipped with sights." He looked at Kate. "So, do we call the cops, or what?"

"You didn't reach Dottie?"

He shook his head.

Deb said, "Reach my mother? Fat chance. You never can reach her. She's never around. Today the police came, so she talked to them forever. She made us look all over the house for Brent's wallet. Of course it wasn't there." She chomped a mouthful of popcorn. Angie sipped the Pepsi.

Billy D said, "We could get the manager."

Kate said, "Why don't you and I buy tickets and go in and look around—just to be sure?"

He said, "But the kids—"

"Hey, we're cool." Deb flashed a wide grin. "I know, we'll go and get your car, Billy. We'll drive it over here." He looked doubtful. "It's fine. We won't tell my mom or Lily."

Billy D said, "See, Kate, I parked back at The Waterfront."

"We got here early," Angie said, "and we wanted to see the old Esprit store. We used to get neat clothes and ride paddleboats and feed the ducks."

"I said I'd drive them. I promised Dottie."

"Come on, Billy, it's only a dumb parking lot." Deb

toyed with a button of his shirt, traced a circle on his chest with a cherry-red fingernail. "Just give us the key, the little ol' key. And Kelly'll come with us too. Okay, Kelly?"

Kelly? In a car with these two? It caught Kate off guard. A headache surged. She remembered Dottie and these girls screaming yesterday while she walked with Turk, something about them totaling a vehicle. And the open-road roar of their engine on the driveway.

"Oh come on, Billy-Willy." Deb pouted.

Kate said, "I think Kelly can sit in our car. You all can."

"Oh, Mom, no!"

Angie said, "She'll be fine, Mrs . . . Kate. We'll walk over and drive right back here to your car. We both have licenses. The speed limit is, what, five miles an hour? Billy has a Land Cruiser."

Deb said, "If you ask me, anyway, you're the ones in danger. You're going in there to hunt the stalker." She shoved in another handful of popcorn and chewed. "Unless we stand here and talk about it all night."

Smart kid. But good point. Kate said, "You absolutely promise to stay in the lot? You'll drive right back here in the lot? And belt yourselves in?" The three nodded like holiday-pageant angels. Kate said, "This will take us ten minutes. We'll meet right here."

They set off for the sidewalk, Kelly between them, her shoulders hitched up to full height. Kate wanted to call out, "Kelly's only in eighth grade" but it would be embarrassing, not safer. She looked at Billy D. "Let's go."

She bought two tickets, and they went in and walked left past the snack bar down the hallway. At the far end, a uniformed teen usher swept popcorn from the carpet. Kate said, "Let's go inside and let

our eyes adjust. Then we can walk down the aisle
slowly, sit down in front, look back up at the faces."

He nodded, and they went into the door marked
Desire Mountain. Inside, the smell of butter popcorn
and sneakers. No more than twenty figures were scattered through the theatre. With Billy D beside her,
Kate paused, waited. Onscreen, a grizzly swept a fish
from a stream with one paw. The bear's eyes were
red, the teeth yellow. The fish bled.

Kate saw a soldier in uniform, a man and woman
midway on the right, a very fat figure who sat alone
to the side crunching nachos, a threesome of little kids
on the front row.

She nudged, and they walked slowly down the aisle,
past an older man with a walking cane in an end seat,
a woman with beehive hair, two guys with bushy side-
burns and baseball caps. One figure on the left who
sat alone looked round-headed enough to be Walter
Sian, but close-up his face was lined, wrinkled—a se-
nior at the matinee.

Down front, Kate touched Billy D's arm. They entered a row and sat. She whispered, "You look
around. Go ahead, turn around." Onscreen, the bear
ran up a mountain while grunting. She heard Billy D.
breathe. He whispered, "I don't see him."

She turned, craned her neck, saw several pairs of
eyeglasses. Did Walter Sian wear glasses? With or
without them, nobody in sight fit his description. The
faces ogling the bear were long, or thin, or had
pointed or flat noses. No candidates for the stalker.

"Maybe he already left. Maybe out those emergency exits."

"Wouldn't you and the girls have seen him?"

"I'm gonna ask." She watched him go to the guys
in the ball caps, then come back. He said, "No. Nobody went out the red exits." She said, "Then let's
go." They made their way up the aisle in silence. From
onscreen, a ferocious growl in Dolby. Billy D glanced

back. Kate did not. The swinging doors opened, and
they stood outside in the hallway. Billy said, "But it
was him, I swear it. Dottie makes us all carry pictures
of him."

"Maybe he saw you too. Maybe he remembered."

The teen usher was just passing. Kate said, "Excuse
me, we're looking for a guy. We thought we saw him
go into *Desire Mountain*. He looks like—"

"Like this." Billy D was opening his wallet. He unfolded a thick sheet, the photo of Walter Sian's face.

"Oh, him?" The usher nodded. "Yeah," he said,
"he was here. He's here a lot."

"At the movies?"

Another nod. "Couple times a week."

"Which way did he go?"

"Uh, well, first a black guy wanted to see a different
movie, so I let him go in. This white guy, him—" he
pointed his broom shaft to the Exit at the end of the
corridor. "Out."

"You saw him go?"

"Out that door."

They sprinted, flung the door open.

Nobody was there. On the pavement outside,
crushed drink cups, candy wrappers. The green sky.
No Walter. They walked around back, where a half
dozen skateboarders were smoking cigarettes. Had
they seen this guy? They glanced at the Xerox. No.
Did Billy D have a light? He tossed them a pack of
matches. No tornado problems on their horizon.

In silence, they walked back around to the front. A
Chevy Cavalier passed, a woman with a backseat full
of kids. Two women with turquoise makeup cases like
tackle boxes got into a car. Nobody else.

Except Kelly, Deb and Angie. The Land Cruiser
doors were open wide, radio blaring. Kate's car doors
were open too. The girls were making themselves
comfy, speakers at full blast. Angie and Kelly danced

on the asphalt. Inside Kate's station wagon, Deb
seemed to be the DJ, turning up the radio volume.

Deb called, "Find him?"

"No."

She shrugged and waved her arms over her head.
"Bummer."

Billy D's voice was drowned by the sheer decibels.
Kate shook her head, then covered her ears. At her
car, she gestured for Deb to get out and shut the
driver's door.

"Aw, Mom."

"That's okay, Kelly. Your mom wants her car
back." Angie stopped dancing. Deb swirled a time or
two. Kate saw the two cigarettes crushed out in her
car ashtray. She signaled for Kelly to get in. "Time to
go, Kel. Billy, I'd like your phone number." She copied it down. "Let's stay in touch. I want to talk to
you."

"Billy only likes to talk about bows and arrows."

"Good to meet you Angie, Deb."

They powered down their windows and called,
"Have a nice evening. See y'all."

Kelly rolled down hers and called back "See y'all
later."

Y'all. Y'all indeed. Kate's head banged. Great day.
Brent gone, the Alhambra in the moonlight, a tornado
watch, the stalker who ran like the grizzly, and Kelly
Banning going South.

Face it, couldn't Kate Banning use a friend, a buddy?
She was home, heating frozen pizza, the tornado watch
lifted, Kelly in her room with the door shut. Somehow
Taylor Evelyn's face came to mind. Kate picked up
the phone, called the Evelyn Gallery. Taylor's butter-
scotch voice was reassuring. She was just closing up.
Did Kate like sushi? How about Goten II, right in
Cummins Station. Half an hour.

As promised, Taylor Evelyn was downstairs in the

subdued lighting of the Japanese restaurant. She sipped sake and fingered her multi-strand pebble-pearl necklace as she scanned Kate's face.

"You're looking mighty glum, Kate Banning."

Accusation or observation? Kate sat down. "I left my daughter with a microwaved pizza and carrot sticks. You have—?"

"Children? Only by proxy. One niece named Blythe, which she definitely is not, if ever a child were misnamed. I love her to death, but the day-to-day would send me into a state of vegetation."

Kate laughed. "Meet yours truly, the human cabbage. So Taylor, it's good to see you again."

"Likewise. I'm here so often I ought to own company stock—and you look like you need a good warm sake." She signaled the waiter. "The tornado watch scare you, is that it?"

"In New England we have hurricanes, and yes, I was worried." The warm wine appeared before Kate, who ordered the sushi special, as did her companion. She looked at Taylor. "Not a great day."

"I heard about that musician. It was on TV."

"Brent Landreth was shot dead in front of his house."

Two fine lines creased Taylor's forehead. "Robbery, wasn't it? That's what TV said."

"It's not clear. His wallet's missing. He'd been with LilyAnn since the beginning of her career. Did you know him?"

"Is he the one with the bow and arrows?"

Kate shook her head. "No, that's Billy D. He's a caretaker."

"—oh, right, I remember him now. The one with curly hair. He seemed like a good guy, actually. Such a Grand Central Station out there." The creases deepened. Taylor said, "Well it's just awful, the killing. And on top of LilyAnn's arm too. She must feel be-

sieged after the door. I understand you talked to
Sonny."

"Sonny Burkendahl, yes I did."

"I suppose he bent your ear about LilyAnn's
brother. I swear it's a turf thing. Sonny's just a little
bit jealous."

"I don't know. Valley Construction has problems."
Taylor's brows arched. The sushi arrived.

Kate touched the tender spot on her scalp and
thought of the Granny White house, the backyard
lumber and weeds. She said, "Clients are unhappy
about construction delays."

"Oh, that old story—whee, that wasabi mustard
catches me every time. Anyway, I learned a little
something about contractors when I expanded the gallery last winter. A permit is a license to mint money
and vanish into the fourth dimension."

And to attempt murder? A question Kate couldn't
ask here and now. She said, "This guy seems out of
bounds even for a contractor."

Taylor sipped her wine, ate a piece of sushi. "So
now you think the contractor brother let the door fall
on his sister? What on earth for?" Kate didn't answer.
Taylor looked at her face. "Oh, you're not at liberty
to say, are you? Hughes probably made you sign a
confidentiality agreement when you started at
Fleetwood."

"Not exactly." But Kate managed to smile.
"Though I'm still working on the . . . the problem."

"But you think the building contractor brother
might have something to do with it?"

Kate shrugged. Avoid a direct answer. She said,
"There's also a bitter ex-drummer who hurt his hand
and feels cheated and literally foams at the mouth.
These days he puts up stage lights. You know the
name Sibbett? Bucky Sibbett?"

Taylor shook her head no.

"How about LilyAnn's ex-husband?"

A firm no.

"You're sure? His name's Keith Grevins."

"Sorry, Kate, they split before my time. In fact, Li-lyAnn started working with me after the marriage failed because the Mosely house was literally empty." Taylor's smile was almost dreamy. "It was heaven. I had trucks coming in from Atlanta, Dallas, one whole collection of Roycroft tables and chests from Utica, New York." Her expression turned sardonic. "Of course, getting action on my invoices proved to be another matter. Anyway, I never met the husband, though I understand his taste ran to Naugahyde and Barcaloungers."

They chuckled. Taylor said, "Isn't this fun, gossip with a twist. So who else is worrying you?"

Kate paused. "Actually, there's a photographer who collaborated on LilyAnn's book, and he's furious."

Taylor Evelyn laughed. "Oh, now that one sounds familiar. He's the one who 'bout went crazy photo-graphing at Mosely. I'd bet it's the guy with the hair."

"Orange."

"It used to be pink, a sort of dirty fuschia. What's his name, Miles Something?"

"Myers Fatenza." Kate wiped her mouth. "You know him?"

"Not personally. I go to LA on gallery business, and several years ago his name was on everybody's lips out there. One time I saw him on a flight—the hair, somebody pointed him out." Taylor ate a tuna roll and looked up. "Fatenza used to be a Hollywood photographer, Kate, a sort of a Herb Ritts type. His male bodies were gorgeous, but the women looked like beef carcasses, and Amanda Havens sued him. I forget the charges, but she'd just won that Oscar. They settled, but it ended his career out there."

"So he came to Nashville."

Taylor nodded and put down her chopsticks. "It's

been a few years." She looked at Kate. "You really want to hear this?"

"Absolutely."

"Here goes. One of my gallery assistants worked for him here in town so I got some insider stuff. Fatenza did a gift book on country music stars—arty shots in sepia, they all posed. I mean, he's no Annie Liebowitz, but nobody wanted to be left out, and the Music Row publicity machines got behind him."

She paused, sipped. "Turned out, the guy is a tyrant. He turned the country music millionaire stars into whimpering puppies, got them to stand for hours in freezing weather outdoors and drag their best guitars over rough tile floors—just crude, ignorant power plays. Deep down, you see, Country Music Nashville has a huge inferiority complex, and he played the part of the big LA photographer artiste and just cowed them."

"That's when LilyAnn Page signed him to a deal." Taylor nodded.

"But his contract terms were terrible."

Taylor chuckled. "And was LilyAnn ever the toast of this town when word got out! Believe me, whatever her negatives, she was Twang Town's sweet revenge that season."

"And Myers Fatenza's career crashed for the second time?"

Taylor nodded. "There was some talk of a lawsuit, and then I think he tried nature photography, maybe a calendar, but it didn't work. What's he doing now, children's birthday parties?"

"Insurance claims."

"Oh, how the mighty get what's coming to them. Once in a while, anyway." She set down her chopsticks. "But how is Kate Banning doing?"

Kate touched her scalp ever-so-lightly. In fact, Taylor was correct, she could not speak freely. She said,

"It's magazines by day, and my teen daughter by night."

"So you need a day off now and then. You need to unplug your brain and sit by a waterfall. You should drive down the Natchez Trace, Kate. We have some spectacular scenery in Tennessee."

"Taylor, I . . . theoretically I could. I'm on flextime. Mostly, it means I work the night shift." She paused.

Taylor brightened. "I know what, let's take off tomorrow. I'll show you spring along the backroads, the violets, the iris. It's the state flower, you know, the iris."

"I wish I could. But there's an office consult, and I have to go out to The Waterfront."

"The river? Oh, *that* 'Waterfront.' Kate, why on earth go to a failed mall? Lord, the bankers in this town knew that place was dead-on-arrival. I was warned never even to consider gallery space out there. It's been through bankruptcy and out the other end. I understand even the movies are going to close down. Don't go there, it's depressing."

"LilyAnn Page is shooting a video at The Waterfront soon. I need to check it out."

"Ah." Taylor Evelyn sat back with a knowing look. "Ah, you're on her safety patrol, aren't you? That's the part you can't talk about, the ins and outs." She dabbed her napkin at the corners of her mouth and put it down on the table. "I heard about LilyAnn Page's accident with the fire and that boy that was killed. I bet you're asking whether this murder yesterday is connected, aren't you?"

Kate said nothing. The server put down the check.

Taylor leaned toward her. "I'll be thankful when you're done with this, Kate. LilyAnn Page is my gallery client, and I feel as though she's been right here with us at this table, in spirit anyway. You and I can talk, but not quite frankly. There's that fallen door and Sonny Burkendahl and now this death, and it's all mixed up and dark as the night."

Then Taylor reached for the bill. "I'm grabbing this, and it's not generous but selfish." She looked at Kate and fingered the bill. "This lunch'll be on your Boston conscience. In New England, you all call it the check. In the South, it's the ticket. And it's my ticket to see you again, because this way, you'll call me back and we'll go out for a drive and have some real fun. Meantime, you stay safe and sane."

CHAPTER TEN

Safe and sane. Great policy. Bright sunny Friday morning, blue sky, no rain, not a hint of a funnel cloud. Just Dottie calling to say the autopsy report showed gunpowder particles "tattooed" on Brent Landreth's skin around the gunshot wound, meaning he was shot at a distance of six to eight inches. Shot, actually, by a full-jacketed 10mm. bullet that pierced his carotid artery and cervical vertebrae.

In her office chair, Kate stared at the wall. Brent, the late Brent, who killed him? The 10mm was an unusual cartridge, its availability somewhat limited. The gun was probably a Bren Ten, which supposedly combined stopping power and penetration, the "best" features of a .45 and a .357 Magnum.

Were common criminals riding the interstates around Nashville with Bren Tens, exiting for fast cash and credit cards in nice modest neighborhoods? Highly unlikely. The Bren Ten was a kind of glamour gun, debuting years ago on *Miami Vice*. It was Sonny Crockett's gun. Was Keith Grevins a *Miami Vice* fan? Would anybody think to find out?

She sipped her coffee and looked across at her red loveseat and pictured a pallet of reds from office furniture to blood. When he was shot, Brent's blood along the flagstone walk on Colorado was arterial bright. The "trail" on the stones was really a fountain spurting as he collapsed, hemorrhaging and paralyzed. The bullet was now at the police ballistics lab, the wallet still missing. Funeral services and burial would be at Mint Spring, Virginia, his hometown. Dottie said Billy D was dispatched to help the widow Suzanne and little Rory, and that police detectives had interviewed Lily-Ann at great length. The stress of the interviews was nearly unbearable, according to Dottie, so Lily remained in seclusion.

Seclusion. Such mystique around the word. Did Lily-Ann weep in her bedroom, stare blankly at a TV screen, page through photo albums, drink, smoke, sing? Who knew? Kate stared at the river. A motorboat passed, four women in windbreakers and scarves, laughing. They had a picnic cooler. Their wake vee'd out behind them. TGIF.

She turned once again to Arkansas. The U. S. Air Force Singing Sergeants were appearing at the Robinson Center Music Hall in Little Rock. How about a feature? And was it too early to plan a *SouthWing* spread on October's Annual State Fair and Livestock Show at the Barton Coliseum and Arkansas State Fairgrounds?

Frankly, Kate hadn't a clue and at the moment didn't give a damn. Singing Sergeants, Livestock, deadstock. Tell the writer to move ahead. Then go through the motions at two meetings with spreadsheets and bar graphs and policy memos in pebble grained folders.

It was nearly one when she headed out to The Waterfront. Traffic was thick, one lane of I-265 closed for repair. She spotted the bright blue roofs, pulled in and parked by an old Camaro and a Honda, both with local Davidson County plates. She copied the numbers in case one of them belonged to Walter Sian. Then she got out his photo, studied the bland features, put him back in her bag, left her car and locked up.

Warm afternoon sun, cool wind. Kate was the sole pedestrian, and the place looked sad. A torn sign read "The Waterfront—Shopping, Dining, Entertainment,"

but the Special Events board was watermarked and
blank. The walkway bricks were loose and missing,
and the once-white outdoor ceiling panels stained and
broken. Surely somebody had high hopes for this project, put life's energy into its success, felt its failure.

She walked out toward the blue-brown water, where
the developers had tried for a docks-and-pilings nauti-
cal fantasy. The ducks and paddleboats were long
gone, ditto the onetime retail mall. Acres of water,
acres of dead plate glass. The name "Esprit," she saw,
was still stenciled on a store window. Inside the former
clothing store were a wheelbarrow, a rake, bags of
mulch, a stack of empty plastic pots. Admittedly, it all
looked like the perfect backdrop for a video titled
"Against the World."

She walked out onto a dock with a little railing at
the end, leaned against it. The wood was still in
good shape, the hardware not yet corroded, the
structure solid. Maybe the whole place was salvage-
able. She looked left and right, watchful, then briefly
leaned out over the water before retracing and moved
along the storefronts.

This place, Kate realized, was not entirely deserted.
Some commerce went on. Vehicles were parked on
the other side, and a few of the abandoned retail spaces
were now business rentals—a sales office, a hair salon,
Nashville Parent magazine, gyros. Maybe ten percent
occupancy with very short leases over the whole
complex.

Would Walter Sian be employed here? Did he put
in some hours and then walk over to the movies at
Fountain Square? Was he a janitor, or handyman?
Out beyond the lake, it was woodsy and weedy. Could
he camp out there in this warm spring weather? Hun-
ker down in a tornado watch?

She took out her photo of him, smoothed the edges,
and began to knock on doors, beginning with the sales
office, then the hair salon. Employees and customers

all shook their heads. She climbed the stairs and tried an engineering office, Gourmet noodle, an accounting firm and the Pentland Sports Group receptionist. No recognition, not even a maybe. Back down, the gyro guys shrugged behind their takeout window. The other doors were locked.

She walked back to the waterfront area. On a plaza side were huge jardinieres of wind-whipped petunias and also outdoor tables and chairs with umbrellas on a deck. From a distance, it could almost look festive. Add a little spring landscaping to perk things up, and maybe a commercial realtor could find an out-of-state buyer for the whole sorry site.

Then Kate paused. A thought, a connection clicked. Sort of clicked. Here was minimal upkeep, but upkeep nonetheless. Groundskeeping. Maybe that was it, the flowers and shrubs. Walter Sian—he served prison time for armed robbery. He stole a car. But he was obsessed by nature and lived in McMinnville, a "landscape capitol."

Here at The Waterfront, could a handyman from McMinnville talk his way into a job as part-time groundskeeper? That wheelbarrow and rake, the pots and bags of mulch, were they Walter Sian's new trademark? Did the Fountain Square usher recognize him because he actually worked here on a regular basis and afterward went to the movies?

She walked briskly but warily back to the Esprit windows, peered in carefully. Nobody stirred inside. If this was Walter's "shed," he could easily have been here just yesterday, and then, at about this same time, headed across to Fountain Square for a late afternoon movie.

So he'd be due back when?—*if* it was Walter? Probably not for days. If he wore a cap or brimmed hat in the sun, it made sense that none of the workers here recognized the photo.

The wind made her shiver. She crossed her arms for warmth.

Next step, verify the name of the groundskeeper, then talk to Dottie. If Walter recognized Billy D yesterday, it made sense that he'd flee, lie low, burrow into some hiding place.

For how long?

The video was first scheduled to be shot out here tomorrow, Saturday. Did the convicted stalker know that? Was he planning his rendezvous with LilyAnn?

Or was Kate Banning fantasizing this whole thing—making a few pots of petunias into mortal danger because she could not figure out who was trying to kill a Queen of Country Music? "Break of Dawn." Break Kate.

She walked the back way toward her car on the Metro Center Boulevard side. No water views here, only asphalt, the enormous parking area. The Waterfront workers were leaving for the day, a trickle of vehicles, the Camaro, a pickup, sedans, an open Jeep with a man driving. Her glance lingered there. It was a man with a buzz cut in a brown Jeep, an army brown Jeep. The driver looked her way, paused, then saluted. She recognized him. It was Turk Karcic.

"So you sent him?"

"Yes."

"You did."

"I did." The phone buzzed. Kate was back in her office. "Of course I did, Kate. Stalker on the loose, Turk's got to check it out. Lily's not going out there unprotected. Turk's the go/no-go guy on this. He gives clearance, we shoot the video. He sees one sign of that wacko, we're out of there. We have two other sites in mind. The production company's working with us on this."

"Dottie, you aren't telling me the shoot is proceeding on schedule tomorrow?"

"Kate, the show must go on."

"My God."

"Listen here, Kate. Brent's funeral is Sunday afternoon, and Lily's chartering a plane for her and the Iron Works and me and the girls too. We'll fly up to Virginia and come on back for Fan Fair. Lily's devastated, we all are. But we're pros."

"So the schedule holds."

"Who do you think's picking up the funeral expenses? Who do you think's covering the whole entire thing?"

"LilyAnn?"

"You got it."

So Brent would be buried on LilyAnn's dime and her schedule too. She who pays the piper . . . So be it.

"Dottie, what about my talking to LilyAnn?"

"Indefinitely postponed."

"It's important."

"It's all important, Kate—important Lily not get more upset when the video's tomorrow and Fan Fair's so close. Anything you need to know about the situation, I can tell you myself. No need to drag her in, not after what the detectives put her through. They came back this afternoon—a million questions about her and Brent. One of them remembered the divorce, so we had all that again."

"Questions about Keith Grevins?"

"Please, Kate, no more. It's in their hands."

"But they asked about him?"

"They asked. Because Keith was . . . you could say notorious back in the divorce days. He made threats. They're investigating."

Best news of the day.

Kate said, "Dottie, I'm worried about Walter Sian showing up at the video shoot. How about calling for a police detail?"

"A Metro officer will be on site for the shoot, Kate. It's a municipal law."

At least that.

"But remember the cops can't do anything unless Walter Sian comes within a thousand feet, and that'd freak Lily out, wreck the shoot. The broken arm's enough. We're looking into private security."

"Who's the 'we'?"

"Turk, of course."

Of course. What to say? That it was weird for Turk to spend a whole afternoon at a ghost town of a mall and yet Kate only caught a glimpse of him at the exit moment?

Dottie said, "So you did ask around out there at The Waterfront? You showed the photo?"

"Dottie, nobody recognized Walter from the photo."

"Seems like we're clear enough, Kate. It was probably mistaken identity yesterday. Billy D's more upset than he lets on. The girls too. I gave them Valiums."

"Dottie, aren't we talking life-or-death?"

"Absolutely. That's why Turk's on surveillance and you're behind the scenes. Call me the minute you've got a real lead. See you tomorrow at the shoot." The line went dead.

She sighed, packed up her tote and went home and put on jeans and a soft shirt and picked up Kelly. The phone rang, Sam to say his bosses wanted to look at a Hawker in Atlanta and a Boeing business jet, a.k.a. BBJ, available in Chicago. He thought he could get into Nashville sometime over the weekend, maybe tomorrow night. Was she doing just fine?

Just fine, except for a bucket of nails on her head and Walter Sian on the loose and Brent Landreth on a cart with a toe tag in the morgue. She started to tell him all this, then backed off. Not now. Stalker? Corpse? Killers? Movies and TV. Roof nails? Nails? It was all about a manicure.

Then Kelly. Plan pasta and beans with garlic for dinner because Kelly liked it and because Kate needed to talk with her seriously about the Fountain Square moment yesterday, about those cigarettes in the car ashtray. Were they hers? Last night they'd got nowhere. Even Kate's mild request after dinner to water the African violets had prompted accusations and high drama.

Had it also prompted watering? Kate now went to the tabletop and felt the pots. Dry. Should she call upstairs, "Kel, before dinner, how about water these violets?" And risk launching the evening in a sour sequel of last night?

Or should she quietly water the plants herself, but thus give Kelly the message that teen tasks were not important? Or just let them die of neglect, twenty dollars' worth of the plants Kate disliked anyway?

Yet twenty was twenty. Since when did Kate Banning throw away twenty-dollar bills?

Why did the smallest thing bloom with ambiguity?

Back off. Relent. Let go. She gave in and watered the violets, simply filled the measuring cup without fanfare and gave every single pot and jar a good soaking drink without any further mental back-and-forth.

Maybe this evening mother and daughter could talk calmly, reach an accord. What was parenthood but an act of faith?

In the kitchen sat the breakfast remains, milk stains and crumbs. The *Tennessean* was on the table turned to the comics page, *Doonesbury, Kudzu, Dilbert.* She hit "Messages" on the phone machine and heard three hang-ups, a pitch for air-conditioning service and then a "Hey Brian, Dave here at Auto-Time Garage about your van—and we gotta get the Ford folks in on this so you quit havin' that electrical trouble. Give us till next Tuesday."

A tiny case study in ethics. Did she owe van-owner Brian a little Golden Rule behavior? The moral compass wobbled, and sometimes you did, sometimes didn't. She got the phone book and looked up Auto-

Time Garage to tell them about their wrong-number mistake, for Brian's sake. They did not say thanks.

Nobody said thanks these days. Not Dottie Skip-with. Not LilyAnn Page.

Not a teen daughter.

Kate cleared the kitchen and put water on to boil for the pasta. Keep it low on the beans, light on the garlic, just the way Kelly liked it. Kate had something else for the teen palate, though not until after dinner. Wasn't it Spock who advised against turning the dining table into a battle zone?

Dining table—more like a trough. They ate fast, both hungry. The cut-up raw veggies crunched loudly. Kate said, "You're all set for tomorrow?"

"Band practice in the morning, box lunch and the service project at the food bank."

"And Caitlin's dad's driving?"

"Her mother is. They changed it. Oh, hey Mom, that condo meeting's tonight, isn't it? The Mitzy people? And you're going, right?"

"Kel, I forgot about it. I have work to do, some insurance magazine to edit, and a file to review."

Then stern orders. "But you have to go to the condo meeting first, Mom. You need to know the neighbors." This from the hope that Mom would strike up a local friendship. It also felt like a parent night at school, home front stuff. Kate said, "Sure, okay, Kel. I'll go."

"And be extra nice to Mitzy. Scratch behind her ears. She likes that."

Kate said, "I'm always nice to Mitzy, even though she went for my ankle last week at the mailbox."

"She didn't mean it."

"Of course not." Kate saw her daughter's plate was empty. She spoke in a quiet voice, warm and calm. "Kelly, before I go, I have to ask you about yesterday, whether those cigarette butts in the ashtray were yours?"

"Mom, no way. They absolutely weren't." Surprisingly, her voice was extra adult. "Deb and Angie, they both smoke. They sat in our station wagon 'cause it's so old and has a cigarette lighter in the dashboard. They think it's cool. They only have an outlet plug in the Land Cruiser. So they used the ashtray. I knew you'd get mad."

Kate smiled. "Kel, I'm not mad."

"A little mad?"

"Nope." They smiled. Kate said, "I need to ask you, did Angie say anything about her father?"

"Her dad?" Kate nodded. "I don't think . . . no, she didn't. Why?"

Kate shrugged. "Somebody thinks they saw him in Nashville a couple of days ago. It might matter."

"She said he lives in Hawaii."

"So she did actually say something."

"Only that much, Mom. Nothing else. I have homework."

"There's just one other thing."

"Lots of math."

"I know. Just a couple more minutes. It was something you said yesterday at Fountain Square. You said 'Y'all'."

Kelly did not blink. Kate repeated, "You said it to Deb and Angie. You said, 'See y'all'."

Blank look. "Yes? So?"

Stay patient. Kate said, "Kelly, southerners say y'all. It's their language." She looked across the table. "That's what you said, 'y'all.'"

Then Kate awaited the moment of horrified repentance, a hand clapped to the mouth.

Instead, Kelly's face was quizzical. Boston born-and-bred Kelly stared and simply said, "So what?"

Kate felt her face flush. She fiddled with her fork. " 'So what' isn't good enough, Kelly. How could you say that?"

"Mom, don't get upset. It's no big deal."

"Of course it is. Words are a big deal. A very big

deal. I earn our living with words. I spend every work day working with words." Kate gestured around the new condo, pointed toward the living room, the plump wheat-yellow sofa with its cheerful throw pillows, the two comfy easy chairs, the coffee table with catalogs that poured in because the average income of households in their Nashville zip code signaled disposable income for cookware, leatherwear, linen ensembles.

"Kel, words make all this possible. My new job here in Nashville, I write, I edit—" But at that moment, Kate heard her voice heading high, a little shrill. Across from her sat Kelly, hair pulled back, her features open and lovely, eyes a bit glassy from a long day. But also puzzled at this big pronouncement from mother.

"I'll just say, Kelly, that in proper English, a yawl is a boat. You saw lots of them in New England. It's a sailboat specifically rigged . . ." But Kate stopped. She hadn't sailed much in recent years. Now she tried to remember what exactly defined a yawl. Something about the helm, whether the helm was fore or aft the main mast . . . ? She couldn't exactly recall. Kate cleared her throat and spoke a little too loudly. "The point is, in our home, in New England, the word refers to boats. At home, a yawl is a boat."

Kelly paused, hesitated. Her voice was low when at last she said, "Nashville's our home now."

And there it was, the nub and the rub. Boston born-and-raised, Kelly was now going over to the other side, to the South. That's what the "y'all" meant.

Kate said, "Kelly, only southerners say 'y'all.' It's their native language."

"So what? I can say it if I want to." Her lower lip moved to a pout. "There's no law against it. It's a free country and we're studying the First Amendment, free speech. And, you know—" Kelly's voice was defiant authority. "I think it sounds nice."

"Six months ago you hated 'y'all.' It was a southern saying you hated. You said so."

"Six months is a long time, Mom. Anyway, I can change my mind if I want to. It helps me fit in. I don't want to be the weird kid from Boston."

"But you are from Boston. It's something to be proud of. And you're going to summer camp in New England."

"I won't say it there."

It took Kate's breath away. North-South schism. And by design, and so poised, so self-assured. She simply sat while Kelly excused herself, murmuring "math." So babyhood's first words, "Mama" and "Doggie," and the cute sayings about the moon made of plastic—this all came down to "y'all." Daughter's first words from Dixie.

Silently she cleared, rinsed the dishes, soaked the pot, refrigerated the ample supply of leftovers.

And wished Sam were here. Tomorrow, tomorrow, and tomorrow.

Anyway, it was time for the condo meeting, and so Kate went, first changing into slacks. Wise move, to show proper neighborly respect. The Fred-and-Alice condo was heavy on flowered chintz, crystal, and porcelain figurines. Other neighbors included twenty-something Andy and Ben, who wore tennis whites and who might or might not be a couple, and Dr. Isabel McKlerk or McGurk, whose doctorate was apparently in education or dermatology, hard to tell which, and wearing a shiny green suit that made her look like a huge potted plant.

Everyone seemed to know Kelly and mentioned the mother-daughter resemblance. Kate smiled. Mitzy, confined to the kitchen behind a baby-gate, growled and yapped her disapproval of the whole thing.

The meeting came to order. It was crime on Fred's mind. Burglary was on the rise, a nearby house ru-mored stripped clean in broad daylight and a boy on his motorbike robbed, also in broad daylight. Fred liked the term, broad daylight, and outlined a plan while Alice brought a tray of coffee and strudel. Something must be done. High on his list were bomb-proof mailboxes.

Mailboxes? Andy thought security meant an electric gate, if it didn't cost too much.

Dr. Isabel suggested they take bids from various security services. "There's Ameritech. ADT . . ."

The coffee and strudel were served, the crust like a laminate. The group fell silent as back molars went to work.

"There's Fail-Safe and Brinks."

Mailboxes, said Fred again, not because of una-bombers but because the U.S. Postal Service remained the carrier of choice for the financial service industry nationwide.

Ben murmured something about monthly Social Security checks.

"Oh, Social Security, that's very far down the road for us," said hostess Alice, her voice in a brittle duet with Mitzy. "Far, very far into our own particular future."

Ben meant no offense.

"Fact is, financial transactions of every kind, dividends, mature instruments, your first-class stamp remains the key."

"So you think, new mailboxes?" Humble tone, Ben making amends for the Social Security age insult.

A starting point, Fred said. Bomb-proof, shatterproof. He passed around a security-products catalog. Everyone sipped their coffee, clear as a lake to the bottom of the cup.

Kate warned she would have to think carefully about major expenditures that might increase the monthly condo fees. Andy and Ben agreed. Fred said peace of mind was priceless. Dr. Isabel seconded that motion.

Double steel mailboxes became the modest start on which all could agree, could placate Fred and Alice. Another ten minutes of chat about the spring weather, polite refusals of seconds on strudel—and insistence that Kate take a piece for Kelly—and the meeting adjourned.

Back in her own unit, Kate called up, "Kel, want some dessert? Apple strudel from Mitzy's place. It's pretty chewy." Kelly appeared in a Celtics T-shirt-nightgown, the logo a reassuring New England message for mom, for herself, for both of them. It hung below her knees, America's contribution to pop culture, the XL shirts that half the female population wore as sleepwear. Kate thought this was Victoria's real secret.

Kelly went back upstairs, strudel in hand to spend the night e-mailing and phoning friends. Then Kate sat and reached into her canvas tote. It was just after nine, with a good hour of editing yet to do. Finish that cycle piece? No, first skim the slushpile folder, and fast. Shouldn't take more than fifteen, twenty minutes to skim the unsolicited manuscripts that came in daily. Maybe something usable from Arkansas? She opened the folder on her lap. A Milwaukee water department cashier on the Jenny Craig diet proposed a body-building diary that would climax in her entry in a triathlon. She was just now in a beginners' swim class at the Y. She hated all forms of exercise, which made for an interesting angle, she was sure, "a very unique inspiring standout article on overcoming great odds."

Pass on that.

Kate shuffled through. Health was big—sun protection, allergies. "Shingles: It's Not a Roof Job." Ick. One on antique tools, a maybe.

She was midway when she saw it. One plain sheet with stick-on letters, schoolroom letters. They were

iridescent blue, silly—and chilling. KATE GET OUT
OR DIE

That was it. She reread, looked around the room as
if a full-dress clown might pop out. KATE GET OUT
OR DIE. The lamplight gave a pearly sheen to each
letter.

Kelly's joke? No, not Kelly. Way too far out of
bounds. She shivered. First-grade stuff, bumpy letters
like crooked teeth—yet packed like a punch to the
jaw. She turned it over. Blank, nothing. She edged a
fingernail under the K on KATE. Peel-away letter.
ATE GET OUT OR . . . .

She put back the K.

Felt stupid.

Felt the violation. A pit viper in her tote bag. Her
sturdy L. L. Bean tote and the file folder vanilla ma-
nila so predictable and safe. She looked inside the
folder where she'd pulled the sheet. It was lodged between a query letter from Spokane and a proposal
from Fort Meyers, Florida. Nothing suggested the
sticker job had anything to do with either query—or
with anything in the entire folder.

Her palms prickled, her armpits too. She got up and
closed the blinds tighter and tried to think. This threat
was lodged in her bag since—at least Tuesday. Yes,
Tuesday after the talk with Sonny Burkendahl, she'd
grabbed the whole folder from her "in" basket and
then toted it around for the next two days, a low priority, an extra pound of paper dragged from office to
car to condo and back again.

And before that?

Before that, hard to say. The mail room was on
Fleetwood's lobby level, street level. Delia sometimes
opened routine mail, sorted it. So did the interns. So
did the temps. Nobody'd said a word about hate mail.

Kate stood with the sheet, squeezed her eyes shut to
picture the mailroom—the canvas sacks, plastic tubs,
separate departmental mail bins for Production, Sales

and Planning, Editorial. The whole area was fairly open. People came through, messengers, delivery men and women. Some were uniformed, others not. Delia greeted everybody.

The sweat from her fingertips now rippled the sheet, her prints forming a pattern along with the stick-on letters. Then it dawned on her, the sheet was not creased, had not been folded. Chances were, it was not mailed but slipped in broadside, and that meant it was local. It meant somebody got into the slushpile.

Was any Fleetwood staffer angry enough to paste up a crude threat and slip it into her batch mail?

Or was this linked to LilyAnn Page? To the Wyoming Steakhouse nails? To Brent's death?

Sticker shock.

She went into the kitchen, walked through the dining area, paused at the stairwell and listened for Kelly. Muffled sounds of music came from inside, tapes and CDs. Friday evening, no homework. Microwave popcorn and friends on the phone and more e-mail, the kids' online chat room.

What about the sanctity of the home?

The sanctity of the office?

She sat back down in the living room chair, too edgy to keep working. Where to put this thing? Not where Kelly could find it. Not where Kate would gravitate to it either. No drawers or cabinets. Not stuck inside a book.

She finally returned it to the folder. The best spot turned out to be the folder it came from. Last place Kelly'd go. Kate could deep-six it in her office files on Monday. Now she set about housecleaning her canvas tote, removed each and every file and paged through, sheet by sheet. A backlog of work, but everything was in order. No more surprises. It was nine-thirty when she got a cloth and Pledge and dusted every surface and vacuumed the first and second floors and mopped the kitchen floor and cleaned the stove and skied on

the NordicTrack for another half hour and then showered to soap off the clammy sweat.

So go to bed. Surrender. At 11:17 get into her own
XL tee, set the alarm for the video shoot and slide
under the covers and give up this day. Give it up to
the neighbor who saw security in mailboxes. Give it
up to Dottie who thought the stalker sighting was mistaken identity. To LilyAnn in seclusion. To Brent in
transit to a final resting place in the Shenandoah
Valley.

And to Kelly who whistled and hummed to records,
bright-eyed and awake as her mother stopped the der-
vish motion and sank down in bed and gratefully
drifted off.

CHAPTER ELEVEN

Saturday morning. The alarm, then the groggy shuffle to the bathroom mirror. Kate brushed her teeth, the face in the mirror not ready to see the light of day. In a terry robe, she went downstairs, opened blinds, put coffee on, reached outside for the newspaper and unfolded it as if a death threat or bomb might be tucked inside. No such thing. She came back up to dress. This being Nashville, makeup was required. Base and eyes, but skip the powder.

Jeans, is that what you wear to a video shoot? The temperature dropped and was forecast to climb into the fifties, the sky patchy gray and blue. Yes, jeans, and sneakers and a navy cable cotton sweater. Kate ran a brush through her hair and ate a bowl of shredded wheat with a banana. She grabbed a light jacket, filled a go-cup and wrote the sleeping Kelly a note. "— back by mid-late afternoon. Can drive you & friends tonight. Hope Sam gets in. Have great day!"

Great day. For Kate, it was a Waterfront vigil. Wasn't she really subbing for the late Brent, her role to be a one-woman alarm ready to cry "Wolf!"?

It was almost nine when she pulled into the blue roof complex. There was an assortment of cars, panel trucks, vans, TomKats catering. She walked around to the water side, saw the rope encircling the perimeter of the video area.

Across that rope was a hive of activity that must have started at dawn. A trailer sat on the outer edge,

perhaps the video company's headquarters. Closer in,
lights were rigged along a storefront strip and on scaffolding erected in fifteen-foot towers at the water's
edge. Cloth partitions in grays and lemon hung from
metal frames, and thick cables snaked everywhere on
the ground. Track was laid like a narrow-gauge rail
line on the concrete and the planking out toward the
dock, and a camera assembly was set to roll on a dolly.
Speakers were set up, cranes and booms, and huge
electric fans on wheels.

Crews were everywhere, mostly young white guys
climbing the scaffolds to install more lights, extend the
track, anchor the cloth partitions, assemble a platform.
Several wore tool belts. They moved on orders of a
rust-bearded man with a clipboard and a battery-
powered bullhorn. A denim-shirted stocky dark man
moved all over the set, touching base with everybody.
It all looked like a ballet approaching chaos.

Kate stood at the edge, recognized no one, ducked
under the rope. A heavyset crewman in a black T-shirt
with a notebook sprang to ask for identification. His
shirt pocket said Blue Sky Productions. Kate spelled
out her name. "You could check with Dottie Skip—"
But his finger had already stopped midway down a
page. He nodded her in and disappeared. She looked
around again. A vacant Waterfront store was opened
up. Folding chairs were set in groupings inside, and
the TomKats crew installed tables, covered them with
cloths and now iced down pails of soft drinks and
bottled waters and carried in baskets of croissants
and muffins.

Kate stood back against a plate glass storefront and
looked for the security detail. The notebook guy, did
he count? And where was that one Metro cop required by law?—yes, over there near the trailer, a thin
woman with long hair and her uniform cap askew. She
wore her gun, cuffs and radio. Her shirt was a little
bulky. Could it be body armor?

Then the trailer itself caught her attention. Its door opened suddenly to admit a man in a leather vest with a garment bag held high and a woman with hair in a dark topknot and a wooden box cradled in her arms. The door closed after them. It was probably LilyAnn's dressing room, then, not video headquarters.

Outside the rope, a small crowd of the curious were gathering, mostly kids in sports team shirts, the Bulls, the Braves. If Walter Sian emerged in this group, his pale moon face would be noticed instantly.

Then Turk Karcic marched in from a side breeze-way. His hair was buzzed to a quarter inch, his twills tucked into tightly laced combat boots. But instead of a shirt, he wore a cardinal-red sweater with gold shoulder boards. So much for undercover. He made his way over the cables toward Kate.

"How you doin'?"

She hesitated. Tell him about the paste-up threat in her tote bag? His shoulder boards gleamed. Forget it. She said, "Okay. Fine. I don't see any extra officers. That guy with the notebook, is he one of yours?"

He shook his head no. "He's with the video crew. Me, I got private security, Kate. Got the outer perimeter guys." He visored his hand across his forehead and scanned the distant fields. "They're all out there in the fields, on the tarmac, five guys. The parking lot's covered too. No uniforms. It's covert."

"You hired all five?"

"Off the night shift at the Farmer's Market. They work for Mallory at night, but today they work for us. They're on patrol. They'll reconnoiter. I'm handling everything. You enjoy the day. Leave everything to me." He moved off.

Sergeant Yukon.

Kate looked back at the trailer, surveyed the scene. No sign of Dottie or LilyAnn. The rust-beard mega-phone man said, "Hit it, Ollie. You ready? Hit it." Then lights came on, banks of blazing lights that

turned normal daylight bright as a pro ball diamond.
The dock now blazed superbright, the very spot where
Kate walked yesterday to lean over the railing. Yet
the megaphone man was not happy. He beckoned
Ollie for a consult, and Ollie in turn had a word with
the crew, a foursome who soon climbed like sailors
in rigging.

Fascinating, although it could be a very long day.
Already it was clear that a video shoot involved micro
steps, much fine tuning. At its uneventful best, it
would be tedious. Absorbing but tedious. No nasty
surprises, nothing lethal, that was the hope. Go ahead,
bore us.

But when would LilyAnn arrive? Noon? Maybe she
and Dottie were both in seclusion until the last minute. Kate looked around, suddenly startled by a windy
roar—the fans being tested, blades whirling big as pro-
pellers. Kate thought of Sam, wished . . .

She stepped into the catering area. A fruit bowl had
appeared, melon and berries. Coffee service too.
"Take what you want. We'll be bringing lunch out
at eleven-thirty." The caterers in collar T-shirts were
brisk, cheerful.

At that moment sound equipment blared. More
testing. It was the voice of LilyAnn. ". . . against the
world, against the worrlllld—" That voice, the
haunting tone that went to the very marrow. The tone
quality was darker now, the voice worn from the
years, scraped by life's undertow—richer. The woman
had a genius to this day. To keep that voice
protected . . . Kate turned to look at the female cop.
She was yawning.

The recording of LilyAnn now burst on and off over
and over again, softer and louder, treble up, bass
down. It could probably be heard over a radius of half
a mile. Was it a siren song for Walter Sian lurking
out in the fields? Would it flush him like wild game

to a scent? ". . . against the worllld . . . against . . .
against . . . against . . ."

Feeling edgy, Kate looked out through the plate
glass across the water, which was rippled by a light
breeze. Birds flew in a wedge, heading north for the
season. Nothing amiss. She scooped some fruit into a
plastic bowl and took a bite of honeydew. It could be
one of those days when you eat the time away.

Maybe a word with, a closeup look at, that cop.
Take a little offering. She put down her bowl, grabbed
a Pepsi, a water, an apple muffin and very carefully
stepped around scaffolding and equipment to the spot
where the uniformed officer leaned her hip against the
trailer. Her nameplate read G. Toffatt, and she wore
smoky dark sunglasses. Kate said, "Good morning,
Officer." G. Toffatt gave the standard curt smile and
hi doubtless learned at the academy. Kate introduced
herself as one of LilyAnn Page's staff. "I thought you
could use a snack."

"Thanks." Officer Toffatt's dark lenses tilted toward
the muffin, though she reached only for the Pepsi and,
to her credit, kept watch over Kate's right shoulder.
She was slim through the hips and shoulders, but her
chest and sides definitely had the padded look of body
armor, an unusual degree of self-protection for such
detail as this—unless the investigation of Brent's death
led to this site, to this very cast of characters. Or unless Turk had led Officer Toffatt to believe that Walter Sian might be armed and dangerous.

Or unless a shootout in these rookie years moved
Toffatt to reach for the body armor after she hooked
her bra every single workday.

Kate said, "This is a specially hard time, Officer.
You must know LilyAnn Page's people are on alert
for the stalker released from prison last month."

Nod yes.

"And you probably know Metro police are investigating the fatal shooting of one of Ms. Page's band

members just three days ago." G. Toffatt pulled the
Pepsi tab and drank as if combining a yes nod with
thirst quenching. If only Kate could see the eyes behind the lenses. Kate said. "I understand robbery is
not completely established as the motive in that
death."

The glasses angled in her direction. She said, "We'll
be ready for all eventualities, ma'am."

Standard cop talk to civilians. Kate unscrewed the
water cap and drank herself. The old police reporter
days were long gone, but things hadn't changed that
much, Boston to Nashville. Good old blue wall. Not
a chink, not a ray of light.

She sighed, stepped away and was back at the catering area when abruptly the trailer door opened. Out
came Dottie and the two girls. So they'd been inside
the whole time. She waved, watched Deb and Angie
scamper forward around the equipment as if it were
their playground. In very tight jeans with bare midriffs
they zigzagged and hopped. "Hi, Ms. Banning. Is
Kelly here?"

"No, not today." Kate was watching Dottie pick her
own way across the wires carefully, head-to-toe in
black. She said to Angie and Deb, "Kelly has band
practice."

"Hey, too bad. She could hang with us. We might
even be in the video. Mick said so."

"Who's Mick?"

"The director. He's pretty cool." Deb had a new
tangerine colored manicure. She wore a checkered
backpack over one shoulder. Angie had a walkman
with earphones around her neck.

Kate said, "Who are you listening to?"

"Queen Latifah." She added, "Hip-hop."

Deb grinned. "Anything but country music, right,
Angie?"

They giggled. "Hey, we'll see ya." They moved to

the muffins, selected one each, grabbed cans of Coke
and Pepsi, fled.

"Kate, g'morning."

"How are you, Dottie?"

"I came out to get some fruit for Lily."

"So she's in that trailer?"

"We've all been cooped up in there since eight-
thirty. Vito just brought Lily's clothes. Camille will do
her makeup soon as she has a bite to eat. These croissants any good?"

"I didn't try one."

Dottie scooped fruit, picked muffins, shrugged and
added a croissant to a plate. Maybe this was the moment to tell Dottie about the paste-up threat. Maybe.

Dottie looked around. "Well, so far, so good."

And maybe not. Kate said, "I see the cop's on
duty."

"Since before eight. Turk gave her the stalker
photo. She's on the lookout."

"He said his men are out in the parking lot and in
the fields."

"Big load off my mind, I can tell you that. And the
girls ought to be okay, plenty of boys to flirt with
during the down time. I made Deb bring her homework. Wishful thinking."

The girls indeed had gathered at a spot where guitar
cases and drums were piled. A lanky man in a soccer
shirt and a muscular one in a tank top hauled drum
cases onto a platform built to look like a dock. Kate
said, "That drum kit over there, isn't that the band
setting up?"

Dottie nodded. "Can you believe it, all that effort
and cost just for a few shots of the Iron Works in the
video." She added, "That's Farley and Steve. Just
watch Deb and Angie make fools of themselves with
those two. My Deb's got the hots for Farley, I know
the signs. Been going on since last winter. He's such

a fix-it guy, he does odd jobs at the house sometimes.
I never thought my own daughter—"

"Are both of those men on LilyAnn's road crew?"

Dottie nodded. "*Men* is right. Those guys are in
their twenties, way too old for high school girls."

"Dottie, I'm trying to figure out the video scene.
Would you just help me for a minute." She waited for
the woman's reluctant attention. "To sort out who's
who, Dottie, are production people and the artist's
people both involved?"

"Uh, not usually this much. Our road crew guys
wouldn't be here ordinarily. A production assistant
would help unload drums and guitars. For today,
though, Lily wanted to hire Farley and Steve, and I
think it's because of Brent. She didn't say it in so
many words, but I think she wants familiar faces
around. It's the comfort factor. Now if we can just get
Lily *in*to this."

"Isn't she in the trailer getting ready?"

"I mean into the music."

"To sing? Won't the band play?"

Dottie stared. "Kate, you don't know anything
about videos, do you?"

Her cheeks got warm. "So she'll lip synch, is that
it? The band will pretend to play?"

"She'll sing along with herself while they shoot.
That's why they're testing the sound system. She'll
sing along to her own recording." Dottie bit her lip.
"When I say in, I mean involved. Mick says Pam Tillis
needed thirteen takes. I tell you, Lily won't go near
thirteen, not with her arm and her state of mind. She's
a pro's pro, but there are limits." She added, "At the
moment Mick's not helping."

"The director?"

"Producer and director, Mick MacIver. He's from
Chicago. He wins awards, and Lily loves his work. But
now all of a sudden he wants to shoot her arm in
the cast."

Dottie picked up two bottled waters by the necks and shook her head. "A thousand promises to keep her broken arm out of every frame, and suddenly today he thinks it might be artistic to have footage of her cast. *Artistic.* I'm in the middle of it. As usual." She sighed. "At least we've got lots of security. Though why Metro Police sent a baby girl rookie, I'll never know."

"Who handled it?"

"Turk."

"I see." Moving off beside Dottie, Kate scanned the scene, saw Turk talking on his cell phone, the field commander.

She looked up at the light rigs. Could a crew member be ready "accidentally" to drop a tool from the scaffold onto LilyAnn Page's head? Could a live wire be readied somewhere here, its voltage lethal? She felt her chest tighten. She said, "Is Kip here? Any of his crew?"

Dottie shook her head no. "Kip's got a couple guys out at the Fairgrounds working on Lily's Fan Fair booth. Almost had to call him out to the house. A pipe burst in the kitchen. Fortunately Turk had some wrenches in his Jeep. We'll have to get the plumber out."

"How about those kitchen knives? They show up?"

Dottie shifted her shoulders uneasily. "I told Marie to replace them. We even looked out by the pool. Billy D checked his archery targets in case somebody decided to practice knife throwing." She shook her head again. "They just vanished into thin air. They'll probably show up the minute we get new ones, isn't that how it goes? I mean, why would somebody take off with kitchen knives?"

Kate looked Dottie in the eye. "A boning knife and a carving knife," she said. "You tell me."

Now Dottie's cheeks flushed. "I better get back to the trailer. 'Dressing room vehicle,' I should say.

That's what the budget line item says. One-day rental, over twelve hundred bucks. Kate, keep an eye out."

"It's almost a blind eye, Dottie. If I just knew a few more basics of a video shoot—"

She paused. "Tell you what, I'll ask Mick to send one of his interns over. Check in with me later."

Momentarily the trailer door opened to receive Dottie and the morning rations. It occurred to Kate, she might have offered to help carry. Deb and Angie, she noticed, were still talking to Farley and Steve. The one in the soccer shirt—Farley?—stepped close to Deb, smiled, opened his mouth as she fed him muffin bites. Angie was lighting up a cigarette.

"Kate? Are you Kate?"

She turned. "Yes I am." Before her stood a young woman in a royal blue ball cap, yellow pullover and khaki shorts. She was fresh-faced, toned up. "I'm Devon. I'm an intern. Mick says you need, like, an interpreter. I'm yours for twenty minutes. Anything you want to know." She checked her watch, which looked submersible to thousands of feet.

Kate said, "So which one's Mick? Is he the man with the bullhorn?"

"Oh no. Mick's dark-haired, there in the denim shirt. The bullhorn's Andy, the director of photography. See, he's telling the gaffer to add heads, and the best boy sees to that."

"Wait. Heads? You mean crewmen?"

She laughed. "Sorry, no disrespect. A head is a light. Ollie's the gaffer—the lighting tech. He tells the best boy to get the head—light—and he does. Like the electric gets the cable. It's a one-day shoot, no rehearsal, so it has to be very organized."

Kate nodded. At that moment a small group in streetwear—no, more like costumes—emerged from a storefront that had brown paper taped over the windows. A short middle-aged white woman in a pink plastic raincoat followed a dark man with fine fea-

tures—Pakistani?—in a sweater vest, with two women
in saris and sandals and a dark man in a long cream-
colored robe and hat, perhaps Nigerian, in the rear.
There was makeup on their faces, the white woman
very white, the Pakistani man in face powder of deep
caramel, the Nigerian deepened to ebony. *Against the
World,* was this "world" global, the United Nations of
LilyAnn Page?

Kate said, "Are those extras?"

"They're actors, Kate. For a one-day shoot, you
can't take a chance on extras. Casting is a big, big
deal even for small parts." Kate watched the denim-
shirted Mick move in to consult with the group. Devon
said, "That's him. That's Mick."

"And he'll coach the whole cast?"

"He'll direct. He's the pumping heart, the captain
of the ship." She said it so proudly. "He's giving the
actors their cues. Then he'll check film stock with the
cinematographer, and that's Jerry. They have twelve
loads of Bolex. They're mainly using two Bolex hand-
held cameras. They'll shoot maybe five, six thousand
feet of film today. They'll shoot thirty frames a second.
It slows everything down for that smooth, dreamy feel.
Also, Mick wants that grainy, aggressive close-up look.
He came out here last week and shot 35mm. stills so
he could plan the day."

Kate nodded. "Tell me more," she said pleasantly.
"Just pretend you're explaining a ball game to a
foreigner."

Devon chuckled. "Well," she said, "in a country
music video, the close-up is everything, *everything* because the artist and audience are so close. This is
not MTV."

"So the country artist agrees to these close-ups."

"No, wait." She anchored hands on hips like an
aerobic instructor. "Start at the beginning," she said.
"First, the label makes a deal for the video. See, this
is Mick's company, Blue Sky Productions. He pitches

the concept to the label, not to the artist. They set the budget based on projected unit sales. This particular video," she said, "it's on a real tight budget."

"You mean low."

She looked at her watch. "Well, Mick went after it anyway. He pitched a great concept. There's always a basic concept, and it rules. This video, *Against the World,* he sees it as inspired by the classic film, *On the Waterfront,* and this famous photographer with rich texturing, Evans Walker."

"Walker Evans."

She blinked. "Okay. Anyway, it's a lot of black-and-white. Mick's concept is courage. In today's world there's a hunger for courage. He'll intercut a montage of courage images from old TV. I mean, Mick himself won't. Some place in Chicago transfers old kinescopes to film. That's postproduction. This will be, probably, a fourteen-hour day. The guys started at four this morning. Mick wanted to work with this particular artist. I hear she used to be tops."

Kate bit her tongue. She said, "The camera equipment, it's under lock and key when no one's using it?"

Devon gave Kate a look. She said, "The Bolex is Mick's pride. He's very careful with the equipment, it's a big investment."

"And Mick does still photography too, like the shots of this location?"

"Some, sure."

"Have you ever seen him use a Nikon?"

"A Nikon? I don't know." Her voice was edged in caution. "Lots of people use Nikons. Why? Why ask that?" Devon squinted, angled her neck, reread Kate's face. "Hey, my twenty minutes is about up. Now you know about the lights, the cast, the cameras, the concept, the schedule." She held up one hand to count off finger by finger. "So Kate, anything else on your mind?"

Kate looked over the scene. Turk was on his cell

phone, Angie and Deb with Steve and Farley in a cloud of cigarette smoke, the trailer like a submarine with hatches closed. Murder on her mind, the clues too few. One Bren Ten slug from Brent Landreth's neck, one scratched lens cap scavenged from a poison ivy patch. A sudden notion that video producer Mick MacIver might alternate Bolex with Nikon and so be yet another suspect? Talk about tapping into Kate's own frustration. Grabbing at suspects, snatching at straws. She said, "Maybe one thing, Devon. All this is Mick's company—" The intern nodded. "So all these workers, they're his employees?"

"Oh, no." She laughed a bit too brightly. "Some are the artist's, for instance Miss Page's band and a couple of her road crew. And Blue Sky hires the makeup and wardrobe people the artist likes best, so they're basically Miss Page's too. But the lighting company, the sound equipment, they're, like, Blue Sky's subcontracts. Look, I better get back now. I'll be around if you have more questions. Bye."

"Bye." Her thanks died in the roar of the huge fans.

Now what? Kate looked at this choreographed scene. So it was basically an odd lot of sub- and sub-sub contracts, practically day laborers. They climbed, they carried, they did heavy lifting. But were any of them under subcontract to kill LilyAnn Page today? Any of them secretly working for Keith Grevins's "productions"? Or Kip's? Or Myers Fatenza's? Could Bucky Sibbett have a political buddy willing to commit terrorist acts to topple the governing queen of country music?

And was there an apprentice here who pasted up death threats with stickers? Who might be assigned to arrange a special bonus "accident" for Kate Banning?

She scanned the water, the new green foliage of the fields beyond. The answers were blowing on the breeze.

And across the set stood G. Toffatt, who doubtless

spent her days checking burglary false alarms, rowdy neighbors, blocked traffic signals. This overtime detail was a nice perc to stretch out a dismal paycheck. She'd keep an eye out for the nondescript face of Walter Sian, but what she knew of Brent Landreth probably came from TV news.

Why that body armor?

At that moment Toffatt straightened up because Mick himself called out, "We're ready." His denim sleeves were rolled, and he tapped at the trailer door. "Ready." Toffatt took a position alongside the door. There were footfalls, and down came LilyAnn Page herself.

In floor-length off-white silks and dark glasses, with her hair down, she looked fragile, breakable, less like a star in disguise than a petite woman who'd gone blind. A thick cast and sling held her right arm, and she put out her left for escort. Kate saw Turk lurch forward in her direction but stop as Mick took her arm to walk her to the set. Toffatt followed a few steps behind as police escort. Dottie brought up the rear. For a moment all seemed stopped for a reigning queen of country music in the opening ceremonies.

Kate moved close enough to see and hear. Lily-Ann's makeup was heavy around the eyes, and she wore a cluster of large silver rings on her left hand and dull silver disc earrings that almost matched the skunk streak. The off-white flowing silk contrasted with the hard lines of the Waterfront complex. The makeup woman with the topknot, Camille, removed the star's dark glasses, which were entrusted to Devon, who casually pocketed them in her shorts. "The windswept look," Kate heard Mick say. "Let's first walk through it. Think Brando and Eva Marie Saint at the Millennium. Think grit. Let's have the fans."

The low roar began as LilyAnn paced off the route while her hair blew and the silk sleeves fluttered. Lights blazed against the storefronts. On cue, torn papers were sifted from big bags by a crew helper and blown into camera range by the fans. Was this a wind-blown gutter effect, simulated trash? Yes.

Two cameramen had moved in close to LilyAnn's body and swept along every contour from the ankles on up. Somehow Kate thought of a strip search.

But something was not right, something about the star's walk. Mick ordered the cameras turned off, then stood beside her, talked, gestured, and then walked back and forth, back and forth as if teaching her how to skate. Then she walked by herself, the cast on her arm half hidden. And walked once again.

But Mick shook his head, took LilyAnn off to the side and walked with her some more, and then signaled for the costumed cast to walk the same space while LilyAnn watched. Forward came the pink rain-coat, the two saris, sweater vest, Nigerian robe—all moving together, not just walking but striding. They had presence. They were actors onstage. Mick ordered a cameraman to film them.

But when LilyAnn tried it, she again looked small, a petite pedestrian. Mick signaled a stop. Camille came forward with her wood box of cosmetics to brush more powder on LilyAnn's face, to touch up her lipstick and add blush. She stepped back. Then more walking. More starts and stops. Another makeup moment.

Then the miracle, the music. Dottie whispered to Mick, who cued the sound system. LilyAnn seemed suddenly to come alive. "Destiny's seasons—" she sang along with the recording. Her voice spoke the soul's ache.

> "—continental drift,
> The planets' reasons why you're free
> With*out* me, without me—
> Against the world . . ."

She seemed magnified, transformed, singing herself

into the identity of the beleaguered, forlorn and love-
lorn yet larger-than-life woman who believed down to
her deepest, innermost self that it was she—she and
she alone—who stood so bravely against the world.

The music somehow made time pass and yet stand
still. The cameras rolled, fans blew, sacks emptied out
their fake trash, which piled up against the plate glass.
LilyAnn sang her song over and again when Mick directed the cast of actors to walk behind her, alongside
and around her, all the while the cameras were un-
loaded, reloaded, with Devon helping to label and
stow the spent film packs.

Now Mick himself took up a camera and shot high
and low, close, closer, closest. LilyAnn seemed oblivi-
ous of the lenses, dwelling inside the world of the
song. Her walking tour an hour ago was just that,
walking, because she was not an actor. The music,
however, was another story. Singing, she entered the
role of the ballad. She became the song.

The day's momentum was now palpable. Kate
looked around. It was warming up a bit, the sky still
a blue-gray mix, the water a blue-brown stirred by the
breeze. The cameras focused solely on LilyAnn, while
the lighting crew in their tool belts stood back snack-
ing and sipping, yet attentive. The TomKats caterers
removed the mounds of leftover muffins and quietly
carried big foil-covered pans from their truck to the
tables.

As LilyAnn sang, the cast of actors, with their filming finished for now, went to the buffet, filled plates
and retreated into the storefront and disappeared behind the brown paper that covered the plateglass. The
Iron Works band members sat on their "dock" platform, the drummer twirling a stick through his fingers
like a baton. Angie and Deb perched on a fake piling,
Deb leaning back against Farley's legs.

Dottie stationed herself by the trailer, her head
turning from LilyAnn to her daughter and back again.

No sign of Turk. Officer Toffatt moved to the rope
line to tell the crowd of kids to keep back and keep
the noise down.

LilyAnn, all the while, sang her song over and over
as the fans blew her hair and her silks. ". . . aching,
aching . . . now you're free, without meeee . . ."

Mick now backed up to take longer shots, the Bolex
in hand as he passed close by Kate, the side of his
face glistening and the back of his denim shirt soaked
with sweat. So Blue Sky meant sweat equity.

Then a break. It was nearly 1:00. Mick gestured,
and the fans and sound system stopped. Silenced, Lily-
Ann Page once again became a diminished figure.
Devon appeared with her sunglasses, and Dottie went
immediately to her side, and Mick too. They walked
her back to the trailer. Toffatt shadowed them. A
TomKats woman followed with a stack of box lunches,
and Camille sat with her makeup chest and a water
bottle on the trailer steps.

Kate turned. Deb and Angie stubbed out cigarettes
on the platform and then joined Steve and Farley and
the Iron Works in the lunch line. Andy took up his
bullhorn to order the lighting readjusted. The tool
belts began to climb the scaffolds.

The focus for the afternoon's shooting, Kate saw,
would now shift. It would be LilyAnn "against the
world" on the ten-foot dock extending over the water.
She would make her way to the end of it, probably
turn and then, with her back to the railing, sing her
title song another half-dozen times against a background expanse of water. Maybe the costumed cast
would join her there. Trust the magic of the camera.
A silty manmade lake at a failed shopping mall would
look like the high seas. A few costumed bit players
might impart a global message.

But the whole thing felt more or less safe. Maybe
that was the seduction, that the video shoot would
pass as planned. Kate strained to see the light crew

up in the scaffolding. Three young guys and a woman—would any of them loosen a "head" to fall on LilyAnn's own? She looked down at the cables, which appeared intact, encased in thick rubber. Could a live, exposed wire be snaked out to that dock, ready to strike? She gazed at the water as if a dorsal fin might cut the surface and circle.

Just then her nostrils prickled. It was a strong after-shave, spicy, clove. She turned. Farley stood arm in arm with Dottie's Deb. He held a thick sandwich. His coarse dark hair was slicked against his head. "Lotsa food," he said, his mouth stuffed. Deb said "Get yourself something, Ms. Banning. It's all free."

Free lunch?

"Thanks, Deb. I guess your mom's still in the trailer?"

"Where else?" She rolled her eyes. "Lily prob'ly needs my mom to cut up her food."

"Because of her broken arm."

"Just like a baby." Deb looked at Farley. "Waa-waa, just like a little doll baby. Waa."

The two laughed and moved away. Kate stepped into the lunch line. There was salad, tortellini, cold cuts.

Someone said, "No little lamb chops?"

"Sweetheart, on this budget, you're doin' good to get bologna."

Uneasy, embarrassed silence.

Kate ate her sandwich quickly, found the restroom, came back out. The Blue Sky notebook guy was telling the crowd of kids not to push against the rope. All faces in that crowd were dark. No stalker. Toffatt stood by the trailer, at the moment biting into her own sandwich. She seemed to be sticking close to LilyAnn. Good. Camille, now gone from the trailer steps, was probably inside repairing the star's makeup for the afternoon.

Which came up fast because the break proved short.

Ollie had satisfied the rust beard with the megaphone that the lights were good to go, and the crew snapped to. Mick once again went calling at the trailer door to escort LilyAnn out. The ritual of the sunglass removal was performed again. The Iron Works settled in on their platform for their own filming.

In moments, LilyAnn walked the dock with Mick, back and forth while the banks of lights on the scaffolding blazed down on wood and water. Kate looked around for Turk, who was nowhere in sight. Maybe he'd gone to the parking lot, perhaps to the fields to be sure his platoon was on alert. She looked out. No sign of the cardinal-red sweater. In silence LilyAnn paced off the steps with Mick.

Midway out the third or fourth time, the two had a close, whispered conversation, with Mick's lips against LilyAnn's ear as if no other soul were present. Mick MacIver's body language spoke seduction, and in moments he gently rearranged LilyAnn's silks to expose the cast on the singer's arm. So "artistic" won out.

All set. Mick himself took up a Bolex. LilyAnn looked ready to walk the full length of the dock in three-quarter profile while Mick filmed every step. The opening bars of "Against the World" filled the air.

> . . . rust out, burnout, gone
> Out of bounds. I take my stand
> Against the world . . .

Once again, her very presence seemed to magnify itself as she swept forth in regal slow motion down the dock. Mick halfway crouched with the camera alongside, and Kate saw the costumed cast had been cued too, to come forth and approach the dock as a track-mounted camera rolled along, filming.

LilyAnn was nearly at the end of the dock now, and

here came the Nigerian, the Pakistani and pink rain-
coat ever so slowly.

> "Against the world, against the world . . ."

The two saris too, but between them someone new,
a man, round headed, his face a muddy gray. Another
ethnic? Racial ID? But his features looked so bland,
undistinguished. He moved with the actors, wedged
between the raincoat and the sweater vest. Yet his
walk was different from theirs, ordinary. It was not an
actor's walk. He wore boots and a sash and sword.
That round, bland face. A half-pirate with sword in
mudface.

Beneath that mud, something familiar. Generic but
familiar, a Charlie Brown type. Something stirred in
Kate's memory. The sword. *"You will feel it like a
scimitar dividing you through the heart and marrow."*
Step by step he got closer, nearer, reached for the
sword. *"I sculpt your flesh and blood and bones as
my own . . ."*

Kate jumped, leaped forward to the dock, to the
actors. "Walter Sian! It's Walter Sian! Catch him!
Hurry, catch—!" She shoved the saris, jammed her
shoulder, saw the pirate flinch, draw back. She
screamed, tried to scream.

> "Against the world, against the world without
> meeee . . ."

The pirate was running, running free. Heading for
the rope. Under it. The crowd parted. He was slipping
out. "Get him! He's running!" The actors had scattered. Kate lunged, tripped on the planks, was grabbed
by Nigeria and the Blue Sky T-shirt. "The stalker!"
She screamed it. "Stalker! Stalker! Get him!"

But the music shut her down as LilyAnn leaned
back against the dock railing now, still singing to her-

self, eyes closed, her cast thrust forward. The camera
lens ate her up—"against the world, against—"

"The stalker! For Chrissake—"

Just then, suddenly, the dock railing itself went
slant. It leaned, it moved, gave way. LilyAnn herself
tilted back. "The stalker!" LilyAnn was falling, her
free arm a windmill in the air. And Kate's own arms,
reaching out, were suddenly pinned back in a hard
grip. It was Officer Toffatt grabbing her as she
watched LilyAnn Page, unsupported, her arm and cast
flailing. Then toppled, falling backward and down into
the water. The cameras rolled in the next seconds,
filmed a cardinal-red streak in a racing dive plunging
for rescue, splashing, light gleaming on gold shoulder
boards.

Frozen, caught in the police grip, the handcuffs
snapping around her wrists, Kate saw two things. One
was Walter Sian running free. The other was Turk
Karcic's feet. The bodyguard sprang into the lake fully
clothed from shoulder boards down, but the lingering
memory was his pale bare feet.

CHAPTER TWELVE

"Calamity," Dottie said. "Fiasco. How many words for disaster?"

Kate kept silent. A shaft of late afternoon sunlight came through the screen door of the office cabin. The fluorescents were on too. Dottie's black leather chair creaked as she rolled it out from behind her desk and sat down. Kate was on a stack chair.

"Kate, I'm humoring you against my better judgment. You couldn't pick a worse time. You know that."

"I know."

"And I'm really sorry about the handcuffs. It was a simple mistake."

"I realize that."

"A misunderstanding." Kate nodded. "That rookie did the best she could."

She nodded again.

"It was that mud that threw everybody off." Dottie pushed back her short hair. "The mudface." She paused. "You're sure it was him? Totally sure?"

Kate hoped her own stare was cold as ice.

"Okay, okay. Sorry. The cops really put you through it, and I'm sure you're twenty/twenty on that. You could pass a polygraph with flying colors."

"It's not about lying, Dottie. It's not about mistaken identity either."

"Just sorry it took so long to straighten out."

"So am I. The mix-up gave Walter Sian at least an extra hour."

"Oh, they'll find him for sure. They'll really be on the lookout now. All those patrol cars, they'll radio every cop and sheriff's department in middle Tennessee. The McMinnville police are on high alert. Everybody saw that sword. The actors, we have eyewitnesses galore. They'll put him away again. If we just had any idea how that s.o.b. got onto the set, sneaking into that bunch of costumes. All those men on security too. And that sword . . . Turk has no idea how he got in."

"Close call."

"Nevertheless, Kate—" Dottie looked stern, ready to point a finger. "Your timing's just terrible. Why force us to have a talk with Turk now? Why not let him be? We all have to fly up to Virginia for Brent's funeral tomorrow, and we all need the rest. I finally got Lily settled down. Billy D took the girls for Dairy Queens. Fact is, she'd have drowned. Drowned." Dottie closed her eyes. "I can see her fall backwards into that lake . . ."

"Dottie, it's four feet at the deepest point. You heard Mick MacIver's assistant say—"

"You can drown in a bathtub, Kate. Lungs can fill up from a one-quart saucepan. I close my eyes, and that's all I see as clear as day. If it hadn't been for Turk, if Turk hadn't been on the spot—" She shuddered.

Kate kept silent. Her watch read 4:32. Turk Karcic was two minutes late. Something buzzed. Fly? No, a wasp up near the rafters. Then an engine outside, a slammed door, footsteps.

He knocked and entered at the same time. "Took time to change out of my wet clothes," he said, striding in fresh fatigues. He reversed a chair and straddled it. The combat boots were back on, spit shined. His chest was puffed out.

"Ladies."

Dottie beamed. "You earned yourself a medal this afternoon, Turk. Hero of the hour. I know Lily will want to thank you personally when she's rested up. Oh, and you too, Kate."

"What I'm there for," he said, not looking at Kate.

The wasp circled, settled on a rafter beam. "Mud dauber," he said.

"What?"

Dottie said, "It's the season."

"Builds its nest out of mud. Here—" Turk went to the fireplace, chose a shovel from the poker and tongs, then stood on Dottie's desk, waited for the wasp to settle, leaped up, whacked it, watched it fall. He tweezed it carefully with his fingers and deposited the wasp among the newest wrappers and peelings in the fireplace. Kate thought of Brent Landreth helping Dottie clean it out just days ago. No more. Rest in peace.

Dottie beamed as if to promise a second medal for valor in combat with a wasp. Turk straddled the chair again.

And Kate was now set to rain on his parade. Drenching downpour on his tickertape. If only Dottie had half an open mind. She said, "Turk, I asked Dottie to get you to come over here. I didn't want to wait."

"It's okay."

"I thought we ought to have a talk without any delay. I told Dottie it's very important."

"Hey, I'm cool."

Kate nodded. She said, "Just a few things about today's video shoot."

"Hey, you want to talk some more about that stalker, Kate, it's okay with me. My position is, thanks to our security detail, we really stopped him cold. Otherwise he could've tried a water approach. He could've tried rooftop. I admit he breached security and remains at large, but we narrowed his options. In security terms, the mission is an operational success." He gave a rugged grin.

Kate paused a moment and then said, "Actually, Turk, I'm not asking you here to talk about Walter Sian. At least not now. I'm more interested in Lily-Ann's fall from the dock. That was an amazing rescue."

"All in the line of duty." His chest expanded another inch.

"And you were filmed."

He shrugged. "Cameras caught it all, I guess. They say cameras don't lie. One picture's worth a million words."

Dottie leaned forward. "Kate, let's save some time here. We know all about the filming. Mick told us. You heard it, I heard it. The cameras caught the whole thing. We'll leave it all in Mick's hands."

Kate was watching the way Turk's chest pressed against the twill of his fatigues. She said, "So Blue Sky Productions will edit the footage—everything filmed up to the point when LilyAnn fell and you jumped in—"

"Dove in."

"—and brought her to shore. *Against the World* will be a video created from footage including the rescue."

Turk nodded. "Anything for Miss LilyAnn. If they want to use me diving in and pulling her to shore, if they think that'll help her out, it's theirs. It's free. I promised to sign a waiver. I give up any claim. I'm in security, not movie acting."

Kate nodded. Dottie jiggled her foot.

Kate said, "If I could just ask you a couple things, Turk?"

"Fire away."

"That dock railing—how do you think it happened to fall?"

He shrugged. "Prob'ly rotted."

"But you were out at The Waterfront to inspect. I saw you two days ago. We waved to one another. Didn't you inspect the dock?"

"I paced it off. I looked around, got the big picture, like if a sniper could take up a rooftop position. That kind of thing. I couldn't check out every board foot, every crack in the cement." He cupped a palm over each knee. "Security doesn't operate that way."

"I see." Kate wet her lips. She said, "I notice you have an interesting background, Turk. I understand you worked in Kansas City last winter?"

"Right. Like I told Dottie. So what?"

"So there's a complication. Dottie might not know you were forced out of your job at Excalibur. And forced out of the Marines too."

Dottie's eyes widened. Turk's gaze narrowed, dazed but sharp. "What's this all about?"

"Yes, Kate, what is going on here? Turk doesn't need this. We know him from Opryland."

"Then I'll change the subject. Let's talk about rescue." Turk nodded. Dottie looked exasperated. "Somebody has to be endangered before a rescue can occur, right? Like a building's got to be burning before the firefighters lift people off the roof." He nodded. Dottie heaved a loud sigh. Kate spoke clearly, steadily. "And LilyAnn had to fall into the lake before you could come to the rescue."

"Yeah, sure."

"And you knew that the video crew would film her on that dock."

"Sure I knew that. Made it part of the security plan."

"So then, Turk, wasn't the best rescue opportunity at The Waterfront that dock with the railings?"

"I don't get you."

"I'll make it clear. Those railings—they weren't loose, were they, Turk?—not until you loosened the bolts."

"That's crazy."

"With the wrenches in your Jeep?"

"I got a whole toolbox."

"Now Kate, you can't slander Turk—"

"Because, Turk, you planned to rescue LilyAnn Page on camera, didn't you? That dive, the red sweater—the camera was rolling, and you looked great. Just the way you planned."

He looked over at Dottie, who frowned and blinked but now stayed silent.

"You see, I was on that very same dock too, Turk. Last Wednesday I leaned my full weight over that railing, and I'm heavier than LilyAnn. That wood was steady as a rock. It didn't budge. Not an inch."

He sat up straight. "Hey Dottie, she's pissed 'cause the cop cuffed her. You gonna let her gang up on me?"

"Turk's right, Kate. We're all upset. Give him the benefit of the doubt." Though somehow Dottie's voice now lacked full conviction.

Kate leaned toward him. "Glad to give benefit of the doubt, except for one thing, Turk. Your bare feet. You took your boots off for the dive. It takes time to unlace combat boots. Preparation time."

"What's your point?"

"I think you staged that rescue."

His face was flushed. "You're nuts." He began to pace, to strut. "Who do you think you are? I oughta get physical, shut your big mouth." He stopped inches from Kate's face and socked a fist into his open palm. "How'd you like your nose fixed?"

Kate sat very still. She said, "Just tell me, Turk— The woman judge in Missouri, the one you rescued. Dottie tells me you'll testify at her trial."

"So what?"

"So suppose we were to look into that story. Suppose I contact Excalibur."

He socked again. "Hell you will."

"And have another talk with Pat."

His thighs flexed, and his shoulders shifted. But now the chest contracted. "What is this? What the hell?"

Kate's voice was quiet and low. "What this is, Turk, is the end of the line. I think your security deal with LilyAnn Page's management is going to end here and now."

"The hell."

They looked at Dottie. All in black, the appeals judge. She did not jiggle her foot but stared at Turk, at Kate, her mouth open, eyes wide. She said, "Turk, what do you say?"

"Crap, my word against hers." He tossed his head. "What'd she ever do for LilyAnn Page?" Yet his shoulders hunched, his chest shrunk as if the air escaped.

Kate said, "Let's just suppose we decide to file a complaint, Turk. You'd face charges of criminal liability."

He tried to snarl. "You're no lawyer."

"Mayhem, for instance, is a form of aggravated battery. The common law of most states treats it as a separate offense." He said nothing. "If convicted, you'd have a criminal record. In real life terms, Turk, that means you couldn't get a night job guarding fertilizer sacks at Home Depot."

His head was sunk into his shoulders. Dottie, for once, looked speechless. The shaft of light shifted. It was early evening. Kate waited a full moment. Dottie seemed suspended, as if awaiting a finale in which she had no part.

Kate said, "But perhaps, Turk, perhaps if Dottie and Ms. Page are willing to be generous, they'll take your past work at Opryland into consideration. On that basis, perhaps they'll decide not to press charges. In that case, you could simply leave right now, no hard feelings."

He sat very still. He looked like a tortoise. "But how 'bout if I promise from now on—"

"Too late for promises, Turk. It's over."

He seemed to absorb this. Dottie blinked. He said, "No trouble? No call to Kansas City?"

"No trouble."

He nodded. A moment passed. "I was hopin' to work Starwood again this season." Kate said nothing. "They had some vehicle theft last year. They're gonna need people." Kate still said nothing. He looked up. "Nothin' to get in the way of that?"

Kate said, "No objections here."

He nodded, looked relieved. "Uh, about the video? I don't suppose . . ."

"Absolutely not. TV viewers will never see you in *Against the World*. Ms. Page will be advised to make certain that footage is preserved only as potential evidence. It will come to light only if you try another stupid stunt. That would include publicity from incidents at Starwood. Isn't that correct, Dottie?"

Dottie managed the slightest nod.

"So, Dottie, as spokesperson for Ms. Page, you need to confirm these terms. Turk will be paid and terminated as of today, right?"

"That's . . . that's right."

"And the video footage impounded. You'll see to it."

"Talk to Mick."

"And Turk will receive salary owed up to today."

"I'll do the payroll."

Then Kate stood. Turk stood. Dottie got up slowly, started into a handshake, pulled her hand back as Turk's own moved forward. The waning sunlight caught his aqua jeweled ring, which reflected on the cabin walls in little spots. He tromped to the door, and the last sound was his Jeep roaring toward the front gate as Dottie hit the electric release button on the wall panel.

Kate sat for a moment in silence. Dottie turned,
and her voice sounded small, almost choked. Kate recalled her words moments later as she stepped toward
the cabin door. "It's up to you now, Kate."

Up to you. The sun flared into a glorious sunset as
Kate stepped outside, the clouds like vast sofas for
heavenly hosts. She gazed skyward as she got in and
started her car. Let the trumpets sound, for Turk Karcic is banished from the realm of the Lily of the Shenandoah Valley. Clever Kate to see the scheme behind
the ten bare diving toes, the pale white arches of the
bodyguard with a rescue compulsion.

It's up to you now, Kate.

Like a ringing in her ears.

Up to you.

But not an iota of comfort as Kate drove along. The
ten-minute triumph in the cabin went flat. Turk was
out, but Brent Landreth was shot dead, and LilyAnn's
broken arm a reminder of three near-misses. Who was
planning number four? Would the cops find Walter
Sian before he came back with his scimitar?

Could Kate even find out who slipped a paste-up
death threat into her Fleetwood mail? She checked
the rearview. Nothing, nobody.

She touched her scalp, still tender from the nails.

On impulse she turned toward Eighth and headed
to the city, parked, keyed into the back door of the
Fleetwood building, punched in her employee alarm
code. She entered the lobby. No Delia at the Fleetwood front desk this late Saturday afternoon. Nobody
on the leather club chairs. Kate forced herself to walk
into the mail room, a version of remounting the horse
that threw you. The vinyl tile floor was waxed, thanks
to the night crew. Not a soul here. No brush-cut intern
gathering envelopes for the Art Department, no temp
in her thigh-high skirt taking directions. No Don Donaghue. Nothing malicious.

Surely none of the workday regulars would harass her, not with a paste-up threat.

She went to her own mailbox, cautiously reached in and—pulled out a flyer for a new take-out service. Wraps, Mediterranean salads. No death threats, no animal skulls or snakeskins from Walter Sian. Though his "gifts" were probably reserved solely for LilyAnn. Kate was at the elevator before realizing she held her breath.

Breathe, Kate. She went to her office, checked out the river, checked her desk, table, seating surfaces, computer screen. She'd locked her files. No sign of disturbance. No e-mail flames. Her Boston fern looked droopy, and she watered it. She left the building and drove home with the radio off, hands on the wheel in the ten and two o'clock position.

Her condo was quiet, eerie. No Kelly, though Sam could arrive at any time. She changed into navy slacks and a white shirt and went into the kitchen. The banana peel from Kate's breakfast lay darkened in the kitchen trash. She closed up the bag and took it outside to dump it and came back in to hear the phone warble.

It was Kelly. Could two friends spend the night, Stephanie and Amanda? Absolutely. Should Kate pick them up, bring them over here? No, Amanda's big brother would drive them over.

"Big brother? Brother? Kel, how old is—?" But the line went dead. It occurred to Kate that she did not even know Amanda's last name. She stood at the phone, took up a cloth and began to clean the earpiece. She cleaned it carefully, thoroughly, minutely. She got a Q-Tip and worked the tiny ridges and grooves. Noteworthy that when life pressed from all sides and threatened to blow out of control, the response was frequently this—small-scale acts, controllable miniatures.

She finished, went to the fridge, dropped ice cubes

into a glass, poured herself a cranberry and soda and
cut a lime wedge and stirred and drank. She checked
the supply of Michelob dark for Sam. She put in a
load of laundry, sought comfort in the hum of the
washer. She ate four Triscuits out of the box and
scanned the morning's newspaper headlines. "Deep
Cuts Loom for State Programs." "Procession to
Honor Veterans." She turned on TV for sounds of
human voices. Ads, ads, ads. Turned it off, looked
outside for any sign of Kelly and friends approaching.
No Kelly, no friends. Mitzy was stalking a squirrel.

What now? Revisit LilyAnn's website? Check out
Myers Fatenza's homepage? Maybe Kip had a site—
Actually, there were a few loose ends. Back to the
hygienic phone, Kate reached into her purse for the
days-old list from the Howard School Building. Loose
ends, tie them in a double knot. She unfolded the
sheet of the residential permits, plus the hair salon.
"Chez Robert. How can I help you?" Mall Muzak
played as a female voice said that Valley Construction
worked only after business hours—when they worked
at all. The crew had not been spotted for over two
weeks. Distinct unhappiness in the voice.

Still no Kelly.

Work the phone some more. Presumably Miss Marjorie Styles's weeds were still sprouting among the
framing timbers dumped in her backyard by Kip's
merry men. But check on the other residential permits
too. Two did not answer, a third had no listing. The
fourth was a high tenor voice. Valley Construction?
No show for the last month and a half. Walls were
broken through, plastic sheeting everywhere, the family camping out in their own home, cooking on a Cole-
man stove. The tenor became a counter tenor. He
planned to file suit. His lawyer was collecting names
of other victims. The voice was flying high above the
staff.

Just as Kate finally hung up, the phone rang.

"Kate."

"Sam!" She said his name again. "Sam!" and gripped the phone, where work and private life collide. "Where are you?"

"Still in Chicago. How's Saturday treating you? How was the video shoot?"

"Uh, interesting."

"How's the bodyguard?"

"Funny you should ask." She sketched the scene.

"And you nabbed that guy for going barefoot. Great move, Kate."

She said, "I thought so too, except it doesn't solve anything. It might prevent another dumb rescue spectacle, but that's all."

"That ought to count."

"Not for long, Sam. Monday she's back here onstage at Fan Fair and signing autographs—and she's a moving target. Listen, there's a ton of stuff I can't wait to tell you in person." She reached for a pencil. "I'm ready for Nashville airport taxi duty. What time are you coming in?"

"Stuck up here tonight."

"Oh, no."

"Can't help it. But I got a great idea. Why don't you and Kelly fly up this evening?"

"To Chicago?"

"I've got hotel discount coupons for the Hilton on Michigan Ave. There's a warm spell. The Cubs are in town. I'll get tickets. We could make it by the third inning."

"Sam, Kelly's got two friends coming for a sleepover."

"Tomorrow morning, then. You can get the first a.m. flight out. There's an afternoon game."

"Sam, I can't. I . . . I have to check some things down here tomorrow." She had planned on him being with her at the Fair Grounds, going over the Fan Fair booth.

The line was silent. "Let me guess. LilyAnn Page again."

"But you're supposed to be here in Nashville. I thought you'd be here."

He said, "Corporate life, Kate. If Hacksaw says stick around town, I stick around. But hey, Wrigley Field, Grant Park, Second City." But his voice had changed tone, from buoyance and intimacy to a cool pleasant distance. "Oh well, nice try."

"Sam, it's . . . it's not just for fun and games down here." But she was reluctant to say over the phone it was about a killer, a stalker, even her job. He would worry too much.

Yet she couldn't let Sam think she'd choose Nashville over a surprise weekend in Chicago with him. . . . Lose lose.

She said, "Sam, there's a kind of pressure to . . . to work on the LilyAnn Page project."

"Kate, don't get coy on me. I saw a TV snippet about the Iron Works guy who got shot. What's going on?"

She sighed, somehow relieved. "Okay, his name's Brent Landreth. He was killed in front of his home. We don't know why. Maybe robbery."

"The TV said random drive-by. You buy that?"

She paused. The easy answer was yes. She said, "It might be connected with LilyAnn's ex-husband. The gun model was identified two days ago, and a detective interviewed her about her ex, Keith Grevins. He was violent during the breakup with LilyAnn."

"So you think he might have done it?"

The line buzzed. She paused again. "Before he died, Sam, Brent told me Grevins was very jealous, that he kept it more or less under control but recently decided Brent was LilyAnn's newest lover. That he obsessed about it."

"Homicide in jealous rage. Sounds like a TV headline, doesn't it?"

She said, "Sam, do you know anything about the Bren Ten?"

"What's this, a gun quiz? It's a semi, right? Wasn't it on *Miami Vice*? Or was that the Tec-9? Sometimes I mix up the glamour guns."

"The Bren Ten fires a .10mm bullet."

"Well, maybe that makes the police work a little easier. The leads narrow down faster. Surely the police are on top of this, Kate. Homicide will find out fast if he owns a Bren Ten. They'll put a trace on him, won't they? Work with the ATF? They have the know-how."

She stared at the kitchen wall, picturing Sam, so confident, so trusting—and so naive. Her savvy Sam, and she'd hit a blindspot. How many parades would she rain on in twenty-four hours? "Sam, not to burst a bubble, but state-of-the-art procedures at the ATF's National Tracing Center haven't changed from my police reporter days when Kelly was in diapers. They're still in the era of electric typewriters and disco balls. They're stuck with microfilm and paper files and the telephone. They operate out of a West Virginia warehouse the size of a supermarket, and these days they're deluged with cartons of paper from retiring gun dealers."

"There's no new electronic syst—?"

"Forget it." She shook her head, as if he could see her. "Congress won't give them the money to computerize. Too many campaign bribes from the gun lobby, I suppose. The chances of finding an original owner are about ten percent because after the first retail sale by a licensed dealer, the trail goes stone cold."

"Assuming it's a licensed dealer and not a street sale or gun show sale, right?"

Quick study, Sam Powers. "Right. Fact is, cops trace guns with legwork, Sam, with in-person questioning. So unless people in Nashville or Hawaii know something about any guns Keith Grevins owns, the odds of

finding out whether the Bren Ten that killed Brent
Landreth belongs to LilyAnn's ex are terrible."

Sam said, "But he's back in Hawaii?"

"Who knows?"

"Still in Nashville?" His voice was suddenly edged
with anxiety.

She cleared her throat. "Maybe. I bet the police
aren't sure either. I just wish I knew."

"Kate, you don't have to know, dammit, it's not
your job."

"Not technically."

"So then, why that tone, Kate?"

"What tone?"

"The one in your voice right now. As if you're
standing watch. As if it's your shift."

She did not hesitate. "It is my shift. I agreed to get
into it. And it's tied into my Fleetwood work. Hughes
Amberson is backing the fanzine project."

"But not a murder investigation conducted by his
coordinating editor."

"Sam, I should never have given you my business
card."

There was no ironic mirth in his voice. "I warned
you about 'Break of Dawn,' Kate. It's too close. It's
getting to you."

"Not really."

"Affecting your judgment. I was afraid of something
like this." He paused. "Then it's her daughter, isn't
it? It's the mother-daughter thing?"

But it wasn't. Kate spoke clearly. "No."

"So—?"

"So it's . . . right now it's more like—her voice. I
mean, the actual voice. I realized it today at the video
shoot. It's been through the mill, and a voice coach'd
probably hear the vocal cord damage. But my part
in this, Sam, it may sound weird, but it's maybe like
protecting a rare instrument. If there are Steinways of
country music, she's one of them. Just wait till you

hear 'Against the World.' The woman can still sing, shape a song, and maybe better than ever. She gives you chills. Not many singers can do that. Nobody else sounds like her. She's got incredible talent." The line stayed open. Kate said, "All those country singers you like to listen to, Merle Haggard, Ernest Tubb, Ronstadt . . ."

"The greats."

"I think she's one of them."

"Maybe."

"She is. Listeners need her."

"Fans."

"Okay, fans. And she needs to stay alive for them. To sing, to make records." She paused, realized it was a Nashville moment for Kate Banning. It measured something. Maybe something about Kate and country music and Nashville. "Sam, I'm trying to help keep that voice alive."

His own was quiet. "You know who I want to keep alive."

"I know."

"I say, let's find our desert island. We'll stock it with albums and listen forever. Someday, okay? Deal?"

"Deal."

She heard him let out a breath. "Meanwhile, Kate, I'll keep the hotel coupons and try to get an afternoon flight down to Nashville tomorrow. You take care. I mean it."

The line went dead with their smacked kiss. Kate stared out her window. Suddenly Kate missed Sam, missed him with her whole self. He felt so far, far away, her lover—lover and best friend combined. She felt lonely and sad and noticed the last dogwood flowers were turning brown. Didn't the radio report something about a dogwood blight? Fungus? Virus? Whatever. Lonely and sad—and still had no real idea

of who was trying to kill the Lily of the Shenandoah
Valley.

Such a relief to hear tires outside on the pea gravel.

Kelly and the two eighth-grade friends were approaching the condo front door, their sleeping bags
rolled, canvas totes and backpacks stuffed with PJs,
cosmetics, Teddy bears and Kermits and music tapes
and CDs. They came inside and giggled through introductions. The elfin Stephanie twinkled, while the wistful Amanda tried not to show her orthodontics and so
smiled in a grimace-like grin with lips literally sealed.

They had a plan—dinner at Ruby Tuesdays, the
three of them. "You're invited too, Ms. Banning, if
you want to." Three girls collectively held their breath
lest Kate mistake courtesy for sincerity. Kelly Banning
was braced for extreme mortification.

"How about if I just drive you?"

Relieved exhalation. So Kate drove them, grateful
for the very ordinariness of the moment, of the route.
It was just after six when she dropped them off at the
Green Hills Ruby Tuesday and faced the suburban
hour to kill, barely time to get back to the condo
before retrieving them. Besides, she didn't want to
rattle around alone. Where to go instead?—the book-
store cafe? The mall? She was hungry. If Sam were
here—?

They'd go to F. Scott's. Maybe a jazz combo would
play. Maybe that's the kind of hour she needed now,
a sandwich at the bar, neutral space, timeout. Anyway,
she was an old hand at sleep-overs and knew what to
expect. Sleep would come after midnight amid a din
of stereo and bursts of laughter and much padding
downstairs to the fridge for snacks and drinks. By
morning, Kate would be groggy, the girls cranky. So
take this hour now, try for a personal treat. No Turk,
no death threats. LilyAnn Page was tucked in, resting.

She turned onto Crestmoor, cut in at F. Scott's, gave
her keys to an attendant and went inside, a sharp left

to the bar, where a piano and bass duo played on the small corner stage.

Just one bar stool was open in a surprisingly crowded room. Kate beelined to it. On the left was a youngish couple having a pre-dinner pale green whatever whipped up in a blender. To the right sat a slender woman in dark linen and a brimmed hat, her face turned away, an iced drink before her, gin or vodka.

The wine list went on forever. Kate pointed to a dry white and ordered an open face ahi tuna and listened to the bass and piano join up and trade off on "My Funny Valentine." She settled in. The bass and piano did a call-and-response, moved out far from the melody line, took turns, got sprinkles of applause for solos. The hat brim nodded to the bartender, who poured a vodka over ice, slipped in a lemon twist and put the fresh glass down before her.

It was a fine-boned left hand reaching out for the vodka, the fingernails surprisingly short, utility grade. The hair was up inside the hat. The jawline, though, and shape of the nose looked somehow familiar. The duo moved into "I Got Plenty of Nothin'." Kate's wine was a little too fruity, the fish just right. The bass went deep, deeper.

"—plenty of nothin'."

It came from the hat, the soft vocal line. Her vodka level was already moving down fast. The bartender looked her way, decided not to offer another. Was this her second? Third? Kate cut a fish bite. Stay out of it. Typical Kate, starting to feel involved.

"Plenty of nothin.'"

She looked around. Not another free seat. Just her luck, a singing lady drunk. So forget it anyway. Enjoy the music and the fish, drink the wine. If linen hat lady must croon vodka jazz notes, let her. Pay no attention.

Except the voice was familiar. Female jazz singers . . . Cleo Laine, Abbey Lincoln. No, nothing like them, except for the dusky mournfulness. "Plenty of—" Too nasal for jazz, too much like country.

But wasn't that it? Country. That was the voice. The familiarity. The deep connection. Kate looked toward the right. The hat, the linen jacket was draped over the shoulders and arm. She leaned further forward, still looking right, and saw the bulked-out arm, the cast. Her pulse rate was up. That mournful voice.

LilyAnn. LilyAnn Page.

The tuna lost its taste in her mouth. The piano broke into runs up and down the keyboard.

She could break into a run herself. Mistaken identity? She looked so far to the right her eye muscles hurt. She said, "Ms. Page?"

The face turned in her direction, eyes unfocused. "Damn lemon," she said.

"Lemon?"

"Damn bartenders. It's s'posed to be a twist, not a piece of fruit. Look a' that." She plunged her fingers into the glass and held up the lemon. "See it?"

"You mean the pulp?"

She licked her dripping fingers. "S'not a twist."

Kate looked to the bartender, who was closing out a tab, his back turned.

"S'not."

She said, "Here—" and reached into her purse for the tiny Swiss Army knife. She pared the pulp away and gave it back. "Okay now?"

LilyAnn nodded, dropped the lemon into her drink. "You be the bartender. You understand all about it."

"Miss Page, my name's Kate Banning. I, uh, I was at the video shoot today."

The eyes tried to focus. "You fall in too?" Kate shook her head. "Got a plastic cast on my arm. Waterproof. Imagine."

"I know about your accident . . . the accidents. I thought you were at home resting."

"Got a funeral tomorrow. Going back to the Shen-andoah Valley. My funeral."

"Isn't it Brent's funeral?"

"Mine. It's mine." She lifted her glass, drank, put it down, swayed as she turned to Kate. "Lemme tell you something. This is the world, this is it. You get to be a legend, they treat you like shit. Def'nition of a legend, they treat you like shit. 'Plenty of Nothin.' Patsy's right, you fall to pieces."

The bass kicked in. She drained the vodka down to the ice, managed to put the glass down, called for another. And then Kate watched the brimmed hat go askew as LilyAnn Page leaned over, pillowed her face on the bar and fell sound asleep.

She was just a bit late getting over to Ruby Tues-days. She did not tell the girls she'd lingered at F. Scott's to pay LilyAnn Page's bar bill along with her own. She did not describe waiting for the taxi—Music City Taxi—and helping the driver wrestle the limp LilyAnn into the backseat, giving him the Mosely ad-dress and the last twenty out of her own wallet. No, she simply apologized, in Kelly's irate term, for "stranding" the three for all of twenty minutes, her penance a good long cooling of the heels at Block-buster and also the ice cream freezer at Kroger.

They were barely inside the door with pints and movies when the phone rang. "Mommmm, for youooo."

It was hard to hear the voice clearly against the slamming freezer door. It was familiar but small, thin. "Dottie? Oh, Dottie, I'm so glad you've phoned. Are you at Mosely? No? Then call Billy D because Lily-Ann's probably home by now, in a taxi, and her car's most likely in the parking lot at F. Scott's. She's been dr—"

But Dottie cut her off. "Kate, I just talked to Suzanne."

"Suzanne who?"

"They found the wallet."

Wallet? Kate blinked.

"Brent's wallet. The police found it in his car."

"The Celica?"

"Between the seats. It was wedged in between. They missed it the first time they inventoried. All his cards and money are inside. They'll turn it over to Suzanne. Kate? Are you there, Kate?"

"I'm here."

"You know what this means."

"It means robbery is out. It means Brent was outright murdered."

"One other thing, Kate. Just so you know, Billy D tells me one of his bows and a couple arrows are missing."

"His archery bows."

"A small one, he says. The small ones are strongest."

"How strong, Dottie?"

"I asked him. He says strong enough to kill a buck at fifty yards."

CHAPTER THIRTEEN

I-FLY-SWA. Kate picked out the touch-tone letters of Southwest Airlines's 800-number. Her fingers twitched. Too much caffeine, too little sleep. Upstairs the girls were still dead to the world. She'd showered, tiptoed down, made coffee and scanned the paper. Now, I-FLY-SWA told her Sunday morning's flights from Chicago's Midway Airport were all on time. Good. She'd be at the gate when the jetway door opened and the passengers straggled out, humanity *du jour*.

She pictured the scene, Sam in sportswear with a small duffel and his jacket slung over a shoulder. She'd nestle against him, cheek against his chest. Then they'd go for brunch and then out to the Tennessee State Fair Grounds to look again at LilyAnn's booth. Sam would help her go over the hot-spot danger zones. He'd promised.

His call came at 10:03 A.M. Yes, he was at Midway and ready to board, but—

"But what?"

"But instead, I'm going to Kansas City today, Kate. Maybe Wednesday. I remember Wednesday's Kelly's band concert—"

"Wednesday? Wednesday . . . What do you mean, Kansas City?" Her voice rose.

His was patient but strained. "You know I'm on call."

"What about your life?" About her life.

He said, "I never know what top brass'll decide to do. They want to fly someplace on short notice, I have to drive. You know that."

"Short? This is no notice at all. This is ridiculous. What are you, the company waterboy?"

"Flyboy." The tone was clipped, tight, proud. "Flyboy."

"I take it back. I'm sorry." The line was silent. "I said sorry."

He said, "You sound tense."

"Of course I'm tense. Too much coffee, not enough sleep. The girls and their blaster music till all hours. And all the LilyAnn flack too. And one of Billy D's bows is missing."

"He plays fiddle?"

"—archery, as in big game hunting. What do you know about bows?"

The line buzzed. "I know about bow-echo winds."

"About what?"

"Strong mid-level winds can push a storm forward, and rain and hail drag the winds toward the ground. The winds show up on radar in a bow-and-arrow pattern."

She said, "That's not helpful."

"Very helpful to us flyboys."

"Sam, I said I'm sorry. I'm disappointed. I counted on you helping with the LilyAnn Page thing."

He paused. "And how about carpentry, Kate? Any odd jobs to do? Plumbing, maybe?"

"What are you talking about?"

"Handyman stuff. Sometimes it seems you want a handyman. Marriage is out, but you like the trappings."

He stopped. Was it true? She felt tears smart.

He said, "Kate?"

"I'm thinking. Trying to think."

"You're not crying?"

"No."

The silence was more than awkward. "Kate? Kate?" He seemed at a loss to go forward.

She swallowed to keep her voice from choking. "I'm fine."

"You're not fine."

She looked outside, blinking. On her leash, Mitzy was squatting in the yews. She turned. "I . . . I can't think straight right now. I'll be ready by Wednesday. Or whenever you get here."

"Wednesday at the latest. Kelly's band concert . . . We'll work this out. I want to."

"I want to."

"Tell Kelly . . . you know, tell her . . ."

"I know."

"And you, Kate, you take it easy. Let the cops do their job. You're a magazine editor. Remember that."

"I remember." She sniffed and said, "You be careful up there."

"Safer than the ground."

"You say." She sniffed again. So much formula, rote back-and-forth. Too little time together, too many gaps to fill. Neither said I love you. The line went dead.

What to do? She mopped her eyes, blew her nose, felt hurt and guilty and then mad. Best-laid plans fell apart. No point moping. Brooding was a dead end. Who to count on?—yourself. I, myself, and me.

She glanced outside. No more Mitzy. Fred was tugging a bag marked "Scott's Green Thumb." Her own palms felt clammy. She thought of the Lily of the Shenandoah Valley weeping for herself in these very Sunday hours at Brent Landreth's gravesite.

And so much safer in the Virginia valley than she'd be tomorrow back here in Nashville.

And Kate Banning had to shift those odds.

It's up to you, Kate.

First, get the upstairs teens moving. It took about an hour from undercover grunts to departures. With

Kelly settled in, Kate put on clean jeans and a shirt and took a right onto Blakemore to drive out to the Fair Grounds.

It was hot today, muggy, the air thick. Kate smelled meat grilling. Those with ID badges came and went in a brisk contrast to the parking lot picnics. She fastened on her badge, nodded to the guard, noticed his shirt stuck to moist skin. In moments she entered the cinderblock building and walked down the aisle of booths. Finishing touches were in process. It looked like a party ready to start.

Except the LilyAnn Page booth looked far behind in its preparation. The Liberty figures were on pedestals and bunting draped, and a stand of potted palms stood to the side along with the lilies. But the pile of wood still lay on the floor. Clark and Babs's shirts and jeans looked as though the two camped here all week. There seemed to be more potted palms than before.

And here was Kip with two of his workmen. He smiled and said hi.

Kate said, "I'm surprised to see you here, Kip."

"Instead of Brent's funeral? I should be up there. Dearly love to be. Virginia's my homeplace too. And Brent . . . that's tragic. Shot for no reason at all. But the booth, the fans, we're way behind, and I'm needed here. 'Fact, I'm way late. I expect Dottie'll be out here to check things out tonight. Lily'll rest up, come on out tomorrow."

Kate said, "I promised Dottie I'd come by today."

He looked earnestly into her eyes. "Good to see you again, Kate. I take it you're well?"

"I am."

"How I regret that accident at the steak house site. Truly I do. We've tightened safety procedures on site." Then he gestured around the building. "Amazing, isn't it, what fan club folks do with a space no more'n twelve feet across." He called to the workers and pointed to the stack of wood slats and panels.

"We were going to set this up. Let's go, guys." At his signal the men bent, lifted, grunted, Kip exerting as much force as the others. Panels slid into grooves, and a form emerged, a kind of box-in-a-box, something like a throne.

Clark said, "At last. Now we can drape it." He went for a bolt of bright blue cloth.

Kip stood back. "Cabinet maker's got nothin' on me. Any cabinet maker'd be proud of this. See?" He pushed a panel to reveal a hidden hinge. "See, it's knock-down."

He slipped off his cap and wiped his forehead on the back of his wrist. "Build a booth, tear it down, sell it for scrap year after year. This time I got smart. This one recycles. It's versatile and flexible. She ought to get five or six years out of it."

"And these holes—?" Kate fingered round drill holes about three inches across cut from wood extensions at each side of the throne structure. "What are the holes for?"

"To support banners or flags or posts to hang stuff, flowers, whatever. She wants an upright, the holes are pre-drilled and ready. A three-inch hole, she can mount something sturdy. And you can mount the whole thing up high or low. There's a spring seat too. Cushioned. Good light steel. Lily'll sign autographs for hours, she needs this. 'Specially what she's been through lately."

Kate stared at the structure. Trap doors? A deadly pitfall? Or her own paranoia?

Kip chuckled. "Relax, Kate. Lily's booth's all screws and pegs. Not a nail in the assembly. Not one nail in the entire module."

Clark was holding a gold wood plaque. "Here's her autograph schedule. She's on tomorrow, noon to two, then on Wednesday two to four. But Kip, how're we supposed to fasten this thing to that door? I can't even budge that door."

Kate stood very still and watched. Kip said, "Simple. It goes on the door like this, see? Let's just make sure that door stand is braced right." He grinned, somehow both sheepish and mocking. "Well, I better get going. Got to get over to the museum today too."

"The Country Music Museum?"

"It's for Lily's Fan Club party on Tuesday night. We're setting up."

Kate said, "But it's a reception, isn't it?"

He laughed, nudged her forward. "Kate, you got a lot to learn. An artist has to do more than mix and mingle. She's gonna put on a little show. We're putting up a scaffold. Kind of a stage."

"What kind of scaffold?"

"Like painters use. Like guys that wash the highrise windows."

Her neck prickled, and her body stiffened. Kate asked how high the scaffold.

" 'Bout twenty, twenty-five feet. Buddy of mine runs a tree service, he's helping me rig it. The Iron Works will be on the floor, but Lily'll sing like a bird in the treetops."

"What about her arm? Her balance?"

"She'll be fine."

"And the hard floor? Will you set up cushions?"

He laughed again. "Kate, that floor's a country fan's delight. All those star medallions."

"It's hard as rock. Twenty-five feet up—?"

"New stars all the time. Gotta let the fans see the stars' names. It's a rollcall of the greats of all time. Hey Xavier, Pablo, let's get going, huh?"

Babs stepped up. She held a notebook. "Kip."

"Babs."

"Kip." She tilted one hip and twinkled. Kate recalled her blush at the mention of his name just days ago. So these two had something going, at least a flirtation. Babs said, "Hey, Kip, I need the new number."

"Don't know it yet."

Babs cocked one eyebrow and thrust out her chest. "You mean you're starting a brand new company, and you don't even know the phone number?"

"Company?"

". . . the way it goes."

"What company?" Kate tried to sound upbeat, casual.

"Haven't you heard?" Babs grinned at Kip. "It's bye-bye Valley Construction, hello KP Builders. This Kip Padgett, he's a man on the move."

On the move. Exiting the Fair Grounds at this moment. Kate stared after him, the boss and his workers. She walked down the aisle past other booths, Brick Hazleton, Jeanie Porter. She heard the hammers and saws, giggles and laughter and "shee-its." Phrases rose in the air. ". . . you mean we got a whole case of glue that won't stick to plastic . . . he said *that* . . . hit number three on the charts . . ." She heard but didn't hear. She saw T-shirt portraits at every booth, Faith Hill, Tim McGraw, Martina McBride.

She saw but didn't see—because the portrait in Kate's mind was a white-haired granny of Granny White, Miss Marjorie Styles, who said certain contractors started up new businesses to escape the law. Was Kip Padgett just such a man?

Just the man to stage his stepsister's plunge? To arrange a fatal fall from a twenty-five-foot scaffold to a rock-hard floor? The man to arrange the star's death in front of her most devoted fans? Kip was "in tight" with Keith Grevins. Did they have a deal?

If the stalker didn't get her first.

If, if, if.

She drove home. It was getting muggier. The AC hummed. Kelly pounced. "I have to go to Radnor Lake. It's for the *Walden* project."

"Today? Now?"

"For the nature journal. I'll take my new camera.

You can include pictures for extra credit. Stephanie has to go too. Can you drive, Mom?"

"Kelly, why this afternoon?"

"It's due on Tuesday."

"Why didn't you tell me earlier? Last week?"

"Because of the stupid violets. And you were at LilyAnn Page's house. Oh, I forgot, Deb's mom called."

"Dottie."

"From someplace in Virginia. I wrote it down."

Kate moved to the phone, punched numbers, waited. "Kate, you nearly missed me. We're off to the airport—airstrip, this is the boonies."

"Dottie—"

"Big news, terrible. Keith's under arrest. They caught him with a gun at the Honolulu airport. That detective who interviewed Lily was nice enough to call. He understands a star's life."

"What kind of gun is it?"

"What kind of gun? Who knows what kind? The funeral today, we're all wrecks. I'm trying to keep LilyAnn together. The kids are miserable. Angie's coming down with the flu."

"It's important, Dottie."

"It's important Keith's arrested. We'll get calls, publicity. The timing's terrible with Fan Fair, the new album."

Kate paused. Let her vent. Force a little patience. Finally Kate said, "What about Walter Sian?"

"Nothing about him."

"So he's still on the loose." The silence meant yes. "Dottie, one more thing. Whose idea is the Fan Club scaffold? Was it all Kip's?"

"The scaffold? . . . why, Clark and Babs's of course."

"Mostly Babs's?"

The line crackled, cut out, came back. "Kate, you got suspicions, let me hear them. You think Babs—?"

"I don't know. I'm concerned."

" 'Concerned' won't cut it, Kate."

"I'm worried about the Fan Club party."

"That's two days off. First things first. But let's keep an eye on Babs."

"What do you know about Kip's new business?"

"Personal growth and change, Kate. Listen, we're off, I'll call you tonight when we get back to Nashville."

The line went dead. Time: 1:22.

Kelly said, "How about Radnor Lake? And you know we're out of milk."

Kate turned toward her, eyes narrowed. Quietly she said, "Call Stephanie and get your camera and your shoes on. And no whining."

"But I—"

"None. Not one bit. You want a favor, listen up. You get an hour and a half at Radnor, from drop off to pick up. I have a schedule of my own to meet. Let's move it."

Kelly moved. Kate drove the girls to the Lake, bought the week's groceries, stopped at the condo to unload and put them away, then picked the girls up again and listened to Stephanie moan about blisters from her new Nikes until she dropped her at her subdivision and drove on.

"Mom, isn't this the long way around? Are you lost?" Sarcasm on the rise.

Nip it. "Would you like to take the bus, Kel? I have an errand at the Country Music Museum. It's a spot check. If that'll inconvenience you, I'll gladly drop you at a bus bench."

"Uh, no. It's awful hot."

"It's June. It's the South. You're not whining, are you?"

Quietly, "No." Kate pulled into the museum parking lot. No sign of Kip's truck. "You want to come in, Kel? No? Be out in a minute." Inside it was cool and dim. No Kip in the foyer. No tourists either. Everybody was bound for Fan Fair. She looked down at the floor. The inset outlines of stars caught a pale light from the stained glass window panels. The names— Marty Robbins, Roy Acuff, Minnie Pearl. And Babs.

"Kate, hi." She came out of a corner with a steel tape measure. "Just making sure everything fits for LilyAnn's Fan Club gala."

"And does it?"

"Oh, you'll be surprised." She flicked her thumb. The steel ribbon recoiled. She had changed into a new T-shirt, crisp and ironed. Her eyes looked tired yet glittered.

Kate said, "Kip's not here?"

"You missed him. He left to go work on the scaffold. Something about the pulleys."

"He'll be back . . . when?"

She shrugged. "Day after tomorrow. It's a late afternoon installation. It'll go over there against the wall. See, fans come at six, but catering's due at four. Also Tennessee Stage and Studio Supply."

Tennessee Stage and Studio? That meant Bucky Sibbett.

And maybe Myers Fatenza on hand to photograph the big moment? Come one, come all?

"Guess we'll see you at the Fan Club party too, Kate."

"Guess you will."

"And the booth looks great now. The module's all draped. Stop by Fan Fair and say hello."

"Count on it."

Then Babs dropped to a crouch and flung out the tape. It zinged, half snake, half razor. Kate backed out, out to Kelly.

"So hot inside here, Mom. People aren't even supposed to leave their dogs in hot cars. I hope my film isn't damaged."

"Don't dramatize."

"Jeez, you're like some drill sergeant."

Turn the key, head out. Kelly held a battered *Walden*. They drove out Seventeenth, connected to Magnolia. "Mom, what's a s-c-i-m-i-t-a-r?"

Kate braked. "What did you say? What did you say?"

"S-c-i-m—" She pulled suddenly right. "Hey. you almost hit that car. What's the word mean? S-c . . ."

"A sword. It's a curved sword. But where—?"

"It's in *Walden*. It goes, 'Stand fronting the sun, and you will feel it like a s-c-i-m-i-t-a-r dividing you through the heart and marrow.' Mom, what's it mean? So weird."

"That's in *Walden*? That's Thoreau?"

"Right here. It's a quarter of our grade. Don't you know what it means? I thought you loved it so much."

"Then it's a quote. It's a quote."

"Of course it is. I'm reading it to you."

Kelly talked on, but Kate now talked to herself. That's why it sounded familiar. The threats, Walter's threats. *Walden*, Walter. Yesterday's Bluebeard was the nature stalker. The missing kitchen knives, did Walter somehow get hold of them?

Her head spun, started aching.

"You okay, Mom?"

"I have a headache, Kel."

"Me too. This nature journal's a headache. I don't know what Mr. Schuchard wants. I'm worried about my grade."

The words swam in, swam off. As mother, she should help separate out the grades, the learning, the curds and whey. The good mother would step in.

But the good mother was not available. The driver was here, and the short order cook—functional Kate, the Kate who turned into the driveway and parked the car. The Kate who put a pasteup death threat on her own back burner. Kelly bounced out, opened the door with her own key.

But Kate sat a moment, a mental kaleidoscope turning to show a pattern. It included Babs and Kip and maybe Bucky Sibbett. Figure Keith Grevins was in a deal with Kip—and Kip in turn dealing with Babs, maybe cutting Bucky in. Fan Fair was a finale in motion—one meant to seem altogether accidental.

The knock-down seating module would play a crucial part. As a prop, it was a deliberate diversion, a reusable unit that Kip could cite as an act of his own good faith. Why, after all, would the dutiful stepbrother design such a reusable structure if he planned to kill his beloved country star sister? The module was evidence of his good faith, of projected years of LilyAnn's Fan Fair booths using the same clever knock-down module over and over again. Meanwhile, LilyAnn was scheduled to crash just like the window washers who fell to their deaths. Grevins probably would be out on bail when it happened.

And all the while Walter Siau was the wild card who copped his mission statement from Henry David Thoreau. Scimitar, cleaver—Walden was a weapons inventory for a fanatic. A stalker's inspiration.

Sweat broke over Kate's back, her neck. If Dottie would just listen, would help. For now she'd move Kelly along and wait up by the phone. From here to Tuesday, two days, countdown with LilyAnn Page flying home to her obituary.

CHAPTER FOURTEEN

She did not expect to wake with a shudder, fully clothed, a crick in her neck—on the sofa. It was 4:03 A.M. No Dottie, no call. Vigil for nothing.

Welcome to Monday. Too early, however, for action. Kate rubbed her neck and clicked on CNN. A blow-dry Congressman brayed about family values and a jowly admiral pleaded for combat readiness.

Combat readiness, just what Kate needed. She stood, stretched, blinked to clear her gritty eyes. Hungry, she went to the kitchen and pulled a snack bag from the pantry and reached in. Human kibble. Ingredients on the package listed guar gum, cheddar sodium bicarbonate, malic acid and yellow dyes #6 and #5. She stopped chewing, tossed the bag in the trash, vowed to pay more attention to the food fine print. She drank a glass of orange juice and decided to hold out until six a.m. to call Dottie. Then she skied the NordicTrack for half an hour, showered, sent e-mails to Arkansas, cycled two loads of wash. Finally it was six.

But Dottie did not answer. How many into-the-void monologues had Kate recorded on that woman's voicemail over the past week? She tried to sound urgent, then called back with a P.S. and spoke the actual word: *urgent.* She awakened Kelly, did the morning routine, the school drop-off, the drive to the office. She wore a twill skirt and cotton blouse, Fan Fair casual. In the lobby and mail room everyone said good

morning as usual. No death-threat paste-ups in her
Fleetwood box to start the week.

Office door closed, she tried Dottie's number at
once, shuffled desktop papers and hit redial every five
minutes, then every three. One more try and then
she'd head out right to Fan Fair.

But just then Kate's own phone sounded. "Kate,
Dottie here. I'm out here at the Fair Grounds. Got a
favor to ask."

"Dottie, I've been trying to reach you. Why
didn't—?"

"Sorry about last night, Kate. We were stuck on
that runway in Virginia forever because of thunder-
storms. Got back really late, it was crazy."

"I see." Kate stared at the sweep second hand of
the wall clock. Best to wait out the usual Dottie blitz.

"—so we got Lily settled down, got Angie into bed,
sick as a dog. Then Deb and I came out here to the
Fair Grounds. Farley too. There were finishing touches,
and he was a big help, Farley. Give the devil his due.
Clark was wiped, a zombie. I sent him home. The
booth's fantastic. You saw it? Fantastic. But I couldn't
stop to call you with all that going on, Kate. No way,
too late. We didn't leave the Fair Grounds till almost
two. Farley stayed to hand out Walter Sian's mug shot
to the night security."

"Dottie, I need to talk to you face to face. Did you
check your voicemail?"

"Kate, I hear you. 'Urgent' is a word I hear pretty
often but not from you. Let's see, you're coming out
here—when, later this morning?"

"Immediately. Is that soon enough?"

"Fine. But Kate, about the favor."

"What favor?"

"Strictly personal, mother to mother. Billy D's already out here, and Maria won't come in to cook till
later. I thought you might pitch in."

"What is it?"

"My Deb's backpack. She left it at Mosely last night, and she just called from school. It's got all her books, her gym stuff. I said I'd bring it over to the high school, but I'm stuck here, so . . ."

"So you want me to fetch Deb's bag and take it to her at school, is that it?"

"She says it's near the kitchen door. Just drop it off in the school office, Kate. She'll be waiting. Whale of a favor. Shouldn't take you more than half an hour. Oh, and would you stop and pick up some ginger ale for Angie? Maybe some Jell-O too? She's one sick puppy. She'll buzz you in at the gate. It'll be a big help. Then we'll talk. Promise. I want to hear all your suspicions about Babs. Meanwhile, set your mind at ease, the security's tops, first-rate. Lily's got a whole police platoon for escort. Remember, she goes on at eleven sharp. Fan fair runs like clockwork, so allow yourself plenty of time."

Click.

It annoyed her and took too long. Took fifteen minutes to exit Fleetwood, another ten to the parking garage, then twenty-five out of downtown and through thick traffic of Green Hills. Checking out Jell-O and two liters of Canada Dry at Hill's felt like forever, then on to Mosely, where she pressed the gate intercom over and over. Wasps buzzed her car window, her arm. It was humid and already felt in the high eighties. She thought of Turk. Mud dauber man. Could he help in a pinch? No. Good riddance.

Finally the intercom voice, scratchy and thin. Open sesame.

For the first time on this gravel drive, Kate veered off to the right to the main house.

Angie came to the door wrapped in a fuzzy pink blanket, her cheeks flushed, hair lank and flat, eyes filmy. Sick, she looked like a very young child.

Kate resisted the urge to feel her forehead. "How are you, Angie? Here, let me—" Kate stepped inside

and went to the Sub-Zero, got ice, found a glass,
poured, handed over the fizzing drink. "Sip that,
Angie. Lots of it. I make Kelly drink gallons when
she's sick. Here, let me top it off. Now how about
some Jell-O? I brought lemon, orange, cherry . . ."
Angie summoned energy to point. "Lemon it is." Kate
filled the kettle, a designer kettle with a bird whistle.
Minutes were passing. She saw the knives in their
holder, the two empty slots. She said, "I need Deb's
backpack."

"Over there."

Set on the floor, it was the checkered pack Kate
remembered from the video shoot on Saturday. Now
the kettle chirped, and she opened cabinet doors in
vain for a measuring cup. "This okay for a bowl. I'll
just . . . need to get going, actually." She poured,
stirred. Those Jell-O colors, talk about dye #5, #6.

"Angie, please try to eat some of this in an hour or
so when it's firm. I have to go. You might need to see
a doctor. I'll tell . . ." But tell whom? Dottie? The
cook? Billy D? The Lily of the Shenandoah Valley?
"I'll tell your home folks."

The child nodded and looked wistful, sad, small and
young. Alone in the big house. Very much alone.

Kate took a deep breath, picked up the backpack,
reluctantly said goodbye, told herself the top priority
was long-term health—was life itself—for Angie and
for her mother.

Because Angela Lyn Grevins would be orphaned if
her father and Uncle Kip carried out their plan. Because as things stood right now, this child was hours
from one more funeral, her own mother's.

Because Kate thus owed it to this sick child not to
stay for bedside duty.

She got to her car and took the gravel drive too
fast, spit pebbles and spun her wheels onto Mosely,
onto Tyne and toward Franklin Road. The car smelled
suddenly perfumed. From spring blossoms? No, from

the backpack in the passenger seat. It smelled like a mix of scents, perfume and herbs. She leaned to sniff. *Chanel No. 5? 19?* She'd edited a perfume issue for Fleetwood two months ago. Either perfume had spilled inside this pack, or it was daubed on.

The latest teen fad?

She sniffed again. Tobacco was in the mix, no surprise there. She drove on, five miles over the speed limit, eight, then ten. It was already pushing ten-thirty in the morning. At a light, she leaned to sniff one more time, then backed off at the unmistakable aroma of *cannabis.*

So the perfume was a cover up. Well, so what? Was it any of her business? At some point Kelly herself might—Kids tried different things. Keep moving.

What other things, though? Accelerating, Kate reached across and felt the backpack. There were books for sure, notebooks, hard rods—probably pens. And something metal and round that clanked. What? She pawed at the canvas, drove one-handed, neared the big brick suburban school, put her left blinker on and pulled into the visitor's lot. It was 10:38.

She cut her engine and yet groped the pack a moment more. What was metal and cylindrical? Of course, cans. Still she was reluctant to unzip the pack and look in. Invasion of privacy. So get going. Dottie asked her to pick up and drop off, period. And Lily-Ann would go onstage in twenty minutes, "Against the World," probably "Break of Dawn" too. Even with the platoon of police, Kate wanted to be there. Get going. If Deb was experimenting, that was Dottie's affair.

But suppose inside this pack were canisters of inhalants? Sprays and fixatives came in metal cans. Kids sniffing—a huge danger. Brain damage, death. Mother to mother, keep school officials out of this. Go straight to Dottie. Give her the pack.

But if the cans were innocent, the contents anything

from hairspray to supermarket squirt cheese—? Kate
Banning would be a laughing stock, the alarmist of
the century. Worse, she would discredit herself, the
former police reporter hallucinating in Nashville. Her
theory about the scaffold could be dismissed as luna-
tic. A chorus of sneers would sing LilyAnn Page crash-
ing to her death.

Forget it. Kate reached across, unzipped the pack
and looked inside. Textbooks, markers, socks, gym
shorts, and deep down zigzag papers and a plastic
twist-tied bag of weed. Okay, marijuana. And the
metal cans—Right Guard and Paul Mitchell hair
mousse.

Relief. Marijuana was the issue. For all Kate knew,
Dottie might light up herself.

She started zipping up the pack—but just then her
hand brushed the hard rods inside the canvas. Pens.
No, they felt too heavy. She pulled one out, then another. Then a third. They were polished bright gold
rods, weighty, about six inches long and each capped
with a little ball. Brass, she'd guess.

Not pens, then, but . . . pins of some sort. For what?
Perhaps a school project, theatre props, a science experiment. She rolled them in her palm, reluctant to
let go.

Hardware? machine parts? So polished. The ball
tops . . . something out of a kit? A kitchen appliance?
Casement window fixtures? No, door hinges. Pins
from hinges, big ones, the kind to fasten something
heavy.

Like a mahogany dining room door.

Like the door that fell, that broke LilyAnn's arm
because the pins were pulled from the hinges.

The loose hinge pins she held in her hand.

Staring, Kate did not move but sat fixed as a statue
while light bathed the brass. It shone like gold as the
chills began, the tingling that spiked up and down her
bones while gooseflesh rose on her arms.

She shivered in the stuffy, hot car, then cracked a window for air, watched a white convertible drive by, a furniture truck, a Jeep. Her sweaty fingerprints smudged the gleaming brass pins stashed here in Deb Skipwith's school backpack.

Had a prank got out of hand? A teen practical joke run amok, with the girls too ashamed, too embarrassed to confess. As for the pack, it was a perfect hiding place, practically a teen body part.

But wouldn't Angie offload these pins before handing over the pack? Sick as she was—assuming she was Deb's partner, the inseparable duo.

Assuming it was both girls.

Assuming.

Kate turned to root inside the pack again. *America, the Story of Democracy, Science for Our World,* a math book, workbooks, a folder of spiral papers, stencils. And then a package of stick-on letters, sheets of iridescent blue, the consonants with extra vowels. Some were missing. The A, D, G, K, three E's, two O's. Puzzle?

It didn't take a genius. KATE GET OUT OR DIE.

So those girls sneaked into the Fleetwood Building? No, it was that day at Fountain Square, the Walter Sian sighting, Kate's car and tote—

And Deb had played the DJ that afternoon at Kate's car radio. Deb the joker? The prankster? Apple-cheeked Deb? In league with Angie.

Or with somebody else? Someone on tour with Lily-Ann? Like Farley? Farley the roadie. Farley the Mister Fix-it. Farley who was out touring much of the time with LilyAnn, who could set up a guitar case avalanche, a bus fire. And then back in Nashville, the dining room door at the Mosely house. Booby traps. All booby traps.

Now Fan Fair. The last one at the Fair Grounds in the wee hours was Farley.

Booby traps.

What could happen?

Police escort for LilyAnn. From stage to booth, what could happen?

LilyAnn would sing and sign autographs. Miss Liberty "Against the World."

What could—?

The kitchen knives. And Billy D's bow.

That hunting bow.

Kate's head spun. It was eleven. LilyAnn was onstage at this moment. Could she be wrong, her yesterday's theory all wrong? A good case, a theory of the case—just make-believe?

Because if the brass rods spoke the truth here and now, her idea was . . . dead wrong. If the hinge pins talked, there was to be no next day, no overnight plan, not one minute of maneuvering left. If the pins talked, Kate had maybe an hour to get to LilyAnn's booth.

Franklin Road to Wedgewood. She gunned it but soon stuck in trickle traffic, lumbering along at twenty in a no-passing zone behind an RV. She dug out her Fan Fair badge, put it on, at last crossed the entrance. WELCOME TO FAN FAIR. A finish line, a starting gate. It was 11:48 A.M.

Where to park? Pavement and fields were filled to the horizon with every kind of vehicle. Trolleys shuttled fans in from faraway lots, and attendants in Day-Glo orange beckoned her to those outer reaches. No, she'd never make it. Forget rules. She pulled over, grabbed her wallet and keys, got out, slammed shut.

"Hey lady, you can't park—"

"Car trouble. Broke down."

"No, but you can't . . ."

But she broke into a run, stuffed wallet and keys into pockets, hitched up her skirt and pumped and listened for footfalls behind her.

"Hey, lady—!"

But the biggest sound was the miked voice soaring out over the air from the raceway. "Sun in the

morning . . . all sailors and cowboys take warning . . ."
It was soulful, throbbing, unmistakable. It was live,
LilyAnn live and alive, still alive.

Kate glanced back. The Day-Glo guy shook his fist,
but nobody chased her from behind. Her shoes were
wrong, stupid office shoes, little heels.

". . . take wwarrnnning." It had to be the set's finale, the signature song of the final onstage minutes.
The fans' cheers rose, "Break of Dawn" their classic
too. The grandstand whistled its approval. You could
hear the whole concert from the parking lot.

But Kate's legs felt like slow motion as she cut left
past a tow truck, Tommy's Wrecker Service. LilyAnn's
voice rose, arched high and lingered as if to defeat
the very heat and humidity. Tommy was inside the
truck cab on his cell phone. Getting orders to tow
Kate?

Would a cell phone network relay word from the
parking lot to the entrance to chase her down? Kate
Banning the BOLO of the hour? Quarter hour?

She reached the entrance, flashed her ID, felt confused. Which way to go, to the raceway stage or the
booth? She looked at her watch. Eight, ten minutes
max. Life or death, grandstand or booth? The air
smelled like cotton candy.

The booth side was a human wall of flesh, tank tops,
legs and arms and hips. Everybody wore a plastic arm
band, pink bracelets by the thousands.

So head left instead. That passage was clear to the
grandstand stairs, the concrete pathways. People there
sat listening on benches, braceleted in rows.

She dashed to the stands and started down the big
steps. Get backstage and head off LilyAnn when she
leaves the stage for transit to the booth. Kate took
the stairs in broken rhythms. Video big screens beside
the stage showed LilyAnn's face, but ahead and way
down on the stage itself was the tiny actual singer, the
miniatures behind her with guitars the Iron Works,

who moved into the instrumental bridge, that soul-
searing melody line.

Searing Kate's windpipe as she gulped this humid
air. Halfway down she almost tripped, grabbed the
hot metal rail, kicked over a Coke cup that splashed
her and—

"Hey."

"Sorry."

"Wyancha watch where . . ."

"Didn't mean to."

She pushed on. Closer now. "Break of Dawn" had
moved into the last chorus, LilyAnn's voice a well of
sorrow and resolve.

Cops guarded the track entrance, and security in
black shorts and T-shirts with lettering—"Polite but
Firm." Kate flashed her All-Access badge, crossed
over a plywood ramp, then through two sets of metal
gates, another ramp and then flashed her ID again just
as guitars rolled out and the voice lofted to the final,
lingering phrase, "until the break of dawwnnnn . . ."

The song was finished, and Kate was backstage inside a big tent with tables, drinks, food trays. And
people with guitar cases, performers. The new act to
go on, the changing of the guard. A male threesome
in fancy outfits with snake patterns. She rushed past,
bumped a table. A tray of macaroons went flying as
she ran to the other side of the tent.

Just in time to see LilyAnn get into a golf cart, the
cart beginning to move.

"Wait." The nick of time.

And to move faster.

"Wait! Stop!"

And Kate ran after it, sprinted in the stupid shoes.
Her calves—

"Stop! LilyAnn, stop!"

But the cart outpaced her, its little green striped
awning jiggling, the cast on LilyAnn's arm draped. All
of it receded before her eyes, her legs.

Then a voice she knew. "Kate, Kate, over here—"

She turned. The figure in black at the tent. Dottie. Too awful, the truth she did not know.

"Kate, hey Kate—"

But Dottie was waving in jerks, like spastic aerobics, cell phoned clapped to her head. "It's Billy D. He thinks he sees Walter. The stalk—"

"Not now."

"But what—?"

"Booth—"

She'd pivoted, backtracked fast, brushed past Dottie at the tent flap as tent people stared and stepped back away from her. Crouched, one picked up handfuls of macaroons. Kate said "sorry" in passing. Stupid manners.

In her ears both pulsing blood and loudspeaker voices. "Mercator recording artists . . . Diamondbacks . . . just a few minutes." The crazed scream of female voices.

Trotting, running, Kate held out her ID at chest level like a shield. Cops and security nodded, passed her back on through, this silly woman dashing in the heat. Again the metal gates, the ramps with her feet thumping.

The grandstand stairs before her were a Matterhorn. Climb that mountain. Run it. She panted now. Her side ached. All those skiers who trained for the season running stadium stairs, but not Kate. Her left calf began to knot. Where was the second wind?

New problem. Between acts, grandstand fans moved out and in. The stairways were clogged. Men, women, children. Backs, arms, hips, sandals, sneakers. They jostled, inched, stood, blocked.

" 'Scuze me."

A mantra, but it took life's breath. " 'Scuze me. 'Scuze . . . 'Scuze . . ."

She slipped sideways, turned for a quick glance at the raceway, the stage, the inner oval. No sign of the jaunty golf cart. Gone. LilyAnn was bound for the booth. " 'Scuze me. 'Scuze." More bodies, endless bodies.

How did she lose her shoe?

Suddenly it was gone, Kate limping, one on and one off. She stopped, searched the steps, the forest of ankles. "My shoe," she called. "My shoe."

"Folks, put your hands together for The Diamond-backs."

"Shoe?"

Fans screaming.

No time. She kicked the other one off, moved stocking-footed now at the top stair, sticky, hot, greasy on her soles. She skidded on French fries.

Then into the grandstand passageway and out to the buildings and sheds. Sweat soaked her clothes. Nylons in shreds. Her feet burned on the asphalt. But which building had LilyAnn's booth? Kate tried to spot the main entrance, get oriented, couldn't. Smells of hot dogs, funnel cakes. Bodies everywhere.

Where was the damn booth?

Around a corner, an information desk? No, it was Buck 'n Bum Western Outfitters, leather jackets with stars and stripes. " 'Scuze me, do you know which building has LilyAnn Page's booth? Do you—?"

Sweet soul. "Well now, Doobie's got our map. Doobie, you still got that map? It's in Crystal's bag? Where's Crystal gone off to?"

Kate fled. Another pass-through. In an open-air shed, the lunch crowd settled. Bright corn on the cob. ". . . I'm wantin' some decent slaw."

She turned, dodged left. Fannypacks and bellypacks, wheelchairs, T-shirts. She bumped past a man in coveralls with a banjo and washboard, jostled an old woman with a cane. A cop took notice, a young one with a thin moustache. He could help.

He could hurt.

" 'Scuze me, looking for LilyAnn Page's booth."

She turned into another dead end, a food cart with Polish Italian sausage, foot-longs, polka dots, stripes, iced tea. Now Serving Cappuccino.

Top of her lungs—"LilyAnn Page's booth? Where is it? Help me? Where is LilyAnn Page's booth—?"

People stared, looked away. The moustache cop was coming her way. The shirts all around her—Brooks & Dunn, TNN The Nashville Network, Turn on to Country CMT."

Her feet were burning. "LilyAnn Page's booth? Where is it?" Her voice hysterical.

T-shirts faced her. Fun Galore, Odessa Chuck Wagon Gang, Jesus Is the Answer. The cop was now waylaid by a huge woman in overalls.

Odessa pointed. "Building's right over there, ma'am. That one."

That one. The cop got closer. Where was the building entrance? A lineup of fans waited along the cinderblock side wall. Follow to the door. They blocked the door, the autograph seekers, a quarter-mile of knees and shorts. Kate pushed ahead, pushed the door."

"Hey, you got to get in line. We all waited . . ."

She shoved.

"End of the line's back there . . . You got to . . ."

" 'Scuze." The air inside hot and wet as breath. The center aisle was jammed. Bodies, sweat, sprays, aftershave, leather, plastic. A boot heel came down on Kate's foot. She jackknifed in pain, staggered, nauseated.

But saw that cop, the same cop nearly caught up. He eyed her. If he detained her, LilyAnn died. That simple. So cat and mouse. She gasped for breath, ducked around a supply cart, got extra seconds. Her foot, was it broken?

Then the voices rising, oohs, a flurry. Ahead she saw a tall boom mike, felt the crowd ripple like so much jelly. "Lily . . . make way . . . it's LilyAnn Page . . ."

Fifteen feet away, it was the police escort and a TV crew and Clark and Billy D too. It was LilyAnn making way to her booth, seconds from her booth.

Her death.

The boom mike led, moved like a mast, the police sidestepping. Over shoulders, by armpits Kate could see LilyAnn now inside the booth, fans waiting. Cameras, autographs.

And the Liberty torches, the tops of the potted palms. The star approached the seating module, smiled and waved to everybody in the moment before sitting down.

Kate shouted, "LilyAnn, No. LilyAnn!"

Then she stiff-armed forward. Second wind, and climbing. These bodies so many stairs. Concrete, muscle, body ramps. Necks, eyeglasses knocked, hats. A big boy fell down, his shoulder Kate's own springboard as she reached the counter, climbed and dived just as LilyAnn Page began to sit.

"Don't sit! Do not!"

Dived. Cast or no cast. Dived and hit her at an angle, grabbed hold at the waist, hung on and tackled and burned her elbows and banged her shins and front teeth. And brought LilyAnn Page to the ground just as a potted palm right above their heads went *thunk*. Fans and cops yelled.

In Kate's ears, the echo, *thunk*.

LilyAnn Page writhed, fought free, sat up and screamed in Kate's face. Screamed in rage and fear, sweat and spit with bulging eyes. *Thunk*. The sound now embedded in her brain. Furious, cops and security swarmed. Fans stared. From the floor of the booth Kate twisted to look. It was just what she'd thought. Just what she guessed. *Thunk*. Most sickening of all. She gagged to see it. *Thunk* as it crossed the spot where LilyAnn was just starting to sit down, where

Kate dived. Now LilyAnn turned to look, gasped, screamed again. Kate retched at the sight. The statue lifted her lamp beside the golden door, but an arrow was buried deep in her breast.

CHAPTER FIFTEEN

"I want a Heath Bar Blizzard, okay, Sam? Remember this time, a Blizzard, not a Breeze. Hey, is something wrong with you two? You're acting very weird, both of you."

"Us?"

"Very weird?"

Kelly gripped her flute. "It's like you're not even talking to each other."

Kate shrugged. Sam shook his head. The air smelled of basketballs and sneakers and band instruments. After the applause, forty kids in white shirts and black pants and skirts were all swarming to their families. The gym floor creaked, the metal folding chairs scraped.

Scraped like Kate's elbows and shins. Her long-sleeved blouse and floor-length skirt hid a patchwork of gauze squares and ointment.

Now parents and kids bunched in post-concert festivity. Kate slid a program in her purse for the Kelly Banning scrapbook, from the preschool years to John Philip Sousa.

Kelly looked triumphant, free in spirit for the first time since Fan Fair Monday. Call it Black Monday that came with the unspeakable knowledge of the LilyAnn affair, knowledge that she, Kelly, could not be spared. "So, Sam," she said, "you took a taxi here."

"Got to the gym right at the downbeat, Kel. Fortunate to get a seat right beside your mother. Don't want her to be lonesome."

He twinkled.

Kate refused to twinkle back, though she noticed his checkered shirt and the suede jacket slung over his shoulder, her birthday presents to him two years ago.

"But did you two have a fight during the concert?"

"Of course not. We were busy listening to you."

"And you sounded just great. The whole band sounded terrific. You're ready for Disney World."

Kelly beamed. "How about the flutes in 'Stars and Stripes Forever'? It's really hard. You have to overblow to hit high A."

"You are always 'A' in my book, Kel." Sam tugged her earlobe.

Kate said, "Kel, I clapped till my hands hurt." Not hard to do with contusions and abrasions, not to mention loose incisors. Now the band instrument cases were snapping shut all around. Kelly twisted apart her flute sections and set them in velvet grooves of the case and closed it.

"So it's off to the Dairy Queen for a Blizzard."

Could a rickshaw please take her to the parking lot?

Yet admit it, her bruises and pains served as a kind of diversion from a deeper ache, from the maelstrom of malice and rage . . . from Fan Fair as a planned killing field. Her hurting body was the refuge of her mind.

"C'mon, Mom, get going. And let Sam drive, okay? He takes the corners faster."

Quiet to the school parking lot, Sam held her passenger door, then watched as she eased into the front like an orthopedics outpatient.

"Kate, what's happened? Are you okay?"

"Just a little stiff from all that sitting." Her smile was a grimace. Her two front teeth moved back and forth when she sucked them. If the root nerves died, would LilyAnn Page become Kate Banning's tooth fairy? Try not to think about LilyAnn. Or Dottie. Or Farley.

Or Deb.

Especially not Deb.

Sam drove slow as a hearse. The roadways felt like the craters of the moon and drew her back into the cocoon of pain. Then Kelly bounced out at the DQ, and again Sam held her door as Kate eased sideways, cradled her elbow. "Kate, I can see you're not—"

"Fine. I'm fine. Well, well, it looks like the Little Leaguers beat us here." She spoke too brightly and avoided his eyes. "Wednesday night, and the joint's jumping."

"Mom, grab that table. I'll wait in line with Sam. You want a small chocolate dip?"

She felt dazed. "Looks like every kid in Nashville is here . . . The ones in red and white, are they a soccer team?"

"Softball."

"Oh, softball, I see. Sure, Kel, small chocolate dip." Kate tried not to limp, sat down with her back to the wall and stared at the gray Formica tabletop and waited.

In moments a tall shadow crossed the table surface. "Madam, may I join you? For a fee, the star flutist agrees to be our server."

"Sam—"

"Kate." His eyes so soft, sad and worried too.

She said, "Don't you start to work that bedside manner with me."

"Love to work the bed with you."

She rolled her eyes. "Forget it."

He sat back. "Okay then, here's a tough love question: did you scrimmage with the Nashville Titans this week?"

"Football?"

"It's spring training time. You blocking? Tackling?"

She met his eyes. Their glance held. "Maybe some of both."

"You're hurt?"

"I'm sore, that's all. It's from spring training at Fan Fair. Muscles I didn't know I had, ligaments."

"Kelly just told me you dived like a movie stunt woman and upchucked on LilyAnn Page at her booth, and broke two of her ribs. Is that true?"

"All true. I did a swan dive and tossed my breakfast all over LilyAnn's country couture. She'll be sore for a while too, and I ruined a pricey new set of sequins and suede—and probably Fleetwood's pilot fanzine project too."

But she fell silent. Why did this Dairy Queen, which was fluorescence-lighted enough for an entire city block, feel as dark as a full solar eclipse? She looked out at the kids crowding round the counter in every style from sports uniforms to baggies. Ages six or seven on up to the teens, every complexion, size, shape, girls and boys. They squirmed, laughed, jostled, Kelly among them. She was talking to a shorter boy in line. He, too, wore black pants and a white shirt. A trumpeter? A girl joined them, strawberry blond. Didn't Kate see her tonight among the saxophones?

But kids one and all. Generic kids from the band concert, from the playing fields, from van backseats and bikes and skateboards. These kids with their sundaes, cones, their cascading chocolate syrup and crushed pineapple could be cast in the Coca-Cola ads, Up With People, "teach the world to sing in perfect har-mo-ny . . ." They were here for treats. And DQ, how American, friendly, harmless. I scream, you scream, we all scream for ice cream.

Why then the eclipse? I scream, you scream . . . Nothing but darkness for the last forty-eight hours wherever she looked. The brighter the kids' voices, the darker.

I scream . . .

"Kate, hey there, yo, Kate."

"Kate what?" She looked across at Sam's face.

"You here? You still with us?"

She stared, then deliberately moved her arms and legs to feel absorbed in the bodily pain.

It didn't work. Two days from the flying arrow, the shock was wearing off, the real ache setting in. She stared ahead and let her eyes cross until the crowd of kids at the counter became blurred. Finally she said to Sam, "Look at those kids." Her voice was flat. "Just turn around and look at them all. Look."

He did. "Okay. I see Kelly's fifth in line—"

"But which ones are natural born killers?"

"What?"

"Those kids. Are any of them natural born killers? Which one of them might move out of fantasy and psychic hurt into actual plans to kill? The boy in the Cubs jersey? The girl standing behind Kelly? How do you know?"

She shivered. He turned back to Kate and took her hands into his and looked into her eyes. "Kate, you have to tell me what's going on. You're hurting— how much?

At the next table a couple shared a banana split. She said, "Kelly's flute case, the velvet insets—?"

He nodded.

"If I could lie down in that velvet for a few days . . . does that answer?"

He nodded. "What happened?"

"You haven't seen TV, Sam? The papers? Radio? The networks carried it. You can't be that out of touch?"

"Kate, I've been cooped up in hangars and offices and buried in Holiday Inns with paperwork on business jets for the last three, almost four days. I busted my tail to get here tonight. Now tell me what's wrong."

If only she could inject the story, put it in a pill or

capsule or a nicotine patch. No Way To It . . . She began a bare bones outline. "But there's related news here. LilyAnn's ex-husband has been arrested for murder."

"Keith Grevins?"

She nodded. "Ballistics tests showed the gun he was caught with at the Honolulu airport was the weapon used to kill Brent Landreth. It's the same Bren Ten. They're sending the bullet to the FBI lab for a few more tests, but they're certain enough to arrest him." She pushed back her hair. "Grevins apparently thought he could sneak the gun through airport security. He was too stupidly jealous and possessive to just throw it away."

Sam tried to look wry. "Well, he paid good money for it."

"And just think of the sentimental value. Great souvenir." She shook her head. "And so now Angie has an alleged murderer for a dad. Consider the Father's Day gift, an hour of billing time with Johnnie Cochran."

"Kate, it's great to hear your irony up and running."

"Oh sure, irony, that'll buck me up."

"Beats sulking."

"You think I'm sulking? Sulking?" She almost hissed. "Here's a fact from the sulking department, Sam: Dottie Skipwith's daughter is in juvenile detention for conspiracy to murder LilyAnn Page. How's that?"

She watched his jaw go slack. "That kid? The one with rosy cheeks?"

"That's right, a sixteen-year-old killer. If she and her partner had succeeded, LilyAnn would be the fatal victim of—are you ready for this?—of a Satellite Titan broadhead." Sam looked blank. "That, F.Y.I., is a space-age arrowhead with a cutting-tip designed for great penetration. It's prized by archers as especially good for elk or larger animals."

He chewed his bottom lip. "Or country music stars . . ."

"Only in season." She looked into his eyes. "You still like my irony?"

He shook his head. "But how did it happen?"

"How? From what Billy D tells me, Deb Skipwith sneaked into his apartment and stole a bow and a couple of wood arrows. Billy didn't notice right away that three aluminum arrow shafts and a screw-in Satellite Titan were also gone. You see, the plan was to blame the death on Billy D."

Sam's brow arched. "I wondered about him from the start, the archery—"

"But he had no motive, Sam. He lives free on the Mosely property. He does his chores and practices on the target range and goes hunting. It all suits him fine."

Kate shook her head. "But Deb thought it would be easy to frame him. She swiped the equipment and cooked up the plan. The execution was left to her accomplice. That's her boyfriend, Farley Eckles. He's on LilyAnn's road crew. He set the actual booby traps, starting with the guitar case."

"And the bus fire?"

She nodded again. "She brainstormed, and Farley did the deeds. I understand she's bragging about taking the bow and arrows out of Billy D's place to kill LilyAnn at the booth. She's confessing and boasting." Kate paused, drew breath. "And as of now, there's not one scintilla of remorse. And that's the real horror." Kate now looked over at the laughing kids, at a tanned teen girl biting a Dilly bar.

Sam said, "You met this Farley?"

"At the video shoot, a two-seconds 'hi.' He's in his twenties, a so-called older man." She leaned across the table, felt her elbow throb, ignored it. "That's the grisly irony here, Sam, that Dottie worried about *his* influence on Deb. She thought Farley was way too old for her daughter, way too worldly.''

"But it's the other way around, is that it?"

She nodded. "Deb's the brains, and God knows what their pact is all about on his side, great sex or S&M or what, but he did her bidding.''

"He pulled the hinge pins too?"

"No. They did that together. But Farley rigged the bow and arrow at the Fair booth module. She thought it up, and he figured out how to set the trap. He was the last one at the booth on Sunday night.''

Sam nodded slowly. At last he said, "Then the step-brother, Kip, had nothing to do with any of it?"

Kate felt her face flush. "No, evidently not. So far, there's no evidence linking Kip to Keith Grevins, who apparently acted alone when he shot Brent. And the booth module turns out to be just exactly what Kip said it is, an earnest effort, like the scaffold for the Fan Club party.''

She shook her head. "Kip is, well, frankly, innocent, Sam. I was way off base. I mean, he could end up in court for grabbing deposit money and abandoning his construction clients. Maybe the money's going up his nose, I don't know. But that's all separate from the archery death trap and the other booby traps.''

Sam frowned. "Still, that's a very big trick to pull off, a hunting bow—"

She nodded. "Absolutely. The key to it was Kip's design for the new seating module for LilyAnn. You see, it has drill holes at the side for flagstaffs and such, and Farley used one of those holes to brace a drawn bow. He rigged a release device to be triggered by pressure on the cushion spring. Sort of a trip wire.''

"So LilyAnn would sit down and—"

"Die.''

"And Billy D would take the blame." Sam paused, nodded. "So the consistent pattern all along is really booby traps." Kate nodded. "But why didn't somebody at the Fan Fair booth see the bow? It must have been obvious."

She shrugged. "Not really. It was hidden in the potted palms. They surrounded it. You'd have to look very closely."

"But weren't there people inside the booth on Monday morning?"

"Yes, Clark and Babs were there, but they were both so tired and worn out from working day and night they weren't seeing much of anything. The Fan Club president was there too, but too excited by the whole scene to pay close attention. Besides, the fans were stopping by for souvenirs, t-shirts and mugs, so everybody in the booth was busy clerking and chatting up the fans."

Sam nodded slowly, rubbed his chin, looked at Kate. "And the death trap was all set and waiting—"

She nodded. He leaned closer to her. She smelled his nice aftershave. He said, "But why? That's the question, Kate. Why?"

Then she looked out past him at the kids and paused and picked a cuticle and looked out again to spot Kelly in the crowd. "Why? Because Deb Skipwith thought LilyAnn Page had stolen her mother away from her."

He blinked. "I don't get it. You described this woman as a kind of mother hen to those two girls."

"Deb and Angie both, yes." Kate nodded. "She chauffeured them for years, prom dress shopped, dental appointments, the whole thing." She shook her head. "But somehow Deb experienced it all as . . . I guess logistics instead of love. It didn't count. Or didn't count enough."

"I don't understand."

"I don't understand either, Sam. You do what you can for a child. You do and do. What the child makes of it . . ." She looked out and saw Kelly first in line, at the counter placing their order. She said, "Raising one, it's all an act of faith. Faith upon faith. Kids are such bottomless pits, and lots of the time the term, adolescent, is . . . probably a polite synonym for a borderline psychopath."

Her sigh was heavy. "But with Dottie and Deb, it all got distorted. Deb evidently believed she was in a contest against LilyAnn, competing for Dottie's affection and losing, barely getting an honorable mention in a race which the Lily of the Shenandoah Valley always won." She bit her knuckle. "I caught a whiff of that bile a couple of times but shrugged it off. I ignored the real clues."

Kate paused, rapped her knuckle on the table. "And in a twisted way," she said, "I think all this was Deb's effort to get her mother back. I think she decided that if LilyAnn was out of the picture, then Dottie would be all hers again. She'd finally have her mother back. It was a plan of vengeance and redemption both."

"And how's Dottie doing?"

"She's crushed. Remember, her Deb also faces charges in the death of that road crew guy, Carnie."

"The one killed by the guitar case."

Kate nodded. "So Dottie's devastated. At least that's what Billy D says. He answers the phone. I've called morning, noon, and night, but Dottie won't talk to me. I left messages. I sent her a card. If she wants privacy, she's got it. I won't camp on her doorstep."

Kate paused, shrugged. "It's funny, for a week or so, I was joined at the hip with that woman. Now it's likely I'll never see her again. I guess that's show biz."

"Atten-hut!" Kelly stood between them. "One small chocolate dip for Mom, one large chocolate dip for Sam, one Heath Bar Blizzard for moi. And Sam, here's your change from the ten, but can I keep it?"

"Nope."

"Please."

"Not a good idea."

"If I shine your shoes?"

"Kelly, stop wheedling and get us some napkins. Please."

"I don't need a napkin. I'm not a baby."

"We need napkins. Us." Already white creamy beads burst the chocolate coating of the two cones. "Besides, it's about manners."

"Manners, shmanners, who cares?" But Kelly disappeared back into the crowd by the napkin dispenser. Sam bit his ice cream. The chocolate shell snapped.

Kate wiped a drip. "Sam, I have to say . . . this has been very hard on Kelly. The last two nights I stayed in her room for hours. She woke up screaming. Constant nightmares. She'd liked Deb, admired her—you know, the older teen thing. She can't absorb what happened. She's got her own version."

"That the girl is innocent?"

"That Farley is the real villain, that he somehow coerced and framed Deb. Kelly is positive this will all come out in court, and that Deb will be found innocent and freed." She paused, licked the cone. "I scream, you scream . . . Sometimes denial works wonders."

"I hear you. I won't punch a hole in Kelly's cloud." He bit a hunk of chocolate, just as Kate did, like some precision drill. Her front teeth zinged.

Then Kelly was back with a mound of napkins. She spooned a mouthful of Blizzard, said ummm, waved to more kids just coming in in the black and white outfits. "Wow, the whole band's here. Joyce, Richie, hi! Hey, Mom, Sam, you guys are dripping all over the place. You look like it's broccoli. You should've got Blizzards. Want a taste? Heath bar's the best. And Sam, did Mom tell you about the stalker?"

"Stalker? No, not yet."

"He escaped from Fan Fair. They're looking for him in Kentucky. All that bad stuff about cleavers and the scimitar sword, guess what?—the stalker got it from Henry David Thoreau."

"You don't say."

"Yes I do. It's in *Walden.* But we're not allowed to use that part in our nature journal. I asked. Only the inspiring stuff, like 'It is glorious to behold this ribbon of water sparkling in the sun.' So boring. It was due this week, but we got an extension. I still want to use pictures. The roll's being developed. My camera's great, Sam. Best birthday present this year."

"Glad it's working out, Kel."

She looked from Kate to Sam. "You two feel better now?"

Dutifully they said they did. Then Kate realized she actually did. She pressed Sam's hand.

He licked his dripping cone as if to tame a wild stream. "Hey," he said, "I've got an idea. How about if we all walk around Radnor Lake tomorrow morning, the three of us? Check out the waterfowl."

"I have school."

"Earlier. Before school. I'll play Reveille on the kazoo and get us all up."

Kelly looked from Sam to Kate. "How about it, Mom?"

"Sounds like Camp Kelly."

"Yeah, and you know what they call Radnor Lake? You ought to like this, Mom. They call it Tennessee's Walden Pond."

"Tennessee's . . ." She managed not to wince. "True fact?" Kelly nodded. Kate took a deep breath. "Okay, it's a deal. I'll get out my old hiking boots from Boston, and we'll all head out at the break of d . . . I mean, at dawn itself. Sign me up for Walden . . . for Walden South."